Until
Then

A Date for Good Luck
A Date for the Hunt
A Date for the Derby
A Date to Play Fore

STAND-ALONE NOVELS

Stripped Bare
Blow
Sexcation

HOLIDAY NOVELS

Santa's Secret
Christmas With You
It's a Wonderful Holiday

Until Then

HEIDI MCLAUGHLIN

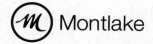 Montlake

Published by Montlake, Seattle

www.apub.com

Amazon, the Amazon logo, and Montlake are trademarks of Amazon.com, Inc., or its affiliates.

ISBN-13: 9781542027366
ISBN-10: 1542027365

Cover design by Caroline Teagle Johnson

Printed in the United States of America

To all those who have let that special someone slip away.
I hope you find them again.

PROLOGUE

Graham Chamberlain pressed the power button on his desktop tower. The guts of the computer groaned, and the monitor flickered to life. The cream-colored device was Hewlett-Packard only by name and not the inner workings. Over the last year, Graham rebuilt, modified, and swapped out every part he could, building himself the ultimate computer. The holy grail of machines. One faster than his roommate's. The competition between them had grown since they decided to live together. Who could build the better system? Who was going to be the one to break the mold? To date, Graham was winning by a hair. Of the five roommates, two were computer geeks—or *nerds*, as the women who often visited called them—and the others worked in banking and finance. Graham hadn't cared about being called a geek, though. He had a love for artificial intelligence and couldn't wait to watch the world evolve with technology. Bill Gates was going to change the world, right along with America Online. Once the display came to life and the icons from installed programs finished loading, Graham double-clicked on the AOL icon and waited. The familiar tones of his modem echoed throughout his room as he connected to the internet. The increasingly popular voice alerted him that he had mail, which brought a smile to his face. Before he could click on the yellow man who looked to be running, multiple messages from women he'd chatted with in various groups popped up. They wanted to know how he was doing, what his plans were for the night, and if he could help them with a computer problem. Since he became an avid user, his knowledge of computers had given him a bit of a reputation online. If someone posted a problem, many people from his buddy list often referred them to "Graham Cracker"—a nickname the love of his life had given him. But right now, it was his email that had his attention. The moment his screen showed his in-box, his smile grew wider. He clicked on the message from Rennie Wallace, his best friend, former hookup buddy, and the one woman he would drop everything for if she asked, which made him the worst possible boyfriend in the history of boyfriends.

Graham met Rennie his junior year of high school, when she visited her best friend, Brooklyn Hewett, in his hometown of Cape Harbor, Washington. From the second he saw her, he was smitten. In love. The week during spring break wasn't enough time for them—at least not in his opinion—and when she returned to Seattle, he made his first long-distance phone call and asked her to his prom.

They couldn't talk as much as either of them wanted due to school and the all-important evening and weekend jobs, but once a week, they took turns calling each other with long-distance phone cards. He remembered the first time he walked into Pinky's, the local tourist shop that doubled as a pharmacy, and selected the paper card off the rack. He was embarrassed—for what, he couldn't pinpoint. It was likely due to the look Old Man McGregor gave him as he rang up and activated the card. Graham felt as if he were doing something wrong. Of course, the look was sterner when he returned a month later and bought a box of condoms.

Rennie and Graham had been each other's first in almost all relationship categories. First kiss. First make-out session under the stars. First person either of them had ever slept with. Graham hoped after they had done the deed, their relationship would be serious, but Rennie was a free spirit and hard to tame. Not that he wanted her to be any different. He just wanted her to be his. For the most part, she was. They confided in each other, became best friends, and often added the "benefits" part of their relationship whenever they weren't dating someone else. When she started looking for schools in California, it made sense for him to do so as well. He wanted to be in the up-and-coming tech world, and Silicon Valley was the place to be. Rennie wanted to be a lawyer. Entertainment law. She wanted to be immersed in Hollywood. The glitz and glam of working in the industry. Only, her idea of the law changed once in school—multiple times—and, in fact, it became a running joke between the two of them. Graham expected a call, once each semester started, about how such and such professor had changed her views on whatever subject they taught. In the time since they had moved to the area, Rennie had gone from entertainment law to environmental, from corporate to criminal, and finally settled on family. Graham had joked she should be a law clerk and float from judge to judge—this way she would never be tied down.

Graham opened his email and took in her words. Since the invention of email and online chatting, this was how they communicated if they were home and both at the computer. As of late, they weren't as close as they once were, mostly due to Graham's girlfriend giving him an ultimatum: her or Rennie. Graham met Monica Watson during his senior year of college at a frat party. They hit it off and started dating. One year turned into two, and two became three. She was in love and ready to get married. Graham was neither. He wanted to wait until they were thirty, settled, and homeowners. He wanted to be free of debt and financially able to support his spouse so that when they had children, she could stay home if she wanted. His mother had when he and his twin brother, Grady, had been born. Monica saw things differently, which Graham respected, but he still wasn't willing to budge on his own life plan.

Monica also hated Rennie, which made life difficult for Graham, and he resorted to communicating with his friend via email or at night when Monica wasn't with him. To complicate matters, Rennie was busy, whereas Graham was a nine-to-fiver and home by six every night, making communication between them hit or miss.

The first email on his screen came from Rennie with a subject line of "Tonight." Graham's heart sank. She was supposed to come over for the backyard party he and his roommates were hosting. He had invited her since Monica was out of town visiting her parents in San Diego, and he missed Rennie. As he sat in his chair, he swiveled slightly back and forth and stared at the screen. He had a sinking suspicion she had to cancel. Still, he opened his email.

From: Rennie Ren
To: Graham Cracker
Subject: Tonight.

Graham Cracker,

I need a raincheck. I'll call you tomorrow. Love, Ren

Graham read over the words a few times before he hit reply. He typed out "No problem" and quickly sent the message. She wouldn't call, and he was okay with that. Truth be told, he was playing with fire by inviting her over. He contemplated answering the chat messages waiting for him but ultimately decided to log off. He hated how much of an effect Rennie had on him and had tried to break the hold many times over the years. Yet, all it took was for her to walk into the room, and his attention would be focused on her—something Monica was very keen to notice.

He went out into the living room of his shared house. Two of his roommates were watching C-SPAN for the up-to-the-minute market updates and taking notes. They had their own fake stock market setup in the house and often tried to entice Graham into investing, even though everyone knew there would never be a payout. He put his money into tech, often jumping on start-ups in the hope that one or two would pay off for him in the future. He would love to be retired by forty and living on a yacht somewhere in the middle of the Pacific.

The house the five of them lived in was a modest Tudor-style home. They each had their own bedroom, with one living in the basement; shared two bathrooms; and split the expenses evenly, with one of them collecting money from the others to pay the bills. Each week, two or three of them would be tasked with grocery shopping. Everyone picked up after themselves. And no one threw a party unless everyone agreed. For the most part, living there was easy.

Graham walked into the kitchen and saw a note taped to the phone. It was his turn to order pizza. His roommates were gracious enough to list what they wanted and how many he should order. He dialed the memorized number, told the girl with the cheerful voice on the other end what he needed, and said he would pay by card. After he hung up, he went to the refrigerator, grabbed a beer, and went outside, where another roommate sat by their firepit.

"Where's Monica?"

"With her parents for the weekend," Graham answered.

"Oh yeah? Is your hottie coming over?" His roommates often teased him for being attracted to Rennie even though he had a girlfriend. Most of them suspected Graham cheated on Monica when she went out of town, but he hadn't. He wouldn't. He respected her even though his attraction to Rennie was undeniable.

"Nah," he said, shaking his head. He worked hard to hide his disappointment, but deep down he knew it was for the best. If Rennie were there, life would be more complicated than it already was.

One by one, people started to arrive at the house. They brought coolers filled with beer and Jell-O shots. Their guy friends brought their current girlfriends, who wasted no time jumping in the pool. That feature alone was why everyone hung out at Graham's—the pool.

It was hot in Cali, and while they had the ocean, having a pool was second best.

It didn't take long for the music to start and for the other roommates to join the growing party outside. People danced, flirted, swam, drank, and ate pizza, which lasted a whole five minutes. Graham sat in his chair because he felt sorry for himself for no other reason than the fact Rennie wasn't coming. A friend tapped him on the shoulder and nodded toward a blonde woman, who stood with a group of friends.

"What do you think of her?"

"Pretty," Graham said. He couldn't see her all that well, but from a distance she looked pretty.

"I've been trying to get her to go out with me for a year," his friend said. "She wants to be friends."

The kiss of death, which Graham knew all too well. He laughed. "I feel ya, man."

"What? Aren't you and Monica going strong?"

He nodded. "Yeah, just want different things right now. I predict the fork in the road is getting closer and closer."

His buddy shook his head. "One of my coworkers is getting married next weekend. He's twenty-three. I don't get it."

"Me neither."

Graham's name was yelled from the back door of the house. He stood and walked toward his roommate. "Your parents are on the phone." Graham stood there for a moment. It was late, and his parents would rarely call him past eight o'clock, even if they had been out with the Holmeses or Carly Woods. He went into the house and directly to his room. After he picked up his phone, he yelled, "Got it!" as loud as he could and hoped his roommate heard him and hung up the other line.

"Hello?"

"Son . . ." The sound of his father's strangled voice was enough to send Graham into a panic.

"Dad, what's wrong?"

He heard his mother wailing in the background.

"Dad!" Graham yelled.

"It's Austin."

"What about him?" Graham grew frustrated between his father's inability to form a sentence and his mother's screaming in the background. "Jesus Christ, Dad. What the hell is going on?"

"There's a storm, and Austin . . . he and your brother took the boat out. The boat capsized—it's bad, Graham. A rogue wave came out of nowhere and took them under." There was more silence from his dad, but he could hear his mother crying louder.

"Dad, is Grady . . ." Graham had trouble getting his question out.

"We can't find Austin." Never in his life had he heard panic in his father's voice. It was undeniable now. Tears formed in Graham's eyes as he searched around his room. He needed to get home, back to his family. He needed to be there for his brother. Grady and Austin had been best friends from the time they were in diapers. There were five close friends, including those two. Bowie Holmes, Jason Randolph, and Graham rounded out the group.

His mouth opened, but no words came out. His tiny fishing community had been rocked many times before with fishing accidents, but not since Skip Woods had a heart attack out at sea had he lost anyone he knew.

Lost. There was no way Austin was lost. Every single guy he grew up with could swim, and if there was a riptide, the people of Cape Harbor would form a human chain to bring him in. His father was wrong.

"Dad, I'm sure . . ." But even as the words left his mouth, he didn't believe them.

The phone was fumbled around, and Graham strained to pick up on the conversation between his parents. There was a third voice, but it was unfamiliar. In the background, he heard sirens and more people talking.

"Dad, where are you? Where's Grady?" Usually Graham could sense when something was amiss with Grady or even when his brother was elated. It was the weird twin thing between them, which often confused outsiders.

"He's in the hospital. He's being checked for hypothermia, a concussion, and is very agitated. But it's Austin; we can't find him. And we can't find Bowie." Graham knew if Austin was out on the boat, Bowie was likely with him. He also knew his family needed him. His brother would definitely need him if Austin wasn't found. "I need to go back down to the docks. We're going back out to search."

"It's not safe if it's raining, Dad. You should stay with Grady," Graham pointed out, knowing full well his plea would fall on deaf ears.

"I won't leave Austin out there alone. I can't do that to Carly. Not to Skip. Your mom will stay with Grady, son. Your brother . . . he's going to be okay, but I have to help find Skip's boy." George Chamberlain was a family man and had taken Austin under his wing after Austin's father passed away. Just as Gary Holmes had.

"I'll book a flight right now." His father hung up, with no other information. Graham was angry and confused. He went to his computer and booted it up. Over the past year, websites had become more popular, and he knew Southwest Airlines had a fairly active site. Plus, their flights were cheap, and there were plenty of them. He could get one by the morning and be home in five hours. While his internet loaded, he went around his bedroom, packing clothes. He dug into his closet and pulled out his wet suit—he would need it if he planned to dive, which he did, unless Austin surfaced beforehand.

With AOL open, he typed in the airline's URL and hit enter. The internet was slow this time of night because everyone was on. He clicked, typed, and pressed enter more times than he could count as he searched for a flight. Nothing for hours, and the earliest was tomorrow night. He could drive home by then. He logged off and remembered his father said they couldn't find Bowie. He couldn't fathom any of this.

None of it made sense. Why would Austin take the trawler out in a storm? Why would Grady go with him? And where was Bowie?

He picked up the phone and dialed Bowie's cell phone. He was one of the few people Graham knew who had one. The phone rang, and by the fourth tone, Graham's frustration started turning into fear.

"Hello?" Bowie answered gruffly into the receiver.

"Where are you, man?"

Bowie paused. "Home, why? What's up?"

Graham knew he wasn't but chose not to dig deeper. "There's been an accident," Graham said hurriedly and with panic. "He's so fucking stupid. The fucker took the trawler out, and it fucking capsized. Fucking rogue wave tipped the boat over. My dad, he's heading out now, and my mom's freaking out. I can't get a flight until tomorrow." The more Graham recalled the conversation with his father, the more worried and distraught he became. The boys were smart, raised better than to play with nature this way. Austin, of all people, knew better.

"Who?"

"Austin, man. Fucking Austin, and he's gone!" Graham screamed.

"What do you mean?"

Graham paused. The word *gone* played over in his mind. Had he spoken too soon? What if Austin was perched on a buoy? Or clinging to a rock? He could be on one of the islands, waiting to be rescued.

"What do you mean, Graham?"

The line went dead before he could answer his friend. He had no time to call him back. He wanted to get on the road and get home to his family. He had one last call to make before he left, and that was to Rennie. Brooklyn would need her.

When Rennie's roommate answered, Graham said, "Is Rennie there? This is Graham. It's important."

"Ren, for you."

Graham counted the seconds until she picked up. "What's up?"

"Austin's been in an accident. I'm heading home."

"Is Brooklyn okay?"

"I don't know," he said. "You and I both know, wherever Brooklyn is, Bowie isn't far behind. Now that he knows about Austin, he'll be by Brooklyn's side." He let the words hang in the air. He and Rennie both suspected something was going on between their friends but never asked either of them. Graham recounted everything his father told him and heard Rennie start to cry. "I'll call you when I get to town to let you know what's going on."

"I'm coming with. Can you pick me up?"

"I'll be there in thirty." He hung up and finished packing. He found one of his roommates and gave him a quick rundown of what was going on and called his boss, telling him what he knew and asking for the week off. He tried to remain positive, reassuring himself Austin would be found by the time he arrived home, and all this panic would've been for nothing.

ONE

Fifteen Years Later

Renee Wallace stood in front of her floor-to-ceiling window, peering out over the Seattle skyline. Her corner office in the First Bank Tower offered her the best view of her beloved city. Small drops of rain, some meeting together and streaking down the tinted windows, made the white and colored twinkling Christmas lights from neighboring buildings and apartments a blur. On a clear night, one she hadn't seen in some time, the view from her office afforded her the ability to see the area of Queen Anne and the faint outline of homes on Bainbridge Island. She missed spring and summer. Even the crisp air and changing leaves fall brought. But it was the dark, dreary winter that kept her from admiring her beautiful city day in and day out. It had been days since she saw the sun, and she missed it. Rennie needed it and longed to be on a tropical island instead of looking out her window as she sipped the gin and tonic her assistant poured and left for her before heading upstairs to the Rhoads PC annual Thanksgiving feast, where Rennie should've been.

Sagging against the glass, she didn't worry that it couldn't hold her weight but was fearful that the emotional baggage she carried might crack the thick panes. She watched the office floor across from her and about eight floors down. Every so often someone would come to the table the other company had set up by the window and load up a plateful of food or make another drink. Her company hired a bartender, caterers, and a DJ to play music meant to get people in the spirit. Men and women would be dressed in black slacks and white shirts, carrying around silver trays, offering champagne and hors d'oeuvres until the sit-down dinner was ready. You were expected to work the room with a smile. Laugh at Bob the copy guy's corny dad jokes, which he had plenty of; feel sorry for Jenny's third cousin, twice removed, because her bunion surgery didn't go quite as planned. Mingle with that ever-annoying coworker you wouldn't talk to on a normal day. Tonight's party was one of three that would happen over the next few weeks. Happy faces all around. No moping, which was why Rennie had yet to join the festivities. Everyone upstairs was living it up, and she felt like she had nothing to celebrate.

By all accounts, she was a fierce lawyer, fighting for her clients and getting them everything she thought they were due. She did her job, her due diligence, and put in her time. She busted her butt for every promotion, being passed up each time for someone willing to kiss a little more ass, someone male. When her promotion had come and her boss asked to see her in the conference room, she had finally felt validated. She was the first woman in the law firm to hold the title of junior partner. She was quickly becoming the go-to divorce lawyer in the city, even though her specialty in college was family law. Her client base was slowly becoming what it had been when she'd lived in California, when she would sit second chair to some of the most powerful lawyers celebrities could hire. Spouses scorned by adulterous affairs. Tech giants who made it big after they were married and now wanted out. They were people married to their careers who had fallen out of love with each other. It was cases like the latter that Rennie preferred. She wanted to work with people to find a happy medium, a smart and healthy resolution for everyone. She hated fighting dirty but would when required. It was those cases, the ones where the media meddled too much because her client had a substantial portfolio or had invented the next best thing, that would catapult her to be the most sought-after divorce lawyer in the area. She would rise to the top and make partner faster than anyone else in the firm.

The day after her promotion, she saw her office for the first time. When she first walked in, she thought her boss was playing a cruel joke on her, possibly showing her what she could have if she were ever to make partner, because there was no way the corner office with a view of the city was hers. He paraded her around the room, showing her the wet bar, the kitchenette with a refrigerator hidden behind the mahogany cabinet and under the black granite countertop. There was a large bathroom that had a black-and-teal-tiled stand-up shower, complete with dual showerheads and the option to switch to the overhead rain shower just in case the Seattle drizzle wasn't enough for her. The bathroom looked like something her best friend, Brooklyn Hewett, had designed. Attached to the bathroom were a dressing room and a space for her to keep extra clothes and shoes. Her boss referred to it as *small*, but the closet was bigger than her one-bedroom walk-up. The more she looked around, the more she surmised this office wasn't for her. He was dangling a prize in front of her, something for her to work toward. To continue the tour, he told her that the couch pulled out into a sleeper in case she needed to stay the night. In that moment, she wanted it. She wanted it all. She could easily see herself spending countless hours in her office, watching the sun set over the sound. She could see her future, sitting at the large desk stained a rich dark brown that almost looked black, curled up on the leather couch under the afghan her grandmother knitted for her in case of a snowstorm. Her future was in this room, and it was within her grasp.

Rennie hadn't believed this was her office, not even when her boss placed the keys in her hand. It wasn't until maintenance installed the gold-plated nameplate outside the door, etched with her name, that it finally sank in. She stayed late the night it went up, well after everyone had gone home and only the glow from the auto-timed night-lights illuminated the pathways to the exits, to drag her fingers across the hollowed letters of her name, *Renee Wallace*. She traced each one until the pad of her index finger was sore. Years of hard work and determination came down to this moment. She had finally been recognized for her worth.

Those feelings lasted about five minutes. It wasn't long after she moved into her new office that her coworkers started mumbling under their breath. According to gossip, the only reason for her promotion was because she had devoted herself to the job. She didn't have kids or a spouse, nothing forcing her to leave at five or six o'clock to rush home. Day cares and schools didn't phone needing her attention. The midnight flu didn't force her to call in sick the next day to care for her child. The doctor's appointments, early dismissals, snow days, or field trips taking time away from other staff wouldn't affect her. To everyone around her, she got the promotion because she was alone, not because she'd earned it.

Years ago, when she was young and hungry for success, right after passing the bar, she made many comments about how motherhood wasn't her thing to whoever asked when she would settle down. Rennie never saw herself with a husband and 2.3 children. The white picket fence wasn't her lifestyle. She wanted a high-rise in the city, the weekend gala fundraisers, and the one-night stands that weren't awkward because both parties knew exactly what they needed from each other. Her passion for sitting in her oversize chair with a cup of coffee and a good book far outweighed any thoughts of dirty diapers and teething rings.

What she wanted now was a ring on her finger. She could still do without a child, but marriage was something she found she wanted ever since she met her boyfriend at a college fair in Spokane, Washington, over a year ago. Rennie was asked to fill in for a coworker and attend the recruiting session and speak to interested interns. Public speaking wasn't her forte, but the thought of getting out of the office for a few days excited her. She never thought a trip across the state would be life changing, but this one was. The staff who had accompanied her to Spokane set up their booth in the convention center and joked with her about how nervous she was. They assured her everything would be fine and the speech she planned to give to prospective interns was spot on. Shortly after her speech, she spoke to the students who stopped by their booth. She handed out flyers containing details about their intern program, the housing they offered, and their hiring process. In the booth next to hers, Theo Wright recruited for a whole other field: forensic accounting. The two of them couldn't have been more different career-wise, yet as the day wore on, they smiled at each other, gravitating toward one another and flirting. Casual conversation turned into drinks at the hotel bar, which turned into dinner the next night. Rennie's staff would later comment on the subtle touches they witnessed her and Theo exchange and how each time they brought him up on the flight home, she would smile.

Theo and Rennie lived four hours apart by car—longer in the winter—and a little over an hour by plane. They often met in Ellensburg, which was halfway for both of them, or Theo would come to Seattle to visit. Rennie rarely went to Spokane, since Theo loved the nightlife in Seattle. The vibe was more his speed, as he always told her. Every other weekend they were together, either at her apartment, skiing in Canada, spending time in the Bavarian village of Leavenworth, or walking hand in hand along the boardwalk on Venice Beach when she would occasionally join him on a business trip to Los Angeles. They were in love. He talked about leaving his job or pushing his company to open a branch in Seattle so they could buy their dream home in the coveted Queen Anne neighborhood. They talked about their future, their desire to travel together to Italy and Greece, and she showed him a condo she wanted to buy in Portugal, giving them a place to escape to when their jobs became too much.

Her promotion changed her dreams, or maybe falling in love had done so. She wasn't sure anymore. She loved her job. She loved Theo. But neither was meeting her halfway. He was demanding of her time, as was her job. With her new role, her responsibilities doubled. She now had lawyers under her, a full office staff, and interns. People depended on her more. When Theo was in town, she was in board meetings or going over briefings. Their normal weekends together turned into her spending hours researching, reading, and highlighting. Plans they had made before the promotion were tossed by the wayside and rescheduled for another date or, more aptly, "to be determined."

She was driven to manage her ever-growing workload and get back on track with Theo, but it was the rumors that made everything worse and had her questioning whether the corner office, pay raise, and gold-plated nameplate were worth it. Of course, the sneers she'd get from her male counterparts who had not been promoted to her current position and the backhanded comments from other coworkers suggesting she was sleeping her way to the top weren't helping. The fact that Theo declined her invite to the firm's Thanksgiving party hadn't squashed the gossip surrounding her. She depended on him to be there for her, to show everyone she was happy and in a healthy relationship—that she wasn't taking part in extracurricular activities with the president of the company or any of its senior staff—and that she could have a career *and* be in a committed relationship.

She sipped her gin and tonic and looked toward the Queen Anne area. There were houses for sale, many in the price range that she and Theo could afford. Brooklyn suggested they buy a fixer-upper and have Bowie do the work. They could flip and invest. Her friend made it sound so easy. They didn't need a lot of room and could buy small, remodel, and move on to something else. When she asked Theo what he thought, he said it would be a waste of time, and he didn't want to live in a construction zone. He, too, made sense. Their time was valuable, and with Rennie's job keeping her at the office longer hours, the last thing she wanted to come home to at night was a dust-filled house. After the first of the year, they'd find the right house—she was sure of it.

Her intercom buzzed, and within seconds, silence filled with music and laughter. The voice of her assistant, Ester, came through the receiver. "Ms. Wallace, are you coming to the party?"

Rennie continued to stare out the window, her eyes scanning the darkened city for any sign of Theo . . . not that she could see him—or anyone, for that matter—from her office. Besides, she knew deep down he wouldn't surprise her, not tonight and not likely over the extended holiday. Their last words had been curt. She would call him later—if not tonight, then tomorrow—and apologize and tell him that once they lived together, things would be different. It was the distance that frustrated them, not their jobs. She would promise to put work aside so they could keep their reservation at the quaint bed-and-breakfast they'd fallen in love with in Vancouver, British Columbia, so they could spend New Year's together. Everything would be on track for them; she'd make sure of it.

"I'll be there in a minute," she told Ester as she stepped away from the window. She placed the glass on the corner of her desk before walking out of her office and closing the door behind her.

TWO

Cape Harbor, Washington, was known for its beautiful coastline, its majestic views, and its quaint style of living, as well as swashbuckling ghosts. Over the years, the story about the pirate ship, the *Grand Night*, sinking a mere thirty feet from the shore grew with each person telling the tale. It was a stormy night, might've been snowing, or was the wind whipping so hard the captain couldn't keep the ship straight? There was no way to tell. What about the ghosts who sat at the bar of the Whale Spout long after it closed, causing a ruckus? As the folklore went, the gangplanks used for the Whale Spout came from the *Grand Night*, but how that came about was unknown. Some say the wind ripped apart the ship, and the wide pieces of wood slammed against local angler Justin Schreiber's boat one afternoon, waking him from a drunken stupor. Others say he was a thief who robbed the ship, taking what belonged to the ocean and bringing a curse to all the fishermen. Whether the tales were true, no one would ever know, but the uncertainty hadn't stopped fortune hunters from coming to the small Washington town with their diving gear, hoping to discover what many before them hadn't—those elusive chestfuls of gold coins and jewels. The tourist shop in town sold magnets, T-shirts, and replica coins and necklaces related to the myth, and the old fishermen who sat in the same corner of the Whale Spout as the fishermen before them had continued to spread the story to anyone willing to sit and listen.

A man sat down at the bar and motioned to Graham. There were very few patrons in the bar tonight; most people were home or traveling to visit relatives for the upcoming holiday. "What can I get you?" Graham asked.

"Whatever you have on tap."

Graham pulled a glass from the counter, set it at a forty-five-degree angle, and pulled the tap of his favorite local brew, the White Elephant Couch, and watched as amber liquid filled the glass. He held it up and admired his ability to create as little head as possible. Beer pouring was truly an art form, at least for him.

"Is it true?" the man asked Graham as he slid the pint toward him.

"What's that?"

"The ghost stories. My buddy has been here a few times and says this place is haunted. Said if I stay until closing, I'm likely to catch the spirit of Blackbird."

"As far as I know, Blackbird never sailed the Pacific." There hadn't been a day since he took over the bar from his father that he hadn't been asked if any of the legends were true. Hearing what others had heard over the years was one of the best parts of his job, and he often wished he could confirm or deny the fables. Was the Whale Spout haunted? Likely. There were too many instances that left Graham wondering. Most often, he'd come in to work and find the barstools tipped over or a water faucet running. Each time, he would thank whoever did it for not touching the taps, because losing a keg of beer would be costly, especially during the winter.

Once Labor Day came and went, the tourism season slowed to a trickle. Thankfully, with the Driftwood Inn reopening, there had been a steady flow of people coming back to the area. Still, most of the people around town were locals who only frequented the town's favorite watering hole on Friday or Saturday nights. Graham thought about limiting the hours during the winter, especially between the months of November and February, but didn't know what he would do with all his downtime. He loved being a bartender, even though his passion lay in corporate America. He missed the challenges and the intricacies of working with computers, of being the tool everyone in his building needed. At night, when he was alone in his houseboat with only the sound of the ocean keeping him company, he thought about giving up the bar and returning to the rat race of traffic jams, meetings, and a cell phone that never stopped ringing. He missed the power-hungry women and the sexiness they exuded when they were asking him for help, as well as the corporate ladder and the feeling that came with being indispensable. He gave it all up, and for what? To be a bartender in an establishment his parents owned? Granted, he was free to do whatever he wanted with the place . . . except sell it. His parents were silent partners, the bankroll that kept the place afloat, mostly for his alcoholic brother, Grady. His twin brother.

Graham continued with his busywork. He lost count of how many times he wiped the bar top down, stacked coasters, and quickly sopped up any inkling of a water drop. The old decking that made up the bar top was rumored to have come from the same pirate ship the door and floor had. Again, rumors spread like wildfire, and he had no idea if it was true, but it was in pristine condition as far as he was concerned. At the end of the summer, once business slowed, he had begged his friend Brooklyn to teach him how to strip and refinish the piece. He wanted to maintain the chunks of wood as long as he could, and the previous finish hadn't held up over the years. He filled the bowls of nuts, restocked the beers he kept in bottles, checked the taps of the newly installed IPAs, straightened the liquor bottles, dusted the glass shelving, washed the glasses, and checked on the old cronies in the corner.

The Whale Spout was Cape Harbor's only watering hole. Not that others hadn't tried to open other bars; they just couldn't compete and often closed within a year or two. Sure, the restaurants in town served liquor, but the locals preferred the one that had been in town the longest. "The OG," as you'd often hear residents tell visitors. Since Graham took over, he'd made a few changes, such as the large-screen projector in the back that aired local sporting events, the smaller televisions at the bar, a better jukebox—because even he knew he had to cater to the women who wanted to dance while their men wanted to be at the bar. He wanted the place to be the hot spot, the happening joint, the place to be, and for the most part, he thought it was.

There were a few other patrons in the Whale Spout, two of whom sat at the bar and four or five guys in the back, playing darts. Each week, there were darts and billiards tournaments and, in the summer, beach volleyball. He always offered cash prizes, the amount determined by the number of entrants.

For the past fifteen years, Graham had been behind the bar. Before him it had been his father, and before his father, his grandfather. Graham wasn't sure if it was his grandfather's intention to create a Chamberlain legacy, but he had. It seemed almost like one hundred years had passed since Floyd Chamberlain bought the Whale Spout. A framed picture of him holding the driftwood sign sat near the cash register, along with similar pictures of the other previous owners. Graham never intended to take over the bar, and it really hadn't been expected of him either. His parents never pushed and instead encouraged him to go to college in California. They secured the loans with the understanding he would pay them back once he landed his first job. His first, and subsequently only, job came in the form of a systems IT analyst and came with a nice Silicon Valley paycheck.

Living in California wasn't exactly a dream but a stepping-stone to something bigger and better. His intentions were to either return to Washington or move to Oregon in ten to fifteen years and open his own security and IT company. Far too often, small businesses and the average computer user didn't protect themselves from cyberattackers, and he had a plan to combat the rising epidemic. After college, he found a couple roommates, four to be exact, to share in the expenses of living in one of the most expensive areas. Carpooled to work to save on the wear and tear of his car, rode his ten-speed bike as often as he could, and opted to have people over rather than going out on the town. Paying his parents back was a priority, and when he wrote the first check out to them, he had done so with pride.

His life, like others around him, changed in an instant. It was one phone call about his brother and a childhood friend. Austin Woods was one of Graham's closest friends. He grew up with the twins, along with Bowie Holmes and Jason Randolph; the five of them seemed inseparable. Austin was destined to be a fisherman. It was in his blood. Grady loved being on the open sea as well, and it only made sense for them to open a business together after they graduated from high school. From what Grady had told Graham, the Chamberwoods Fishing Company did well. They were thriving, at least until one fateful night when Austin took their boat out in the middle of a storm. It rained a lot along the coast of Washington, especially in the northern portion, but there had been a record rainfall that year, and the waterline had risen to new levels. Most everyone was smart enough to keep their boats docked during a storm—even Austin knew the risks. Still, he went out and took Grady with him.

Graham would never forget the way his father screamed into the receiver with his mother crying in the background—not only for her son, but for Austin as well. It was heart wrenching, and it made him nauseous. He never knew what true fear felt like until he was on the road, driving north. Swallowing had become difficult, his breathing labored. Graham's hands ached from the death grip he had on the steering wheel, and his back screamed out in pain from the cramped quarters of his small car. Any other day, he would've been happy to have Rennie by his side, but not because of these circumstances.

The trip from Palo Alto back home took eighteen hours between traffic and stops to fill up, eat, and use the bathroom. They took turns driving, worrying about their friends, and sitting in silence because they ran out of things to talk about. The history between the two of them was palpable. They had an unmistakable attraction to each other and gravitated toward one another when they'd end up someplace together, which had also caused problems in Graham's relationship with his girl-friend at the time, even though he had never been unfaithful. When neither he nor Rennie had a significant other, they were often together but never could quite break out of the friends-with-benefits zone.

When they arrived in Cape Harbor, they went to work. He down to the docks to aid the search party for Austin, and she to Brooklyn to comfort her best friend. Graham couldn't quite remember when Rennie had gone back to California; he could only recall how much he missed her. He would make one more trip to Palo Alto, but only to quit his job on the spot and move his stuff out of the house he shared. The drive back had taken him half a week. He was going back to his hometown to help his twin and put his life on hold. He wouldn't hear from Rennie again until the day she walked into his bar just a few months ago. Since then, whenever he had too much time on his hands, he thought about her. Everyone around him was happy for Bowie and Brooklyn, who had found their way back to each other after fifteen years. Their relation-ship was anything but a fairy-tale romance. For most of his life, Bowie had been in love with Brooklyn, who had been in love with Austin and Bowie. Years later, Carly Woods, Austin's mother, enticed Brooklyn to return to Cape Harbor to renovate the inn she owned. Brooklyn returned with her fourteen-year-old daughter in tow, throwing everyone around them for a loop. Everyone, including Brooklyn, had believed Austin to be Brystol's father, but Carly had known otherwise and had kept the child's paternity a secret, until she made a deathbed confession. Not that it mattered. Bowie had a second chance with Brooklyn, and he wasn't going to pass it up.

Graham wondered when his own moment of happiness would come. Sure, he could pursue any of the women in town, but none of them intrigued him as much as Renee Wallace. From the day he met her, many years ago, she'd always understood him. Unfortunately, time and distance forced them apart. For a moment, when Rennie returned, he thought they could reconnect. They did, but only as friends. She was happy, in a committed relationship, living in the city and doing what she loved, and he was a bartender with nothing on the horizon. He had nothing to offer her and was certain she knew this.

Still, when Rennie sent a text to their "CH Bitches" group chat, his hope spiked. She was on her way to the inn, coming for Thanksgiving. Graham looked at his phone and typed, Is Theo joining you? His finger hovered over the arrow that would send the question. Should he send it? He thought on it until the door to the Whale Spout opened, and a family walked in. He quickly erased his words, pocketed his phone, and sighed. The holidays meant more time at his parents', a place he'd rather not be. His mother would fuss over Grady, and his father would pretend his sons had perfect lives. The Chamberlains had mastered the art of brushing problems under the rug, and because it was the holidays, Graham was expected to play his part as the dutiful son and brother.

Graham tended to his customers, picking up on bits and pieces of their conversations. They were traveling north and took a wrong turn, ending up in Cape Harbor. They asked him if he knew of a place to stay. He told them about the Driftwood Inn and volunteered to send a message to the owners to let them know a family would be up after dinner. He retrieved his phone and looked at the group chat again. Someday, he would tell Rennie how he felt. But until then, he'd keep his feelings hidden.

THREE

With Thanksgiving being the next day, the last place Renee wanted to be was in a partners' meeting, listening to some kiss-ass financial guy tell the staff of lawyers how to do their jobs. The bottom line: there wasn't a single attorney who went into a case trying to lose, yet the man standing at the front of the conference room, with his pin-striped double-breasted suit neatly pressed and his jacket buttoned, had the gall to inform her and her colleagues how much the firm would earn if they were to come away with victories. She was being harsh but with good reason; she was ready for a minivacation, and she counted down the minutes until the office officially closed for the holiday. Not to mention, she handled divorce, not civil or criminal cases. Her fee was set by the firm and paid for by clients. As much as she wanted to leave at noon, she would wait until the lunch rush in the city died down before driving north to Cape Harbor. Now that Brooklyn and her daughter, Brystol, were so close by, Rennie wanted to spend as much time with them as she could.

Finally, the money guy closed his binder, and Renee did the same, only for the CEO, Lex Davey, to stand, button his suit jacket, and walk to the front of the room. He presented a rundown of cases he would like to see closed by the end of the year, and she had three of them. She thought about each one, mentally questioning if it were possible, and concluded that two could settle out of court, but the third was contentious. She represented an author who separated from her husband over a year ago, and he refused to sign the divorce decree until he was guaranteed a portion of his wife's royalties, citing he was part of the creative process and had provided content for every book written while dating and throughout the marriage. He was even laying claim to novels written during the separation. Renee tried to get the couple to come to a peaceful resolution, but the husband refused and had since hired his own attorney. Still, she had hoped the four of them could come to an agreement, and when talks broke down, she knew court seemed increasingly likely. A hearing date had yet to be set, but Renee was ready. As far as she was concerned, it was her client who had created the content, put in countless hours of typing, stressed over queries with agents and subsequently acquisition editors, marketed herself on social media and in the public, and worried about sales, all while raising their family and maintaining her health. What had the client's husband done? Told a few coworkers to read his wife's book? To Renee, that did not constitute enough to take a percentage of earnings, past or future.

"Ms. Wallace, an update on the Soto case?" Lex Davey owned the firm but was not an attorney. His wife started the company many years ago, and when she passed away, he took over. Now he sat three floors up in an office big enough to be a house, worrying about laws he knew nothing about, courting women, and entertaining politicians.

She sat up straight, opened her binder, and dragged her finger down the color-coded tabs until she reached a red one marked "Soto" and flipped to the section. She knew the case by heart, but for some reason, Lex Davey shook her to the core. Maybe it was the way he leered at her when they made eye contact or how he would make comments regarding her clothing. His words often bordered on harassment but were never enough to fully cross the line. Telling her she wore a nice skirt or saying she looked good in a particularly colored blouse was technically harmless. Words were words, but it was the looks he gave her when he said such things that made her feel uneasy. Thankfully, she only had to converse with him minimally and normally only during meetings. She cleared her throat and gave a recap of how the case had progressed.

"Any chance for a settlement?" Justin Baylor asked, another junior partner who was about five years younger than Renee but surprisingly made partner in his second year with the firm.

She tilted her head slightly, as if she would signal *no*, but stopped. "My client, as you can imagine, would like to protect her assets. She was the one who put in the work and doesn't feel her ex is entitled to anything at all. We have offered him one percent; he has countered with fifty-one, which would give him full control over Mrs. Soto's artistic work, and this is out of the question. The man has done nothing to improve or contribute to my client's business, and—not that it matters—Mrs. Soto writes under a pen name and has very rarely spoken about her husband in any public manner. She is not damaging nor enhancing his reputation, and therefore he should not benefit from hers."

"What about thanking him in acknowledgments?" one of the partners, Donna Pere, asked. She and Donna had a good bit of history. They met at Santa Clara Law when Renee was in law school and Donna was teaching a summer course on ethics. They stayed in touch, and when Renee needed an internship, Donna brought her on at the firm she worked for. Rhoads PC enticed Donna with a job in Seattle, which opened the door for Renee to return home. The interview had gone well, and Donna had raved about her ability, but the wait to hear whether the firm would hire her kept her on her toes. It took two months for the board to decide her fate.

"Only if he can make the claim that she included him in 'Many thanks to my family.' If the judge agrees, we're going to see a lot of people coming out of the woodwork to sue for royalties."

"Sounded like an open-and-shut case when you signed on," Lex pointed out. Renee wanted to ask him what he knew about open-and-shut cases, but she held her tongue. Another time, another place for outbursts such as those. Instead, she smiled, nodded, and shut the binder, hoping to convey she was done talking.

Lex then asked, "Anyone have anything we should know about?" He made eye contact with each senior and junior partner sitting at the table. All were quiet until he came to Donna, who sat upright. She cleared her throat and looked down at her notes.

"A friend of a friend asked me to look into a civil case as a favor. There was a car accident over the summer in which the driver ended up paralyzed. The parents of the driver want to sue the bartender that served their daughter alcohol, saying they never checked her ID. They admit she was already drunk when she entered the establishment and contend the liquor served made her more impaired, and therefore she shouldn't have been served nor allowed to leave without someone taking her keys or a car being called for her."

"Was she with friends?" Renee asked.

"She was."

"Are they being sued?" Renee shocked herself with her question. One reason she went into law was to fight for injustices. She thought she would practice criminal law and spend her life defending the innocent, but after one of her internships, family law had captured her attention.

"They aren't," Donna responded.

"If the young woman had friends with her, why didn't one of them drive?" Lex asked. Renee wanted to know the same thing.

"A joyride gone bad?" The way Donna spoke made it sound like a question and like there was more to the story, and it seemed Lex felt the same way.

"Let it go; it sounds like a loss for us." Lex stood and abruptly ended the conversation. "Happy Thanksgiving," he said in a cheery voice. "By the way, Christmas bonuses will come earlier than normal this year."

She gathered her things in her arm and held them precariously as she read the messages on her phone. Emails from clients complaining about missing child support payments or spousal support. There was a hint of desperation in each email, and her heart went out to her clients. The holidays were upon them, and people counted on those monthly payments. She also had a slew of text messages, mostly from Brooklyn, who was, per her typed words, OMG SO EXCITED TO SEE YOU! The message made Renee smile. Once she was in Cape Harbor, she could relax and let the stress of work drift out into the ocean. Four days of nothing but her friends, shopping, wedding talk, and Christmas decorating were exactly what she needed.

She stopped at her secretary's desk. Ester Singer had been with Rennie since she started at Rhoads, and she insisted Ester come with her when she was promoted to junior partner. Ester looked up as Renee approached and, as coyly as possible, slid the ad she was perusing under her keyboard.

"Any good sales?" Renee asked. She never wanted to be *that* boss, the one who chided their employees for taking mental health breaks, and yes, she considered looking at Black Friday ads a mental health break.

"Anything in particular you're looking for?"

"My niece is fourteen. What do teens like these days?"

Ester pulled the hidden advertisement out from under her keyboard and flipped rapidly until she came to the page she was looking for. She turned it toward her boss. "I get one for my daughter every year, and she loves it." Ester pointed to a box of sample perfumes. "You get thirteen of the most sought-after fragrances, all designer, and the best part is they get a full-size bottle of their choice, all for sixty-five dollars."

Renee took the paper out of Ester's hands, almost as if she couldn't believe what she'd been told. Sure enough, the fine print said the same thing. "Is it worth it?"

"So worth it."

Renee made a mental note to get one for Ester. She knew she was a single parent, and Renee tried to do what she could to help. "What else?" she asked. Ester continued to flip and point out what the hot items of the season were.

"I'll text you a list, Ms. Wallace."

"Thank you, Ester." Renee asked her to email the attorneys whose clients had missed their necessary payments for the month, and once she did, she could go for the day. "Have a happy Thanksgiving," she said before disappearing into her office.

She sat at her desk and texted Brooklyn. Do I brave the traffic and leave now?

Brooklyn Hewett: Bowie says there's an accident and to wait.

Of course, there is.

Renee pushed her phone aside and shook the mouse on her desk to wake up her computer. She had depositions to go over in a custody dispute, briefs to write for the tiny humans she was a guardian ad litem for, and she needed to read through a stepparent adoption case, but the only thing she wanted to focus on was her solitaire game. She clicked "New" and watched as the computer laid out the board for her, groaning when multiple red cards in a row flipped over. Renee preferred a mix; it was easier to build a sequence that way. As tempted as she was to click "New" and get another board, she accepted the challenge and started moving her mouse from one spot to another.

Halfway through her game, Ester came on the intercom and told her boss she was leaving and to have a fun time shopping, and then there was a knock at her door. She closed the application, pulled up a random file, and acted as if she were knee deep in reading. "Come in."

She hadn't bothered to look to see who walked in, figuring it was Donna or someone who needed something from her. Out of her peripheral, she saw something move and turned her head slightly to catch a glimpse. What she saw had her moving her chair around so she could face forward. Someone stood at the front of her desk with a large bouquet of roses.

"You can set those down," she said as she stood up to reach for the small white card that contrasted with evergreen and lush red of the partially opened rosebuds.

The person holding the vase lowered it, and as he did, Renee's eyes went wide, and her mouth dropped open. "Theo," she said breathlessly. He barely had time to set the flowers down before she was in his arms. His hand rested softly on her lower back, and his other went around her shoulders. Theo brought Renee into his embrace and tilted his head as her hands encased his neck. They looked at each other, both smiling before closing the gap. The kiss started off soft. A small brush of the lips until Theo pulled her forcefully against him and let out a slight growl. Her breath left her body in a quick gasp, and then his tongue plunged into her mouth. Once their lips parted from each other's, she cupped his face with her hands and tried to slow her breathing. "I thought you couldn't make it to Thanksgiving."

"I can't," he said, and her exuberant demeanor changed instantly. He touched her chin lightly and said, "I changed my flight plans so I could have a brief layover. I only have a few minutes before I have to be back to the airport."

"You didn't have to do that, but I really appreciate it."

"I wanted to see you before I flew to Japan. I wish I didn't have to go."

"Me too," she said as she took him by his hand and led him to the couch in her office. She fixed him a drink and then took the spot next to him. She kicked off her heels and brought her legs up onto the sofa.

"Do you want me to massage your feet?" he asked her.

"No, I want to lean my head on your shoulder and absorb as much of you as I can."

"Me too, sweetheart." Theo patted her knee three times and then rested his hand there. He had quirks, much like anyone, and a few bothered her, such as the knee pat. It was always three. And he never wore jeans, shorts, or sweatpants. He always ordered for her, and it was often a meal for them to share. At first it really irritated her, and she figured if she gave him a list of foods she didn't like, he would be mindful. Most of the time he was but was also insistent she try new things. She hated seafood, and he would often order it for them until she reminded him she wouldn't eat, and no amount of persuasion would change her mind. But in the grand scheme of things, these were all minor annoyances when it came time for them to be together. His job kept him busy, and the distance between them often seemed greater than it was.

Thinking about his love for seafood made her laugh.

"What's so funny, sweetheart?"

"You're going to the land of sushi. You'll be in heaven."

Theo grinned. He had a great smile, and it was one attribute that attracted her. "But I will miss turkey, stuffing, and all the fixings."

"Not to worry, my love," she said as she brushed her fingers through his hair. "I'll make you your own dinner when you come back."

"I'll look forward to it."

They stayed in this bubble until Theo had to catch a taxi back to the airport. He insisted Renee not come with him, telling her it was more reasonable since she had to travel north, and the airport was south. After he left, she went to her window and, once again, looked down at the miniature-size people bustling along the sidewalks. She could never pick him out but liked to think she could. She saw someone in the same cream-colored trench coat Theo wore and set her hand on the windowpane. "I'll miss you," she said aloud.

FOUR

The repeated sound of a foghorn finally woke Graham from a restless sleep. He lay in his bed, nestled under the weighted blanket his mother had given him for his birthday. When he unwrapped the heavy present, he was confused until she told him she thought it would help him sleep better at night. He wasn't aware he was having trouble sleeping until he started using the genius invention, and now, most nights, Graham slept well, always waking up refreshed. Unless Grady was on his mind. Graham missed his brother. Their parents missed their son.

There were times when Graham thought everyone would be better off if Grady had died the night of the accident. Grady felt the same. The life he had known, the one he wanted, no longer existed, and no matter how hard he tried, he would never be the same.

Every year downtown Cape Harbor closed Third Street for the annual Austin Woods Memorial Celebration. The town would come together to memorialize not only Austin, but also other fishermen lost at sea, but it was Austin's tragic death that spurred a couple members of the town to create the event in his honor. Vendors would line the street, selling their goods, and the stores would keep their doors open and their storefronts looking fresh, hoping to entice a tourist or two. The football field at the high school would become a carnival. There would be Jet Ski races in the bay, and a 5K race. Everyone in town loved the event, except those who suffered the most. Those people stayed away from downtown and only met on the beach for one night of drinking and reminiscing by the bonfire.

It had been five years since Austin and Grady had their fateful accident, and nothing had been the same since. Graham, Jason, Monroe, Bowie, and Mila sat quietly around the fire, a few feet from the Driftwood Inn. Every so often, Graham would look toward the massive windows and wonder what Carly Woods did while all her son's friends were outside, near her home, but never had the courage to go knock on her door. His brother had survived, when her son had died. He often thought of what he would say to her or her to him. The last time they had spoken was at Austin's funeral.

When Grady finally joined the group, he stood on the cusp and watched while everyone stared at him. They, too, had no idea what to say, especially on the anniversary of the accident. This particular year had been a milestone. Graham heard people around town saying, "Wow, I can't believe it's been five years." He could. He lived with the aftermath every day. He saw the pain and anguish in his brother, as if those words were written on his face.

"Grady." Monroe finally broke the silence among the friends. Graham watched as his brother looked everyone over and made the decision to head toward the shoreline. Monroe stood to follow, but Graham held his hand up.

"I'll go."

Graham left the bonfire and trudged through the sand until he caught up with Grady. They walked quietly, side by side, until they reached the surf. The brothers stood there, absorbing the peace and quiet.

"Can I tell you a secret?"

"You can tell me anything, Grady."

"Most of the time, I wish I had died on the boat that night."

Graham let the words sink in. He couldn't imagine his life without his twin. On the other hand, he hated what Grady's drinking had done. Not only to himself, but to their family as well. Graham put his arm around his brother's shoulder and pulled him closer. "Someday, I hope the demons go away, Grady. I miss my brother and my best friend."

Grady inhaled harshly, almost as if he fought back tears or even rage. "I miss him, too, but he's long gone, Graham. He's buried out at sea with Austin."

Those words haunted Graham. Ever since Grady spoke them, Graham had been at a loss for how to get through to him. To get him the help he needed even though he didn't want it. Some nights were worse than others. Graham had a lot of anger and resentment toward Grady and even Austin. If they had made better decisions, his life would be different. It would be where he wanted it to be. When nights like this existed, nothing worked. Graham would simply avoid crawling into bed and would opt for the sofa or the chaise on his patio, although he found he never really slept when he was out there. He loved the ocean, but it haunted him as well.

The foghorn sounded again, and Graham groaned. He had hoped the weather would clear for Thanksgiving, that maybe the rain would stop, and the sun would come out . . . anything Mother Nature could do to help improve the day he dreaded already. He glanced toward his sliding glass door. Long black curtains hung, blocking any light from seeping into his room. Beyond those doors was a deck facing the water, with two chairs and a small table. It was where he went to think and relax. Where he often sat in the early hours of the morning, watching the ships leave port, and where, when he had a rare night off from the bar, he'd watch the sunset.

Living on a houseboat had its challenges but also had many perks. Friends came to visit but rarely stayed. His place was small, tiny by most people's accounts, yet perfect for him. Space was an issue, and he barely fit himself. If his shoes had a bit too much lift, he'd brush his head on the low-lying ceiling. He had to duck under doorways and slouched when he had to do the dishes. The bathroom wasn't big enough to do much in either. Graham had to replace the showerhead with one that came with a detachable hand shower, and when it was time to shave, his arm brushed against the wall. His bedroom wasn't anything to write home about, either, with his bed taking up most of the space. His bedroom was by far the biggest space, occupying the full length of the house. When he bought the houseboat, there had been two bedrooms. He and Bowie removed the wall between them to give Graham more space. He had a small closet, a little storage, and still washed his clothes at his parents'. Still, he wouldn't give up the houseboat for anything. He loved living on the water and felt at peace there. The quiet, serene moments were worth the hassle of missing modern-day amenities.

Graham threw his covers back and sat up slowly. His head already throbbed, and he would bet money the pain was only going to get worse as the day went on. He rotated until his bare feet touched the hardwood floor, and his toes wiggled, which made him laugh. Before him, the black-covered sliding glass door called to him. As much as he wanted to confirm the doom and gloom, the foghorn warned him that coffee and aspirin were more important. Still, he stood and made his way the few steps from his bed to the door and pushed the curtains aside, sighing. He longed for summer, when the sun lingered high in the sky and cast an orange-yellow-red-and-pink glow over everything. When he could look out from his room and have to squint, and he could feel the heat penetrating through the glass. He had months until those days would return, and until then, he would have to cope with the winter blues.

Graham placed his bare feet onto the planks of his narrow stairway. Brooklyn called it a floating staircase, held together by suspension cables to give off the illusion of a bigger houseboat. The perfect concept for tight, confined spaces.

He made his way to the kitchen, flipped a switch to turn on his water pump, and waited. Outside, the single mom who lived across the dock from him appeared. Shari and her two boys, Bryce and Brayden, moved to Cape Harbor a few years ago from somewhere on the East Coast. Other than saying hi when Graham saw his neighbor, he didn't know much about her. For the most part, they kept to themselves. The day Shari and her boys moved in, the youngest boy decided to see if he knew how to swim. He jumped off the dock before anyone had any inkling he was even thinking of doing so. Graham reacted instantly and dove in after him. Now, every time he was outside, Brayden teetered on the edge to get a reaction out of Graham. One of these days, he was going to pretend to push him in to tease him.

Shari glanced toward Graham's houseboat and waved. He returned the gesture and pulled up on the handle to turn on the water. It spurted a few times before gushing a slow but full stream out of the faucet. He filled the reservoir of his single-serve coffee dispenser. Another gift for his birthday; however, this one was from Brystol. She had asked him to take her shopping so she could buy something for her parents, and when she saw him fiddling with the coffee maker, Brystol told her dad she wanted to give it to Graham. In the time since Brooklyn returned to town with her teenage daughter, Graham had adopted the role of doting uncle and appreciated the gift. The only downfall—he had to fill the canister each time he needed a refill. Still, it was better than using instant coffee or the old percolator pot his father kept stored in the garage with all their camping gear.

With his reusable pod filled with coffee grounds and the button pressed to start brewing, Graham went back upstairs to grab his phone. Notifications of emails, sports reports, and text messages from his mother filled his screen. He cleared them away and put on a pair of sweatpants and a sweatshirt before heading back downstairs. The one hard lesson Graham learned early on about living on a houseboat was to always use the handrails. Often, a gust of wind would blow against the house, or a powerful wave would crash into the bay, rocking his house back and forth. One knock to the head was one too many for his liking.

Downstairs, his coffee maker spurted out the last drops of freshly brewed coffee, which he carried out onto his deck. It was cold—the wind blew slightly—but it was the quietness that grabbed his attention. The ocean was calm, barely any movement, and the seagulls that usually hung around the pier didn't seem to be anywhere in sight. Graham reached into the small aluminum garbage can he kept on the deck and scooped a handful of salmon pellets into his hand. He let them go slowly, watching each bunch hit the water. The plunk, plunk, plunk echoed, yet no fish rose to the top. He finally opened his hand and released the rest, expecting to see hungry fish clamoring to swallow every piece, but nothing. Migration had happened. The salmon had gone back to the rivers for the winter.

He drank his coffee as he looked out over the horizon. He shivered from the cold and opened his phone to look at the weather app. It was going to be in the midforties and had dropped to the low thirties overnight. It seemed colder, for some reason, and Graham deduced it was because his subconscious was looking for an excuse to stay home.

After another cup of coffee, he finally texted his mother back, confirmed he would be there for dinner and that no, he wasn't bringing a date. There wasn't anyone in town who caught his eye, and the person he would like to be with was in a committed relationship. He still struggled with his feelings toward Rennie. There were times when he wished he had pursued her back when they were in California and times when he was glad he hadn't. Graham had a lot of baggage in the form of his brother and wouldn't wish the burden of caring for an alcoholic on anyone. As much as he wanted to put off the holidays, they were upon him.

Graham finished his coffee, washed his mug, and changed the light bulb in the bathroom. He showered quickly, dressed nicely in a cobalt-blue button-down and a pair of relaxed-fit jeans—a far cry from the look he had when tending the bar—and made his way over to his parents', which took him about ten minutes. When he walked in, the smell of roasting turkey made his stomach growl.

Johanna Chamberlain stood over a boiling pot with a wooden spoon in her hand. She wore an apron that read "Kiss the Cook." Graham did as it asked and placed a kiss on his mother's cheek.

"Smells good in here." Graham rested his hand over his rumbling stomach. He hadn't eaten earlier because he knew he would need the space for dinner.

"Thank you. Your father is in the den. There's sausage, cheese, crackers, and chips and dip in there. Drinks are in the cooler on the sunporch." She paused and looked at her son. "Have you heard from your brother?"

The question gave him pause. Grady lived with his parents, and Graham had expected to find him sitting next to their father, watching football.

He shook his head slightly. "He didn't come home last night?"

His mother continued to stir. "He hasn't been home in a couple of days."

Graham placed his hand over his mother's. She stopped moving the wooden spoon, turned, and looked at him. "Why didn't you tell me?" he asked.

"I didn't want you to worry. You have so much going on with the bar . . ." She trailed off.

"He's my brother." The day Graham returned home after the fateful phone call was the day he put Grady before everything else in his life.

Graham excused himself and went outside. He pulled his phone out of his pocket, brought it to life, and pressed Grady's number. It rang and rang until voice mail picked up. "Hey, call me back. If you need me to come and pick you up, let me know." He hung up and held his phone in his hand. Across the street, a group of teenagers playing a game of flag football got his attention.

"Okay, Austin, you're going to linger near the line for a bit and then take off like you're late for dinner. I'm going to fake a handoff to Bowie, circle around, and send a pass your way. On three." The three of them clapped, and Graham moved toward the makeshift line of scrimmage. He crouched down, called his audible, and prepared to get the football from the center.

"Chamberlain steps back," he said as he moved backward. "He looks to his left, to his right. He fakes a handoff to Bowie Holmes and fires a bomb downfield to Austin Woods. Woods catches the ball and dodges a tackle by Jason Randolph." Graham threw his arms up in the air and danced around when Austin jumped over the broom handle they used as a goal line.

Grady dramatically fell to the ground.

"Get up, sore loser," Graham heard Austin say to his brother.

"Every year. I give up," Grady lamented. He sat up and pointed at Graham. *"Next year, I get Austin on my team."*

"Whatever you say, Grady." Graham walked over and held his hand out for his brother, helping him up. The friends huddled together and on three chanted, *"Forever."*

Graham brushed the back of his hand over his wet cheek. That was the last time the five of them played together. By summer, Austin would be gone. The Thanksgiving following the accident, no one even suggested the boys get together and play. Their forever had ended. He went back into the house, kissed his mother on the cheek again, and went into the den to visit with his father.

George Chamberlain yelled at the television with a string of curse words to rival any sailor. He sprawled back in his recliner, jerking slightly when the mechanism locked into place. He pointed the remote control at the screen and mumbled incoherently.

"It's not even the Seahawks," Graham said as he sat down on the couch. Instantly, his body sagged and relaxed.

"It's football. It doesn't matter who's playing," George bellowed after another round of his yelling at the television subsided. Graham knew his father's statement to be false. His dad was a die-hard Seahawks fan and flew a flag out front for everyone to see. That particular act of showmanship always confused Graham. It would stand to reason most people in Washington would be fans of their professional teams, and he could understand if someone had moved to the state, such as his neighbors, but they would display their hometown team, unlike the locals.

Graham liked to consider himself impartial, something he'd learned while working at the bar. He never wanted to pressure his employees or patrons to root for one over the other and respected all the sports fans and whatever teams they supported. With that said, because he ran a tourist-town bar, he subscribed to the most expansive sports providers in the market so he could appease his customers.

Graham paid attention to the game, cheered when required, and greedily helped himself to the appetizers. When his pop was empty, he'd get up and get a new one, along with a beer for his dad, and the men would continue to watch the game until it was time to eat. Every so often, Johanna would come into the room, say something about the officiating while wiping her hands on her apron, and disappear back into the kitchen.

"Where's your brother?"

"Not sure." He spoke quietly as he took his phone out of his pocket, hoping to find a message from Grady. Nothing. He sent him a text message, asking him to call. He waited for the three conversation bubbles to appear; they never did. He typed out a message to his friend Monroe, asking her if she had seen Grady.

Monroe Whitfield had grown up with the twins and had always had a crush on Grady. From early on, when Grady and Austin decided to start a fishing company back in high school, Monroe said she had no plans of ever leaving Cape Harbor, and everyone knew it was because of Grady. Her younger sister, Mila, couldn't get out of there fast enough. After the accident, Roe tried to fix Grady, show him he could still have a life, but he pushed her aside as he had done to everyone else. Yet, she still lingered, often showing up with him in tow after no one had seen him for a few days. She always knew where to look.

Monroe Whitfield: I haven't seen him in a few days.

Okay, thanks

Monroe Whitfield: Is everything okay?

Nothing is ever okay, he wanted to say to her.

He's late for dinner.

Monroe Whitfield: I'll keep an eye out.

That was precisely what Graham didn't want her to do, to interrupt her Thanksgiving to look for his drunk-ass, irresponsible brother.

Don't, Roe. He's an adult and needs to figure things out on his own. I'll see you later at B's.

Monroe sent back a sad-faced emoji, and Graham pocketed his phone. He felt like shit for ruining her holiday, even though she would never admit it to him.

"Maybe Grady should move in with you."

Graham turned his head slowly until his gaze fell upon his father. "What?" he croaked out. "I don't have enough room."

"Move," his father suggested gruffly. "Grady needs his family to be supportive."

"What Grady needs is rehab and therapy, and he needs for his parents to accept the fact he's an alcoholic. Besides, doesn't he live here?"

"Dinner!" Johanna's voice rang out, cutting through the tension-filled den. "Come on—come eat."

Graham didn't hesitate and followed his mother into the dining room. He sat in his usual spot, across from the empty chair where Grady would sit when he arrived. His mom would sit to his left, with her back facing the kitchen, and his dad would soon be to his right.

Their table was small, fitting the four of them cozily, but add anyone else, and it would feel crowded. The tablecloth was plastic and had turkeys, cornucopias, and leaves printed on it. A plate of sliced turkey sat in the middle of the table, and without giving it much thought, Graham reached for a piece of the crispy baked skin—his favorite.

"Do you want to talk about work?" his mom asked as she set down the bowl of mashed potatoes and took her seat.

"Not really. No offense, but I see you almost every day; I think you know about everything that goes on there."

"Okay, what about your love life? Ever since the Holmeses became grandparents, I've grown rather jealous. I see Linda out and about with Brystol all the time and wonder when I'm going to get the opportunity."

Graham sat in silence as he listened to his mother's pleas. At times, he longed for a companion, especially after seeing his best friend Bowie reunite with Brooklyn. He had never given much thought to parenthood, though. Truthfully, none of his friends had. It was almost as if that ship sailed for everyone when Austin died. Somehow, he took a piece of each of them with him, and none of them had ever fully recovered.

"I don't know, Mom."

"Maybe you should try a dating app or something," she suggested with a shrug.

"Yeah, I'll think about it." He stopped talking as soon as his father walked into the room. The moment George sat down, it was time to eat. Throughout dinner, his mother sighed, and Graham suspected it was because the chair across from him remained empty.

FIVE

Waking up to the sound of the ocean, the waves crashing against rocks, and the booming echo of the foghorn was a happy reprieve from the normalcy of car horns, screeching tires, and loud voices, most often arguing with someone over a parking spot. It took Renee only a split second for the realization to set in—she was in Cape Harbor, and for the next few days she was Rennie, the outgoing, wild, and fly-by-the-seat-of-her-pants person she longed to be in Seattle. Here, among her closest friends, she could be herself and not worry about the facade of being a professional. She could snort at the corny jokes and add her sarcastic two cents when someone talked about their current existential life crisis. Here, a few hours north of her hustle-and-bustle life in Seattle, she was free.

She rolled over and took in her room. She was on the third floor, at the end of the hallway. The converted rooms were the Driftwood Inn's version of a suite and had the most privacy from the busy reception area. Her room had a sliding glass door and balcony, whereas other rooms only had windows that opened to let the ocean breeze in. The bed had an antique wrought iron frame painted white, set up against a navy wall. Across from the bed, the shiplap wall held lantern sconces and a piece of artwork she was sure Brystol had created of an anchor made from seashells. The room was different from when Carly Woods had owned the inn. Rennie wasn't sure when the inn had been constructed but remembered clearly the decor. She had spent one summer cleaning rooms for Carly and hated all the brown fake wood that was everywhere. Part of her missed the old look, mostly because it meant Carly would still be around and Brystol would have her grandmother.

The soft knock on her door caused her to sit up in a flash. Her hand went to her head, as if to push back the impending headache. Coffee: she needed it—and fast. "Whoever is there, you better have your own key and a cup of coffee for me." She heard the mechanical lock adjust and suspected the person on the other end was her best friend, Brooklyn Hewett.

The door crept open slowly, and long wavy brown locks made their appearance before Brystol stepped into the room with a mug in her hand.

"Brystol." Rennie sighed and held her arms out for her niece. It hadn't been very long since they had seen each other, but since her two favorite people returned to Washington, Rennie had been trying to spend as much time as possible with the mother-and-daughter duo. The teen made her way to Rennie, set down the mug, which was filled to the brim with coffee, and crawled into bed.

Brystol rested her head on Rennie's shoulder and wrapped an arm around her waist. "I've missed you, Aunt Rennie."

Hearing her niece's sweet voice brought a smile to her face. She kissed the top of Brystol's head and adjusted so she could look into her breathtakingly beautiful blue eyes. "I miss you every day and am so happy your mother decided to stay."

"Me too."

The two rearranged the way they were sitting, and Brystol handed Rennie her coffee. "I knew you needed this."

She nodded and inhaled the aroma. "This is why you're my favorite niece."

Brystol chuckled. "I'm your only niece. Oh, get this. We were talking about family in my social studies class, and so I list everyone, right? Well, Tessa Cary raises her hand and says you're not really my aunt. She literally argued with me in class over it."

"Who is Tessa?"

Brystol rolled her eyes. "Like, the most annoying girl in school . . . and the most popular." The last bit came out in a much-quieter voice, bringing back memories from Rennie's high school days. She took a few sips of her coffee and set the cup down on the nightstand next to her bed.

"Here's the deal, B. We're family because we say we are. I've known your mom for most of my life, and the day you were born is the day I became your aunt. I'm your aunt because I say so and because you say so. Who cares what Tessa Cary thinks? She's not in our family, is she?"

Brystol shook her head.

"Besides, she sounds like a mean girl."

"Oh, she is." She rolled her eyes again. "We like the same guy, and it sucks."

"Does this guy like you or her?"

Brystol pushed her glasses up the bridge of her nose. "He likes both of us. Says he can't decide."

Rennie rolled her eyes in dramatic fashion, and Brystol giggled. "Run, girl. Run!" she screeched. "You don't need a guy messing with your feelings. He either likes you, or he doesn't. If you're going to date . . . wait, does your dad know there's a boy?"

She shrugged. "He's been over before, but he's scared of my dad."

"As he should be. What's his name?"

"Seth Sabine."

"Well, Seth sounds like a politician." Rennie adjusted her pillow and held out her arm, inviting Brystol to cuddle. "Honestly, B, before you find the right guy for you, you're going to kiss a lot of frogs, figuratively speaking. The point I'm trying to make is, don't waste all your emotions on this guy if he's not willing to do the same for you."

Brystol sighed. "You're right. I'm so happy you're here."

"Me too, B. I really needed this minivacation. Now, tell me . . . does Simi have those amazing cinnamon rolls downstairs?"

Brystol sat up straight and nodded excitedly. "Yes, but you better hurry. We have a lot of people staying here, so they're going fast."

"I'll be down in a few, okay?"

They got out of bed at the same time, and Rennie walked Brystol to the door. After shutting it, she picked her phone up off the dresser and scrolled through her notifications. All quiet on the work front. She mentally calculated Theo's flight to Japan and figured he would be landing soon. Rennie turned the ringer on, opened her music app, and took her phone into the bathroom. She wasn't worried about missing the cinnamon rolls, because she knew either Brystol would save her one or Simone would make another batch. Simone was good like that.

After her shower she added tinted moisturizer to her face, opting to go makeup-free while away from meeting with clients for a few days, and pulled her wet hair into a french twist, securing it with a couple of bobby pins. She dressed in black leggings and an oversize sweatshirt, opting for comfort before she sat down for Thanksgiving dinner later. After placing her phone in one of the two side pockets her leggings had, she sent a silent thank-you to whoever created the pants she wore, because she hadn't wanted to carry her purse everywhere. She slid her key card into the other pocket and headed toward the lobby. In the hall, she passed a family of four chatting excitedly about driving north to Canada for some skiing. She couldn't help but smile, knowing she and Theo were going to do the same thing for New Year's. Instead of taking the elevator down, mostly because she didn't trust it even though Bowie swore it was the best-working elevator this side of the harbor, she took the stairs. More exercise was going to be one of her resolutions in the coming year. Her office had stairs, and there wasn't any reason she couldn't use them, other than convenience. In the elevator, she could type out an email on her phone, return text messages, or scroll through social media. Taking the stairs meant paying attention. The last thing she wanted was to trip and fall on concrete steps.

As soon as she came to the grand staircase, the smell of every breakfast food imaginable surrounded her, and she envisioned a plate of crispy bacon and eggs, an ooey-gooey cinnamon roll with cream cheese frosting, another cup of coffee, and some orange juice to help fight against pesky germs. A side of fruit and yogurt would do her some good as well.

Rennie stood on the imaginary divider between the reception area and the dining area. She glanced at the tables, each one full. The sight of families on vacation during the holidays no longer surprised her. Once her parents retired from their jobs, they sold their home, put most of their stuff in storage, and began traveling the globe. The first holiday Rennie spent without her parents was hard, but she grew accustomed to them being away.

A perk of knowing the owner was the liberties Rennie could take. Walking into the kitchen like she worked there was one of them. As soon as Simone came around the corner and saw Rennie standing there, she held her arms open for a hug.

"Simi." Rennie sighed when she saw the woman she considered to be a part of her family. "Happy Thanksgiving."

"I'm so happy you could come."

Rennie inhaled deeply, taking in the way Simone smelled like cinnamon and baked fruit. She released her hold and stepped back. For as long as Rennie could remember, Simone Dowling had been a figure in their lives. As a young teen, when Rennie would visit, Simi would drive them to the movie theater or make them lunch. Simi never meddled but always had an opinion when asked. When life changed, she became Carly Woods's caregiver, and she helped take care of Brystol when she would visit over the summer. Simi was the one person who stayed on, despite the inn closing. Who made sure Carly had everything she needed. Rennie never knew Simone's title until Carly's will came across her desk and the document referred to her as *confidante*, but she had been and continued to be so much more to the family.

"There isn't any other place I would rather be right now." Rennie spoke the truth. Being in Cape Harbor meant being with family.

"You must be starving. I heard from our overnight desk agent you came in late last night." Simone motioned for Rennie to follow her. They walked out of the kitchen and into a little alcove, which had a small table and a couple of chairs in the corner. "Sit here; I'll get you some breakfast." In a flash, she was gone, leaving Rennie with her thoughts and a view of the ocean. Off in the faint distance, she saw a ship, and it reminded her to pull up her calendar to see where her parents were. *Australia.*

"That's right," she said to herself. She typed out a quick text to her parents, wishing them a happy Thanksgiving and asking that they send pictures when they could.

Simi returned with a trayful of options and set it down in front of her. "Brooklyn is helping a customer, and then she'll be right in. Can I get you anything else?"

"Just your Christmas list," Rennie said.

She waved her off. "Don't be silly. I have everything I want."

"Yes, but sometimes it's nice to get new socks or something."

"Meh, don't you worry about me."

Rennie watched as Simone walked toward the kitchen. She would buy presents for her, whether she gave a list or not. It was nice, though, to have some sort of idea what people wanted when she went shopping over the weekend. Rennie thought Simi would like the perfume sampler as well, but then it occurred to her she loved the way Simone always smelled like pastries.

Rennie was midbite when her name echoed off the walls. She quickly set her fork down, stood, and launched herself into her best friend's arms. To anyone looking in, it would seem the two hadn't seen each other in years, not weeks.

"I can't believe you didn't come to the house when you got in last night." Brooklyn sat down and poured herself a cup of coffee from the carafe.

"I didn't want to wake you or interrupt the baby-making process."

Brooklyn blushed. "I'm fairly certain the factory is closed. Besides, I was looking forward to a late-night gab session."

"There's always . . ." Rennie paused and thought about the next couple of days. They would go to bed early tonight to rise at dawn to shop on Black Friday. It was tradition and not something she would pass up. Then they would be exhausted after shopping all day and go to bed early, which left them Saturday. "Saturday night?"

"It's a date. Wait until you see the ballroom. Bowie and his crew have been working nonstop since yesterday to get it ready for Friday. The tree is gorgeous, and all the decorations came out exactly as I wanted."

"Were you able to get the room booked for the month of December?"

"Yes, almost every night is booked, and twice on the weekends. It's been so crazy. I will never fully understand why Carly closed the inn. It's taken hardly any time to bounce back. Most nights we're at capacity on the hotel side, and we've started advertising for beach weddings."

"My interior designer is becoming a party planner. I'm not sure how I feel about the career change," Rennie deadpanned. She glared at Brooklyn for a long beat before cracking a smile. "All joking aside, we need to talk about your wedding."

Brooklyn squeezed Rennie's hand. "I know. I can't wait. But first, the holidays, and then it's all wedding talk. I want to make this one special for Brystol and Bowie—and Simone as well. I know she misses Carly."

"Speaking of, any idea of what I can get her?"

"Bowie and I have made lists, picked up on little hints here and there. We are thinking of sending her on a cruise or somewhere tropical after the holidays. She's working so hard and never complains."

"Oh, I bet she would love a nice trip. I should ask my parents what they recommend."

"Are they home?"

Rennie shook her head and took a sip of her coffee. "Hanging with the koalas right now. It's weird. I miss them, but I don't. I'm a horrible daughter."

"No, you're not. You've adjusted—that's all. But yes, ask your parents what they suggest, and I'll get it booked."

Rennie sent another text to her parents. After she set her phone down, she returned to her breakfast. In between bites, she asked, "What are the plans for today?"

Brooklyn turned her phone toward Rennie and rattled off the list of things that had to be done to set up for Thanksgiving dinner. "The dining room needs to be set up buffet-style. All the linens changed. Plates, utensils, and all the necessities set out."

"Well, put me to work."

"You're on vacation, Ren. I'm not going to make you work."

"You didn't ask; I offered. Besides, what else am I going to do?"

Brooklyn closed the screen on her phone and looked into her best friend's eyes. "What's going on? You haven't mentioned Theo since I sat down."

Rennie sat back in her chair. Her fingers fiddled with the handle of her mug. "Theo's in Japan or about to land, and I don't know. When I see him, I'm happy. I'm in love. But when I'm here, it's like he doesn't exist, and I'm okay with that too. I don't know. I'm sort of weirded out by this revelation." She picked up her mug and finished the rest of the warm coffee.

"Don't be mad at me for what I'm about to say."

"B, I could never be mad at you." She leaned forward and rested her elbows on the table.

"We feel like Theo doesn't like us much."

The words lingered in the air as Rennie watched Brooklyn. Her friend looked embarrassed and possibly regretful for saying what she had. Rennie couldn't fault her, though, because she had seen signs pointing in this direction. There had been a few trips in the past few months where Theo suddenly canceled, and when he had come to Cape Harbor, he acted as if he thought he was better than everyone else, which bothered Rennie.

Rennie tried to form a proper response. One that would appease everyone, but she had a tough time finding the right words. She could make excuses for Theo, but that was all they would be. She didn't see him changing anytime soon. Still, Brooklyn was her best friend, and she wasn't willing to push their relationship aside for anyone.

"He'll come around. I think he's a city boy who doesn't know how to let loose sometimes. We have to teach him." Even as she spoke, she wasn't sure she believed her own words.

As soon as the dining room cleared out, Rennie and a couple of the hotel staff got to work on setting up the space with long rectangular tables for Thanksgiving dinner. Despite all the guests staying at the hotel, only a handful would join them for dinner. Brooklyn had spoken to Rennie at length about what to do over the holidays and decided serving dinner would be best. They would do the same at Christmas. It was how Carly always ran the Driftwood Inn, and Brooklyn wanted more than ever to have the inn relive its glory days.

By the armful, Rennie carried linens, boxes of utensils, and plates to the tables. She organized, stacked, reorganized, and practiced how the line would move. She wanted everything to be perfect because she suspected Brooklyn was under a bit of stress.

She slowly ticked each item off the list and even found time to sneak into the kitchen, where she found Brystol and Simi making pies and had her hand slapped when she stole a cookie off the tray. Throughout the day, she kept busy. She helped check out guests who were leaving and showed the newcomers to their rooms.

Around midafternoon, she found herself on the back porch in one of the rocking chairs, watching the surfer who braved the rain. She could never get the hang of surfing. One had to be able to balance on a board while it moved up and down. She could barely keep upright on a normal day. Watching the man outside brought back memories she had long buried, at least until last summer, when she saw Graham again for the first time in years. When he sat down beside her at the Whale Spout, their past flooded her senses. The way they used to be together, the on-again, off-again friends-with-benefits couple. When they were together, they flowed seamlessly, as if made for each other. Through their years as friends, they had taught each other everything about the birds and the bees. There wasn't much they weren't willing to try. Now, every time she visited Cape Harbor, she longed to see Graham, to be near him. Oftentimes, he stayed away, and she suspected it was because of Theo. Deep down, she thanked Graham for being the levelheaded one, because she wasn't so sure she could control herself around him. Rennie loved to flirt with Graham. She had done it the night she returned to Cape Harbor without reservation and despite being in a relationship with another man. She couldn't help herself. Graham made her feel. When he was around, she had butterflies in her stomach, and her heart pounded a bit faster. When they hugged, her body melded to his, and she clung to him, almost as if her life depended on it. As much as she wanted to go back to those carefree days, she couldn't. They were adults now. They had responsibilities and commitments to others.

Still, as she sat there gazing at the surfer, she couldn't help but think about the spring break their junior year of college. A bunch of them pooled their money and decided to rent a house Rennie had seen an ad for on campus, which promised an amazing view, access to the beach, and the beds to sleep ten. The owner described the house as small but cozy. Turned out to be a one-bedroom shack a foot away from the beach with an RV-size refrigerator and a bathroom you had to back up into to use.

Rennie stood there with her backpack slung over her shoulder. Everyone around her was quiet, most likely stunned by what they were seeing. "Um . . ." She didn't know how to finish her sentence.

"What did the ad say again?" Graham asked as he ran his hand through his hair.

"Comfortable house on the shores of Malibu, sleeps ten," Rennie muttered.

"Maybe ten outside," one of Graham's roommates quipped.

"Maybe there's more around the corner." Rennie spoke with optimism. She refused to believe what she saw. There was no way she'd fallen for a con. Yet, with each step she took into the house, her demeanor changed. What she saw when she opened the front door was it. The house was nothing more than a shack. She turned to her group of friends and tried to smile. "At least we don't have to walk far to the beach."

People grumbled. Some talked about getting their money back, but it was Graham who took her into his arms and told her everything was going to be okay. "Why don't we head to the store and see if there are any tents or pop-up shelters."

"And chairs and a cooler, because we don't have those either," someone yelled while another added, "And I'm not paying any more money."

She could never ask anyone to give more than they already had. This was her fault. She should've driven out and inspected the place before she sent the owner money through Western Union. She was too trusting, something she would have to work on before law school.

Graham and Rennie drove to the nearest store, the one that had every possible inflatable toy somehow pinned to the storefront. Inside, Rennie walked up and down each aisle, trying to find everything they would need. There were ten of them now, but she knew others were coming. She filled her arms with air mattresses, Koozies, and a couple of inflatable chairs. When she caught up with Graham, he had five or so bags of ice in his arms, and he pushed Styrofoam coolers with his foot.

"What are we doing?" She sighed.

"Making a bad situation better."

"I feel so stupid." Rennie wanted to cry. She wanted to go back to her dorm room and hide until school started.

"Don't. You didn't know."

When they returned, Graham took over. He told the group that if they were uncomfortable with the accommodations, they could leave, but that they were all responsible because they had all agreed when Rennie read them the ad. Rennie smiled. Graham had a way of making her feel better. After she unpacked everything, she found the courage to tell her friends, "If you want to use one of the air mattresses, you're responsible for blowing it up." A few grumbled, but in the end, everyone did their part.

"Come on." Graham took Rennie's hand and pulled her behind him. He had on his wet suit, and the arms slapped his butt with each step he took. They walked toward the surf, trudging through the sand.

"You're not going to try and teach me again, are you?" she asked when they stopped by a surfboard.

Graham laughed. "No, I lost count of how many times you've fallen off the board. I thought we'd go out and just sit for a bit." He took the board from the sand and dropped it into the water. Rennie climbed on and sat cross-legged toward the front while Graham pushed them out into the water and finally slid onto the board.

They were quiet for a while, each lost in their own thoughts as the waves moved them around. Up and down. Up and down. For Rennie, being on *the surfboard like this was almost like a carnival ride, except waves were unpredictable.*

"You can't let our friends get to you," Graham said. She turned and faced him.

"I know. I feel bad, though."

He shrugged and scooted closer to her. He reached for her hand, and she gave it willingly. This weekend they would be more than friends; she was sure of it. "I don't like seeing you sad, Ren." He leaned forward and pressed his lips to hers. Their kiss deepened, and their hands tangled in each other's hair. That was until a wave washed over them. Rennie and Graham laughed, but the tone had been set for the weekend. They were both single and could finally be together.

Rennie startled at the sound of a door slamming. Her lips tingled. A reaction from the memory? Or something else? She couldn't be sure. She looked over her shoulder to see who headed her way, but no one was there. She sat back in the chair and continued to push herself back and forth as she watched the man out on the beach take a break from surfing.

She checked her phone, expecting a text from Theo, but there was nothing. Her parents had replied to her earlier message. They sent her a picture of them holding a koala bear and wished her a happy Thanksgiving and asked that she wish Brooklyn and Brystol one as well. They passed along the name of their travel agent and suggested Simone take the cruise they were taking in March to Europe. Rennie frowned at the idea, mostly because she would like to spend some time with them but couldn't fault them for living their lives.

SIX

Thanksgiving dinner at the Chamberlains' was awkward. The three of them were silent except for the clanking of the silverware when it hit a plate, the murmured requests when someone needed a dish passed to them, and Johanna's sniffles. Each time Graham would look at his mother to confirm his suspicions that she was crying, she would look away or make an excuse to get up. On the other side of him, his father, George, stared at his plate, saying nothing. Grady had done this. He put his family through hell most days, but not showing up for Thanksgiving was a new low, even for him.

Graham fumed. He wanted to find Grady and beat the shit out of him. His brother needed some sense knocked into him. He needed help. Grady needed to wake up and see what he was doing to their parents. Enough was enough. His family had done nothing but enabled his addiction, and this was how Grady repaid everyone. His absence. Usually, Graham wouldn't care, but their parents did, and he hated seeing his parents upset.

After dinner, when his father began watching the next sporting event on television and his mother insisted Graham do the same, he chose to help her with the dishes instead. He suggested she clear the table and put everything into containers while he finished carving the rest of the turkey, making sure to separate the meat from bone for the soup his mother would later make. Once he finished, he filled the roasting pan with hot sudsy water and moved it to the stove, where he turned the burner on low. It was a trick he learned from his grandma many years ago, the best way to remove stuck-on food. He also filled the sink and started washing the dishes his mother brought to him.

"We have a dishwasher, you know." Johanna pointed to it.

"I know." As much as Graham wanted to head over to the Driftwood Inn to be with his friends, he didn't want to leave his mother so soon. He figured he would try to prolong his dish duties by handwashing everything.

"Well, at least put some gloves on."

He held a hand up and laughed. "I think my manicure will survive the dishpan-hand look."

His mother swatted him with a towel and went back to work. They made small talk with hushed voices. She didn't ask any more about Grady or about Graham's love life. Instead, she talked about a vacation she wanted to take but was having a difficult time convincing George to go on. He was worried about Grady.

"Always worried about Grady," Johanna stressed. "At some point, do we give up?"

Graham stiffened and looked out the kitchen window. In the fifteen years since the accident, he had never heard his mother ask such a question. He removed his hands from the water and dried them with a dish towel. He turned and found his mother sitting at the small table where she and George ate most of their meals. Graham took a mug from the dish rack and filled it with coffee and took it to his mother. He pulled the vacant chair out from under the table and sat down.

"Grady needs professional help, Mom."

"I know," she said quietly as tears escaped her eyes. Her hands wrapped around the mug. She lifted it to her lips and took a sip. "I've tried talking to your father, but he's in denial. He doesn't see the prolonged damage. There were times when you boys were growing up,

I couldn't tell you apart. So many of the same features—your eyes, cheekbones, and the way you'd wear your hair. When I saw Grady the last time, he looked nothing like you, and I had to take a step back. My baby boy is in trouble and has been for years, and I've been blinded by the notion he'd get better on his own or this was his way of coping."

"What do you mean, last time? Isn't Grady living here?"

She shook her head. "I haven't seen him in weeks, Graham."

"Why didn't you tell me?"

She tried to smile, but her cheeks barely lifted. "I didn't want to burden you."

"Mom, he's my brother. I worry about him too."

"I know, but he shouldn't be your problem. He's mine and your father's."

Graham was at a loss for words. Her thoughts differed vastly from his father's. George wanted everyone to look the other way when it came to Grady. On the surface, George needed to believe he had the perfect life.

"I thought that with Brooklyn back, Grady would change. That her presence would bring him some closure," Johanna stated. Graham knew this wasn't the case. Grady was upset with Brooklyn and blamed her for Austin's death.

"If you could convince him—"

"To do that?" Graham asked.

"To go to rehab."

"I've tried. He won't listen. I told him I'd drive him, be there when he got out."

"Try harder, please. For me? So much has been lost; I just want my son back."

"And I want my brother back." Graham longed for the days when his brother was his best friend. Granted, over time, they'd grown apart, but they'd always had each other's backs. He wanted more than anything to help his brother overcome his demons, to help him move on.

Graham hated feeling as if Grady was a lost cause, but there were also times when he thought Grady could use a month or two in jail, under lock and key. He was sure it was his brother who had broken into the bar over the summer, but Graham couldn't prove it. As much as he tried and told the police who he thought busted the door open and stole hundreds of dollars in liquor, nothing ever came to fruition.

Graham went back to the sink and finished the dishes, packed his leftovers, and kissed his mother goodbye. He sat in his car, looking at the house he had grown up in. So much had changed—and not for the better. He and Grady had so many dreams when they were teenagers. No one ever faulted Grady for wanting to be an angler. Most everyone embraced it. If anything, people turned their noses up at Graham for planning to leave Cape Harbor. Grady had been supportive of Graham's career choice, and he of Grady's. Now, all Graham wanted to do was find his brother. And when he did, he was going to ask him to finally pull his head out of his ass.

He started his car, and at the same time, his phone rang. He expected it to be Bowie asking him where he was. The display showed an unknown number. He declined the call, switched his car into reverse, and pulled out of his parents' driveway. He'd made it to the corner when his phone chimed with a new voice mail. He sat at the stop sign while his car idled and wondered what kind of telemarketer would leave a message on a holiday. His curiosity won out, and he pressed the button to listen.

"I'm trying to reach Graham Chamberlain. My name is Traci Birk, and I'm calling from Port Angeles General. If you could return my call . . ."

Graham's heart plummeted. He pressed the callback number and waited. Ring after ring, he sat there while his heart raced and his palms sweat. By the time someone picked up, his mouth was dry and parched. Images filled his mind of his brother lying somewhere alone—or worse, dying or already gone.

"Port Angeles General, how may I direct your call?"

"Yes, I need to speak with Traci Birk. I'm returning her call."

The operator asked Graham to wait while she transferred his call. He needed to turn around, to head back to his parents, but he felt trapped, paralyzed with fear. After what seemed like an hour, Traci picked up.

"Traci speaking."

"Um, hi, yes, this is Graham Chamberlain. You left me a message a few minutes ago."

"You were listed as an emergency contact for Grady Chamberlain."

"Is my brother . . . ?" Graham stopped, unable to bring himself to ask the question that sat on his tongue. "Is he . . . ?"

"Unfortunately, I can't say much over the phone, other than you and your family should come to PAG. The doctor on staff will be able to fill you in."

"Can you tell me if he's alive or what happened?"

"I'm sorry, Mr. Chamberlain—it's out of my purview to say."

Graham thanked her, hung up, and flipped a U-turn in the middle of the road. He sped toward the house, pulled back into the driveway, and left his car running. He ran toward the front door, threw it open, and yelled for his parents.

"Graham, what is it?" his mother asked as she rounded the corner.

"It's Grady. We have to go."

"What do you mean?" Her voice cracked.

He shook his head slightly. "I got a call from the hospital in Port Angeles. Grady's there. We have to go. Where's Dad?"

"What's all the commotion?" George asked. He ambled into the room and yawned.

"George, we need to go with Graham."

"What in heavens for? The game is on."

"Dad, Grady needs us," Graham said. "He's in Port A. We should go now."

George waved Graham off. "That boy will find his way home."

"Not this time, George. Get your coat, and get in the car. Graham will drive us."

George looked from his wife to his son. His eyes were like a Ping-Pong match, going back and forth. Graham waited for the realization to settle over his father, and when it finally did, his face went pale.

"What happened?"

"I got a call. They said to come to the hospital."

Once the words sank in, George rushed to put on his shoes while Johanna put her coat on. Graham went into the den and turned the television off and made sure the oven was off as well, in case his mom had forgotten. He flipped the light switch for their walkway and waited for his parents to exit.

"I should drive," George said as they approached Graham's car. Graham wanted to chuckle, but his father was serious. The elder Chamberlain prided himself on being the best driver of the household.

"Not a chance." Graham held the passenger door for his mother and waited for her to be safely inside before he shut it. He ran around to the driver's side, got in, and reminded his dad to put his seat belt on.

Graham drove out of town, north toward the highway. It would take them approximately three and a half hours to get to Port A if they caught the ferry at the right time. He couldn't be sure the ferry ran today and couldn't very well ask his parents to look the schedule up on his phone. He took his phone out of his pocket and asked the artificial intelligence to call Bowie.

"Hey, what's up? Are you on your way over?"

"Can you look up the Port Townsend ferry schedule to Coupeville?" he asked, avoiding his friend's question.

"Everything okay?"

"I don't know. Grady is in Port A General. My parents and I are heading there now."

"Holy shit, Graham. What happened?"

"Not sure—they won't tell us over the phone."

Bowie didn't speak for a few moments, and when he came back on the line, he gave Graham the schedule. The ferry ran on a limited schedule because of the holiday, and Graham would have to time his arrival to make it across to Coupeville.

Graham thanked Bowie, hung up, and pressed the gas pedal a bit more. His mother wouldn't be fond of him speeding, but he needed to hurry. In hindsight, he should've gone the other direction, but he'd thought he would save time by heading north.

During the drive and ferry ride, no one spoke. Graham held his mother's hand most of the trip, and when they were on the boat, his father refused to get out of the car. Graham needed fresh air. He needed to think. He went to the top deck, where very few people were, and stood against the railing. The harsh wind beat against his face. If he wasn't already in pain from the ache he felt, the wind might've hurt. He tried to think about anything other than Grady's cold dead body lying on a table. Since the fateful accident, Graham's outlook on life was far from positive. He saw the bad before the good. He expected nothing to go his way, and when it did, he looked for the underlying message. Bad luck and shitty outcomes followed him like the plague, especially when his brother was involved.

When the port came into view, Graham headed back to his car. The windows had fogged over, which led him to believe his parents had argued while he was gone. Growing up, his father never uttered a nasty word toward his mother. That all changed after the accident.

At first, Johanna catered to Grady. She coddled him. She made his breakfast, lunch, and dinner. Did his laundry, cleaned up his messes, and sat outside the bathroom door while her son threw up the copious amounts of alcohol he had consumed hours before. She spent hours on the phone with Graham, crying, asking her son repeatedly why this happened to their family. They were good people, never caused harm to others. And yet, everything fell apart around them. Graham had never had an answer, and he never would.

George, on the other hand, spent hours at the bar with his son. When he wasn't working, he sat on the stool next to Grady. In George's mind, he helped Grady cope the best way he knew how and refused to believe he enabled his son in any way. He was his friend. They were best buds. A voice of reason wasn't what Grady needed at that time. He had lost his best friend in a tragic and traumatic accident, barely surviving himself. Grady needed support, and George provided it, pint after pint.

The Chamberlains each saw their son in a vastly different light. Johanna wanted her son in rehab. George denied Grady had a problem.

Back on the road, Johanna tried to make small talk. Graham would answer and offer an opinion, but George stayed silent. Every so often, Graham would look at his father in the rearview mirror and try to figure out what the man thought. Was he scared? Was reality finally setting in? Graham wanted to know, but there was no way George would express his feelings. He wasn't that sort of man.

An hour later, Graham pulled into the parking lot of Port Angeles General. The hospital was new and looked practically like a shopping center. It wasn't one of those monstrosities you would find in a big city but a two-floor, well-designed building with a view of the mountains. Regardless of its facade, it was a hospital, and they had been summoned there because something happened to Grady.

Inside the main entrance, Graham went to the reception desk and gave the woman his name and told her he was there to see his brother. She asked the names of the other two people in his party and typed them into the computer. Name tags printed out of the machine, and she handed them to Graham.

"Go down this hall, and take the elevator on your right to the second floor. When you get to ICU, press the button on the intercom, and give them your name."

"ICU?" Johanna asked. "What's wrong with my son?" Her voice quivered.

"I'm sorry, ma'am—I don't have that information. They can help you on the second floor."

"Thank you," Graham said as he placed his hand on his mom's shoulder and directed her toward the elevator. The doors opened immediately, and they stepped in. Graham gave his parents their name tags and peeled the backing from his before adhering it to his shirt. His stomach flipped and flopped on the ride up. Silently, he let out a prayer. Intensive care meant Grady was alive and not on a slab in the basement. There was still some hope.

When they stepped out of the elevator, they followed the signs down the hall, which seemed to take a year. Everything moved in slow motion. Graham stood at the double doors keeping him and his parents from entering the ICU and pressed the button on the intercom. When asked, he gave his name.

The double doors opened to a waiting room. Four other people were sitting; one was asleep, and the rest were watching television. His parents sat while he paced.

Up until now, Graham had no idea he was Grady's emergency contact. The thought had never crossed his mind, and while he waited for the doctor to come out, he checked his phone. Other than "Home," no one would know who to call if he were in an accident. What had Grady done to make sure someone knew to reach out to Graham?

The second set of double doors opened, and a doctor came out. "Chamberlain?" Graham stepped forward just as Johanna and George stood.

"What's wrong with my son?"

"Follow me, please."

Graham wanted to reassure his mother that this was protocol. The doctor wasn't going to tell them anything with other people lingering around. There were privacy laws and etiquette. Inside the unit, there was a large semicircular desk in the middle of the room. The nurses there had a line of sight to each room, although some had their blinds pulled. The noise was what caught Graham's attention. Everyone was quiet except for the machines. The static beeping, the whooshing of breathing machines, and crying filled the void of people talking among themselves. As he followed the doctor, he fought back the tears.

The doctor took the Chamberlains into a small room. There were three chairs, and even though Graham wanted to stand, the physician motioned for him to sit down. "I'm Dr. Field and have taken over Grady's care while he's in the ICU."

"What happened to my son?" Johanna asked.

"Grady came in earlier this morning via ambulance. He was found on the side of the road, suffering from an overdose."

"Oh, God," Johanna gasped.

"My son doesn't do drugs," George added sternly.

Graham stayed quiet.

"The officers who found him were able to bring him back with naloxone. However, he coded in the ambulance on his way here."

With each bit of grave news, Johanna cried out, while George continued to deny that his son was a user. Graham held on to his mother and internally criticized his father for being so damn naive.

"What's Grady's prognosis?" Graham asked.

"His organs are shutting down. Grady has severe deterioration of his liver and pancreas. Right now, we have him in a medically induced coma to flush his system and hope we'll be able to grasp how much internal damage has been done. If Grady survives, he will need a strict lifestyle change."

"Meaning what?" George asked.

"Meaning he needs to go to rehab, Dad. It's time you accept that Grady is an addict and get him the help he needs before it's too late," Graham ground out. "If this isn't your wake-up call, I don't know what is." Frustration poured from Graham. Grady should've been in rehab years ago.

"Dr. Field, what are Grady's chances of survival?" Graham asked.

"Right now, low."

"And if he does survive?" Johanna asked.

"Without rehab?" Graham and Johanna nodded. "He won't make it."

Dr. Field left the family in the room. The tension between them grew until a nurse came to get them. They would only allow one in at a time. Graham told his mother to go.

When Graham and George went back to the waiting room, George walked through the second set of doors, claiming he needed something to drink. Graham let his father go. They both needed space away from each other to cool down.

He sat down and pulled his phone out of his pocket to text Bowie with an update, only to find a text message from Rennie: I'm here at the hospital. Where are you?

SEVEN

The dining room at the Driftwood Inn had five circular tables set up, all dressed in cranberry-colored linens. Most of the tables had filled with guests or employees of the inn who didn't have any family and opted to stay at work for Thanksgiving dinner. Brooklyn and Simone had gone above and beyond to make dinner special for everyone. Every possible food someone could want to eat sat on the rectangular tables surrounding the room, and all around, people chatted and got to know the strangers beside them—in the true spirit of Thanksgiving.

Rennie sat back in her chair and placed her hand over her stomach. She was full, having eaten one of the best meals of her life. A few morsels lingered on her plate, and even though Rennie lacked the energy to lift her fork, her index finger did the job for her and scooped the last bit of mashed potatoes off her plate. She stuck her finger in her mouth and moaned.

"I don't know what you put in these potatoes, Simi, but they are the best thing I've ever tasted. You should open a restaurant."

"Don't give her any ideas, Ren," Brooklyn said. She lay back in her chair and mimicked Rennie.

"It's an old family recipe," Simone responded with a smile.

"Can I join your family?" Rennie asked. Simone and Brystol laughed.

"You'll give it to me, right, Simi?" Brystol batted her eyelashes at the woman who had helped raise her over the years.

"Of course." Simi cupped Brystol's cheeks and gave the teenager an adoring smile. Rennie enjoyed watching the two of them together. They had a fondness for each other that was hard to come by lately.

As people finished dinner, they came over to the main table and thanked Brooklyn and Simone for dinner. Brooklyn told everyone that it was all Simone and her team who deserved the credit. She also reminded them to come back for pie or to take a piece to their room, as room service would be off for the night.

"Pie? How can you even mention dessert?" Rennie whined. She wanted pie. A slice of each one if she had her way. Earlier in the day, she had her hand slapped by Simone when she was caught trying to sneak a piece. As far as Rennie was concerned, she could live off cookies, cake, and pie and never eat a regular meal again, if she wouldn't balloon to five thousand pounds.

"It's always pie-thirty somewhere," Bowie said as he stood and went over to the table of desserts. Rennie watched him like a hawk. Her mouth watered when he returned with a piece of pumpkin pie with a mountain of whipped cream on top.

Brooklyn pulled the plate away from Bowie just as his fork touched the whipped cream. "What are you doing, woman?"

"We're waiting for Graham to get here."

Graham.

The sound of Graham's name made Rennie pay attention. She sat up a bit straighter and ran her hand through her hair to make sure there wasn't a strand out of place. Thankfully, she had changed her clothes for dinner. Although she still had on a pair of stretchy pants, she looked normal.

Wait, why do I care?

Rennie's thoughts gave her pause. Why did she care if Graham came over? Rennie had a boyfriend. She was in a committed relationship. Yet, since the day she walked into the Whale Spout five months ago and saw her Graham Cracker, he had been on her mind. Fifteen years she'd spent missing him because her best friend had asked her to stay away. Rennie had regrets, and there had been many times over the years when she'd picked up the phone to call or would fall down the rabbit hole of social media and spend hours looking him up online. And there were times when she remembered how he ditched her, ignored her after everything happened. How, when he went back to California, he packed up his stuff, quit his job, and left without a single word to her. They never had a proper goodbye, at least not one that meant anything. The last time Rennie saw Graham, all those years ago, they were in the parking lot of the church after Austin's funeral. Rennie had to leave to go back to her job. They hugged, and Graham promised to call when he got home at the end of the week. The call never came, and Brooklyn left shortly afterward. It seemed their lives in Cape Harbor were over, along with any friendships they had established.

Over the past few months, there were times when Rennie was in Cape Harbor, and she had chosen not to see Graham. Not because she had been mad at him, but for her own peace of mind. Rennie noticed that when she hadn't seen Theo for lengthy periods, her thoughts moved on to Graham. Rennie likened those moments to her past, when she and Graham would practice the friends-with-benefits role. Their relationship had always been easy. They gravitated toward each other, flirted relentlessly, knew each other's thoughts, and often finished each other's sentences. Their friendliness toward one another was often an issue when they were exploring other relationships. When Graham had a girlfriend, Rennie was always friendly. A little bit too much, and her exuberance often caused problems with Graham. Toward the end, when she was busy with law school and internships, she distanced herself from Graham. Mostly out of respect for his girlfriend at the time.

"Speak of the devil." Bowie pushed away from the table with his phone in his hand and disappeared down the hall. Rennie watched until he was out of sight, wondering why Graham called instead of showing up.

"I'm exhausted," Brooklyn stated for all to hear. When Rennie looked at her, she had her arms stretched over her head and yawned. "Four a.m. is going to come so early."

"We could sleep in and wait until Cyber Monday," Rennie suggested. "The sales are just as good, and we don't have to get dressed, fight for a parking spot, deal with traffic, or carry bags through busy malls." All valid points, even though she wanted the one-on-one time with Brooklyn.

"True, but I like to touch what I'm buying. I want to see the box, read the fine print, and make sure the product is quality."

"You mean unlike the snuggly blanket you found online that only fit a Barbie doll?" Brystol asked her mom.

"Exactly!" Brooklyn exclaimed. "This is why I can't be trusted to shop online." She looked directly at Rennie. "And don't even get me started on reviews. You know most of them are fake anyway."

Rennie scoffed but secretly agreed. She had been burned a time or two with deals that seemed too good to be true, and when the product arrived not to her liking or the specifications on the website, she had to battle some foreign entity for a refund. Black Friday shopping would commence in the morning.

Bowie came back into the room and paused as he held his phone in his hand, looked from the device to the table where his family and friends sat, and moved slowly toward his seat.

"What's wrong?" Brooklyn asked as Bowie sat next to her. She reached out and put her hand over his.

"It's Grady." Bowie paused and glanced at his phone. "He's in the hospital in Port Angeles."

"Was that Graham? What did he say?" Brooklyn fired off her questions in rapid succession.

"He asked me to check the ferry schedule, and he'd let me know. Nothing else."

"I'm going to drive over," Rennie blurted out.

Brooklyn turned sharply toward her friend. "Why?"

Rennie stood slowly as she composed her thoughts. Her gut told her she needed to be there for Graham. Sure, they weren't as close as they used to be, but he was still her friend. "I don't know. I just need to be there for him. Make sure he and his parents are okay."

"I'll go with you. I know George. He's probably sitting outside. He hasn't dealt with Grady very well," Bowie added.

"Okay," Brooklyn sighed. "You guys go—keep me updated."

Rennie saw the disappointment in Brooklyn's eyes. Was it because Bowie decided to go, or was it because Rennie was leaving, and it likely meant no shopping trip for tomorrow? The drive alone would be at least seven hours round trip.

Against her better judgment, Rennie took the elevator back to her room. She hated small confined spaces and especially feared metal boxes that rattled, squeaked, and shook. She was in a hurry, though, and wanted to get on the road. She changed into a pair of jeans and an over-size sweatshirt, packed her yoga pants, grabbed her laptop and the book she recently started, and threw her toothbrush in her bag just in case. Rennie had no idea what to expect but wanted to be prepared in case it meant a restless night in one of the uncomfortable waiting-room chairs.

She took the stairs on her way back down, and instead of walking through the ballroom and to the secret door, Rennie went out the front door of the inn. She hadn't expected to find a valet driver working on Thanksgiving night and had planned to get her car from the parking lot. She also hadn't expected to find Bowie waiting for her.

"I figured I would drive. I know the roads a bit better, and I have a feeling George will want to come back to town later."

Rennie nodded and slid into the front seat. She closed the door, buckled up, and sighed. "Am I being presumptuous?"

"It's hard to say. We don't know what we're going to find. For all we know, they could be on their way home."

"Do you think that?" she asked.

Bowie shook his head. "No. I think if Grady was in the hospital and it wasn't urgent, Graham takes the long way around. As it is, I have a bad feeling."

"Me too." Rennie knew only what Brooklyn had told her about Grady. When she saw Graham, his brother was never a topic of conversation, and she understood why. Grady's outburst over the summer had left a bad taste in her mouth. He had been volatile toward Brooklyn while they sat around the bonfire meant to honor Austin, pointing his finger and slurring his words as he cursed at her friend, telling Brooklyn it was she who should've died, not Austin. Rennie had been warned that Grady was the town drunk, and he proved everyone's words to be true that night. She didn't want to think about what Grady had done to land himself in the hospital.

Rennie and Bowie passed the time in the car talking about Christmas and what he could get Brooklyn. While he drove, Rennie pulled up the ads for all the home-improvement stores and rattled off a list of tools Brooklyn would love. Bowie suggested Rennie buy a fixer-upper and have Brooklyn help her restore the home, and Rennie countered with how the handy-dandy couple needed their own reality show. They sang songs that came on the radio. Rennie and Bowie talked about Brystol and how fast she was growing up. Bowie spoke about his fears when it came to boys, recalling the way he was when he first met Brooklyn.

Rennie smiled when she thought about meeting Graham for the first time. She remembered the moment when Brooklyn told her she was moving north and how heartbroken she had been. The beginning of her junior year of high school depressed her. She missed her best friend. However, when spring break came, Rennie's world changed with her first trip to Cape Harbor. She met Graham and fell in love for the first time.

At some point during the drive, Rennie fell asleep. Bowie shook her gently to wake her up when he pulled into the parking lot. She made sure to take her bag with her and pulled her phone out and sent a text to Graham. I'm here at the hospital. Where are you?

"I texted Graham to find out where he is," Rennie said as she and Bowie walked into the hospital. A security guard put his hand up to stop them.

"I'm sorry, but visiting hours are over."

"Oh," they said in unison. Neither of them had even thought about restricted hours.

"Do you have family here?"

Rennie nodded. "My brother-in-law was admitted earlier. I'm bringing my husband a change of clothing." She patted her bag for emphasis.

"And you, sir?" The guard directed his attention to Bowie.

"I'm a cousin. I'm here to pick up my aunt and uncle to take them home. They're elderly."

Rennie liked how quick Bowie was on his feet. The guard asked for their names, and once again, Rennie lied. She had an answer for him, too, if he asked why her identification read Wallace instead of Chamberlain. The guard gave Bowie and Rennie name tags and said they had to wear them at all times. He pointed to the general waiting room, where other families had gathered.

The waiting room had the open-concept feel to it. You could see staff walking up and down halls, hear the intercom and the click the doors made when people swiped their key cards. There was one television suspended in the corner and set to a news channel. The volume was off, but those interested could read the subtitles. They sat down away from others and waited for Graham.

"What if Grady hurt someone? What if someone in this area is waiting for word on a loved one Grady hurt?"

"Don't think like that, Bowie." Rennie had the same thoughts but didn't want to express them. One of them needed to remain positive.

"I can't help it."

Neither can I.

Rennie spotted Graham, the tall dirty-blond-haired man with green eyes whose crooked smile could make her heart skip a beat, coming down the hallway, and she rushed over to him. She wrapped her arms around his waist and pressed the side of her face to his chest. "I'm so sorry." Her words were automatic and heartfelt. Regardless of everything going on in their lives and the separation between them, she would always care for him. "What happened?"

Graham pulled away and clasped his hand with Rennie's. "I see Bowie over there. I might as well tell you both at the same time."

She nodded, and they walked toward Bowie, who pulled his friend into a hug as soon as Graham neared.

The three of them sat down, with Graham in the middle, who continued to hold Rennie's hand. "Grady was found on the side of the road. He overdosed, but the officer who found him had Narcan. He coded on his way here. They revived him . . ." Graham paused and covered his face with his hands. Rennie put her arm around him and hugged him as best she could. She considered telling him everything would be okay, but the words would be empty. Graham cleared his throat and continued to speak, telling them everything the doctor had said. "Bottom line, if my brother survives, it's going to take a miracle and then another one to get him into rehab."

"He didn't hurt anyone, did he?" Bowie asked.

Graham shook his head. "Not that I know. My mom is with Grady now, but I asked one of the nurses, and she said she wasn't aware."

Rennie's grip on Graham's hand tightened. She couldn't imagine what he felt or the thoughts going through his mind. She was an only child, and Brooklyn was the closest she had to a sibling. When Austin died, she had done her best to be by Brooklyn's side but couldn't put her life on hold. Not like the friends Brooklyn had in Cape Harbor.

"You guys didn't have to come up here," Graham said.

"I wanted to be here for you," Rennie told him. He looked into her eyes, and she felt her heart beat faster than it should. They had an undeniable connection, one she never questioned. One she never thought she had, too, until recently.

"And I figured George would be itching to get out of here," Bowie added with a hint of humor.

Graham laughed. "You have no idea. He's so lost in his head, thinking Grady is fine. Even when a doctor tells him his son is going to die if he doesn't get help, my dad doesn't believe what he's hearing."

"When you've lived in denial for so long, it's hard to overcome the emotion and face reality. I'm sure he acted the way he did because he was afraid to lose Grady," Bowie said.

"Well, now he has no choice." Graham sighed. "Anyway, I'm sure if you offer him a ride home, he'll take you up on it. You guys really didn't need to come all the way here."

"You need us. You would've done the same." Rennie squeezed Graham's hand to bring her message home.

At Graham's suggestion, they took the stairs down to the cafeteria, where they found George watching television. He was gruff with his hello but perked right up when Bowie offered to take him back to town. It was clear to Graham that his father was uncomfortable and wanted to go home, which made him angry. He should be there for Grady. George should stay for his wife.

"Dad, before you leave with Bowie, you should stop in and see Grady. And say goodbye to Mom."

George grumbled some unintelligible response, which Graham took as a "Yes, son, you're right," even though he knew his father would never say such a thing. He sensed his pleas fell on deaf ears when it came to his father. Graham thought about pressing his father for a solid answer but knew it would only piss the old man off, so he turned his attention toward Rennie. He pulled her into a hug and thanked her for coming. She pulled away and shook her head. "I'm not leaving you, Graham."

EIGHT

The shrill sound of the phone ringing jolted Graham out of bed. One hand fumbled for his phone, determined to stop the noise before his roommate woke up, while the other hand worked to remove his entangled legs from the bedding.

"He . . . ," he croaked. Graham cleared his throat and took a deep breath to calm his rapidly beating heart. Before he could regain any semblance of composure, he looked at the clock and saw that it was shortly after three in the morning. Who could be on the other line this early—or rather, late? Was something wrong with his mom or dad? His brother? "Hello?"

"Graham."

Rennie. His mind relaxed. It wasn't uncommon for her to call at all hours of the night. Most of the time, she'd forgotten what time it was because of her all-night study sessions and would call him when she couldn't fall asleep.

"Hey, Ren," he said quietly, so as to not wake his roommate. Graham kicked his blankets straight and lay back down, bringing the comforter over his head to give himself some privacy, of which his dorm room offered none.

"Graham Cracker, I need you."

Graham's heart stopped. Was this the moment he had waited for after all these years? Did Rennie feel the same way? Or was this another booty call, to which he would give Rennie Wallace anything she asked?

Graham was a fool's fool. While he was smart—top of his class—when it came to Rennie, he was as stupid as they came. She could tell him to jump off the Golden Gate Bridge, and he would ask her to name the date and time. Graham was in love with her. Rennie wasn't in love with him. Not the way it mattered, at least.

"What's wrong?" He closed his eyes and imagined her with him under the covers with only a flashlight illuminating the space. They had done that once or twice, back when they were in Cape Harbor and Rennie visited for the summer after their junior year of high school ended. The group had gone camping along the river. The guys were going to fish all day while the girls sunbathed and swam in the river. According to everyone's parents, the boys needed to stay in their own tents. The same went for the girls. Of course, everyone agreed until they arrived at the campsite and paired off.

"I think I'm in trouble."

"What happened?" Those five words woke Graham up. The grogginess he felt dissipated quickly.

"I don't want to say over the phone. Can you come here?"

"I'm on my way." He hung up and sprang out of bed. He dressed in the dark, thankfully remembering where he had left his sweatpants from the previous day. He found a T-shirt hanging out of his drawer, sniffed, and determined it was clean before slipping it on. He spun around his room, trying to recall where he kicked his sneakers off. Graham got down on his hands and knees and felt around in the darkness until he found them.

When it came to clothes, disorderly *was the word used to describe Graham. However, he always seemed to know where everything was. He kept his wallet and keys in a dish on top of his dresser, which made them easy to find in the darkness.*

Outside his dorm room, he slipped his shoes on and walked down the hall as quietly and quickly as he could. If his resident advisor saw him leave, he would ask questions. The dorms had curfews, and his RA was a stickler for the rules. With the recent spike in gang-related activity, San Jose State

University wanted their students to be safe. Leaving at three in the morning to drive to Santa Clara University wouldn't fall under the safety category.

The motion-sensor lights on campus forced Graham to stay in the shadows until he reached the parking lot. He had an excuse ready if campus security stopped him: he needed antacids. Graham was a pro at faking a stomachache.

Graham's four-door silver Honda came to life on the second try. He slipped it into reverse and pulled out of the parking spot, purposely keeping his lights off until he faced away from the dorms. When he came to the intersection to leave campus, he turned his lights on and signaled to merge onto the road and drove the little over seven miles down the road to Rennie's school. He parked near the student center, a place where he was unlikely to get a ticket, and walked through campus to her dorm. He hoped Rennie would be in the vestibule waiting for him. Otherwise, he had no chance of getting into her dorm.

As he grew closer, he saw her sitting on a bench. He sat down beside her and placed his arm behind her. She burrowed into him and clutched his T-shirt with her fist.

"What's wrong?"

"Nothing," she told him. "I just needed to see you."

Graham sighed. He suspected the guy she had been seeing dumped her, broke her heart because, according to her, he was the one. Graham hated every guy she dated. None of them were ever good enough, not when he was the one who wanted to be with her. Someday, Graham would take a chance on telling her, to put himself out there to her finally. He longed for a time when they would be more than friends with benefits, although he wasn't willing to give that part of their relationship up anytime soon.

Graham adjusted the way he sat on the bench and held Rennie close to his chest. When it came down to why he was there, with her, it wouldn't matter, because when she needed him, he ran to her.

Rennie shivered, and his grip tightened. "Do you want to tell me why you called at three a.m.?"

She picked her head up off his chest and angled herself to look at him. "Can't a girl just call her best guy to come over when she needs him?"

"Aren't you dating what's his face?"

"You know his name is Thomas."

"Right, Tommy," Graham said with disdain.

"Thomas," she corrected. Graham didn't care. They weren't friends and never would be.

"Whatev', Ren." He quieted and tried to pull her back to his chest.

"Anyway, we're not really dating anymore. He moved to Venice to start some print shop or something. Told me to give him a call when I graduated, and we'd hook up."

"What an idiot," Graham mumbled. Rennie jabbed him in his side, and he flinched. "Sorry, can't help it. You're so much better than he is, and you're better off without him. He brought you down to a level I didn't like to see." To Graham, Thomas was beneath Rennie. He didn't have a car and used Rennie for a ride everywhere. No life ambition other than smoking weed and vegging out in front of the television. Graham had caught him mocking Rennie one time for her career choice, saying lawyers were nothing more than politicians trying to take away people's rights. Rennie couldn't see through Thomas's bullshit, though, and that bothered Graham.

"Wanna go up to my room?"

He did. He would never turn her down. Graham nodded and held her hand all the way back to her room. When they entered, her desk light was on. "Where's Kim?"

"With her boyfriend."

Graham kicked his shoes off and crawled into Rennie's twin bed. He was tired and needed sleep. Rennie snuggled into him and laid her head on his chest. "Do you like me?" she asked him.

He inhaled deeply and let his breath out slowly. "You have no idea how much, Rennie."

"You're the one guy that'll never leave me, Graham."

She spoke the truth.

Rennie lifted her head and kissed a path from Graham's neck to his lips, and then Graham took over. He made love to Rennie that night and the following and continued to do so until he crossed paths with Monica Watson, the one woman to turn his eyes away from Rennie.

For most of their friendship, at least through college, he had been by her side when she needed him. "You don't have to stay, Ren. I don't know how long I'm going to be here with my mom."

"I'm not going anywhere, Graham."

He finally accepted her offer and nodded. He was grateful for her and their friendship and had missed her over the years.

When George stood and declared it was time to head home, the four of them walked back up the stairs and out the main entrance of the hospital.

"Dad, I really think you should stay. If Grady wakes—"

"Grady's fine," his father said gruffly. "All this nonsense about an overdose. My boy doesn't even do drugs." He stormed past Graham and right to Bowie's car. Graham stared, unsure of what to think.

Bowie's hand came down on Graham's shoulder and squeezed. "He'll come around."

"I doubt it. His son is upstairs, dying, and he wants to go home."

"Are we ever going to go back to normal?" Bowie said as he walked toward his car. Graham didn't have an answer for him, because he knew nothing in Cape Harbor, or at least his family, had ever been the same since the accident. It was like his father believed Grady was still a carefree twenty-two-year-old with his life ahead of him and not a middleaged man known as the town drunk.

Rennie and Graham waved as Bowie honked on his way out of the parking lot. Graham reached for Rennie's hand, and she gave it willingly. They passed by the security guard, who commented, "Happy to see you found your husband."

"Husband, huh?" he said to Rennie after the guard was out of earshot.

"Visiting hours were over, and I had to be quick on my feet. Bowie's your cousin. The guard said we could stay as long as we waited in the general waiting room."

"Gotcha. Well, we're going upstairs. I want to be there for my mom if and when she comes out of Grady's room." Graham let go of Rennie's hand when they entered the elevator. She followed him toward the ICU and leaned her head against his shoulder while they waited for the doors to open. Inside, one other couple was sitting—actually, sleeping—in the chairs.

"They look so uncomfortable," Rennie said quietly.

"There's nothing comfortable about hospitals." Graham could count on one hand how many times he had been in one.

They sat down, and within seconds, Rennie opened her bag and pulled a myriad of items out. She handed Graham a thriller. "This might interest you," she said. "I can't read it at night, because it'll give me nightmares."

Graham took the book from her and flipped it over to read the back. He chuckled. "Why would you buy something like this?"

She shrugged. "I'm trying to broaden my reading palate."

"With reading something that induces nightmares?" Graham looked over at Rennie, and she looked away. "You're crazy, Ren. What else do you have in that bag of yours?"

Rennie held it on her lap and looked inside. "Let's see. I have some protein bars, a pair of yoga pants, my laptop, a couple of cases I'm working on. Pens, pencils, notepads." She looked up at Graham. "Want to play tic-tac-toe or hangman?"

"Not really," he said with a smile. "Thank you."

"For what?"

"For being here. For coming even though you didn't have to."

Rennie set her bag on the floor, turned in the chair, brought her leg up, and hooked it under her knee. "When Bowie told us why you called, there wasn't any question of where I needed to be—or wanted to be, for that matter."

"I'm sure at the inn, tucked nicely in a warm cozy bed, instead of sitting in these uncomfortable chairs."

She nodded. "Or I'm sitting next to my friend because he needs me more than I need a feather-filled pillow."

Graham smiled. He loved that she was there, waiting with him. He leaned his head against the wall and watched her. There was a time in his life when he wanted to marry her but never dared to say anything. Now, she was back in his life and with someone else—such was his luck.

NINE

The overhead lights illuminated, which caused Rennie to stir. She moved slightly, and her eyes shot open from the ache she felt in her neck and back. She sat alone in a small room, surrounded by orange pleather chairs, a table stacked with magazines and day-old coffee cups, and a muted television. The whoosh of the double doors reminded her of where she was—the hospital with Graham.

Her hand found the back of her neck, and she applied pressure to the kink and moved her head back and forth to loosen the muscles. Memories from last night—or more like hours ago, it seemed—replayed in her mind. Graham and Rennie played games, challenging each other in trivia and working together to solve brainteaser puzzles. The last thing she remembered was giving him an earbud and resting her head on his shoulder so they could watch a movie together. At some point, she acquired one of those white hospital blankets, which now pooled around her waist as she sat up straight. Her phone sat precariously on the armrest of the chair next to her. Someone had plugged it in for her. No, not someone, but Graham. Rennie bent forward and reached under her chair to feel for her bag. If Graham had thought to charge her phone, he would've hidden her bag as well. A sense of relief washed over her when she felt the leather straps.

Where had Graham gone?

Rennie stood and gathered the blanket into a fold and set it on the chair near her phone. She bent at the waist and touched her toes, stretching her back, and then stood upright and reached her hands above her head, elongating her torso. She repeated this until she felt the stiffness start to dissipate.

With great reluctance, she reached for her phone. After she arrived at the hospital the previous night, she put everyone and everything out of her mind, except for Graham. She tapped the screen and groaned at the number of text messages. She opened the app and expected to find at least one from Theo, but there was none. Graham, Brooklyn, Brystol, Ester, and a couple other coworkers. She opened Graham's first and read it: in Grady's room with my mom, text me when you're awake. Rennie did. She opened Brooklyn's next, expecting to read a long rant about missing their shopping trip: Let me know if you need anything. Even though Brooklyn hadn't put her feelings into the text, Rennie knew she was upset, and rightfully so. They'd had plans, and she had pushed them aside. Rennie replied: Thank you. I'll call you soon. She opened Brystol's next: OMG! I'm working at the bar today! Rennie was confused because her niece wasn't old enough to be in a bar, let alone work in one. However, she let it go because she didn't want to bother Brystol at work or whatever she was out doing.

The double doors swung open, and Graham walked out. "Good morning," he said to her as he walked toward her. He stopped shy of giving her a hug, which Rennie desperately wanted but couldn't bring herself to initiate either.

"Morning. Any update on Grady?"

Graham shook his head slightly. "No, still in the coma."

"Well, I suppose that's for the best. His body needs time to heal. How's your mom?"

"All things considered, she's okay. They gave her a cot to sleep on, and one of the nurses brought her breakfast."

"That's sweet of them. Want to go grab some coffee?"

Graham motioned for Rennie to lead the way. She picked up her bag and slung it over her shoulder. When they were out in the hall, away from the ICU, the hospital seemed livelier. People milled about. Patients walked up and down the hall with their IV carts, there was an orderly singing as he came toward Graham and Rennie, and an expectant mother was waddling her way toward the maternity ward, yelling at her husband because he was doing tricks in a wheelchair.

"I'm going to use the restroom," Rennie told Graham as they approached the door. She went inside, used the facilities, changed out of her jeans and into her yoga pants, which she should've done hours ago. At the sink, she washed up, brushed her teeth, and combed her hair. Rennie glanced in the mirror and recoiled. She looked tired, with dark bags under her eyes. She pinched her cheeks to bring some pinkness to them and smoothed tinted moisturizer all over her face to give her pallor some color. When she opened the door, Graham was resting against the wall with his phone in his hand.

"Hey, what's this about Brystol working in a bar? I'm assuming it's the Whale Spout?"

Graham pushed away from the wall and met Rennie in stride as they headed toward the elevators. "Krista called this morning to tell me the busboy called out sick." Graham paused and rolled his eyes. "Brystol likes to come down and help out occasionally, so I asked Bowie if she could work today."

"You're paying her, right?" As soon as the words came out of her mouth, Rennie regretted them. She knew Graham would do right by Brystol and pay her.

"Of course." He laughed. "I would never expect her to work for free."

"I know. I don't know why I said anything."

They stepped into the empty elevator, and Graham pressed the button for the basement. He continued to look at his phone while Rennie watched the floor indicators light up quickly and then dim. When B lit up and stayed, she clutched the strap of her bag and waited for the doors to open.

They stepped out and got right in line with the rest of the people. The smell of eggs, bacon, freshly baked pies, and coffee made Rennie's stomach growl. She placed her hand over her midsection and looked around to see if anyone had heard the loud rumblings.

Judging by the look on Graham's face, he had. "We might as whale eat while we are down here."

"Did you say *whale*, or do I hear things?"

"Nope, I said it." He shrugged.

Rennie laughed. "You're a nut," she told him. Once it was their turn in line, they each took a tray and set it on the tubular tray slide. Each station she came to, Rennie wanted whatever was cooked there. Hash browns, pancakes or french toast, fruit, yogurt, and oatmeal. With so many options, she had a hard time choosing, so she took one of everything. By the time she reached the cashier, her tray was nearly overflowing. Rennie looked down at her food and started to question her decisions.

She found a table with a view of the snowcapped mountains. Graham sat across from her with nothing on his tray. "Where's your food?" she asked.

He tilted his head slightly toward her tray, and her eyes followed. She had heaps of food, most of which she wouldn't eat. "I figured you had enough for the both of us and knew you would be mad at yourself for being wasteful."

Graham was right. Rennie slid her tray to the middle of the table. "Everything looked so good. I don't know what I was thinking."

"No worries," he told her as he pierced a piece of sausage with his fork.

"How was Thanksgiving? I meant to ask earlier."

"Fine, given the circumstances of Grady not being there."

"How's your mom? I mean, how has she been? I've been meaning to stop by when I visit."

Graham stilled. His fork lingered between food and nothingness. "She's probably the strongest person I know. Do you remember the night we left to drive to Cape Harbor?"

Rennie nodded. She would never forget that night or the drive back to Washington. For hours upon hours, silence filled the car. They only spoke when it was time to stop or eat or when Graham suddenly slammed his hand against the steering wheel and screamed out "Why?" over and over again.

"We didn't know all the details on the drive home. We didn't know that my brother had been pulled from the water by a rescue boat and given CPR. The medics revived him, and once they were back to the dock, instead of getting into the ambulance, Grady dove back into the water. Friends, people who were there because word spread fast that there was something wrong, went in after him. He fought people, screaming at them to let him go. It was only then that he mentioned Austin." Graham used the fork to move eggs around on the plate. It was as if he was trying to avoid making eye contact with Rennie.

"Why didn't Grady tell them about Austin as soon as he was conscious?" Rennie leaned closer to Graham. "Why didn't the rescue crew know about Austin?"

Graham looked up and set his utensil down. "I don't know. I've asked Grady over the years about that night. He's never come clean about what happened."

"I feel like there's something you're trying to say here."

He shrugged. "We know Austin left Brooklyn that night, broke up with her. We know he called Bowie and told him to go to Brooklyn. Grady has said it was Austin's idea to take the boat out, but what if it wasn't? What if it was Grady's idea? We've had many accidents with our fishermen before, but none of them have turned out like Grady. Ren, he's so far gone. What if this is guilt eating away at him?"

Rennie sat there, stunned. For the past fifteen years, she had known the story about Austin being the one to take the boat out on the raining night. She hated what-ifs, but Graham's made sense. Of course, both thoughts were plausible, and only two people knew the truth. One was slowly killing himself, and the other was still missing and presumed dead.

She reached her hand out and took ahold of his. She wanted him to know she was there for him. So much of their lives had changed the night the call came in. There wasn't a doubt in her mind if the accident hadn't happened, she and Graham would still be in California. With him there, it gave her an excuse to stay. Once he left and never returned, she was alone.

Graham tossed his napkin on the table, and Rennie followed suit. He carried their trayful of dishes and half-eaten foods to the other side of the cafeteria and obeyed the instructions for composting, sorting, and where to put everything else.

On their way back to the ICU, Graham's phone dinged with a new message. He glanced at the screen and frowned. "What's wrong?" Rennie asked. Tempted as she was to look over his shoulder, she refrained from doing so.

"My mom says the cops are here to talk about Grady."

"The cops? Why?"

Graham typed out a message and pocketed his phone. "I don't know. Last night the doctor said he was found and brought by ambulance, but he never mentioned the police needing to speak with us."

Rennie pulled Graham into an alcove and asked for all the details. She listened intently as he recounted what the doctor said when they arrived yesterday. After he finished, they made their way back to the ICU, where they waited for the double doors to open. They bypassed the waiting room and followed the nurse. The moment Rennie saw Johanna, tears formed. It had been years since she had seen Graham's mother, a woman she had grown very fond of while growing up. The two women hugged for a long time. "I'm so sorry," Rennie whispered.

They pulled away, and Johanna sat back down while Graham introduced himself to the two police officers in the room. Rennie stepped forward and held her hand out. "Renee Wallace. I represent the Chamberlain family."

The two gasps she heard behind her were something she'd expected. Graham hadn't asked her for help, but from the moment he mentioned the police were there to see them, she knew they would need it. There was no way she was letting this family battle the legal system alone.

"I'm Officer Hook, and this is my partner, Officer Frey." The tall blond officer pointed to his dark-haired equal.

Rennie sat down and pulled her notepad and pen out of her bag. She crossed one leg over the other and looked at the officers, who sat across from her. She smiled and mentally prepared herself for part of the law that wasn't her forte. At best, she would take all the notes she could and then hand the case off to a colleague.

"I'm a little fuzzy on why you're here," Rennie started. "Are you checking my client's medical status?"

"No, ma'am," Officer Hook stated. "We're here to place Grady Chamberlain under arrest." Johanna inhaled deeply, and Rennie glanced at her.

"Under arrest for what?" Graham's tone held anger. Rennie placed her hand on his leg, which she hoped reassured him she could handle this.

Rennie wasn't up to date on criminal justice but knew the state had implemented overdose laws. Grady had OD'd and been found in time, which luckily for him meant he was clear and free from any charges.

"Surely you're not filing charges against my client because he overdosed on the side of the road."

"Yesterday evening, when we came upon Mr. Chamberlain on the side of the road, we thought he needed help. When we approached the car, we saw many empty bottles in the back and could smell alcohol on him, which would be an automatic arrest for driving under the influence of intoxicants. I took his driver's license, which had expired, and went back to my patrol car to call it in," Hook said.

"I stayed at the car. I noticed some damage on the front end and decided to inspect it. I found blood and fur encrusted into the bumper, which looked fresh. I radioed the game warden to be on the lookout for an injured or deceased animal on the side of the road. I went back to the driver's side of the car to ask Mr. Chamberlain what he hit, and that is when I noticed a bottle in his hand. His eyelids were fighting to stay open, and he started convulsing and foaming from his mouth. I called for Hook to assist in a naloxone injection. It took two doses to bring him back," Officer Frey added.

"I then radioed for an ambulance," Hook finished their recollection of events while Rennie wrote everything down. She would have to refine her notes later, but for now, the scribbled text would suffice.

"What are you arresting my client for again?"

"DUII, possession, driving without a license, valid registration, and insurance."

While these charges weren't her field of study, she knew the last three charges would never stick. Those were the easiest to take care of. The other two would be a challenge. She folded her hands and set them on top of her notepad. "I'm not sure if you are aware, but my client is in a coma. I can call you when he wakes, and you can make the arrest, or you can waste taxpayer dollars by putting an officer by his door."

"That won't be necessary, ma'am. The nurses will let us know when Mr. Chamberlain is awake. We only came by today as a courtesy to the family so they aren't caught off guard when we return to arrest him." The officers stood and made their way to the door. As soon as it shut, Rennie sighed heavily.

"What does all of this mean?" Johanna asked. "I don't even understand, because Grady doesn't have a car. Where did he get a car from?"

Her question lingered in the air. Rennie, of course, had no idea. She looked to Graham for clarification, but he looked as confused as his mother.

"Grady is in a lot of trouble," Rennie stated.

"But you can help?"

"Mom, Rennie does family law. The charges against Grady . . ." Graham stopped talking.

"Graham's right. This isn't my expertise, but I have colleagues who deal with this sort of stuff every day. Grady will be in good hands." Even as Rennie said the words, she didn't believe them. Grady was in a lot of trouble, enough to land himself in jail if they didn't face a sympathetic judge or the right assistant district attorney. Rennie hoped a plea deal could save Grady from such a fate.

Rennie excused herself and went back to the waiting room. She wanted to keep the case in house and cochair, even though one wouldn't be required, and she lacked the experience with this side of the law. She scrolled through her contacts from work and tried to recall any particular crossing they may have had. Rennie came across a few names and jotted them down. She would speak to them on Monday when she returned to work. For now, she sat in the waiting room and looked up case law on her phone because she was going to do what she had to in order to protect the Chamberlains and help Grady.

TEN

The horn sounded outside of Graham's window. Two short bursts, and then another two. And then more followed. Ships passing in the sea. He groaned and reached for his phone to turn off his alarm clock. He hadn't even made it to six o'clock. He was exhausted—both mentally and physically. The long holiday weekend had turned into one he would love to forget. However, with his brother, Grady, still in a medically induced coma and his mother holding a vigil at Grady's bedside, the memories would never fade. Graham lay in bed and stared at the ceiling. *How has life ended up this way?* he wondered. And what was the breaking point for him and his family? For Grady?

Graham stretched, and his muscles protested—some strained and caused him to ease up. For the past few days, he, along with Rennie, had slept in the waiting room, despite Johanna telling them both to go home. Graham wouldn't leave his mother, and for whatever reason, Rennie wouldn't leave Graham. And he loved her for it. All weekend, she had been by his side, being the voice of reason and the person he could lean on, and when the police showed up, Rennie took over—no questions asked. Graham didn't know where he or his family would be right now if it weren't for her.

He finally rolled out of bed and set his bare feet on the cold wood. He shivered and reached for the pair of sweatpants he had left on the floor. Somewhere, he had slippers but had yet to dig them out of his closet because he didn't want to admit that winter was upon them. He hated the cold and often longed for the warmth of California, even though some winter days were chilly in San Jose. There were very few of them.

A full day of worry and work faced Graham. Thankfully, Krista Rich, Graham's only other full-time server/bartender, filled in for him over the weekend and had made sure the Whale Spout stayed fully operational in his absence. Since he had taken over, he had yet to take a vacation, and while the idea of going away for a week or so excited him, he never took the opportunity. Spending the last four days in a hospital waiting room wasn't the kind of escape he longed for.

Graham braved the cold floor and lumbered downstairs to his bathroom, used the facility, and hopped into the shower. His mistake was forgetting to turn on the water pump. He stepped out of the shower, walked out of the bathroom free as the day he was born, and went into the kitchen to flip the switch, having forgotten the blinds were open.

His neighbor Shari was at the end of the dock, and she happened to turn at the right moment. Graham waved like he had done every time he had seen her since she moved in. Her mouth dropped open, and Graham stared, wondering what she was doing. He stood there for a long minute before realization sank in. His mouth plummeted to the ground, and he covered it in horror and then concealed himself as much as possible as he ran back to the bathroom.

He muttered a string of obscenities as he ducked into the shower. He was mortified and hadn't accounted for anyone being near his end of the dock. His next encounter with Shari was going to be mighty awkward. He could see it playing out in his mind. Blushed cheeks and garbled hellos as they passed by each other with little to no eye contact. He wasn't even sure if he'd be able to muster a friendly wave after what had just happened.

When he finished, he dried off, wrapped the towel around his waist, and peeked out the bathroom door, angling to see who, if anyone, was near his windows. With the coast clear, he hightailed it up the stairs, slipped on the hardwood floor, and tumbled down to the ground. He smacked his knee and thigh and finally came to rest on his ass. Out of breath, he huffed, "Just call me Grace."

Graham took a moment to compose himself. He was flustered and needed to get his head straight. He blamed Grady. Everything wrong in his life was Grady's fault. It seemed rude to blame his brother, and deep down Graham knew he could've made changes. No one ever told him he had to stay in Cape Harbor. He did out of obligation, and it was easier to blame Grady than to accept Graham had given up.

He dressed in boxers, jeans, and a band T-shirt from the early '90s. He put on his socks and his "date" boots, grabbed his phone, and went back downstairs and into the bathroom. He stood in front of the mirror and noticed for the first time in his adult life that he had bags under his eyes and had no idea how to get rid of them. Graham picked up his metal container of hair cream, scooped a blob onto the palm of his hand, and rubbed his hands together and then through his hair. Since Rennie's return into his life, he'd started caring about the way he looked. She made him want to care.

Graham planned to grab breakfast at the diner. He figured Peggy had heard something about Grady and wanted to set the record straight before the rumor mill ran rampant with made-up facts, even though the last thing he wanted to do was tell anyone what happened to his family.

The dock wobbled when Graham stepped out onto it. The choppy water usually meant a storm was brewing and would reach land soon. Another part of fall turning into winter that he hated. He passed by Shari's houseboat and walked a bit faster. He kept his head down until he reached the ramp that would take him to land. The parking lot was half-full, and someone backing a truck down the boat ramp was ready to off-load their boat. Graham looked behind him, surveying the water, and shook his head. After Austin's death, the mayor put a lot of restrictions on when boats could go out, and today looked like one of those days.

He drove into town, and while he usually parked behind the bar, in the alley, he found a spot in front of the diner. Graham pulled in and shut off his Hyundai Santa Fe. Brystol teased him about his choice of transportation, calling it a "dad car," but it served its purpose for Graham. He could carry supplies from his runs to the food wholesalers, deliver kegs easily for parties, and transport his parents if need be. There were times when he thought about buying something bigger, like Brooklyn's Tahoe, but he didn't want a car payment.

It was well after nine in the morning, and cars lined the street. Graham considered this to be a good sign of things to come for the Whale Spout's lunch rush, which hopefully trickled into dinner. Monday night was dart night, and most of Bowie's crew would be down for their weekly tournament. Graham craved the normalcy of his job. He wanted to be near people but was unprepared to hear people talk about Grady. Towns were small north of Seattle, and word traveled fast.

As soon as Graham stepped into the diner, Peggy waved. She went to the coffee urn, placed a white mug underneath the spout, and pulled the handle. Graham sat at the counter, on a cracked red vinyl stool nearest the door, and picked up the menu even though he knew he'd order the same breakfast sandwich he always did.

"I'm hearing some scuttlebutt," Peggy said as she set the mug down in front of Graham.

He inhaled deeply and nodded. "Which is why I'm here. I need two things from you."

"Name 'em."

"I don't want people saying anything else about Grady, so if they ask or you hear something, just say he's sick and in the hospital, okay?"

Peggy leaned closer to Graham and asked, "What's really going on?"

He did the same. "He's sick, Peggy. He's in a medically induced coma in Port A. My mom is up there with him. She won't come home, which is part of my second request for you."

A customer walked in, and Peggy stood upright. She greeted them and said she'd be over to help them in a minute. When they sat, she leaned back down onto the counter. "He in trouble?"

"You could say that." Graham didn't want to offer up any more than he needed. "When you're off, do you think you could go over to my parents' and help me pack some things for my mom? She's staying with Grady, and I can't get her to come home."

"Where's your dad?"

"In denial," he told her, wishing it were a real-life place so he didn't have to deal with him.

Peggy nodded. "Tell me what time, and I'll be there."

Graham told Peggy he had to rearrange the schedule at the bar but was hoping to be out of there by dinnertime. He planned to go back to Port A tomorrow after work and would continue to do so as often as he could until Grady woke up. Graham also had to find a way to get through his father's thick skull but was at a loss on how to do such a thing.

He ordered his breakfast, and while he waited, he pulled his phone out of his pocket. He had missed a call from Rennie, and his heart sank. What could've happened from the time he dropped her off at the inn last night until now? He chose to text her back. He didn't want to interrupt her day, and he also didn't know if he could hear her tell him any more bad news. Graham sent Rennie a quick **What's up?** and then closed the app. Talking to her sometimes made him feel like they were back in high school. He thought about the days when he would flirt heavily with her. He missed those days. Life had been so easy.

Peggy brought Graham's breakfast sandwich out on a plate. She took his mug and refilled it but never asked any more questions about Grady. Graham ate quickly, left a ten on the counter, which more than covered his food and coffee, and left her a generous tip. When he got outside, he went back to his car and drove it around the back, freeing up space in front for a patron.

Graham parked in the alley, parallel along the edge of the pavement. Most of the merchants parked back there, giving them easy access to their back doors. He unlocked the rear door to the Whale Spout and stepped into the cold dark space. He fumbled for the light switch, moved it to the on position, and closed his eyes as the overhead fluorescent lights flickered until they illuminated the room. He referred to this space as dry storage and the recycling area, where he kept the bar's stock of paper products, trash bags, and cleaning supplies. The room was barely over a year old, and he'd had Bowie build it after a series of break-ins, which he believed to be carried out by his brother. Ideally, Graham would've preferred to install a reinforced door facing the back alley. However, the building where the Whale Spout lived was old and not in the best shape. Bowie's suggestion was to build a room blocking immediate access to the bar, which he could reinforce with newer construction. Graham agreed, knowing even though the multiple-door system was a pain in the ass, there was no doubt they needed security. He pushed his six-digit code into the keypad, waited for the mechanical lock to slide away from the doorjamb, and stepped into the original yet smaller back room of the bar.

Stacks of boxes, crates, and kegs gave him pause when he entered the room. He had forgotten to do inventory on Wednesday and had planned to do it Friday after the holiday. Graham fully expected to find a list of items Krista took from the back room to cover what she needed up front. He would worry about it later.

Graham went around turning on the lights, the fryers, and the grill, along with the dartboards and jukebox. He flipped the sign from closed to open and made sure he unlocked the door. He wanted people milling around, coming in, and eating. Graham needed the distraction, anything to take his mind off his brother.

He found himself standing in the middle of the bar, jumping out of his skin when the door flew open. He swore aloud to the ghosts who haunted the Whale Spout, quite certain he could hear them laughing at him, calling him a scaredy-cat. Normally, the haunting didn't bother him, but he was on edge with everything.

Luke, Bowie's black Lab, took advantage of the door being open and strolled into the bar. Graham laughed and went behind the counter to get him a treat. Seconds later, Bowie stepped in and pulled the door shut behind him. "Morning," he said as he sat down at the bar.

"Isn't it a little too early for a drink?" Graham said to his friend.

"Aren't bartenders supposed to serve their patrons any time of the day?"

"I'm turning over a new leaf," he replied, smirking. Still, he set one of his custom-made coasters down and asked Bowie what he'd like to drink. Bowie ordered water and agreed with Graham. It was too early to drink. "Are you working today?"

"Yeah, starting a remodel at the old gristmill. Someone from Texas bought it."

"What are they doing with it?"

"Turning it into a house."

"That'll be cool, especially if they run the water mill."

"How's Grady?"

"Shit," Graham said as he reached for his phone. "I meant to text my mom and have her call me." He sent a message to his mom, looked to see if Rennie had texted him back, and, when he saw she hadn't, set his phone down. "When I left last night, he was still in the coma. The doctor hoped they'd be able to bring him out of it today or tomorrow, although his organs are pretty damaged."

"If he recovers, it'll be a long road ahead for him."

"If," Graham repeated.

Don, one of the three cooks employed at the Whale Spout, announced his arrival, which earned a loud bark from Luke. He came into the bar and filled his large plastic cup with pop and said he'd be out back cleaning. Graham wondered how busy they were over the weekend. He needed to pull the register tapes and check profits.

"You heading back to Port A tonight?"

Graham shook his head. "Tomorrow after work. I have to sit down with Krista and see if we can make some changes to the schedule. Tonight, Peggy is going to help me put some stuff together for my mom, and I'm going to try and get my dad to go up there."

"Still being stubborn?"

"Like a mule." Graham sighed. "Do you ever wonder how things could've been different?"

Bowie nodded. "Every day. I look at Brooklyn and ask myself why I didn't follow her or harass her parents about where she was. I let her go and tried to move on. I lost fifteen years . . ." A couple people walked in, and Bowie stopped talking. They sat at the end of the bar, away from Bowie. Graham went to them, tended to their needs, and came back to his friend. "What's plaguing you?" Bowie asked Graham.

"Grady, obviously. My dad for being in denial. Rennie. She stepped up big time at the hospital, and I hate that I can't be with her." As soon as the words came out of his mouth, Graham wanted them back. He glanced at Bowie, whose eyes widened.

"What?"

Graham shrugged. "Ever since this past summer, when she walked in here and announced herself, I'm back to where I was before everything happened."

"Do you love Rennie?"

It was a question Graham often asked himself. Deep down, he knew the answer, but it wouldn't matter, because she was in love with someone else. "I could say yes, but I'd be an idiot for even thinking that way about her. I could say no, but I'd be lying to myself."

"You should tell her."

Graham shook his head. "No way. She's in love with Theo. I'm not going to tell her anything, because what we had was high school and college; it's Brooklyn's return, and subsequently Rennie's as well, that's dredged up these feelings. Before, we had a fling. It worked for us." He shrugged. "Now we're adults. She has a life, and mine's in limbo. I'm not about to confuse her."

"Well, sometimes I think she needs a little confusing. And for the record, Brooklyn has a feeling things aren't great between Rennie and Theo. Maybe you can be the knight in shining armor. I'd be happy to give you some pointers."

Graham reached into his own bowl of popcorn and threw a handful at Bowie. Luke was like a sniper and moved lightning fast to inhale the pieces on the floor. He sat at Bowie's stool and begged for another morsel. "Now look at what you've done," he said, reaching down to pat his dog on the head. "I'm going to head out. Call me later if you get any news on Grady."

"Will do." Graham watched as Bowie left, and another group walked in. A party of four sat at one of the tables, while another party of two sidled up to the bar. "What can I get for you?"

"Anything local on tap?" the young man asked.

Graham nodded and pointed to the chalkboard. "Everything on the board is local. Domestic is bottled."

"Great, I'll take the Muddy Moose Stout."

"And I'll have a white-wine spritzer," the woman said.

Graham asked to see their IDs and, after a thorough inspection, handed them back and started his routine. Everything for him was automatic, from grabbing the right glasses to pulling the tab and tilting the pint glass at the perfect angle to pouring the right combination of white wine and sparkling water. As much as he hated the bar, the work was easy, and he was a natural. There were times when the rowdies came in, or he had to cut someone off—those days proved to be stressful, but he was a mindful bartender and owner. If he felt you had too much to drink, showed signs of being drunk, or had an overall feeling someone shouldn't drive home, he called for a cab and notified the local police to come down and hang out. He felt having the police in the bar sent a strong message to the patrons. He didn't want an accident on his hands, and Graham was more than willing to help people get home safely.

The bar was like Pandora's box in the sense that once the door opened and people started coming in, others followed. By midafternoon, the place was about full. Not the type to look a gift horse in the mouth, Graham busted his tail to keep everyone happy.

ELEVEN

Rennie found herself standing at her office window, watching the snow fall to the ground. The accumulation was minimal but enough to cause concern and some panic among the locals if the temperature stayed below freezing. The somewhat-warm temperatures from the holiday weekend turned frigid overnight. She crossed her arms and shivered. After spending the past few days with Graham, she'd thought a lot about their past, especially in California. They had been close, more than best friends, but their lives had been turned upside down with a tragic event, and they could never find their way back to each other. Not that she'd tried, and she was certain Graham hadn't either. One moment had changed everything.

She turned back to her desk and eyed the stack of reference books she'd pulled from the office's law library when she'd arrived. Next to the books sat her notes from the weekend, reports she'd found online, and the information from the arresting police officers. Grady's arrest would happen as soon as he woke from his coma, which Rennie suspected could be any day. From what she read online, medically induced comas lasted about two weeks. Most doctors felt this gave them enough time to assess and administer the necessary actions to make the patient stable. If Grady's doctor kept him sedated for the duration, his arraignment would be shortly before Christmas. Rennie wanted to handle

Grady's case because she felt she knew what was best for him and the Chamberlains, but she wanted guidance from one of her coworkers.

Next to the pile of reference books sat the files of her other clients—her paying clients. They needed more, if not all, of her attention, and she entertained the idea of hunkering down in her office for the night. She didn't need to be out in the elements and had a change of clothes in her office. Staying would also give her uninterrupted access to the library and the firm's database of cases.

Theo had returned to Spokane the night before. He was supposed to fly to Seattle, spend the night, and return home in the morning, but somewhere along the line, his company messed up his flight, and he had texted his apologies to Rennie, with promises of making up for their lost time. They would spend Christmas together, he promised her, waking up in her apartment and opening gifts before heading up to Cape Harbor for a few days and finally traveling north to Canada. Four nights in Whistler, complete with snowcapped mountains, endless skiing, spa treatments, and hot toddies by the fireplace. Theo was the skier, more so than Rennie. She would venture out for an hour or two and do a couple of the low-level runs with him, but she looked forward to some good old-fashioned relaxation. She'd already booked a manicure and pedicure, as well as a mud bath. And couple's massage and quiet dinners by candlelight for them to share. She wanted their getaway to be perfect, magical. When she told Brooklyn of her New Year's plans, Brooklyn teased, saying Theo was going to propose. Rennie brushed her off but secretly wanted Theo to slip a diamond onto her ring finger.

Rennie had held her hand out and waited for the smile to come. It hadn't. Lately, she felt a disconnect with Theo and wondered if they wanted the same things out of life. An engagement seemed to be in their future, their next step, but Rennie wasn't sure if she wanted it now. In the past few months, her emotions had been all over the place. Pure excitement from seeing Graham again after all those years. Joy and happiness from spending weekends in Cape Harbor, although Theo wouldn't accompany her, to contentment when she snuggled on the couch with Theo, alone in her apartment. *Contentment* wasn't previously in her vocabulary, and the thought made her feel old.

Her intercom buzzed, and she walked over to her phone, pressing the button. "Yes, Ester?"

"I'm sorry to bother you, Ms. Wallace, but your mother is holding for you."

My mother?

"Thanks, I'll take her call," she said, mentally calculating the time difference and wondering if something was wrong. They texted on Thanksgiving, and her mother hadn't indicated anything was amiss.

"Hello, Mom. Is everything okay?"

"Renee, we're going to have a white Christmas."

She looked over her shoulder and made a face even though her mom couldn't see it. "I doubt it. The snow is barely sticking."

"Not you—your father and I."

Rennie rolled her eyes and sat down at her desk, wiggled the mouse to bring her computer to life, and followed the path to start a solitaire game. It was mindless and helped her pass the time through her mother's idle chitchat.

"How so?" she asked. She learned a long time ago not to count on having her parents around, especially for the holidays.

"Your father wants to go to Alaska. We'll be there until after New Year's."

Alaska is close to home, Rennie thought. "I can't wait to see you."

"What do you mean?" her mother asked.

Of course. Rennie closed her eyes for a moment before turning her attention back to her card game. She moved cards back and forth, purposely making her mother wait. When her board cleared, she pumped her fisted hand and clicked to start a new game.

"Nothing. I just thought you'd come home to visit if you were in Alaska."

Her mother sighed. "I'll look at the calendar and see if we have time. We're heading out on a monthlong cruise to the Mexican Riviera afterward."

"No worries, Mom. I love how you and Dad are enjoying your retirement."

"You should join us on our cruise." The suggestion, while nice, was impossible.

"Maybe next time," she replied. "Listen, Mom. I gotta run."

"Oh, Renee, you work too hard. You need to take a break."

She hated the name Renee. Her parents, Theo, and her coworkers all referred to her by her given name, but she preferred Rennie. Yet, it only ever stuck with the Cape Harbor crew and college friends.

"Theo and I are going away for New Year's. Up to the mountains."

"But you hate skiing. I don't understand why you'd take a vacation if you don't love the destination. Relationships are about compromise."

"I don't mind it. It's just not my favorite activity. Besides, Theo loves to ski. I'm happy being in the spa all day."

"All right, dear. I have to go. I'm tired, and your father and I have a big day planned. We'll talk soon. Love you." Before Rennie could respond, her mother hung up.

Rennie sat back in her chair and swiveled to look out the window. She replayed her mother's words in her mind. She couldn't recall a time when her parents fought or even had a disagreement. To her, they were always even keeled and happy. Rennie wanted a relationship like her parents'.

Her intercom buzzed again, and she pressed the button so Ester could talk. "Just your friendly reminder about the staff meeting. Your lunch is in the conference room."

"Thank you, Ester."

Rennie gathered her binder, along with her notes on Grady's case, and made her way down the hall to the conference room, which filled up quickly. She found an open seat, but before she sat down, she searched the various food items on the table, looking for her name. She grabbed her salad, went over to the drink cart, picked out a Sprite, and went back to her chair.

Unlike their quarterlies, where the discussions centered around money and bottom lines, this meeting was about their cases and who needed help with research, depositions, or investigations. If Lex Davey was anything, he was nosy. He wanted to know everything, give input on cases—as if he knew what he was talking about—and instruct the lawyers on how to settle or hit it out of the park for the big bucks. Unfortunately, the staff had no choice but to appease him, but at least he provided lunch once a week.

Rennie dug into her salad, trying to eat as much as she could before she had to talk. She tried to listen to her coworkers, to see if she could offer anyone help and to see who could help her with Grady's case.

"Renee, you're up. What do you have, and do you need any help?" Lex asked her.

She set her fork down and moved her salad away so she could flip through her notes and recount the controversial divorce case she had. "The Sotos have a mediation meeting after the first of the year. Mr. Soto has stalled on talks, which we are using to Mrs. Soto's advantage. She wants to wrap this up because she has a contract she's waiting to sign for another book series. I've also taken a pro bono case for a family I grew up with. Ester filed the contract today. An arrest and arraignment are imminent."

"What's the case? And since when do you practice criminal law?" Lex interrupted.

Rennie tried not to let his behavior get to her, but the man was rude. She cleared her throat and told the conference room about her weekend and what the charges would be against her new client. Rennie made eye contact with a few of her team members who specialized in criminal cases and hoped they'd volunteer some of their time. If not, she would beg.

"I don't practice criminal law, but under the circumstances and knowing what the family wants for their son, I believe I can get my friend the help he needs."

"I'm confused," Lex huffed.

"What's confusing? Surely I'm not the only lawyer in the firm to help out a friend or take a case as pro bono." She stared down her boss. He side-eyed her, which Rennie didn't like.

"Pass it off. Don't waste company time on something like this." Lex moved to the next partner, effectively shutting her down. He pissed her off, and she hated the way he spoke to her. Rennie had no intention of passing the case off to anyone. She would represent Grady because it was what she'd promised his family.

While she stewed over the way Lex treated her, she continued to pick at her salad. She took notes on a few of the cases her colleagues spoke about and intended to send them case files she had recently worked on, and she worked hard not to roll her eyes when Lex talked about how to practice law, spoke about ethics and the legal system. He knew nothing. As soon as Lex adjourned the meeting, Rennie gathered her things, steadied her salad on her binder, and walked back to her office.

"Renee, wait up." She turned to find Jefferson Perkins coming toward her. He fell in step beside her.

"Hey, Jeff. What's up?"

"Your pro bono, what's up with it?" They entered her office, where she set her binder down but held her salad bowl in her hands. Jeff motioned for her to continue eating, and she did.

After she swallowed, she told him again the story of Grady but added the accident and the fifteen years of alcohol abuse.

"Do you have a strategy?" he asked her.

"I'm waiting for him to wake up. Once arrested, I'll appear on his behalf and go from there."

Jeff nodded. "At his arraignment, ask to skip the preliminary hearing. Tell the judge your client is entering rehab. That'll give you at least ninety days to get the case in order and plead him out to misdemeanors."

"Really?" Rennie asked, stunned. "Will that work?"

"He's a first-time offender and is unlikely to face jail time if he's in a treatment facility."

"Thanks, Jefferson."

"No problem. If you want me to sit second chair, let me know."

Rennie thanked him again as he left her office. She felt reassured and confident, knowing she had cocounsel to assist her if need be. Ester stood in her doorway with a folder in her arm. Rennie had a new client waiting for her in the conference room.

"What do we know about Ms. Futter?" Rennie asked as she reached for the folder. Ester filled her boss in and followed her to the smaller, cozier meeting room. She shut the door behind them, pulled the blinds closed, and sat across from Rennie with her pen and notepad, ready to take notes.

"Hello, I'm Renee Wallace. You must be Ms. Futter?" She shook hands with the trembling woman.

"Yes, but can you call me Leah?"

Rennie nodded. "I know you've already spoken to my assistant, Ester, but I'd like for you to tell me what's going on."

"My husband and I recently separated. I was under the impression we were going to go to counseling to try and work things out, but I lost my job, and the same day, he served me with papers." Leah Futter slid the trifold stack toward Rennie. She opened it and scanned the document.

"It says here he wants full custody of your children. How old are they?"

"Five and three."

"Just babies," she muttered. "Why did you and Mr. Futter separate?"

"He had an affair, and now he wants our children to live with his girlfriend."

Rennie nodded. She loathed people like Mr. Futter and would love nothing more than to take him down a peg or two. "We can take your case, but I won't be your acting counsel. I'm going to assign you to one of my staff members. They'll keep me apprised through the process, and Ester will always be available to answer any questions you have." She set her hand on top of Ms. Futter's and squeezed it. She then looked at Ester and asked, "Can you see if Charlie or Barbara is available for a consult?" Ester nodded and exited the room.

"I'm deeply sorry you're going through this, but we'll make things right for you. Unfortunately, the fact that your husband cheated will have no bearing on your divorce, but the fact that you're unemployed does. Do you have another job lined up?"

"I've been looking, but it's hard. I'm sad a lot."

"I can understand."

Charlie Raymond, a bright young lawyer on team Wallace, entered the room. Rennie made introductions and then stepped out. On her way back to her office, she ran into Donna, who followed Rennie into her office and shut the door behind her.

"Hey, it looks like the Soto case is going to close soon—that'll be a relief." Donna's words caught Rennie off guard. She had just told everyone during the staff meeting that they were heading to mediation after Christmas. Nothing about mediation screamed resolution. However, Rennie played along.

"The husband is grasping at straws. She was the breadwinner for only a small part of their marriage. He's lazy and doesn't want to work." Rennie sat at her desk and motioned for Donna to sit across from her. "And I just finished meeting with a new client whose husband cheated, moved in with the mistress, and now wants full custody of the children. The wife, who is now our client, is blindsided. She thought they were going to try counseling."

"Who did you assign the case to?"

"Charlie. She's hungry, and I think she can handle it and really send the husband through the wringer."

"Listen, Lex isn't happy about your pro bono case. Wants me to dig a little to see what's going on."

Rennie wanted to roll her eyes. "Since when are my cases monitored?"

"They're not. It's just the pro bono side. You know how Lex is."

"Fine," Rennie huffed. "I'll make sure to do the work on my own time and use vacation days when I have to go to court." The fact that Grady's case had become a sore spot pissed her off. The firm took pro bono work all the time and had their first-years volunteering for legal aid. This case wasn't out of the ordinary.

"I don't get why it's so important to you, Renee. Surely your case-load keeps you busy."

Rennie shook her head. "Like I said, family friends. I've known them most of my life, and they need my help. I won't turn my back on them."

She watched Donna. For what, she wasn't sure. Rennie found it odd that her decision to take a case was up for questioning. In the years she had been at the firm, and in her time as a junior partner, she had never seen another lawyer experience this sort of embattlement. Donna seemed to have gotten the hint that Rennie had nothing left to say regarding the case and excused herself, but not before giving her a veiled look as she exited the room.

TWELVE

George Chamberlain sat on a barstool at the Whale Spout, nursing a pint of beer. He'd walked in shortly after eleven in the morning, sat down, and ordered. Graham watched his father like a hawk and wondered what was going on in the older man's head. His father had yet to go to Port Angeles to visit Grady since Thursday, despite urgings from his mother and himself. As much as Graham hated the drive, he made it three to four times a week, mostly to be with his mom, and each time he went, he asked his dad to come along. The answer had yet to change from no to yes, and Graham wasn't going to ask anymore. Grady's doctor intended to wean him off sedation today and felt it would be nice to have his family there.

"Want something to eat?" Graham placed his hands on the bar and leaned down a bit to look his dad in his eyes. Over the past two weeks, George had put on weight from the fried foods he ate and, as far as Graham knew, had only moved from his recliner to meet the young kid who lived down the street, who George had conned to bring him food every night from the fish fry. "I can have Peggy bring something over for you. Something that isn't fried."

"I'm fine," George said gruffly.

Graham knew he was anything but fine, but the stubbornness often won when it came to his father. Graham continued to set up the bar, making sure it would be ready for Krista when she took over for the rest of the day and night. She had taken on more hours, which allowed Graham to travel back and forth to the hospital.

A few old-timers walked in and sat next to George, who perked up at the presence of his friends. Their boisterous chatter echoed throughout the nearly empty bar. Graham served the other two men and told them the kitchen was open if they were hungry, but he left them alone for the most part. He wanted his father to relax and be happy when he offered to give him a ride home later.

Krista arrived within the hour. She met Graham at the bar and nodded toward his father. "Does he know yet?"

Graham shook his head. "Honestly, I hoped he would've drunk a couple more beers before we left. He's going to be angry with me."

"He'll get over it. Here." Krista handed Graham a clear plastic bag with a blanket inside. "My mom put this together for your mom."

"Wow, please tell her thanks." He flipped the bag over in his hands and looked at the intricate designs of the patchwork quilt. "She'll love it," he said confidently.

"You should probably go. Traffic is going to be a bitch, no matter what time you leave." Krista was right. Graham was very thankful for her. She'd stepped up and taken over most of the day-to-day operations for him while he helped his mom deal with Grady. He owed her big-time and would have to figure out a way to repay her. When he hired her, she was part time, someone to fill in for him when he needed a day off, but over the past few months and more so in the past weeks, she had become a valuable employee.

Graham went to his father, placed his hand on his shoulder, and waited for the two men beside George to stop complaining about the weather and how Mother Nature needed to get her head straight. One day, it was snowing; the next it was fifty and sunny. They wanted the sun because that meant they could get a head start on the fishing season.

"Dad, you ready?" Graham prepared for his father to give him flack about leaving so soon. There wasn't any reason either of George's friends couldn't take him home when he was ready. Much to Graham's surprise, his dad finished his pint of beer and said goodbye.

George followed his son through the bar and into the back room. He was aware of the break-in that had happened over the summer, and even though Graham blamed Grady for it, George would never believe his son would steal from the family business. Graham never pushed the issue. At the time, he'd wanted to call the cops to have the place dusted for fingerprints but wouldn't go against his father's wishes. So, Graham left it alone and made the necessary modifications to secure the old bar.

"What's that?" George asked of the bag Graham carried. He showed it to his dad.

"Krista's mom made it for mom."

"What for?"

"Um . . ." Graham paused. He'd assumed it was to keep her warm while she stayed in the hospital with Grady. He knew women liked to sew and knit and often gave pieces as gifts, and he had also heard of prayer blankets, but as he held it in his hand, he wasn't exactly sure. "I don't really know."

Graham opened the car door to the back and set it on the seat and then opened his door. He slid into the driver's side and waited for his father.

"Your mother does that."

"Does what?"

"Makes things for people, like casseroles. She meddles."

Graham reminded his father to buckle up, and then he started his car, intent on ignoring the jab against his mom. He drove slowly through the alley, keeping in mind the other vehicles parked back there. He pulled out onto Third Street and turned left.

"Where are we going?"

"I need to stop at the bank." The lie fell easily. His father said nothing as Graham drove down the road. When he passed the bank, his father noticed instantly.

"You missed the bank."

"I know." Graham pressed the gas pedal and picked up speed. The signs changed from twenty-five to thirty-five and then fifty.

"Where the hell are you taking me?"

"Grady needs you today. He's going to need his family when he wakes up."

"Graham, if you know what's good for you, you turn this car around right now and take me home." His father spoke sternly, and if Graham had been younger, he might've listened. As it was, it was time for George to accept Grady's issues.

"No can do, Dad. Mom and Grady need us, and we're going to be there for them. You always talk to me about how I need to be a better brother; well, now's the time for you to step up and be a better father."

"Don't you dare—"

"I did," Graham cut his father off. "You need to accept that Grady is an alcoholic, that we've enabled him for years. If his overdose isn't a wake-up call, I don't know what is, but it's time we stop pussyfooting around Grady and get him the help he needs before he does something we all have to pay for."

"Your brother is fine."

"Except he's not, and deep down, you know he's not. I get there's some pride there—you don't want people looking down on you—but let me tell you something; they already do."

"You don't know what you're talking about." George angled himself away from his son and looked out the window at the passing scenery.

Graham nodded and ended the conversation for now. His father was thickskulled and prideful. It was going to take a lot to get through to him.

When they arrived at the ferry booth, Graham showed the attendant the pass he had purchased and took the ticket with his lane assignment on it and drove to the line. They were right on time and boarded instantly. He shut his car off, pulled the lever of his seat, and reclined.

"Who's Roxy?" His father's voice broke through the silence between them.

Graham knew exactly who she was. "She's a local. Friends with Grady. Used to hang out with us when we were younger. How do you know her?"

"She's called the house looking for Grady."

Graham sat up and readjusted his seat. He hadn't heard of his brother and Roxy dating, but it made sense. By most accounts, Roxy Jean Wilkins was trouble. She originally hailed from Anacortes, and when she was seventeen, her parents split. Her father moved to a small shack that straddled the town lines of Cape Harbor and Skagit Valley. When they were teens, they used to think it was funny. If you were on the left side of the house, you were in Skagit Valley, but go to the bathroom, and you were in Cape Harbor.

When Roxy would stay with her father, she would come into town and hang with the locals, which included the Chamberlain twins, Bowie, Austin, and a few others. She was never one to hang out with Brooklyn or the Whitfield sisters, and if you asked any one of them what they thought of Roxy—well, their thoughts wouldn't be pleasant.

Rumors about Roxy swirled through the towns. Some said she dealt drugs, others said she had a hard life, some people stretched the truth about her, and a few said they understood her, while others pretended they didn't know her at all. Most of all, Roxy was an opportunist, and Grady's downfall was her opportunity to try and fit in with the tight-knit group from Cape Harbor. She'd hung around more in the last couple of years, always with Grady.

"What did you tell her?" Graham asked.

"Nothing—he isn't home, and it's none of her business."

Graham laughed. His father was right; Grady's whereabouts were none of Roxy's business. They finally agreed on something.

"Does your brother like this lady?"

"Don't know, Dad. Grady and I haven't spoken much over the past few months." His father mumbled something under his breath and went back to being quiet until they arrived at the hospital.

Because it was visiting hours, they didn't need to check in with security. Graham made sure to walk side by side with his father to prevent him from running off. He felt like he was herding cattle trying to get his father to go where he needed him to. When they arrived at the doors to the intensive care unit, Graham pressed the button, like he had done many times over the past couple of weeks, and gave his name and waited for the doors to open. They walked in through the second set and followed the path toward Grady's room.

"George," Johanna breathlessly said when she saw her husband. She left her son's bedside and wrapped her arms around George. "I'm so happy you're here." Graham let his parents have their moment while he went to visit Grady.

He sat down and held his hand. Whatever nutrients the doctors fed Grady had done the job of making him not look so sickly. His cheeks had filled out, and his skin looked natural and not like death. The last time he'd seen himself in Grady was back in California, months before the accident.

"I can't believe this is your place." Grady walked all over the house and finally into the backyard, where he spotted a couple of women lounging by the pool. *"You've got to be kidding me,"* he said to Graham.

"Benefits of having an in-ground pool." Graham set his hand down on his brother's shoulder and jostled him around. *The twins laughed and high-fived each other.*

"Damn, I can see why you love it down here." Grady tilted his head toward the sun and smiled. *"Sun, women, more women."*

Grady sat down between the women and introduced himself while Graham kept his distance. He wanted his brother to have a fun time while he visited.

"Holy shit." Graham looked over his shoulder and smiled as his girlfriend approached. Monica had yet to meet his brother—or his parents, for that matter. When they had come for graduation, everyone had their plans, and it didn't seem right to mix the two families at the time.

"Hey, how was work?" Graham asked as Monica sat down on his lap. Not in the chair beside him, like he would prefer.

"Good—glad to be out for the weekend." Monica kept glancing at Grady, hinting that Graham needed to introduce them. He tapped her on the thigh, a signal to get up so he could as well.

"Grady, come meet Monica."

Grady came over with his hand held out. "Nice to meet you. My brother talks about you nonstop."

Monica beamed and placed her hand on Graham's cheeks and squeezed them while making kissy faces at him. Monica was ready to take their relationship to the next level. She wanted marriage and babies and had a timeline of when it all had to happen. Graham wanted to wait, enjoy the single life, and chill with his roommates for a bit longer. Plus, he wasn't exactly on the same page as Monica. He had lingering feelings for Rennie, which wouldn't go away no matter how hard he tried.

Grady went back to flirting with the girls by the pool, and Monica eventually left, although she put up a stink about Graham taking Grady out to the bars later. The possessiveness Monica had over Graham was a quality he didn't appreciate, but he knew it stemmed from his relationship with Rennie.

When evening rolled around, the Chamberlain twins and Graham's roommates boarded a train for San Francisco and hit the town running, and Grady quickly learned what Cali life was all about.

By the time the weekend was over, Graham was exhausted. He took Grady to the airport and made him promise to come back in the fall, once fishing season concluded.

"You never made it back," Graham said to Grady.

Dr. Field and two nurses walked in and went right over to Grady. The nurses started messing with the machines and the tubes running in and out of Grady's body.

"We are weaning him off the sedation meds," Dr. Field said. "Grady could wake up within hours, or it could be a day or two. We've done everything we can to repair some of the damage to his organs, but he is far from stable. His pancreas, liver, and kidneys are severely damaged from the continued alcohol abuse. Before he's discharged, we'll insert a feeding tube through his nose and into his stomach. He needs a liquid diet to maintain weight."

"So, he can't eat real food?" George asked.

"No, he can eat soup, ice cream, anything soft. He won't be able to digest anything heavy. No meats, pasta, those types of things, at least for right now."

"When can we take him home?" Johanna asked.

"Mom," Graham said, cutting her off. He shook his head slightly, as if to remind her Grady wouldn't be going home anytime soon. "Sorry, Dr. Field, please continue."

He cleared his throat and began speaking again. "We're recommending inpatient rehab for at least three months, if not longer. The severity of Grady's addiction is one of the worst I've seen in years, and I'm not confident he won't need to stay longer."

"He doesn't need any help," George blurted out.

"Mr. Chamberlain, I can respect that you feel this way about your son, but he's going to die if he drinks another drop of liquor or injects his body with any more heroin. He will suffer a massive heart attack, or his death will be slow and painful from each organ shutting down. Honestly, I'm surprised he didn't pass away already."

Harsh as the words were, Dr. Field was right to say them to George. He, as well as Grady, needed a reality check. A slap in the face, as it was.

The family needed to band together to help Grady or accept that their son and brother was going to die.

After the doctor and nurses left, time all but stood still for the Chamberlains. George paced the room. Johanna sat by Grady's side and held his hand. Graham needed fresh air, and when he stepped out of his brother's room, he saw the two police officers who had found Grady on the side of the road.

"Unbelievable," Graham said as he stood next to them. "He's not even awake yet, and you're here to arrest him."

"We're just doing our jobs, Mr. Chamberlain."

"He's sick," Graham reminded them. "He can't go anywhere."

They nodded but said nothing else. Graham stormed out of the ICU and pulled his phone out of his pocket. He pressed Rennie's name and waited for her to answer.

"Hey, Graham Cracker."

He closed his eyes at the sound of her nickname for him. He desperately wanted her. In his life, by his side, in his bed. He had to find a way to stop thinking of her as more than a friend, or he was going to fall off the deep end. "They're bringing Grady out of the coma."

"That's great news. I've started working on Grady's case. I met with a colleague today, and he gave me some advice. I should be able to handle everything."

"The police officers from the other day—they're here."

"What? Why? To arrest him?" Rennie seemed frantic. Graham could hear papers shuffling around, and she muttered some obscenities. "They can't arrest him right now. His arraignment would need to be within three days, and he'll be in no condition to leave the hospital. Shit."

Graham held the phone to his ear and waited for Rennie to come to her senses. He tried his hardest not to laugh but pictured Rennie running around her office—without her heels on, for some reason—with the phone cord knocking papers and books off her desk.

"Okay, I'm going to call the chief in Port Angeles and talk to him. I have a plan, but I want to talk to your parents about it. Is your dad on board yet?"

"Possibly. I think Dr. Field scared the life out of him."

"Good. I'll clear my schedule and see when I can get up there. Call me if anything changes, okay?"

"I will, Ren." They hung up, and relief washed over him. He felt confident Rennie would get Grady the help he needed. When the bar had been broken into, Graham wanted his brother in jail, but after seeing the difference of what two weeks of sobriety had done for him, Graham knew rehab was the best place for Grady.

Graham went back to Grady's room and suggested his parents take a walk, at least to go and get something to eat and to get some fresh air. Johanna took George by the hand and led him out of the room.

The blue plastic chair next to Grady's bed was as uninviting as cleaning the bathroom at the bar after a busy Friday night. Still, Graham sat down in case Grady woke. Even though phones weren't allowed in the ICU, Graham slipped his out of his pocket and pulled up a game he often played to pass the time.

He sat there, with nurses coming in and out of Grady's room, and waited. He spoke to his brother, telling him about the weather and how he had to tighten down the houseboat the other night because the waves made him seasick. At some point, Graham rested his head on Grady's bed and fell asleep.

Graham felt something brush through his hair. It reminded him of when he was little, and he would lay his head down on his mother's lap, and she would comb her fingers through his hair. He lifted his head, and Grady's hand fell away. Graham glanced at his brother and saw his eyes fluttering open.

"Grady," Graham said his name softly. "Can you hear me?"

Grady groaned and tried to speak. He reached for the solid tube coming out of his mouth, but Graham stopped him. "Let me get the nurse." He pressed the call button, and immediately, a nurse came in. She smiled at Grady, turned the switch off, and started talking.

"I'm going to remove your breathing tube, but you have to wear oxygen for a little bit. Nod if you understand."

Grady nodded.

The nurse instructed Grady to breathe out as she removed the tube and encouraged him to cough. Graham gagged while watching the procedure. "I'll page Dr. Field and have him come check on Grady."

As soon as the nurse left, Grady reached for Graham and beckoned him to come close. He tried to ask "What happened?" but could barely say either word. Graham sensed his request and sat back down in the chair. He contemplated waiting for their parents, but he had something to say to his brother.

"You messed up, Grady. The gig is over. The drinking, the drugs— it's all done. You're going to rehab if Rennie can keep you out of jail."

"Jail?" Grady's voice was scratchy and barely above a whisper.

Graham leaned forward. "You're going to be arrested. Honestly, it's the only thing that can save your life right now."

THIRTEEN

The drive from Seattle to Port Angeles would take three hours. With traffic, Rennie looked at a four- or possibly five-hour drive. In the early hours of the morning, long before the sun rose, she got in her car and headed west. Her client Grady Chamberlain would be arrested in his hospital room and arraigned the next day. He faced multiples charges, all of which Rennie hoped she'd be able to plea down to misdemeanors as long as her client went to rehab. Their encounter today would be the first time she'd interacted with Grady since his outburst over the summer, and she wasn't sure how their meeting would go. Graham had done his best to prepare her for his brother's defiant attitude and the woe-is-me mentality Grady had. She had also spent considerable hours with Jefferson, going over the game plan. If this case went to trial, he would sit second chair with Rennie, in case she needed him. One thing was for sure—Grady's case reminded her why she had never gone down the criminal route; she was torn between what she felt was an obligation to the Chamberlains and taking someone who could harm another off the streets. Her ethics told her Grady deserved jail for breaking the law, even though it was unlikely he'd ever see the inside of a cell. Meanwhile, her heart told her Grady needed help and a second chance, and she could help him obtain one.

Rennie pulled into the parking lot of the two-story hospital and parked next to Graham's car. She looked over, surprised to find him in his car. Rennie exited her vehicle and went over to Graham's. He was asleep and looked peaceful. Her fingers itched to touch his face, to follow the fine lines in his forehead, and to feel his scruff against her skin. She held back, though. Rennie was committed to another man, and the relationship she and Graham had years ago had washed out to sea.

She tapped lightly on the window. Graham startled. He looked around until he saw her, and a slow smile crept over him. He pressed the button on the door handle and dropped the window that was separating them.

"Good morning," she said. "How long have you been in the parking lot?"

Graham ran his hand over his face and groaned. "All night. I slept out here while my parents stayed with Grady. What time is it?"

"A little after nine," Rennie replied. "Want to go to the diner down the street and get breakfast? We have a little over an hour before everything is scheduled to go down."

He chuckled and shook his head. "You make today sound like a mob hit." He motioned for her to get into his car. She walked around the front and was surprised to find the door already ajar for her. "Thank you."

"For what?" Graham asked as he started his car and pulled out of the parking spot.

"For opening the door. For trusting me with your brother. For being my friend."

Graham remained silent for the one-minute drive. He found a parking spot close to the door, and after he turned off his car, he was out in a flash. By the time he reached the passenger side, Rennie was out and standing there. His face fell; she saw the dejection instantly. Rennie would pay more attention when with Graham. When she was with Theo, the little things like opening and holding doors or letting her walk in front of him never really happened. There were times when Rennie wondered if it was because of the way their relationship started—in between the sheets—and that he never had to woo her or vice versa. Graham had always been a gentleman from the day she met him as a teenager, and it would seem he never lost that part of him.

Rennie stepped into the diner first and greeted the hostess, telling her she had two in her party. Graham followed Rennie toward their booth and set his hand on her lower back. A familiar sense of longing washed over her, but she ignored it. Her feelings for Graham needed to remain buried. Their time had come, and they had missed their chance.

They ordered coffee to start and both glanced at the menu. Rennie's mouth watered when she read their special for the day: pancakes with berry compote. She made up her mind when she pictured a pile of whipped cream on top of the berries.

"Do you know what you're getting?" she asked Graham as she set the menu down on the edge of the table. She picked up her mug and brought her coffee to her lips, sipping gingerly.

"Steak and eggs. It'll keep me full until dinner."

"You don't plan to eat lunch?"

He set his menu on top of hers and wrapped his hands around his cup of coffee. "I think my stomach might be in knots around lunchtime."

She understood. Many of her clients forgot to eat before court because of nerves. There were times when a loud stomach growl would interrupt a cross-examination or a summation. The first couple of times she'd heard the sound, the noise caught her off guard. Now, Rennie didn't falter. Her professionalism saved a lot of face, especially when it was her client.

The server came by, and they placed their orders. Graham looked pensive, completely lost in thought. "What's on your mind?" Rennie asked him.

"The past," he said as he made eye contact with her.

Rennie nodded. It had been on her mind a lot too. "I think because we've spent so much time together in these past few weeks."

"I'm glad you found someone like Theo." Graham's words sent a jolt through her; she was taken aback by his admission. "He's a good guy. I may not like him, but Bowie does, and Brooklyn speaks very highly of him."

"He's different from our crew." She glossed over the fact that Graham said he didn't like Theo. She was curious but didn't want to know the reasons why. "He didn't grow up on the beach with bonfires and close-knit friends. He's a skier. That's his thing. I've been trying to mix both of our lifestyles, but it's hard."

"How so?" Graham took a sip of his coffee and the whole time never took his eyes off Rennie.

"He's not a fan of sand in places it shouldn't be, whereas I don't care. I'm not a fan of skiing. I'm not a fan of the snow, but I'll go because it means something to him. I'm hoping that after our New Year's trip, he'll be more amenable to the beach."

"Shouldn't he go to the beach because it means something to you?" Graham countered. He was right, but Rennie would never admit it aloud.

The server returned in the nick of time, saving Rennie from having to answer Graham's question. She smiled at the waitress and licked her lips in anticipation as she set her pancakes down.

"Are there any pancakes with the whipped cream?" Graham chuckled at his joke.

"Be quiet, you," Rennie said to him as she set her napkin in her lap. She used her fork to take a heaping scoop of the fluffy white concoction off the top and hummed in response when sweetness hit her taste buds. "This is the best."

"If you say so."

"I do. So, we talked about my love life. Tell me about yours. Are you seeing anyone? Maybe your cute bartender?"

Graham cut into his steak. He stabbed a piece of meat, added ketchup and some hash browns to his fork before stuffing it into his mouth. Rennie suspected he planned to avoid her questions, and she had no intention of letting him do such a thing. So, she waited. Her foot tapped against the tiled floor, and she watched his every move.

"Stalker much?"

"Answer me."

Graham sighed. "I'm not seeing anyone. I haven't dated in a while. Krista is happily married."

"Why aren't you dating?"

Graham pushed his food around on his plate and kept his eyes downcast. "I'm the brother of the town drunk. Not exactly bring-home-to-Mom material."

Rennie's heart sank. Graham was 1,000 percent the man you brought home to your parents. She knew this early on and never hesitated to introduce him to her parents. "I'm sorry." She reached across the table and squeezed his hand. Rennie waited a long moment before asking, "Whatever happened to what's her face from college? I thought for sure you'd get married."

"Monica?"

Rennie nodded.

"Grady happened," Graham stated matter-of-factly. "After the funeral, shit went south fast. My parents needed help. We all thought Grady was going through this phase. He needed me, so I stayed. There was nothing here for Monica. The idea of giving up her career to live in a small-town tourist trap wasn't something she wanted, and I couldn't blame her. I didn't want it, either, but here I am. You ask me why I'm not dating. If Grady isn't the obvious reason, it's also because I have nothing to offer someone."

"That's not true, Graham."

"Isn't it, though?" He looked at her pointedly. She couldn't decipher if the jab was directed at her or in general. For all she knew, it was both, because when she came through the door of the Whale Spout over the summer, she flirted with him heavily and led him on.

"We should eat," she said, diverting the topic of conversation back to food. "We have to go soon."

Graham agreed and dug into his breakfast, finishing it in no time. Rennie dawdled, taking only a few bites before her stomach revolted. She should've never asked Graham about his dating life, even though he opened the door when he brought up Theo. She knew better. Brooklyn had tried to set Graham up with a couple of her clients around the state, but nothing ever came to fruition.

He was busy.

Something had come up.

The timing wasn't right.

Graham had excuse after excuse when it came to getting out there in the dating world. Rennie thought about asking Bowie about Graham's love life, to find out if he'd dated before she'd returned to Cape Harbor, but she knew better than to meddle. Besides, deep down, if she found out he'd stopped dating after she'd made her surprise visit, she wouldn't be able to live with herself.

They drove back to the hospital and made it to Grady's room, shrouded in awkwardness. She hated the negative tension between them and wanted to back him into a corner and demand he tell her how he felt. Doing so would require her to come clean about her feelings, and there was no way she was ready to admit that the past couple of weeks had sparked something deep within her. She missed the ease the relationship with Graham had and wished her connection with Theo could be the same.

Rennie walked into Grady's room with a smile. She greeted George and Johanna with hugs and gave Grady a small wave, while everyone in the room made idle chitchat. She explained to everyone what was going to happen today and how tomorrow would go in court, and then she asked for a moment alone with Grady. Once everyone left, Rennie shut the door and stood at the end of his bed. He sat up in his bed, still dressed in a hospital gown, with wires coming out of the top. His left hand had an IV attached, and there was a small tube coming out of his nose.

"Hey, Grady. Long time no see."

"From what I've been told, the last time you saw me, I was drunk." His voice was hoarse, and it sounded like it hurt him to speak.

Rennie nodded. "In the past, right?"

Grady shrugged, which wasn't a good sign for Rennie. She needed him on board with the plan, which was to avoid jail time. Of course, the deal would hinge on Grady going to rehab and staying in a facility until he was healthy enough to function in society again.

"First thing I want to know is how you're doing. Do you need anything?"

He appraised her for a moment, almost as if no one had asked him how he was doing with everything that was going on. "I'm okay," he told her. "A bit scared."

"I hope I can ease your fears. When the police come in, they're going to Mirandize you. Listen to the officers, and tell them you understand. They shouldn't ask you any questions, because the charges pertain only to you. You didn't cause any harm to anyone else or personal property. Can you tell me where you got the car you were found in? Your mother seems to think you don't have one."

"My friend Roxy sold it to me."

"Where did you get the money, Grady?"

He shrugged. "Bartered for a few things that I don't really want to talk about."

"You know anything you say to me stays between us. I work for you, not your brother or your parents. Will the district attorney know something about this car that I should know?"

"No, it was just personal stuff between Roxy and me. She sort of had to get it out of her name because of child support or something."

Rennie nodded and typed a note into her phone. "Okay, when the police come in, I've asked that they not cuff you to the bed. It's normal practice in some places, but I feel it is unnecessary in this situation. Tomorrow, we'll go to court, and you'll plead not guilty—"

"I was just in a coma, and now I have to go to court?" Grady interrupted.

"Yes, it's standard procedure. You can go, or we can ask for a video arraignment, but your doctor would need to sign off on the request. Would you like me to ask Dr. Field?"

Grady shook his head slowly. Rennie continued, "After you plead not guilty, I'm going to ask that we go to trial."

"I have to go on trial?" Grady blurted out.

"Not usually for what you're being charged with, because we'll work out a plea deal, but setting a date is a formality. Did your parents talk about treatment?"

Grady nodded.

"And you're going to agree to enter rehab?"

He glanced at Rennie, and for a moment, she thought he was going to tell her no. He nodded slowly but seemed to lack the enthusiasm she sought. "Grady, it's rehab or jail."

"Or death," he countered.

"Yes, there is that."

Their conversation ceased when the door opened, and Officers Hook and Frey sauntered in. They tipped their hats toward Rennie and stood on either side of Grady's bed. They stated Grady's Miranda rights, asked if he had any questions. When he told them no, they said they would be by tomorrow to take him to court. Once they left, Rennie invited the Chamberlains back into the room.

"It's over?" Johanna asked.

"Only until tomorrow," Rennie said. "The officers will be back in the morning to take Grady to court for his arraignment. We'll meet there. It'll be quick, and then he'll be transported to rehab. The center will allow you a few minutes to say goodbye."

"So, I can't see my son whenever I want?" George asked.

"Not whenever, no. There is special visitation each week for family members and family counseling. I suggest, for Grady's sake, everyone takes part. I think we're in a unique situation where people still hurt from what happened all those years ago."

"We don't need family counseling," George blurted out. "I'm not going to let some shrink tell me how to raise my boys."

Rennie glanced at Johanna, who looked embarrassed, then over at Graham, who hung his head. The family dynamic with the Chamberlains was odd. Johanna wanted her son to get all the help he could, Graham wanted his brother and his life back, and George refused to believe there was anything wrong with his kid. And Rennie was in the thick of it, trying to do right by all parties involved.

Rennie excused herself and left the family to talk. She was tired and in need of a nap and suddenly eager to get to the hotel Ester booked for her. In the parking lot, she turned at the sound of her name. Graham jogged toward her and didn't stop until he had her cocooned in his arms.

"Thank you," he whispered.

"I'm just doing my job." She knew she was going above and beyond, but the idea of not helping Graham or putting Grady's fate into someone else's hands never crossed her mind.

Graham held her tightly. She could hear and feel his heart pounding and smell the sandalwood in his cologne. He also smelled like the beach, which, to her, meant warmth and sun. Rennie inhaled deeply, needing to remember the moment.

"I should really go," she said, motioning toward her car. "I'll see you tomorrow?"

He stepped away from her and nodded. Tempted as she was to ask about his accommodations for the evening, she held back. Rennie needed to put some distance between herself and Graham. It would be best for both of them.

The next morning, Rennie rose with purpose. She called for room service and sat at the small round table in her hotel room, going over her notes. It wasn't necessary, as an arraignment took minutes. However, she would be prepared for anything that came her way. The only other time she had gone to an arraignment was back when she clerked. She had entered a plea, agreed with the restitution set, walked out, and switched to family court.

Her phone rang, and she smiled at the sight of Theo's picture lighting up her display. "Well, hello," she sang into the receiver.

"You're chipper this morning. I love hearing the confidence in your voice." Nights prior, they had sat on the phone, and she told him how her research into criminal law had sparked something in her, how it had brought to life the idea of opening her own firm and becoming a general practitioner. She wanted to help everyone or at least be selective in the cases she took. Family law was still her passion, but she liked the idea of helping in other areas.

"I am confident, Theo. I know it's silly because it's a preliminary hearing, but there's this thrill. I don't know—I'm excited to stand in front of the judge and enter a plea for my client."

"I get it, my love. There is nothing more satisfying than telling a client their books are exactly where they need to be, that no one is stealing from them."

Rennie chuckled at the thoughts that rolled around in her head. "You know, we could open a firm. I could take to trial the people who embezzle from your clients."

"I like the way you think, Ms. Wallace."

"Why, thank you, Mr. Wright. I do believe we could make a powerful team."

"And a team we will become. Listen, I have to get to the office, but I wanted to wish you good luck or whatever. I know you said things should go smoothly, but I wanted to let you know I'm thinking of you."

"Thank you, Theo."

"I love you, Renee."

"I love you too." They hung up. Rennie held her phone in her hand and thought about everything she had said to Theo. Telling him she loved him had become an automatic response for her. They had dated for about four months when he told her he was in love with her. It had happened after they had made love. He had looked her in the eyes and said the three words women often longed to hear. Except, Rennie preferred not to hear them after sex. She felt the words meant more if they happened naturally and not spurred by other acts. Rennie returned the sentiment because at the time, she was in love, or at least that was what she thought. Since her frequent trips to Cape Harbor, she had started to question her feelings for Theo, which hadn't made her very happy.

Rennie dressed the same as she would for any other court hearing. She wore a navy-colored knee-length skirt with a matching blazer and a white blouse. She curled her hair, gave herself a natural look with her makeup, and dabbed on a light-pink-tinted lip gloss. When Rennie felt complete, she stood in the mirror and practiced the few words she would say today. For the life of her, she couldn't understand why she was so nervous.

"It's because it's Graham," she said aloud in her room.

She grabbed her bag, then checked out of the hotel and made her way to her car. The drive to the courthouse was quick, as was getting through security. When she reached the courtroom, the Chamberlains were waiting. Johanna sat on a wooden bench, while Graham held up the wall beside her and George paced.

"They took Grady out in cuffs." George pointed his finger at Rennie.

"Dad, knock it off. It's not Rennie's fault."

"She said they wouldn't do that. It's embarrassing."

Johanna stood and confronted her husband. "Our son is an embarrassment, George. It's time you see him for what he is—an alcoholic and drug user. If these past two weeks haven't proven this to you, I don't know why you're even here."

Graham and Rennie separated the married couple. George wouldn't budge, but Johanna went back to the bench and wiped away her tears.

"This type of arguing—it's not good and can't happen here," Rennie told them. "Although cuffing Grady is excessive, they had the right to do it, and I think it's because I asked for favors which benefitted Grady. Our country is fighting an opioid crisis right now, and if Grady hadn't taken the drugs with the officer standing right there, he'd be facing a DUII charge only. He needs help, and that is what we're going to get him today, but I need everyone on the same page. Okay?"

George ignored Rennie and walked down the hall, away from his family. Graham said nothing and sat down next to his mother. Rennie understood the enormity of the situation in front of her. It was one thing to know and think a family member had an addiction, but it was something else entirely to be face to face with it—and with your hands tied.

The bailiff opened the doors, and everyone waiting for court filed in. Rennie and the Chamberlains took a seat on the left side of the courtroom, and while Rennie waited for Grady's case to be called, she went over her notes.

"State v. Chamberlain is up next."

Rennie rose and walked to the defendant's table. An officer of the court escorted Grady in, without cuffs, which pleased her.

She introduced herself to the assistant district attorney, Kate Martell. "I'd like to talk to you about a plea, but I am requesting my client be remanded to the Port Angeles Rehab Center for at least ninety days."

"He could get help in jail," Kate pointed out.

"He could, but it's a matter of life or death." Rennie handed the ADA a letter from his doctor backing up her statement.

Kate nodded. "No prelim?"

"No, straight to trail and revisit for a plea?" Rennie pushed.

"I can work with this."

"Docket number 20 1 0005 9, the State of Washington v. Grady Chamberlain. One count of driving under the influence of intoxicants, possession of a narcotic, driving without a valid driver's license, registration, and insurance," the bailiff read aloud.

"Mr. Chamberlain, how do you plead?" the judge asked.

"Renee Wallace for the defendant, Your Honor. We plead not guilty and request a trial date."

"No prelim?" the judge asked.

"No, Your Honor."

"How's the state feel, Ms. Martell?"

"The state agrees to move to trial but requests Mr. Chamberlain be remanded to PAR for extensive rehabilitation as outlined by Dr. Field." Kate handed her copy of the letter to the bailiff. Rennie was on pins and needles, anxious for the outcome they needed.

"Ms. Wallace, I do believe this is your first time in my court. Welcome."

"Thank you, ma'am."

"Your client is willing to enter rehab?"

"Yes, Your Honor."

"Very well, ninety days at PAR. The court will set a trial date for then. Adjourned."

The escort returned for Grady. Rennie told him she would be up to see him soon and that they could speak over the phone if necessary.

She went to Graham and his parents and suggested they go over to the center to be there when Grady arrived.

Graham walked Rennie to her car. "I owe you," he told her.

Rennie smiled and set her bag down. "You don't, and neither does your family. I'm happy I can help, and I'm so glad Grady is finally getting the medical attention he needs. I think this is going to be a good thing for you and your family."

His hand jutted out and rested on her hip, only for him to pull it back. Rennie wanted his hand to stay there and chided herself for wanting something from Graham when she had Theo to think about. "You've already made a difference in my family, Ren. My dad . . ." Graham paused and pulled Rennie into his arms. "He's a better dad because of this, and you were instrumental in making my family stronger. Thank you."

"I'd do anything for you, Graham." The words she spoke were true. There were very few people she would do anything for, and Graham was one of them.

Once she was in her car, she headed toward the highway, eager to get back to the office. Traffic was going to be a nightmare, but she had already taken one day of personal time to be in Port Angeles and wasn't keen on rocking the boat with Lex. Rennie phoned Ester as soon as she was out of town and asked her to set up a call with Kate Martell, to call the court and get a copy of the transcript, and to touch base with the rehab facility to make sure Grady settled in.

By the time Rennie reached Seattle, it was close to the end of the day. She planned to put a couple hours of work in at the office before going home and crawling into bed. When Rennie reached her office, she found Ester putting dinner on her desk. "What's this?" she asked as she set her bags down.

"My way of making your day better."

"Oh, Ester, you're a godsend. Thank you." Rennie opened the to-go box, and her stomach growled. She hadn't eaten much of anything all day and was famished.

"It's not much," Ester said.

"It's a delicious sandwich and perfect," Rennie told her in between bites. "How did everything go yesterday?"

"Great. No issues. Donna's looking for you, though."

Rennie sighed heavily. She had suspected as much. Ester went back to her desk, only to ring Rennie's intercom. "Donna's on her way."

"Thanks for the warning." She secretly loved how close the other assistants were with each other, although it backfired a time or two.

"Knock, knock." Even though Donna said the words, she knocked on the door as well. She entered and closed the door behind her. "We missed you yesterday—and today, for that matter."

"I took some personal time."

"Oh, aren't you going on vacation soon?"

In all her years at the firm, no one had ever questioned her time off until now, and Rennie didn't like it. "What can I do for you?" Donna Pere was Rennie's mentor. Rennie respected her, but the level of respect had gone down the past few weeks.

Donna sat in the chair across from Rennie and smiled. It was evil, condescending, and Rennie expected something was about to be said that she wasn't going to like. "How's your pet project?"

Rennie hated the term *pet project*. She felt it demeaned anything she or another lawyer chose to work on. Pro bono work wasn't a project; it was helping people who needed a good attorney to represent them. Donna had taught her as much over the years.

"It's great, actually. We had court this morning; everything went as planned."

"Who is it, if you don't mind me asking?" Donna kept her ankles crossed and leaned onto the armrest. The red suit she wore was a designer label, no doubt Ralph Lauren or someone equally as talented.

She had nothing to hide. "Grady Chamberlain. We grew up together."

"Chamberlain . . . sounds familiar," Donna said.

"Doubt it. Family from up north, Cape Harbor."

Donna snapped her fingers and pointed. "That's right—Cape Harbor. Graham Chamberlain, right? He owns some whale bar?"

"Uh-huh." Rennie was on edge. She didn't like where Donna was going with this. Rennie had never brought Graham up to her, not even when they lived in California and not since she'd been in contact with him.

"You have to drop the case."

"Excuse me?"

"No biggie . . . just that in my civil suit, they're suing Graham." Donna dropped the bombshell, as if it was an everyday occurrence for Graham to get sued.

"I'm sorry, what?" Renee could barely get the words out without choking.

"Oh, I thought you knew. Graham served alcohol to a minor, let her leave the bar without a ride, and now she's paralyzed. We discussed it last month."

"No," Renee said sharply. "You told us about the case, not who you were suing. How come Graham doesn't know this?"

"We haven't filed yet, but now that we know his brother is an alcoholic, it bolsters our case. Clearly, your friend has a penchant for serving alcohol when he shouldn't."

Renee couldn't believe her ears. "You can't use what you learned in our conference room against my client."

Donna's laughter stopped, and she turned stone cold. "Drop your case, Renee. It's in direct conflict, and I *will* use it."

"I'm not dropping my case, Donna. Graham is my client and has been for years. I'm sorry, but your civil suit has to go elsewhere." In the trash was where Rennie wanted to tell her to put it.

Donna stood, straightened her skirt, and set her hands down onto Renee's desk. Her mentor's gaze was menacing, terrifying. "Lex agrees—drop the case."

"I won't," Renee fired back.

The senior partner smirked as she stood and walked out of the room. Even though she hadn't slammed the office door, Renee still jumped nonetheless. A lawsuit was the last thing Graham needed right now.

Rennie called Ester into her office. "Hey, can you get me a copy of Donna's case, the one involving the paralyzed teenager?"

"Of course."

As soon as Ester left her office, Rennie began to pace. Deep in the recesses of her bag, her cell phone rang. She searched for it and answered without looking at the caller identification. "What?"

"I'm not sure how to respond."

Shit. Theo hated rudeness. Rennie closed her eyes, inhaled deeply, and counted to ten. "I'm sorry. Long day."

"I was calling to see how court went."

Rennie smiled. "It went really well. My clients are happy. How was your day?"

"Busy. I have to go to San Diego for a couple of days and wanted to see if you wanted to go with me?"

She did. She wanted to go sit on the beach and bask in the warm sun. Work plagued her, though. Rennie had to talk to Graham about this other lawsuit, and there was a lingering suspicion that something was off at work. "Oh, Theo, I would love to, but I'm so busy right now."

"I see." She sensed disappointment in Theo's tone, which angered her.

"No, I don't think you do. It's a great luxury you have, being able to travel. I can't. My clients need me, and I already have a vacation booked this month. I can't drop everything on a whim and leave, Theo. You know this."

"I understand."

"Do you? Because right now I feel like you don't."

"Believe me, Renee. I do. I just wanted to offer because I know how much you enjoy the coast."

He made her feel like an ass. She slumped over and rested her head on her desk. "I'm sorry," she said quietly into the phone. "It's been so long since I've seen you. I feel like we have this disconnect, and I want nothing more than to go with you."

"I know, love. Soon, we'll be together for a nice long week. Nothing will interrupt us."

His words brought a smile to her face. "I can't wait."

"Excuse me, Ms. Wallace?"

Rennie's head popped up at the sound of Ester's voice. She had papers in her hand, which Rennie believed to be the complaint against Graham. "Theo, I have to call you back. Love you," she said and hung up.

Ester came forward. "I don't know what's going on, but some of us have noticed Ms. Pere acting weird, especially around you, and when you asked for this case, it's clear there's a conflict with the parties involved." She handed the documents to Rennie. "I printed it out instead of emailing."

"You're smart, Ester. Thank you." Ester turned and walked toward the door. "Hey, if you don't mind, can you keep your ears open but nose clean?"

Ester smiled. "Already on it."

Rennie read the complaint and wished she had taken her criminal law classes more seriously. She understood the jargon but not how Graham could be responsible. She looked at the clock and calculated the time it would take her to get to Cape Harbor. To go now or wait— the decision weighed heavily on her mind. She yawned and rubbed her eyes. Rennie was tired, exhausted from the drive, and needed to go home. Cape Harbor would have to wait.

FOURTEEN

For the first time in a long time, Graham was back to work, and he was happy. Ecstatic. The Whale Spout gave him a sense of purpose, belonging, even though running a family-owned business, especially a bar, in a tourist town was the last thing he'd ever wanted for a career. However, he loved it. He loved the regulars who frequented the bar, the groups of people, from the fishermen to the locals—who for generations made the Whale Spout their only watering hole—and he adored the tourists. They were what made living and working in a small town enjoyable. And, it took Grady almost dying for Graham to figure out it was time for him to move on. The only question that plagued him was, "What does it mean to move on?" He didn't have the answer, and he was certain he wasn't going to find it scrawled in messy handwriting on the bathroom stall door. It was Rennie who brought about this sudden change in him. He'd lain awake the previous night, staring at his ceiling—which, as of late, was a common occurrence for him—and thought about how his life could've been different.

Graham pulled in front of the house he shared in the wee hours of the morning. He had driven straight from Cape Harbor, surviving on convenience store coffee, fast food, and chips. Graham was long past the point of exhaustion, mentally and physically drained. His life altered in ways he'd never thought possible. Graham was too young to lose one of his closest friends, and knowing he would never see or speak to Austin again hurt. The pain cut him deeply.

It had been two weeks, maybe even three—Graham had lost count since he had last been in California. He'd also lost his job, in the sense he'd been demoted back to entry level, a position he hadn't even had coming out of college. It was the most his employer was willing to offer since he had exhausted all his vacation and sick time. They were angry, and while he understood, none of it made sense to Graham. His best friend went missing, was declared dead, and all Graham had waiting for him back in California was a demotion and a pay cut to go with it. He, too, felt like he'd lost everything.

And then there was Grady.

His brother drank himself into a stupor every single night. The first couple of nights, Graham and Bowie were right there with Grady, matching drink for drink. They'd close the bar down and make their way down to the docks, where they'd yell for Austin until the sun came up or the police took them home. The next night, they'd start all over again. It was their way of coping, of helping Grady get through an unbearable time. They had all lost Austin, but Grady took it the hardest. He'd been there and had been unable to save his best friend and business partner.

After the funeral, it was time to get back to life. Only, life as Graham knew it was never going to be the same. He had to make a decision, one he never thought he would have to make at the age of twenty-two. Stay in California and work two jobs until he could get back to where he'd been, or go home. Home meant he'd be with his friends, his brother, and his parents. Home meant Rennie would still be there because of Brooklyn. But what about Monica? Did he love her?

He did.

Graham opened the front door of his house as quietly as possible. He tiptoed down the hall and opened his door. He flipped his light switch on and gasped loudly. There was someone in his bed, but who? His heart raced, pounded forcefully with each step he took toward his bed. Graham leaned over the covered lump to peer at their face. His body relaxed when he saw it was Monica. He sat down on the edge of his bed and sighed heavily. Graham hoped to slow his beating heart and not to wake his girlfriend.

Monica stirred. Graham turned to look at her from over his shoulder. He missed her while he was gone, but he also enjoyed the time he spent with Rennie. These two women owned him, but in different ways.

"Hey," she said softly as she reached for him. Monica rolled over and held the blankets open for Graham. He kicked his shoes off, slipped out of his shorts, and pulled his T-shirt over his head. The moment their bodies met, his lips were on hers, and her hands pulled him close. Graham needed Monica. He wanted to feel like himself again, the person he was when he was with her and who they were as a couple in San Jose. They were in love, they had a future, and he prayed she would go with him back to Washington, where they could start their lives. Monica and Graham made love until the sun rose, and though he was tired, he couldn't close his eyes and find sleep.

Graham kissed Monica's temple and told her over and over again how much he loved her. Tears fell from his eyes as he searched for the words that would change their future. Monica rolled onto her side and pushed her fingers through his hair.

"What's wrong?"

"Everything," he told her. "I lost my friend, someone I thought would always be around when I went back to visit my parents. He's gone. My brother is a wreck."

"I'm sorry I couldn't be there for you."

"I know."

Monica wiped away his tears and placed a kiss on each cheek. Graham was surprised she hadn't asked about Rennie yet. When he'd received the call, he hadn't called Monica to tell her until he had to stop for gas. His only focus was getting home. When he called, they argued because Rennie had gone with him.

"Is there anything I can do?" Monica asked.

"Come with me."

"Where are you going?"

The words pained him, but he had made his mind up on his drive back. His brother needed him. *"Back to Cape Harbor."*

"To visit? Of course I'll go. I'd love to see where you grew up."

He shook his head slightly. *"I need to go home, Monica. My brother needs me."*

Monica opened her mouth to say something but stopped. Her eyes darted back and forth, and her fingers fiddled with the hem of the blanket. *"What you're asking—"*

"It's a lot. I know," Graham interrupted. *"And I'm torn, Monica. I don't know what to do, but right now, staying isn't an option. I can't afford my rent here anymore—"*

"What are you talking about?" It was her turn to cut him off. She sat up and pulled the blanket to her chest. *"What's going on?"*

"I didn't have the time to take, and they demoted me at work. An entry-level job in one of the fastest-growing markets isn't going to pay my rent. I'd have to get two full-time jobs just to make ends meet. As is, I'm living paycheck to paycheck but surviving. I've exhausted what little savings I had driving back and forth. And then there's my brother."

"He survived, right? Is he hurt?"

"Not physically. Emotionally, yes. He needs me."

"I need you, Graham. We have plans for our future. We have a life here."

"I know, and I need you, too, but I don't know what to do. I have to go home."

Monica crawled out of bed and searched for her clothes. Graham watched her get dressed, wishing she'd come back to bed with him. *"Where are you going?"*

"Home," she stated. *"I have to work."*

He was silent.

"Will you at least think about what I asked?"

Monica came over to Graham and placed her hands on his cheeks. His hands rested on the back of her thighs. He looked up at her and sought her eyes for the answer he desired. She leaned down and kissed him.

"I'm sorry," she whispered against his lips. She kept her mouth on him as tears fell from her eyes. "I'm so sorry, Graham. I love you, but I can't go."

Before he could reply, she was out of his door and out of his life.

What if Monica had come to Cape Harbor with him—where would his life be? He would've asked her to marry him if she had moved. If Brooklyn hadn't left, would Graham and Rennie be a couple? He could play this game every day and night, and still, the outcome would be the same. He put his life on hold for his brother when no one asked him to, and now he was alone while everyone around him had moved on.

Life passed by, and Graham was no longer willing to sit on the sidelines and watch. He was going to put himself out there. He would download every dating app he could. He would allow his mom to set him up, and he would reach out to Monroe Whitfield and ask if she had any single friends.

As if on cue, Monroe walked through the door, looking as cheery as ever with her strawberry-blonde hair pinned away from her face and in a ponytail. Graham went to her and kissed her on the cheek. "It's great to see you."

"You too." The lifelong friends embraced for a moment.

"Here for lunch?"

"Yeah, and I was hoping we could talk."

Graham already knew she wanted to talk about Grady. Roe, as her friends often called her, always had a soft spot for Grady, even when they were growing up. Graham motioned for her to take a seat while he stepped behind the bar to grab her a menu. He took it over and sat down across from her. "So, Grady?"

"Yeah?" She nodded.

Graham recounted the court hearing and the treatment facility Grady was living in for at least the next three months.

"Are you and your parents happy?"

"We are, and I honestly believe Grady is as well. It took a while, but our dad has finally accepted Grady's situation and is willing to go to family therapy to help Grady. I expected Grady to beg our dad to get him out of there yesterday, but he didn't. He's not happy, but I think he, too, realizes this is life or death, and he wants to get better."

"Oh, this is so good to hear."

"Hey, how come you're not in school right now?"

"Winter vacation." Monroe threw her hands up and cheered. "This year has been rough. These third graders know everything."

"I can't even remember third grade." Graham laughed. "How's my neighbor Shari fitting in?"

"She's a doll. Everyone loves her." Graham asked Monroe what she wanted for lunch. He placed her order, poured the pop she asked for, and went back to her table.

"I think I'm going to start dating," he told her. "I may need your help."

Monroe chuckled. "Graham, you work in a bar. I've seen women throw themselves at you all the time. You're just too caught up in your head to recognize what's happening."

"Really?"

She playfully rolled her eyes and giggled again. "Don't worry. I'm sure I can convince Brooklyn to come down one night. We can scout some possibilities for you."

Graham stood and kissed her on the cheek. "I knew I could count on you." He returned to work but checked on her often. Throughout the day, his friends came in to eat, chat, and see how he was doing. It was like a new leaf turned over with Grady going to rehab. The black cloud of Austin's death and Grady's demise lifted. There was a fresh new life in Cape Harbor.

By the time Rennie walked into the bar later that night, the Whale Spout was packed with bodies, with barely any space to move. The weekly dart tournament had drawn a bigger crowd than average—not that Graham cared. He welcomed the noise, especially a week before Christmas. It wasn't until Rennie squeezed her way in between two patrons and ordered a beer that Graham realized she was there.

His face fell, and he quickly turned away, hoping she hadn't seen his reaction to her. He would never purposely hurt her, but right now, she represented Grady. The good, the bad, and the ugly when it came to him.

Graham popped the top of her bottle, set it on a coaster, and slid it toward her. "You want a tab?" he asked her.

Rennie nodded and motioned toward the end of the bar, giving Graham no choice but to follow her. She rose onto her toes and told Graham what she knew about the lawsuit. At first, he had a hard time hearing her and asked that she repeat herself, because surely there was no way in hell someone would sue him. He was, without a doubt, a diligent bartender and owner. He would never serve a minor, let alone let anyone leave if they'd had too much to drink. There had to be a mistake.

Graham walked away and toward the back of the bar, disappearing behind the door. Once he was in the storage room, away from anyone who could hear him, he fisted his hands and let out a guttural scream. The veins in his forehead popped out. They throbbed from the pressure building. He screamed again and banged his fists against the concrete wall, not caring if his knuckles cut open.

"Why?" he yelled into the room. "What the fuck did I do to deserve this?" He would never get an answer, because there wasn't one anyone could give him. He paced the room, small as it was, and recounted every young patron he could. His hands fisted in his hair as the faces of past customers blurred together. Graham would never be able to remember each person he saw over the summer.

Graham gave up pacing and slumped against the wall until he reached the hard floor. He kept his knees to his chest and let his tears fall silently. He wasn't a big crier, but he was past the point of holding them back. Every part of his body hurt. His hands throbbed from hitting the wall, his head pounded from exertion, and his body ached. He hadn't felt pain like this since Austin died. He wasn't sure how much fight he had left in him. It was like he had won the biggest battle of his life when it came to his brother, only to face another army, ready to attack. Only this time, they threatened his livelihood.

When he returned an hour later, he found Rennie waiting on tables. She came and delivered unwelcome news, and when he left to go cope, she stepped in and helped him. Rennie saved him again.

The crowd had thinned out from earlier, but there were still quite a few people lingering. He owed Krista and Rennie an apology for ditching them, but he needed time away, time to process how the hell his life turned out the way it had. What he needed was a redo. He'd give anything to go back to the moment he decided moving home was the right thing to do.

Throughout the rest of the night, Rennie waited tables while Krista managed the bar and Graham bussed. He liked the change in scenery, the grunt work. It kept his mind on the task at hand, and he didn't have to chat with anyone. When he was behind the bar, he doubled as Cape Harbor's therapist, listening to everyone's problems while avoiding his own.

It was midnight when Krista clocked out. Graham offered to clean so she could go home. Graham followed the last patrons to the door. Two old guys, lifers in town. They had been part of the team who looked for Austin. Days on end they had gone out, searching. He twisted the lock on the door and rested his head against the wood. Graham sighed heavily, but it did nothing to curb the anxiety building. Now that everything was quiet, he could hear his thoughts, and he hated them. There was no way he had done the things someone was accusing him of . . . or had he? He could admit there were times when he second-guessed handing someone a drink, where he watched them throughout the night to make sure they weren't drunk and verified their ride status before they left the bar. He had a local taxi service on speed dial and used it often, and if he suspected someone was sharing drinks with someone underage, he never hesitated to call the police. The last thing he would ever want was for someone to be hurt as a result of his negligence.

He pushed off the door and made his way over to Rennie, who was sitting down at one of the tables, with her feet up. Rennie was crazy to work in heels, but Graham expected nothing less from her.

Graham sat down next to Rennie. "Tell me everything you know," he said as she handed him her phone. The print was tiny and hard to read with the dim lighting in the bar.

"Right before Thanksgiving we had a quarterly meeting, and one of the senior partners, Donna Pere, said she had a friend of a friend whose daughter was in an accident and is now paralyzed. She went on to say the family wants to sue the bartender for negligence. I asked why her friends let her drive in the first place, and Donna called it a 'joyride turned wrong' or something to that effect. No one really said much because people wanted to leave for Thanksgiving.

"At our staff meeting last week, I mention my new case and how I may need some help because it's criminal but that my clients are family friends. The owner, he's kind of on my ass about it being pro bono, which is stupid because everyone takes pro bono cases every now and again, and from what I can tell, Grady's case is easy as long as he cooperates. But Donna, she tells me Lex—the owner—wants her to dig around a little because he's not happy with the freebie.

"Fast-forward to yesterday. When I get back from Port A, Donna comes to my office and asks where I've been, which I don't get because I'm a junior partner—I can come and go as I please. Anyway, she asks about the criminal case, and I finally tell her who it's for, and it's like this light bulb moment for her, and she tells me I have to drop the case because her client is suing you for serving alcohol to a minor. We argue back and forth for a minute until she gets this look on her face and tells me to drop the case or else, pretty much, and that she plans to use the information I told the team about Grady against you."

"Can she?"

"I don't think so, but I'm not a criminal lawyer, so I'm not exactly sure. I had Ester pull the client file, which is what you see on my phone."

Graham glanced at Rennie's phone in his hand. "Why didn't you call me last night when she told you?"

"I know I should've, but yesterday was a good day for you and your family. I didn't want to ruin it. I didn't even go in to work today—sent an email that I was on vacation until after the first of the year and went shopping."

"So now what?" Graham asked.

Rennie sighed and looked at her friend. He could feel the pity rolling off her in waves and hated it. "Now, we wait for someone to serve you papers. It could be the sheriff or a process server, and then we fight. I'll ask Jefferson to take your case, but I'm not sure if he's willing to go against Lex."

"But you are?"

She nodded. "I am, but I don't know what I'm doing."

Graham was worried. He didn't want to lose the bar—or worse, end up in jail or with a debt he couldn't pay. He looked at the document on her phone again and noticed the date. It stood out, but for the life of him he couldn't remember why. Graham fished his phone out of his pocket and scrolled through his calendar.

"Ren, I don't know if this means anything, but the night of the accident—it's the day after someone broke into the bar."

"Did you report the break-in?"

He shook his head. "I figured it was Grady, and if I was right, my dad would've flipped. I had Bowie put in a new door and stuff but left it alone."

Rennie's hands covered her mouth, and her eyes darted around. Graham waited for her to tell him what she was thinking and wondered if they were on the same path. There had to be a connection. What if Grady was the one distributing the alcohol? If he was, how much more trouble would he be in?

"What are you thinking?" Graham asked Rennie.

"I think I'm going to place a call to my private detective, see what he can dig up on this girl."

"I can't afford that, Ren."

"Don't worry about it; we'll figure something out. In the meantime, I'm heading up to the inn to start my vacation."

Graham liked the idea that Rennie would be in town for a bit but quickly remembered she had plans after the holiday with her boyfriend, which meant he would be around as well. He pushed those thoughts aside because despite everything, he was going to put himself out there and find someone to spend time with. No more dwelling.

FIFTEEN

Falling snow would've been the only thing to make Rennie's morning at the Driftwood Inn seem more magical. When she rose, she stepped out onto her small balcony and inhaled the salt air. A fine mist, coupled with fog, had settled over the harbor, and out in the distance, she could hear the warning horns from harbor patrol, reminding boaters the water was unsafe.

Rennie dressed, put on light makeup, and pulled her hair into a ponytail before she made her way downstairs. Christmas music played overhead, and she found herself singing along to Burl Ives as he told the story of Rudolph the Red-Nosed Reindeer. It was funny to think about how refreshed she felt after being away from the city for one day, even with the looming civil suit against Graham. Everything she knew about the law told her that if the lawsuit made it to a judge, it would be years. Rennie would do anything she could to help Graham out of his current dilemma, and that included calling the man she used for her cases, private investigator Walter Shuff. She and Walter had worked together for a couple of years, and he always yielded valuable information for her. This time, it wouldn't be a spouse Walter had to look into, but a family whose teenage daughter drove drunk, crashed her car, and, as a result, was paralyzed.

When she reached the bottom of the stairs, she saw that the lobby looked like the North Pole. Santa walked in with a red sack slung over his shoulder, and a parade of children all dressed in their cutest holiday outfits followed behind. Rennie suspected that if she looked out the window, there would be a sleigh and reindeer in front of the inn, because her Brooklyn didn't do anything half-assed.

As tempted as she was to follow Santa, she veered toward the dining room and ran into Simone. "Oh, good morning, Rennie. I didn't know you were here."

The women hugged. Rennie breathed Simone in, smelling the cinnamon, apple pie, and warmth that Simone carried with her. "I decided to come up and spend Christmas here."

Simone squeezed Rennie's bicep. "I bet Brooklyn is happy you're here. I know Brystol will be. Go on into the kitchen, and I'll make something for you."

"Thank you, but I think I'm okay with coffee. I sort of want to check out what's going on in the ballroom."

Simone's eyes went wide. "Oh, you should. Brooklyn is so ecstatic about the turnout. There are so many kids from here and the neighboring towns. I swear I made two thousand sugar cookies."

"You're so good to them, Simi."

"They're my family. There isn't anything I wouldn't do for them," Simone said with a wink as she disappeared into the kitchen.

Rennie poured herself a cup of coffee and picked up a doughnut off the tray and made her way into the ballroom. She couldn't believe her eyes. Inside, the ballroom was a winter wonderland. Garland with white lights and red ribbon covered every window casing. Every chair had bows made from tulle, and each table had a wreath centerpiece with votive candles, lit and shimmering. There was a large tree in the corner, decorated elegantly with wrapped presents underneath, and beside it sat a throne with red velvet cushions. At the other end of the room, families stood in line as they waited to have their portraits taken in front of the picturesque backdrop. Rennie was in awe of her friend's talent.

"Morning, Ren." Bowie came toward her and kissed her on the cheek. "Brooklyn is over there, in the corner, if you're looking for her."

"Thanks. This place looks amazing."

"It's all Brooklyn," Bowie told her as he looked in the direction of his fiancée. "She's the visionary. I just do what I'm told."

"You do more than that, Bowie. You love her, and that's all she's ever wanted."

"Me too." Bowie exited the room. Rennie stood there for another moment, absorbing the magic, before she made her way through the crowds of people. She reached Brooklyn, and before the two hugged, Rennie set her coffee down, knowing she would likely spill once she and Brooklyn were together.

They hugged tightly and rocked back and forth a bit. When they parted, Rennie said, "B, I can't believe you did this. I've seen most of the houses you've redone, but this by far is your masterpiece."

Brooklyn had a delighted look on her face. "I think this project has been my favorite so far."

"I can see why. You've brought the North Pole to Cape Harbor. Not only are the kids excited, but the parents look very happy. Heck, I even want to join in the fun."

Brooklyn pointed over Rennie's shoulder. She turned and followed to find her niece sitting at a table with both sets of her grandparents. "You can sit with them if you'd like."

Under normal circumstances, Rennie would gladly sit with Brooklyn's family, but Rennie wasn't feeling herself. She was worried about Graham and Grady, even though Grady was in the best place he could be at the moment, and she felt a strong disconnect with Theo . . . her thoughts went to him immediately.

"What's wrong, Ren?"

She shook her head slightly. "I may have forgotten to tell Theo I came here." Rennie felt about two feet tall. A sense of guilt washed over her. As of late, she was insensitive toward Theo and absentminded when it came to him. "Fu—" She covered her mouth to keep the slur trapped inside.

Brooklyn took Rennie by the arm and pulled her toward the back of the ballroom, through the glass door, and out onto the covered balcony, away from the party. "Spill."

"I don't know, B. Things are off between us. It's like when you're on the highway, and you see a sign for the town you want to go to, but you stay on until the next exit—I feel like Theo got off on the first exit, and I kept driving. We're not on the same page for anything, which is stupid because nothing has changed between us, except I haven't seen him since before he went to Japan." Rennie sighed heavily. "I just think we are both overworked, and everything will be fine once we go on vacation after Christmas."

"Isn't he spending Christmas with you? Honestly, Ren, when you called and said you were coming, I thought something had happened between you because I didn't expect to see you until Christmas morning. I know it's only a couple days away, and I love you dearly, but why aren't you with Theo?"

Rennie stared at her friend, hoping the answer would appear on her face. It didn't, and Rennie had no idea what to say other than "I don't know. I need to go call him."

Back in her room, Rennie threw on her oversize sweatshirt, picked up her phone, and went out to sit on her balcony. She pulled her legs to her chest and dialed Theo's number. Her call went right to voice mail. She tried again, only to get the same result. By the third call, she opened her mouth to leave a message but thought better of it. They needed to talk. He would see her missed calls and call her back, hopefully sooner rather than later.

Her thoughts drifted over the past month, and she tried to pinpoint when her relationship with Theo slipped. It could've been Thanksgiving, when he hadn't called. Not that she would've noticed, because she was busy with Graham and Grady's situation. It seemed everything was fine before then, but why the change in her? Admittedly, it wasn't because she had spent an uncomfortable weekend at the hospital with her friend, regardless of their past. Something bugged her, but she couldn't put her finger on it.

Rennie's phone rang, and Theo's face displayed on her phone. She held it in her hand for a moment and looked at him before answering. "Hey," she said.

"Hi. What's so urgent?" he asked in a hushed tone.

Rennie paused. No "Hi, love" or "Hello, sweetheart," and he whispered. Why would he whisper if he was in his apartment?

"Where are you?"

"At home, why?"

"Why are you whispering?" Her tone was accusatory and demanding.

"Sweetheart, what's wrong?" he asked sweetly. Rennie heard a door click and wondered what was going on. Why was he short with her and speaking in hushed tones?

"Is there someone there with you, Theo?"

"Renee, what is going on?" His demeanor changed to forceful and serious.

"Nothing. It just seems like you're whispering and being secretive."

"I'm busy," he said. "I'm trying to pack for San Diego."

Rennie's teeth clamped down on her lower lip as her mind said "Fuck." She had forgotten about his trip. Even worse, she'd told him she couldn't go, and yet she'd taken vacation early because her boss had pissed her off. "Oh, right. I forgot about the trip."

"You forgot I was leaving?"

"No, it slipped my mind. Anyway, I just wanted to talk. I miss you, Theo."

"I'll be in Seattle in a few days, and then we'll be in Canada together."

"Yeah."

"What is it?" he asked. She could tell him where she was and have him drive to Cape Harbor, or she could go back to Seattle. The thing was, she had already brought all her Christmas presents with her, along with her work, and she really didn't feel like being alone. She stood and leaned over the railing. Down below, she spotted a couple of guys milling around on the beach. For a moment, she thought one of them could be Graham coming to hang out with Bowie, but Graham was on his way to Port Angeles to see Grady for family therapy. Why was Graham at the forefront of her thoughts suddenly?

"Renee?"

"Yeah, I'm here. Sorry, just thinking."

"About?"

"About Christmas."

"What is there to think about? We have a plan."

Rennie sat back down and sighed. She had to rip the bandage off, no matter how bad it was going to hurt. "Theo, I'm sorry. I have a lot on my mind lately and decided last night to drive up to Brooklyn's."

Theo was silent for much longer than Rennie thought he would be. She opened her mouth to say something but decided against it.

"Let me see if I can understand this. I ask you to go away with me, and you tell me no because you have to work and then the next day decide to go to Cape Harbor?"

She was the worst girlfriend in the history of girlfriends. "I'll make it up to you, Theo. I'm sorry. When I thought about coming here, I should've called you and made arrangements to meet up. When you come back, fly into Seattle, and I'll pick you up, and then we can wake up the next day, order room service, and never leave my room."

Theo cleared his throat. "I don't want to spend Christmas with your friends, Renee. You know this. I only agreed to drive up Christmas afternoon because I want to make you happy. Waking up in a hotel is not how I want to spend our holiday together."

"I'm sorry," she said quietly. "I'll go back to my place. Everything will be as planned." As she said the words, tears pricked in her eyes. She wanted to spend time with everyone she loved, even her parents, but they were who knows where. Brooklyn and Brystol were her family, and this was where she wanted to be. Why couldn't he see that?

Theo sighed. "Don't. We'll compromise. I'll come up, but I want you to do me a favor."

"What is it? I'll do anything to fix this." She would. She loved him that much to do whatever he asked unless it meant giving up her family in Cape Harbor.

"I know we talked about my company opening a field office in Seattle. It's looking more and more unlikely. I hate the distance between us and want to wake up to you every morning, Renee."

"What are you saying?"

"After the first of the year, I'd like for you to look for jobs in Spokane. I know it's not what we discussed, but it makes the most sense."

Um . . . no, it doesn't.

"Theo, I'm not sure what to say."

"Say nothing," he told her. "Think about it. Look at firms that might interest you, or look for office space and think about opening your own firm. Peruse neighborhoods with big fancy houses you want to live in. After the first of the year, you'll come over here, and we'll tour. I'll take you to all my favorite spots. We'll go ice-skating at the park and make love by the fire. Love, I think this is for the best."

She didn't, and she didn't foresee her mind changing anytime soon. "Okay, I'll think about it."

"I love you, Renee. I'll call you when I get to San Diego."

After she told him she loved him in return, they hung up. Rennie stayed in the chair and let tears stream down her face. She loved where she lived, her job, and being close to Brooklyn. If she moved, she'd be six hours away, and her weekends at the inn would come to a halt. Rennie wasn't sure if she was okay with that.

She went back into her room and changed into sweats. Rennie was content to hang out by herself for a bit. She opened her laptop and searched through her streaming service to find a rom-com to watch. As luck would have it, each movie she was interested in had to do with weddings or babies, neither a topic she wanted to think about.

Rennie closed her laptop and picked up her phone and scrolled through her contacts. When she reached Walter's name, she pressed the icon and put him on speaker.

"Hello?"

"Walter, it's Renee Wallace. How are you?"

"Merry Christmas," he said instead of answering her. Walter was a retired police detective who couldn't give up the job. He started doing investigative work to keep his mind fresh, and Rennie used him as much as she could. "To what do I owe the pleasure on this fine day?"

He made her smile. Every time they spoke, he had this way of cheering her up. "I have a job for you." Rennie opened her folder on the Chamberlains and gave him a full rundown of everything going on.

"So, you want me to look into this girl, her friends, family, and the days leading up to the accident?"

"Yes, I have a hunch that it was my other client who provided the alcohol." She explained that Graham and Grady were twins, and even though extensive alcohol use made Grady look older, the men still looked very similar.

"I'm intrigued."

Rennie laughed. "I knew you would be. Start after the first of the year. My client hasn't been served yet, but I'm expecting it any day."

"I'm on it. Have yourself a merry Christmas."

"You too, Walter. Give Lois all my love."

Rennie felt a huge weight lift off her shoulders once they hung up. Walter would uncover the truth, which would undoubtedly point the finger at Grady. However, if Rennie remembered correctly, the burden of proof would fall on the plaintiff, and the way Rennie looked at this case, it was a lot of he said, she said. However, she would confer with Jefferson after the first of the year to make sure.

Feeling a bit better, she went back to her laptop and turned on a movie. She lay down, and it wasn't long before she dozed off. When she woke, the credits scrolled on the screen, and there was a suggestion for a similar movie waiting for her. She reached for her phone and found a message from Graham.

Graham Cracker: I owe you dinner. Tonight? My place?

Without hesitation, she told him she'd be there.

SIXTEEN

"Is that a snowflake?" Graham's mom pointed to the windshield. "Oh, there's another one," she said, only for the wipers to clear the window. "Turn those off, Graham. I want to see if it's snowing."

"If he turns the wipers off, Johanna, he won't be able to see. And if he can't see, he's liable to drive up right into the damn ocean. Let him drive," George shouted from the back.

For whatever reason, whenever George sat in the back of Graham's SUV, he felt the need to yell to the passengers up front. He didn't speak loudly. He screamed because he said no one could ever hear him. Graham heard him plenty but chose most of the time to ignore his father.

In the days since Grady's hospitalization, George Chamberlain found himself at odds with his wife and other son. Johanna and Graham refused to play by George's rules when it came to Grady, and each had put their foot down. Graham wasn't sure what changed his father's mind, but he suspected it was when the doctor told them, without a doubt, if Grady didn't get sober, he was going to die. It wasn't an *if* but a *when*.

When Graham picked his parents up for family therapy, he expected George to grumble, to claim illness, or to declare there was a can't-miss game on television. Still, he surprised his son and wife by walking to the car and climbing into the back seat without any prodding. Of course, the situation was this: if Johanna and Graham wanted George to go with them, they were going to have to deal with his constant yelling.

You're driving the wrong way.

You didn't stop at the stop sign long enough.

Are you sure you're going the right way?

Did you buy a ticket for the ferry?

We won't make it in time.

Put the game on, will ya?

The demanding tone, gruffness, and volume of chatter gave Graham a headache. If it wasn't his father saying something, it was his mother and her eagerness to have a white Christmas.

"I don't think it's snow, Mom." Graham leaned forward and looked out the window toward the sky. It was gray, overcast, and trying to rain.

"Someday, I would love a white Christmas," she said quietly as she gazed out the passenger window.

"We can take a ride east if you'd like," he said, offering to take his parents to the mountains. "We could rent a lodge and have a nice quiet Christmas. No outside distractions." Even though he offered, he knew his mother and father would never take him up on it, nor would it be feasible this close to Christmas to find an available lodge to rent.

"It sounds nice, but your father would never go for it. He can't stay away from that damn television or the Loyal Order of the Sasquatch. Did you know they don't like women in there? We're allowed, of course, but every time I walk in there, the place goes silent. It makes me wonder what they're talking about."

"If I had to guess, I'd say women," Graham said through laughter. He loved how worked up his mother became over his father's Sasquatch group. A couple of times a year, the group came into the bar for lunch. They always chose to sit in the back, and anytime Graham or any of the staff members got too close, they'd zip their lips.

His mom swatted him and laughed. "Knowing your father, he's in there complaining about having to make his lunch when I go out with the gals."

"You're talking about me like I can't even hear you, Johanna."

"I know you can, George," Johanna huffed.

"Well, what do you and the gals talk about?" Graham prodded as he drove toward Port Angeles.

Johanna blushed at Graham's question. "Women stuff."

George and Graham chuckled. "So, it's okay for you and the ladies to talk about us, but we can't talk about you?" George asked as he leaned forward, sticking his head between the seats.

Graham had seen a slight change in his father, one he attributed to Grady's most recent accident. He would never wish harm on his brother, but in a way, he was thankful for everything that happened Thanksgiving weekend. George and Grady needed a wake-up call.

She brushed him off. "It's not the same, and you know it. We talk about new cleaning products we're using or how we got a certain stain out of a shirt. You silly men . . . well, who knows what you guys go on and on with for hours."

"Talk about sports, who caught the biggest fish, and how retirement is treating us."

Graham smiled. For the first time in a while, he enjoyed spending this time with his parents when they were like this. It had been a long time since he had seen his father act playfully toward his mother. He even saw his father hug his mom the other day, which made Johanna cry, and when Graham asked her why she had tears in her eyes, she said it had been years since he'd touched her.

When they pulled up to the ferry booth, Graham showed the attendant their reservation. After they parked on the ferry, Graham helped his mom out of the car and held on to her until they were seated on the top deck. Surprisingly, his father followed. Their last trip on the ferry, George had stayed in the car. As soon as the boat pulled away from the port, Johanna excused herself, telling Graham and George she had to use the restroom, and left the two of them alone.

The Chamberlain men looked out the window, watching the passing scenery. A young boy stood next to George and pointed out the window. "What do you see?" George asked him. Graham turned his attention toward his father and watched him interact with the young boy.

"I think I saw a whale."

"No way," George said.

"Yes, sir. Right out there." More people congregated to where they were sitting. People lined the wall, looking out the large pane of glass, and while it was freezing outside, people rushed out to the side of the ship to get a better look.

Time moved faster than Graham expected, and he was startled by the captain's voice as it rang out over the loudspeaker, telling everyone to return to their cars. George stood and asked Graham, "Where's your mother?"

"She should've been back by now from the bathroom."

Together, they scanned the people moving toward the stairs and finally found her resting against the bar with a cocktail in her hand. She was in deep conversation with a woman Graham had never seen before.

"I see her, Dad. Why don't you go down to the car, and we'll be there in a minute?" George and Graham parted ways. He went to his mom and touched her elbow. "Sorry to interrupt," he said. She jerked in surprise and smiled brightly at him.

"Oh, honey. Let me introduce you to Cindy. Her daughter, Lacey, just moved to Cape Harbor. Have you met her yet?"

Cape Harbor was small, and normally when someone new moved to town, Peggy from the diner knew about it first. It was like some odd rite-of-passage sort of thing. When people arrived, they stopped in and introduced themselves to Peggy, and the grapevine in town was strong. A neighbor of Lacey's would've told Peggy, and Peggy would've announced it to the community. Still, Graham hadn't heard a thing.

"Sorry, no. Come on. We have to get to the car. We're almost to the dock." He tugged lightly on her elbow, but she didn't budge. She was still carrying on a conversation with Cindy. His eyes went wide when they exchanged numbers, and this woman handed his mom a piece of paper. When they finally said goodbye, and she was out of earshot, he asked his mom what that was all about.

"Oh, nothing, really. We got to talking."

"You exchanged numbers?"

"I'm going to go to her book club. It's in Skagit Valley."

He opened the door for his mom and waited for her to get situated before closing it and rushing over to the other side. "And on the piece of paper?"

"Oh, that's for you. It's Lacey's number. You should call and ask her out."

"Sweet heavens, Johanna, what did you do?"

She turned in her seat and looked at her husband. "I've done nothing wrong, George. A mother is supposed to help her children out every now and again."

"Not when it comes to dating. Graham's a big boy. He can find his own dates."

He couldn't, but that was because he hadn't really tried. He told Krista he was going to, though. He was going to start dating and living his life.

Johanna turned back around and said, "She's twenty-seven, never married, and, according to her mother, ready to settle down."

"She's a little too young, but what could one phone call hurt?" Usually, age didn't bother him. Lacey was ten years younger, depending on when her birthday was, but that wasn't what made his jaw tic. His mother was trying to set him up with a stranger . . . Graham took a deep breath. Something like a setup could work well in his favor.

Graham held his hand out and waited for his overly eager mother to put the slip of paper in his hand. She did, and he pocketed it without looking. The least he could do was call her, explain the situation, and offer to show her around town, although if she'd moved over from Skagit Valley, there was a good chance she knew her way around Cape Harbor. His mother's intentions were good, if heavy handed. There were things she wanted out of life, and lately, it was to become a grandmother. And unless Grady had a child they were unaware of, the future responsibility fell onto him. Nothing out of the ordinary—it seemed every substantial burden rested on his shoulders.

"Boy, you're giving your mother a complex. Be prepared for your phone to ring off the hook with all her friends' single daughters and granddaughters." George chuckled from the back seat.

"You hush, George Chamberlain," Johanna fired back.

The part of Washington they were in was lush and green and bordered the Olympic National Park. However, most of the drive until they reached Port Angeles was nothing more than small towns. Some run down. George was lively during the ride, telling his companions random facts about the towns they drove through, most of which were probably tall tales he had learned from a friend or two. Most of the towns had been forgotten, left alone after people moved to the mainland or down south for work. The economy was based mostly on tourism, which, when you were trying to have a family, didn't necessarily pay the bills.

Graham pulled into the parking lot of the rehab facility; the tension in the car became palpable. For three hours, as a family, they were able to forget the reason they had taken the road trip to begin with and just feel normal. The Chamberlains were back to reality, with a family therapy session waiting for them. He parked, turned off his car, and waited for his parents to meet him around front. His mother had an expression on her face, one he hadn't seen since she sat down by Grady's side while he was in the ICU.

"It's going to be okay, Mom."

Graham held the front door of the center for his parents and was shocked to hear his father speaking into the intercom. He thought for sure his dad would do everything in his power to make this trip miserable, but George kept surprising his son. The second set of doors clicked, and the three of them made their way inside and to the reception desk, where they were told to wait.

George's leg bounced up and down, and Johanna placed her hand over her husband's knee to keep it still. "You're making me nervous, Georgie," she said.

"I am nervous," he told her.

"Me too," Graham said to his parents.

A young woman came out to get them. They followed her through a set of double doors that only opened after she punched in a code and swiped a key card. She showed them to a room that was colorful, like the rainbow. It had a couch, beanbags on the floor, pillows scattered everywhere, and somewhat comfortable-looking chairs. The room had a view of the outside, and there were posters on the walls, all displaying messages with positive reinforcements.

Johanna sat down and encouraged her two men to do the same. "This room feels nice," she said. "I really hope Grady is embracing the help."

"Me too," Graham stated.

"He better. This is his last chance," George blurted. Johanna and Graham looked at him askance. He shrugged. "Doc said, right?" They both nodded. "All right, then. He better figure it out, because I'd like to have my son back."

Graham wanted to jump up and down. He wanted to fall to his knees and thank whoever showed his father the light, because if they could show Grady a united family front, maybe, just maybe, they could all heal together.

The door opened, and Grady and his therapist walked in. Grady sat in the chair closest to their mother. Compared to the last time Graham saw his brother, Grady looked a bit healthier but still had sunken eyes and hollowed cheekbones. He was clean shaven, his hair combed, and he wore hospital-issued clothing. Grady didn't say hi or offer anyone a hug. Instead, he looked down at the ground and let his therapist do all the talking.

"I'm Sonny Andrews." He shook hands with everyone before sitting down. "I want to thank you for coming, as it is imperative for Grady's recovery to know his family supports him."

Dr. Andrews relaxed in his chair and looked at each of them. "I want to go over what Grady and I have been working on. When you're an addict, you have many wars within yourself. Not only is your body fighting against your decision to get clean, but the war also makes you second-guess yourself and the people surrounding you. Grady is slowly working through events and has accepted that his road to recovery is going to be harder than anticipated. He has some anger issues to work on, self-deprecation and esteem issues, and the overall feeling that he doesn't belong on earth.

"I ask that you listen, answer his questions, and tell him your fears and how we can work together to make Grady's time in rehab more meaningful. Grady, you indicated earlier that you'd like to start."

He nodded, moved his hospital-issued shoes around, and cleared his throat. "My family thinks I'm a failure, and I believe they wish I would've died that night."

That night. The one that haunted everyone.

"Oh, Grady," Johanna choked out. She reached for his hand, but he pulled it away. Graham saw how his brother was breaking their mom's heart.

"Why do you feel this way, Grady?"

"I can see it in their eyes. I can sense it when I'm around them. They don't want me anymore."

"That's not true," Johanna said. "We want you, Grady. Why do you think we've been doing what we have all these years?"

"Which is what, Mrs. Chamberlain?"

Johanna stilled. Graham watched as his mother shut down. She would never admit to an outsider their part in Grady's addiction, but Graham would. "We've enabled from the beginning," he started and glanced quickly at his father. "At first, we called it *coping*. What he experienced the night in question—we never actually knew how it affected him; we only assumed, so we drank with him. We got him drunk, held him while he vomited all over the place, picked him up in the middle of the night, and drove him home. I can admit it was nice forgetting everything or at least putting a foggy haze over what transpired. But then, weeks turned into a month, which turned into two, three became four, and a year later, he was still drunk, and we still enabled. It's been a very long and difficult fifteen and a half years, and Grady hasn't seen a sober day since, and until recently, my family has always given him a safe place to drink."

"That would be the Whale Spout?" Dr. Andrews asked.

Graham nodded. "The bar has been in our family for generations. I now co-own it with my father, and I firmly believe the reason my dad won't relinquish the rest of his ownership is because he wants Grady to be able to drink there freely."

"Do you disagree, Mr. Chamberlain?" All eyes were on the patriarch of the family. George was uncomfortable under the scrutiny but nodded.

"I didn't want my son to go without or for him to be one of the people you see on the street corner. I tried to protect him. I thought if he had a roof over his head, warm meals, and clean clothes, he would someday come to his senses. I can see now the mistakes I've made." Johanna placed her hand in George's and kept it there.

"Grady, do you blame your dad for your addictions?"

He shook his head.

"Graham, Grady told me about an episode which happened over the summer on the beach. He said you hurt him."

Graham tensed as his parents made eye contact with him. He cleared his throat and said, "This past summer, a friend who had disappeared after the accident returned. Grady blames her for Austin's death. I think her return triggered something in him, because he changed a lot. He became more manic, demanding, bordering on violence. We were having a party on the beach, and he went after her. I tackled him to the ground to get him away from everyone."

"Grady, how did that make you feel?"

"Like my brother chose his friends over me."

Partly true, but Graham wouldn't admit it. He wanted Grady far away from everyone because when he was around, he caused a scene. What he had done to Brooklyn was inexcusable.

"I was trying to save Grady. Others were there and protective over the woman he went after. It wasn't going to end well for him."

"Have you always tried to protect Grady?"

Graham nodded. "Up until this past summer, and then I stopped caring."

"Why's that?" Dr. Andrews asked.

"Because after the incident at the beach, I suspected he was using but couldn't confirm anything, and one morning, I got to work, and the back door had been busted in, cases of beer and booze gone. I didn't want to think it was my brother, but when he didn't show up to the bar day after day, those suspicions grew. I told our dad Grady wasn't welcome in the bar anymore."

Dr. Andrews looked from brother to brother and then to their parents. Johanna was quiet, dabbing her tears, while George sat stone faced.

"Grady, is there anything you'd like to say?"

He was quiet for a long time. The whole room was silent except for the sound of the second hand moving on the old analog clock attached to the wall. Grady's legs swayed back and forth; he looked agitated, uncomfortable.

"Grady?" his therapist nudged.

"I resent Graham for always thinking he's perfect."

Graham scoffed. "Are you serious right now, Grady? You resent me? I harbor so much ill will toward you for not pulling your life together and moving on. I gave up my life, my chance at happiness, for you. And all you do is shit on me constantly. You stole from my business and won't even admit it. I defend you to everyone in town when they call you a lowlife, a bum—it's me telling them you're trying to find your way again. But the only path you're following is the one that leads to the next bottle. I came back for you, Grady, because you needed me, and look where that's gotten me."

"Graham," Johanna said his name quietly as she rested her hand on his arm.

"I'm sorry, Mom, but it's true. I was happy in California, and I should've stayed. I lost my girlfriend because of him. My job, my friends. Everything. I put Grady first, thinking he'd snap out of it, that he'd realize what he was doing to himself. He had a company to run and people who depended on him. Instead, he let it all go. He gave up on himself, his dreams, and took us down with him."

Graham was frustrated, and yet he felt relieved. When he glanced at his parents, they were crying. He held his mom's hand tightly in his while Grady rocked back and forth, mumbling. "Say something, Grady," Graham demanded. "Don't waste our time anymore. Prove to us this therapy session is worth us driving all the way over here."

Grady looked at his brother. His eyes were still hollow and void of emotion, but the whites of his eyes were no longer bloodshot, and he was looking more like Graham than he had in years. "You think I want this? Do you think I want to sit here and listen to how much of a loser I am?"

"Then fix it," Graham challenged. "Take the opportunity to fix your life before it's too late."

"Easier said than done, brother. You've always been the one with goals; all I wanted to be was a fisherman with my best friend, and now he's gone."

"And why is that, son?" George asked. "Why didn't you stop him that night? You knew the risks, and yet you did nothing to stop him."

"You don't think I tried, Dad?"

George stood and threw his hands up in the air. "We don't know because you won't talk to us. No one knows what happened—not the full story. You've kept it bottled up, and it's eating you alive. Tell us so we can help you."

"Grady," Johanna interrupted as she looked from her husband to her son. She took a deep breath and turned toward him. "Austin has been gone for a long time. It's time you move on. It's time you grow up and stop blaming him."

"Mom . . ."

"I'm sorry, son. I am, but I'm tired. I'm so tired of all of this. The late-night phone calls, the sleepless nights wondering if you're coming home or not—and if you're not, whether you're safe. I'm old, and I shouldn't be. I want to take vacations with my husband. I want to be a grandmother and have babies all around me—none of which will ever happen if you stay like this. Our family, it's broken, and it needs to heal. We *need* you to heal. We can't keep doing this. I know you have nightmares about that night, Grady. We all do. We were there when you were pulled from the water. I held you, cold, shivering, and crying out for Austin. I watched day after day while my husband, sons, and friends went out into the water, searching. I prayed with the moms, cooked the meals for the volunteers. I will never forget those days and weeks, the look on Carly's face . . . or yours . . . at Austin's funeral. And I'm not asking you to forget, but I am asking you to move on, to see past that night. You need help, Grady. Maybe we all do. I am begging you because I want my son back."

Johanna got up from her seat and walked out of the room. George, Graham, Grady, and Dr. Andrews sat there, stunned, until George stood, called after his wife, and asked her to wait. When the door shut, everyone jumped.

The air was thick with tension as the brothers stared at each other. No words were exchanged between the brothers, at least none Dr. Andrews would be able to hear. The twins had their own language, and when Grady dropped his head, Graham knew his brother received his message loud and clear: get clean, or don't come home.

Dr. Andrews asked Graham if he were willing to return for more sessions. As much as Graham loathed the idea, he said he would. He wanted his brother to get better. He missed his best friend and for the last fifteen years had felt like a piece of him was missing. Whether or not Grady and Graham liked it, they were connected and needed each other to feel whole again.

Graham stood and went over to his brother. He held his hand out, and when Grady placed his hand in Graham's, he pulled his brother up into his arms. They hugged for the first time in fifteen years. Tears came instantly for Graham when his brother tightened his arms around Graham's waist.

"I love you, Grady."

"I love you too," Grady replied.

When the brothers parted, Dr. Andrews had a smile on his face. "I call this a breakthrough."

Graham nodded. "There have been a lot of unsaid things over the years. I just want this guy to get better." He slapped Grady on his shoulder. Graham took his leave and found his parents in the waiting room. He filled them in on the last bits of the conversation and told them they had to come back. George grumbled but agreed.

In the parking lot, Graham saw a woman who reminded him of Rennie. He didn't know what spurred him to pull out his phone and send her a text, inviting her to dinner, but when her response came instantly, he smiled. He also looked at the number on the piece of paper his mother had given him and put Lacey's name and number into his phone. The last thing he wanted was to send his jeans through the wash and lose her number. He suspected Lacey's mother, Cindy, had already told her Graham would call, and he wasn't about to let his mother down.

For most of the ride back, the mood in the car was somber. George sat up front, fiddled with the radio until he found a sports talk channel, and then proceeded to argue every point brought up. Typically, this would be an annoyance. Graham didn't care. He felt like a stack, not a ton, of bricks had been lifted off his shoulders when he confronted his brother, and he looked forward to going back next week. There was a glimmer of hope when it came to Grady, and while he knew he shouldn't look too far into it, he couldn't help himself. He was honest earlier when he told Grady he wanted his brother back. He did.

After Graham dropped his parents off, he stopped at the market and picked up dinner. He would toss a couple of steaks onto the grill, along with some sliced potatoes, and make a salad. Before he checked out, he picked up a bottle of red wine and made his way home. His family couldn't afford to pay Rennie, but he could make her a nice dinner to thank her for everything she had done for his brother and what she was about to do for him.

SEVENTEEN

White lights sparkled on the outside of Graham's houseboat. The sight of them gave Rennie pause. Not many single men decorated for the holidays, let alone the outside of their homes, especially those stationary in the water. Still, seeing lights brought a smile to her face.

Rennie stepped onto the patio and raised her hand to knock. The door opened before she had a chance. Graham stood on the other side, looking devilishly handsome and happy. It had been a long time since she'd seen him smile brightly, and it warmed her to think she was part of this change.

"Hey," he said as he held the screen door open. "Thanks for coming on such short notice."

"It's not exactly short when you have nothing to do." She started to take her coat off and felt his hands on her shoulders. The gesture was automatic for Graham, and her thoughts instantly went to Theo and how his and Graham's manners were so opposite. She shook her head to clear her mind and shrugged out of her jacket. "Thank you."

"Of course." Graham disappeared up his floating staircase, leaving her to explore his house. The houseboat had an open-concept feel. It was small yet cozy, with a love seat, a coffee table, and a chair that she pictured Graham sitting in and reading a book. The kitchen sink and stove faced the dock, and across from the counter was a small table set for dinner. She half expected there to be a candle burning, but that would send a romantic message, and they were friends. Best friends, if Rennie had to put a label on their relationship.

Graham came thundering down the stairs with a smile on his face. "What do you think?"

"It's cute."

He laughed. "It's small, but I like it. I've thought about buying a house, but I love living out here. Come on. I'll show you the rest."

Rennie followed Graham through the living room and out onto the deck. It was wide and comfortable with two adirondack chairs, which had afghans thrown over the armrests; a grill; and a space heater.

"I like to sit out here," he told her as he motioned toward the heater. "It can be downright chilly, but it's refreshing."

Graham took Rennie back into the house. He showed her the all-too-small bathroom before taking her upstairs. She remembered Brooklyn saying something about building Graham a staircase, some-time in the fall. "Is this safe?" she asked as she put her foot on the first step and wiggled.

"It is. If not, blame your bestie."

Rennie climbed up after Graham, and when she reached the second floor, her eyes went wide. The bedroom wasn't grand by any means, but the view from the second floor was what caught her attention.

"You wake up to this every day?"

"I did this morning. I haven't in a long time. I've kept my blackout curtains closed. But last night, I left them open, and this morning I watched the sunrise. It was the best damn feeling I've had in a long time, and I have you to thank for it."

"Me?" She pointed her finger at her chest.

Graham nodded and stepped closer. For a brief moment, Rennie thought he was going to kiss her, but he brushed by her and went to the sliding glass door. He opened it and stepped out. She followed and placed her hands on the railings. The first-floor deck was nice, but the view from Graham's bedroom was breathtaking.

"What did I do?" she asked him, needing to know what spurred the change in him.

"Rennie, I'll never be able to thank you for what you've done for my family."

"I didn't—"

Graham held his hand up, and she stopped speaking. "You did, and you didn't have to. You went to bat for Grady, protecting him from jail. I'm not sure where he would be if you hadn't stepped in. I believe in the trickle effect. Because Grady is in a better place, my parents are happy. My dad, he bantered back and forth with my mom. He admitted he enabled Grady. These things may not mean much to someone on the outside, but they do to me. My family will never be the same, but we're moving toward what hopefully is a new normal."

"I don't know what to say, Graham. I didn't do anything out of the ordinary." Even as she spoke the words, Rennie knew she lied. Usually, clients came to her. She never sought anyone out. But when the police came for Grady, she jumped into action, even though she knew nothing about criminal law.

Graham pulled Rennie into a hug, and her heart raced. She shouldn't be excited by a hug, let alone his touch, but she was. Rennie rested her head against his chest, and she could hear his heart thumping. They held each other tightly, and the slight sway of the houseboat made it seem as if they were dancing. They hadn't danced in years. The last time was at a frat party in their junior year of college. That was also the last time they had been intimate with each other. Graham met his girlfriend a week later.

"Hey, what are you doing here?" Rennie asked as soon as she saw Graham sitting on the bench outside of her dorm room. She sat down next to him and set her backpack on the ground.

"I met someone."

"Get out of town, Graham Cracker. Are you serious about her?"

He shrugged. "I like her a lot."

"Tell me about her," Rennie prodded.

"We met on the quad. I had to leap over her to catch a football. She screamed, and I thought I hurt her, so I checked on her."

"Total pickup move. I've done it before." Rennie laughed. Graham did as well.

"It worked. I've seen her every night since."

Rennie's shoulder bumped Graham. "Are you in love?"

He turned and looked at her so intensely she had to avert her gaze. She swallowed hard and waited for his response. "No, but I like her. I want to see where it goes."

"Then I'm happy for you, Graham Cracker."

Later that night, when Graham didn't call her like he usually would, Rennie cried herself to sleep. Many times, over the years, she had wanted him to pick her. She wanted to be the one he kissed last before he went to sleep at night and the first when he woke. She never considered he would meet someone else, and now that he had, she knew they would never be the same again.

Graham was the first to let go. "Sorry," he said as he stepped away.

"For what?"

He shook his head slightly and looked at her. "We should eat. Dinner is warming in the oven."

Rennie wanted to stay and find out what Graham was sorry for, but he had other ideas. Years ago, she would've tackled him on his bed, straddled his hips, and tickled him until he told her. They were adults now, living completely different lives, and this time around, she was the one in a committed relationship.

She lagged behind Graham, and as she descended the stairs, she got another look at Graham. He wore an apron with the image of a bare-chested man with chiseled abdominal muscles.

"What is this?" she asked, barely able to control her laughter.

He stood there with his arms held out wide. "What do you think? Does it look like me?"

Rennie shook her head and dabbed at her eyes. "Where did you get this from?"

"Krista and her husband gave it to me for Christmas."

"It's priceless," she told him as she went to the counter. "What can I do to help?"

He nodded toward the bottle of red wine. "Glasses are in the cupboard if you want to pour." Rennie uncorked the bottle and poured two glasses. She carried them to the table and went back to the kitchen. She helped where he thought he needed it and told him everything smelled amazing.

They sat down, and she held her glass up for a toast. Graham did the same. "To old friends," he said before she could start.

"Yes, old friends." They clinked glasses and each took a sip.

They ate dinner with very little chitchat. When they finished, Rennie helped Graham wash dishes and asked if she could make a cup of coffee. With a warm mug in her hand, she went out to the patio and sat down. Graham joined her a few minutes later.

"I could fall in love with this place."

"The view is beautiful," he told her. Rennie turned to look at him, only to find him staring at her. She blushed at his compliment.

"Do you ever wonder . . ." She didn't need to finish the sentence.

"All the time, Ren."

As of late, she'd wondered too.

The vibe in the car was contemptuous at best. Rennie was an expert at holding a grudge—even though Theo showed up to Cape Harbor, it was two nights after Christmas. She couldn't believe her eyes when she opened the door to her room. She expected Brooklyn, Brystol, or Graham to be there, but it was Theo. Even though he came with two dozen red and white roses and a teardrop-diamond necklace, he had ruined their holiday. Or his boss had. Rennie didn't care where she put the blame.

Anger didn't scratch the surface of what Rennie felt when Theo phoned her on Christmas Eve to let her know he had to work. She called bullshit on his story and demanded to know what the hell was going on, because no one would make their employee work on Christmas, and she couldn't understand why Theo wouldn't tell his boss to shove it. This was their second holiday missed because of his job.

Aside from Theo's absence at Christmas, he had a lot to say about the potential lawsuit against Graham. Renee had always kept her cases to herself, only talking strategy with the partners from her firm, her clients, and the paralegals she often worked with. When Theo snooped through her file, one she had left open on the small table in her hotel room, he suggested she stick to what she knew. Another bout of anger rolled over her. Theo knew nothing about law. He was a numbers guy, always looking for discrepancies. Everything coming out of Theo's mouth pissed Rennie off, to the point she contemplated canceling their trip.

Rennie was at her tipping point. She was upset about Christmas, his desire to stay in Spokane, and his butting into her business. They were gearing up for a fight, and that was something they had never done. Little disagreements here and there, but never a full-blown argument. They were a cohesive unit, always on the same page, until recently, and she desperately wanted to get back to where they once were.

Rennie toyed with the diamond that nestled in the hollow of her neck as Theo drove toward Whistler. His car rack was filled with skis—apparently, he needed different kinds depending on what the terrain was like—and the back seat held their luggage, which was slightly oversize with the snowsuits. Her suit was white with a royal-blue stripe down the side. Theo had picked it out last year after seeing it in one of the stores he frequented. He had a new suit and had encouraged her to also buy a new one, but she couldn't bring herself to do it. The one she owned had hardly been worn, and it was like brand new.

Once they made it through the border checkpoint, the ride to Whistler was smooth sailing. The talk radio program Theo wanted to listen to filled the silence between him and Rennie. She had zoned out, choosing to watch the scenery as it went by. Traffic was light, and every car they passed or that passed them seemed headed for a similar destination.

"Lots of people are skiing this weekend."

"A lot of people take vacation around this time. It makes sense with the back-to-back holidays." She couldn't help but take a jab at his comment.

"Renee, I know you're upset—"

"I have a right to be," she interrupted. "First Thanksgiving, where you don't even call, and now Christmas. We had plans."

"You're right, we did, and then you changed them without even consulting me. How do you think that made me feel?"

"I had a rough week at work; I needed to get away," she told him.

"And I'm trying to make a name for myself with my company."

"Oh please, you've been there for years, Theo. Someone lower can work holidays."

"If it were—"

"Don't say easy. Thanksgiving, I understand, but not Christmas."

"You're forgetting the snowstorm."

"Right," she muttered. Where he lived, it snowed heavily versus the rain where she was. That was another reason she didn't want to move east. She wasn't a big fan of the snow. It was pretty, but she preferred it off in the distance, not at her doorstep. She continued to look out the window, hoping she'd be able to get out of the funk she was in. Forgive and forget; she needed to do that, or her attitude was going to ruin the weekend.

She placed her hand on Theo's thigh, and when he put his hand down on top of hers, she looked over and smiled. She was determined to make the upcoming weekend one to remember. He adjusted the station to something she liked, and she started singing along to the tune. Before long, they were pulling into the circular drive of the hotel, and the valet was opening the door for Renee.

"Welcome to the Grandview Hotel," he said as he reached for her hand.

"Thank you."

"What name is the reservation under?"

"Wri—"

"Wallace," Theo interrupted. He met Renee on the passenger side of the car, smiling. He put his arm around her and handed the keys to the valet.

"Why is the room under my name?" she asked.

"I'm not sure," he said. "When I made the reservation, I think it had something to do with all those appointments you booked. Your name is showing on the email."

Renee and Theo walked through the double doors and were immediately enveloped by warmth and liveliness. The hotel was bustling with skiers, and the decorations were still festive but without overdoing it with leftover Christmas cheer. She could hear a fire crackling nearby, and the front desk clerk seemed to love her job. She confirmed the appointments booked for Theo and Renee and offered a free upgrade to their honeymoon suite, which had a jetted tub with a view of the mountains.

"Just think, my love, when I'm swishing down the slopes, you can watch while you soak in the tub."

Renee rested her hand on his chest and rose up on her tippy-toes to give him a kiss. "Sounds about perfect to me."

The clerk handed Renee a printout of her appointments, along with their keys. She gave them brief directions of where to go and told them the bellhop would be up shortly with their luggage and that they could store their skis in the ski room until they were ready to hit the slopes.

They held hands as they walked to the elevator, and every few steps, Theo would stop them so he could kiss her. Each kiss grew more and more passionate. "I think when we get to the room, we should see exactly what it means to be on our honeymoon."

Renee agreed. "I think we need to, Theo. I feel disconnected from you."

"I agree, darling, but first, let's get a drink."

Instantly, her mood soured. Could he not wait to drink until after they made love or, better yet, call for room service? Reluctantly, she followed him to the bar and sat down on the stool next to him. The bartender was the exact opposite of her favorite one, Graham. He wore a white shirt with black bow tie and black pants. He didn't spin the bottles on his fingertips like Graham, nor did he repeat the orders. And he worked much slower. Graham could take multiple orders and make as many drinks at the same time, whereas this man would focus only on one customer at a time.

"What can I get you?" he asked Theo.

"Two chardonnays," he said, without asking if Renee was okay with his choice. She wasn't. She wanted something hard and powerful, something to leave her body with a zing. She watched as the bartender painstakingly opened the bottle of wine, found two glasses, and bent down to pour the exact amount in each one. He scooped the glasses up by their stems, situated them between his fingers, and, with his free hand, set two coasters down in front of Renee and Theo, followed by their wine.

They reached for their glasses at the same time, and Renee paused with hers midair. She waited for Theo to make a toast or say something to start their vacation off, but he drank and did so greedily.

"Thirsty?" she asked after taking a sip.

"I guess I was." He finished the glass and motioned for a second. Renee thought about doing the same but wasn't feeling it. The wine wasn't what she wanted. When the bartender came back, she spoke up. "I'll take a vodka tonic, please." She slid her glass of wine to Theo and smiled.

"Vodka?"

She nodded. "I need something a little stronger."

"Huh" was all Theo said as he picked up the glass in front of him. He downed it quickly. He ordered his third before Renee even had her tumbler of vodka.

She sipped her drink, growing more irritated the longer they sat at the bar. One drink, and then they should've been in their room, reconnecting. There was something wrong; she could feel it in her bones. Or maybe she wanted something to be wrong. Ever since she'd started hanging out with her old friends from Cape Harbor, she'd started second-guessing her life. She felt as if she were two different people. Renee versus Rennie, and she wanted to be Rennie.

After Theo finished his fourth glass, she asked for the check from the bartender. Theo started to balk, but she put her hand up. "We have plans, Theo." Renee signed the bill, adding the charge to their room, and grabbed ahold of his arm. He was drunk, and she was pissed.

In the elevator, he leaned against her and professed his love for her very sloppily in her ear. Theo wasn't known for holding his booze well, and wine was one of the worst. Renee knew once they entered their hotel room, he would pass out. The elevator dinged, and the doors opened. There was a couple waiting to enter, and they gave a wide berth for Renee to help Theo navigate his exit. She smiled softly at them, only to have them scowl at her.

"Judgmental assholes," she muttered when her back faced them.

"Who?" Theo asked with a slight slur.

"The people waiting to get on the elevator. They're judging you because you're drunk, but honestly, so am I." They stopped in front of their door, and Renee fished the key card out of her purse.

"I'm not drunk, baby." Theo pawed at her, grazing her breasts with his hand. "I'm going to make love to you," he said rather loudly. She shushed him as she slid the plastic card into the metal key holder and pushed down on the handle to open the door. She held it open with her foot and slowly guided Theo in.

"Theo Wright, is that you?"

Renee turned toward the voice and saw the same couple who gave her and Theo a dirty look approaching them. Theo stumbled slightly, righted himself, and every ounce of color in his face drained. He tried to clear his throat, but it sounded more like someone was strangling him.

"Karen, Chad, wh . . . wha . . . what are you doing here?" he stammered.

It was Karen who spoke while eyeing Renee. "We're on vacation, and who might you be?" The question was directed solely at Renee.

She opened her mouth to speak, but Theo cut her off. "Hotel staff," he said. "She was just helping me to my room."

Renee's eyes went wide as his words settled in. He was looking at the ground, and this Karen person was glaring at her. Karen tilted her head to peek into their room. "Where's Angela?"

Renee's heart hit the floor. Her mouth ran dry, and tears threatened to expose themselves. "Who?" she asked any one of the three of them, although Chad had yet to say a single thing. Theo finally lifted his head and looked at Renee. His eyes spoke volumes to her. The tears she had been holding back flowed like a waterfall. She let the door go, and it slammed shut on Karen and Chad.

"Renee," he said her name softly, but she wasn't listening. She walked into the room, looked around at the beautiful scenery outside their large picture window. The desk clerk had been right; you could see people skiing down the mountain from their room.

On the table near the window sat a bottle of champagne, and next to it a dozen roses. For months, she'd questioned things around her. The hushed phone calls, missing important events, the excuses. Each time he chalked it up to work. Without a word to Theo, she grabbed the bottle of champagne and flung it toward the wall. The shattering was unsatisfying, and she sought out more things to destroy. The chair was next. She picked it up and heaved it at Theo. Even in his drunken stupor he was able to dodge the flying wood. The chair crashed into the wall and stayed fully intact when it landed on the floor. The only visible damage was the deep gash missing from the wallpaper.

Weak hands clamped down on her arms, and she moved out of Theo's grip. "Don't fucking touch me."

"I need you to listen."

She turned and saw the man she had fallen in love with standing there looking defeated, and she didn't care. Not about him or what he had to say. Yet, he spoke anyway.

"This isn't what you think."

"No? So, you're not married? Engaged to someone else? Have a girlfriend? What the fuck is it, Theo?"

He sighed and studied something on the floor. She stepped closer and bent slightly so he had no choice but to look at her. "What is it, Theo? Let me guess—you're going to leave her but haven't had the chance?"

He said nothing.

"Answer me!" she screamed, and he flinched. "Give me your sorry excuse so I can leave."

"Where will you go?"

"That's none of your business," she told him. "Are you married? And what I mean is, do you live with your wife, Theo? Are you fucking married?"

He nodded.

"Un-fucking-believable. You had no fucking right to put me in this situation."

He reached for her, but she pulled her arm away. "Don't touch me."

"Baby, listen."

"I'm not your baby, your sweetie, your love, or your fucking darling. To you, I'm nothing. I don't ever want to see or hear from you again."

"You don't mean that, Renee."

"Oh, I do, Theo. You're a piece of shit. You cheated on your wife and did so without even telling me about it. You didn't give me an option as to whether I wanted to be in a relationship with a cheater. News flash, I don't! I would *never* do something like that to another woman. I don't care how much I liked someone."

She went to get her bag and pulled the handle so she could drag it behind her and grabbed her purse from the edge of the bed where she'd dropped it.

"Renee—"

"Don't talk to me. Don't call me. Don't even come to see me. You and I—we are *done*." With those last words, she left the hotel room. She sensed Theo would come after her, so she followed the sign for the stairs. She picked up her suitcase and carried it, making it down a few flights until her emotions overtook her. In the corner, surrounded by gray cinderblocks, she pulled her phone out and sent a text to Graham: I'm in Whistler at the Grandview Hotel. Can you come to get me?

Graham Cracker: Everything okay?

No, please hurry.

Graham Cracker: I'm on my way.

Rennie pocketed her phone and slid down the wall, pulling her knees to her chest and letting out the most agonized wail she had ever experienced.

EIGHTEEN

Graham was in the back room doing inventory when his phone dinged. Seeing Rennie's name pop up made him smile, but the words to follow changed his demeanor instantly. She needed help. Worse, she had gone to Canada for vacation, and now she needed him. He didn't want to think of everything that could've been wrong; all he thought about was how quickly he could get there, even though a million questions swirled in his mind as he entered the bar, told Krista he needed to leave, and asked if she could close for him tonight and open in the morning.

"Of course—is everything okay?" Krista was aware of the issues surrounding Grady, and since her employment with the Whale Spout had begun, Graham had considered her a friend.

"I'm not sure," he told her. "I'll let you know if I won't be back tomorrow. Otherwise, I'll be in by the time your shift ends."

"Okay," she agreed without hesitation before heading back to the customers and her daily to-do list.

Graham left Cape Harbor right away, only stopping to fill his gas tank and grab a coffee. Something terrible must've happened to Rennie for her to call and ask him to come get her. It would take a lot for her to bail on a vacation she had really been looking forward to and which had barely just begun.

When he reached the border, he showed the Canadian agent his enhanced driver's license, thankful to at least have this documentation to cross international lines. He had let his passport expire years ago, after never having used it. He didn't see a reason to have one.

"Where are you heading?" the agent asked.

"To Whistler. I have a friend there who needs a ride back to the States."

"When are you coming back?"

Graham thought for a moment. He wasn't sure but imagined their return would be right away. "After I pick her up," he said. "Although, if it gets too late, we might stop at a hotel along the route back."

"Will you be spending any money while you're in Canada?"

"Yes, on gas and food." Shopping, although beneficial with the exchange rate, was not on his list of activities.

The agent handed Graham his license back and told him to drive slowly, letting him know that due to the recent weather pattern, snow-caps were falling off cliffs and could hit the roadways. Graham thanked him, rolled up his window, and drove away slowly. He adjusted his digital speedometer to read kilometers, turned the dial on his radio up, and set his cruise control. Getting a speeding ticket in Canada was not something he was willing to do, no matter what.

When he was about an hour out, he stopped to use the restroom, unable to hold it any longer. He also bought a couple of pops, bags of chips, and candy bars. He passed by the small travel-size bottles of wine and thought Rennie might need one but decided to wait until he had her safely in his car. Before he got back on the road, he sent her a text letting her know how far away he was, and she replied, letting him know she'd be outside waiting for him. He thought about asking her what was going on but refrained. She'd tell him on their way back or sometime later, if she wasn't quite ready. He wasn't going to press her. Graham knew Rennie well enough to know she'd talk when she was ready.

It was dark by the time Graham pulled into Whistler. His GPS directed him to the Grandview Hotel, and when he pulled into their circular drive, the valet came to his door to greet him. Graham rolled down his window and spoke. "I'm here to pick up a friend." The passenger-side door opened before the valet could acknowledge Graham. He smiled at the man. "And now she's in my car. Thank you." He rolled up his window and turned his head toward Rennie. "Hey."

"Just drive, okay?" She pushed her suitcase over her shoulder and onto the back seat before reaching for her seat belt.

"Okay." He did as she asked, driving out of Whistler and leaving the ski resort behind them. Rennie sat there with her head leaning against the window and with her eyes closed. Every so often, she would whimper, and he would place his hand on her arm or squeeze her hand. She never shied away or woke up.

When he pulled into a gas station to fill up, Rennie startled awake. She looked around, almost as if she were dazed and wondering how she got from the hotel to Graham's car. Her hair was a mess, her eyes were red and puffy, and he could tell she had been crying. He squeezed her hand once more before he got up to pump the gas. She followed shortly after, telling him she was going to look for a bathroom. He kept his gaze on her as she entered the store, watched as she asked the clerk a question, and followed her until she disappeared. Once the tank was full, he replaced the nozzle, waited for his receipt, and went into the store. Rennie was still in the bathroom. He thought about knocking but wanted to give her the time she needed to cope with whatever she was going through. When she came out of the restroom, she found him in an aisle.

"Are you hungry?"

She shook her head.

"You should eat something, Ren."

She reached for a doughnut and then put it back. She glanced up at Graham with tears in her eyes, and he nodded. "Okay. Let's go home."

He wished Brooklyn were with them, because he wanted to go hunt Theo down and ask him what the hell happened to Rennie. Whatever he had done, it was bad, because he had never seen his friend like this.

He opened the passenger-side door for her and waited until she was in before closing it. He then opened the door to the back seat and rummaged through the bag of goodies he had bought earlier and placed them on the console. Graham closed the door and went around to the other side. He leaned in, opened the pop, the candy, and a bag of chips and set it out for Rennie. "When you're hungry," he told her and then did the same for himself.

Traffic was light heading toward the border. At times, Graham found himself counting the oncoming cars to keep his mind occupied. He talked to Rennie, which was more like talking to himself, because she wasn't answering him. She also wasn't providing any sort of commentary to keep the conversation flowing.

"Do you remember our sophomore year when we had that really minor earthquake? I don't think it even registered on the Richter scale." He laughed. "You were on campus, hanging out, and we were getting ready to go to some frat party or something. Was it the toga party?" He looked at Rennie for confirmation, but she was gazing out the window. He continued, "Or maybe that party was later. Anyway, so you and I are walking, and we're goofing around. We had pregamed, and we're feeling a bit tipsy, but then I started leaning toward the right, and you the left. People were falling, and a few people were screaming, which I didn't get. I had no clue what was going on, and you were on the ground, laughing.

"When someone hollered out we had an earthquake, I was like 'That was it?' because I barely felt anything, and I remember when I told my mom I wanted to go to California for school, she freaked because of all the earthquakes, and I had to remind her they were more south. Of course, you called your mom and told her all about it; she called the Hewetts, and Brooklyn's mom told my mom, who thought the ocean had swallowed the campus. She told me to come home right away because San Jose was dangerous."

He glanced at Rennie again, but she hadn't moved. Graham's head was on a partial swivel, going from watching his friend to the road and back again. He thought about pulling over or finding a hotel, any place where he could hold her until she was ready to tell him what happened back in Whistler. As he drove, signs for the border came into view, and he pressed the gas pedal a smidge more to increase his speed.

"I'm going to need your passport," he told her.

Rennie rummaged through her purse, pulled out her passport, and handed it to Graham without a word. She continued to stare out the window with the angriest look he had ever seen on her face. For as long as he'd known her, she'd always been the type to brush her emotions under the rug, and if someone upset her, she sought revenge, which was why she made a damn fine lawyer.

Graham inched his car forward, waiting his turn at the border. For some reason, he was nervous, afraid they weren't going to be allowed back into the United States. He knew it was silly to think such a thing, but the thought tickled the back of his mind. When the signal light turned green, he slowly let off the gas and pulled up to the border agent.

"Passports or enhanced IDs," the man said gruffly. Graham handed them over. "Where do you live?"

"I live in Cape Harbor, and she lives in Seattle."

The agent bent forward to look farther into the car. "Roll down your back windows." Graham did as he was told. "How long were you in Canada?"

"Only a few hours."

"What was your business there? Anything to declare?"

"I went and picked up my friend, and no."

The agent waited for Rennie to say something.

Without looking at the agent, Rennie said, "I drove with a friend to the ski lodge in Whistler. I couldn't stay, so Graham picked me up."

Graham grew irritated with Rennie. She had to know she looked suspicious when she didn't make eye contact with the guard. Graham waited, his fingers gripping the steering wheel while the agent typed on his computer. The temptation was there to ask what the screen read, in the hope of making light of the fact his passenger acted fishy and slightly rude.

After what seemed like an hour, the border agent handed Graham his ID and Rennie's passport back and told them to have a nice night. As soon as he was away from the station, he floored it. They technically had an hour until they were home, but forty-five minutes or less if Graham had anything to say about it.

He thought about bringing up some old memories, like the time they went to prom their junior year and Rennie was so nervous she stabbed him with the pin for his boutonniere. She jabbed the needle so hard into his tuxedo jacket it went right through and poked him in the chest. His mom had to work to get the tiny bit of blood out of the white shirt, and Rennie felt so bad that she told Graham he could stab her back so they'd be even. He never took her up on her offer but would have liked to right about now.

They pulled into the marina parking lot. Graham parked and shut his car off. The only sound around them was the strong wind coming off the ocean and waves crashing against the rocks. Overhead, a lamp softly illuminated the space inside the car. He took off his seat belt and angled his body toward Rennie, only to find her asleep. He sighed, got out of the car, and made his way to the passenger side. He opened the door slowly and made sure he caught her before she fell out. Graham reached in and pushed the red button on her seat belt, untangled her, and somehow found a way to scoop her up into his arms. She whimpered.

"I've got you," he said as he kicked the car door shut.

Carrying a full-size human down a single-person ramp was not easy, but he managed to do it, and when he approached his door, he did so without a clue of how to get her inside without waking her up. On the off chance he forgot to lock his door, which he did often, he used the small outside table his mother insisted he put out for decoration to prop his leg up to support Rennie's body weight so he could safely wiggle his arm out from under her legs. He sighed again, this time in relief, when his door opened. He repositioned again and was able to carry her inside.

The stairs to his bedroom were daunting, and as much as he wanted to carry her up there, it would be impossible. He'd surely whack her head or legs, waking her up, and walking up sideways was unmanageable. The couch was the only answer, at least until she woke up, and then she could move up to his room.

"We're at my house, Ren," he told her as he laid her on the couch. "When you wake up, if you want to go to Brooklyn's, I'll take you." He said the words as though she could hear him. Graham covered her with an afghan his grandmother had made many years ago and kneeled next to her, brushing her hair away from her eyes. "I don't know what he did, but I'm here when you need me."

With those words, he went outside and back to the car to get her things. When he walked back into his houseboat, she was on her side, her back facing him. He was tired, but his concern for his friend outweighed his need for sleep. Instead of going upstairs to sleep, he brought his weighted blanket and comforter down from his room. He added the comforter to Rennie, knowing the afghan wouldn't be enough, and he settled into the chair for what was going to undoubtedly be the most uncomfortable night of sleep he had ever had.

NINETEEN

Rennie woke to the smell of freshly brewed coffee, the sound of birds squawking, and the . . . ocean. It took her a long minute to remember where she was, and when she rolled over to verify her surroundings, she almost fell off whatever she was sleeping on, her back screaming in protest, and her legs flailed about until one planted firmly on the ground. She sat up and looked around for Graham and saw him sitting on his patio, reading the newspaper. The sliding glass door was open a smidge, enough to let the cool ocean breeze in. Next to the couch sat her suitcase. She stood, picked it up, and made her way to the bathroom, afraid to turn on the light. The last thing she wanted to see was how wretched she looked or what Graham had to see when he picked her up last night. Rennie closed her eyes, flipped the light switch on, and braced her hands against the ledge of the counter.

When she opened her eyes, she saw pain, suffering, and anger staring back at her. Her eyes were bloodshot and puffy, her cheeks stained with makeup.

When she stared at her reflection, she thought back to the last twenty-four hours and how everything fell apart . . . or had it? Maybe life had finally come to fruition. Maybe there was a deeper meaning to what she was feeling.

The knock at the door startled her. "I'll be out in a minute."

"The pump's on so you can shower. There are fresh towels under the sink. Can I get you anything?" His voice was so kind and caring. She owed Graham an apology for how she acted last night—how she ignored him when all he tried to do was get her to talk to him. Yet, he never gave up. She'd heard every word he had said to her.

"Coffee, please."

"Of course, Ren."

Because his place was small, she could easily hear him walk the few feet to the kitchen. She heard him fumble around, likely popping another pod into the coffee maker or setting a cup under the dispenser. She turned on the water for the shower, undressed, and stepped into the stand-up. The water felt good, and as much as she wanted to stay under the hot spray for an eternity, she knew from Graham's stories that hot water on the houseboat didn't last very long. She washed her hair and body, using his soap even though she had her own in her suitcase. But there was something about the way Graham smelled. It appealed to her, comforted her.

When she emerged from the shower, she pulled her damp hair into a bun and dried off. She dressed in a pair of lounge pants and an over-size sweatshirt belonging to Graham, which she had found hanging on a hook behind the door. Her cup of coffee was sitting on the counter, along with a blueberry muffin, when she came out of the bathroom. She took her breakfast outside and made herself comfortable.

"Nice sweatshirt."

She pulled the fabric to her nose and inhaled deeply. "It smells like you."

"And that's a good thing?" he asked. Graham closed and folded the paper and set it on the table between them.

"It's a great thing," she replied. "It's comfort, and I need that right now."

He nodded and took his cup back into the house and into the kitchen. Again, she heard him fumbling around, making another cup for himself. She watched the harbor and counted five boats trolling around. There was also a couple in two kayaks who were staying reasonably close to the shore. "Isn't that dangerous?" she asked when she sensed Graham's presence. She closed her eyes when she felt a blanket wrap around her shoulders.

"You're going to catch a cold with your wet hair," he told her as he sat down. "And yes, it is dangerous, which is why I've been sitting out here since I saw them walk down the dock over there."

"It's too cold, choppy."

"And not a lot of people around. If anything, they should be near the pedestrian beaches, where people are running, where they're visible. They're risking a lot by being near the marina. Most of the boats around here are for leisure and docked for the winter. Foot traffic these days is very minimal."

"I bet they got them for Christmas."

"I see *you* got something new for Christmas."

She turned sharply and glared at Graham. What would possess him to say such a thing to her? Her penetrating gaze obviously didn't faze him as he sipped his coffee.

"It is hard to miss. It looks like you have a piece of ice hanging from your neck."

Her fingers instantly went to her necklace. Somehow, she had forgotten about it and even showered with it on. It had been hiding under her shirt when she had been analyzing herself in the mirror. Surely, if she had seen it, she would've taken it off. No, ripped it off, which was what she was doing now. She tugged until the chain dug into her neck and let out a bloodcurdling scream as she tried to yank it away from her body.

Graham's hand stilled hers, and in one swift motion, he had the chain away from her skin. The thin gold metal dangled from her clasped hand, and the diamond cut into her palm. She stood and walked the few inches to the railing and dropped the necklace into the water.

"How very *Titanic* of you," Graham quipped.

"You can just call me Rose."

"As long as he's Jack . . ." Graham paused. "No, I want to be Jack, but you're moving over, because I refuse to drown."

Rennie found herself laughing as she sat back down. She expected regret to take over, but what came was a feeling of relief, and again, she laughed. She laughed so hard tears came out of her eyes, and she had to bend over to curb the ache forming in her side.

"Care to share the inside joke?"

"Oh my God, that necklace was probably a couple of thousand dollars, and I just dropped it into the water."

"Want me to get some scuba gear and go look for it? It's not very deep."

"You're serious, aren't you?" Deep down, she knew he was.

"For you, yes."

She shook her head. "No, I don't. I don't ever want to see it again."

"You could pawn it," he told her, and while the thought was appealing, her desire to never lay eyes on it again was stronger.

"I think I'm good."

"Well, now that you're talking, want to tell me what happened?"

She tore her eyes away and looked out over the water. The kayakers were still in the area and hadn't ventured far enough out where they'd need to be rescued. "Do you ever wish you could take your house sailing?"

He laughed. "No, the thought has never crossed my mind."

"Oh, because it's crossing mine right now. I want to be out there, away from the world."

"Okay," he said. He got up and went into the house. She heard muffled voices and wondered who he was talking to. He came back to the patio and rested against the railing. "We need to go to the store, or I will, but three docks down is Bowie's boat. We can take it out."

"Did you tell him I was here?"

"Yes."

"Why?"

"Being as I've picked you up in Canada when you're supposed to be with someone else, I imagine that someone is going to come looking for you. It's better this way. Bowie and Brooklyn won't tell anyone where you are."

"How long can we be out there for?"

"Depends on what we're doing. What do you want to do?"

She stood and pointed. "I want to be away from people."

"Okay," he said. "I can do a couple days until Krista will need a day off. I might have to send her to Hawaii or something after this. She's been covering my shifts a lot lately."

"She's a good employee." Rennie paused and then looked at Graham. "Okay, can we go?" She felt like a heel asking him, but she needed to get away. She needed to be someplace where no one would find her.

"Of course."

Together, they walked over to where Bowie's boat was and undid the tarp. They worked as a team to fold it as small as they could get it for storage. Graham stepped onto the transom and stowed the tarp in one of the cabinets and climbed the steps to the bridge to start the engine. Rennie followed, and Graham asked her to go down the stairs and into the accommodation area to see what they would need for blankets and such. She made a mental note of items to take from Graham's and met him back in the upper salon, where the galley kitchen and primary living space was.

"We need some bedding," she told him. "There's only one bed, though."

He laughed. "There are two rooms down there, and the couches fold out," he told her.

"Oh, okay. Well, there's some bedding, but I'm not sure how long it has been in there."

"We can bring some from my house—come on." He placed his hand on her arm and helped her step off the boat. He left it running, likely because they weren't going very far and were coming right back.

At his house, they gathered what they needed, and Graham packed. She heard him make a phone call, and while she wanted to listen, she kept herself busy instead, rummaging through his cabinets.

"What are you looking for?"

She jumped at the sound of his voice, almost like she had been caught snooping. She wasn't, and she hoped he knew she would never do something like that. "Provisions."

"Not here. I wasn't planning to be home much, so I don't have anything except a couple bottles of beer."

His words gave her pause. She was keeping him from something or someone, and she couldn't do that to him. "I'm sorry, Graham. This was a mistake. I don't mean to keep you from your plans or whatever."

He chuckled. "If you call working at the bar *plans*, I must really live a sad life." He went to her and leaned his hip against the counter. "Krista is going to cover for me. It's going to cost me extra, but it'll be worth it."

"How do you know?"

"Because you're my best girl, Ren, and you need me right now."

She moved toward him until her head rested on his chest. She wrapped her arms around his waist, and he did the same to her. She felt his lips press to the top of her head, and her body relaxed against him.

"Come on." He let go of her and removed her hands from him. "We have enough gas to get to Kiket Bay. There's a marina around there somewhere. We can get gas, food, and the provisions we need."

"Are you sure you want to do this, Graham?"

He didn't say anything as he reached for her hand. He led her out onto the front porch, closed and locked his door. They picked up their bags, with Graham carrying most of them, and made their way over to the boat.

When they arrived, Bowie's slip neighbor was getting ready to untie his boat as well. "Morning, Mr. Reser."

"Morning, Graham. Taking the Holmes Forty-Two out, I see?"

Graham's hand pressed into Rennie's lower back, and he helped her onboard but didn't follow. "For a few days at least," Graham told the man. "What about you?"

"The missus wants to spend New Year's Eve out on the water, away from the crazies."

"Sounds smart. Have a good time, Mr. Reser. See you next year." Graham climbed aboard and winked at Rennie as he passed by her and disappeared down below. Rennie was climbing down the steps to get the last bag when the man spoke up.

"He's a good man."

She paused and looked from the man to where Graham had been a few moments before and back at the man. "I know he is. Someone like me doesn't deserve someone like him—that's for sure."

"Happy New Year."

"You too," Rennie said. She bent down and picked up the last bag and gave the man a wave before ascending the stairs to the upper salon, where she found Graham putting a few things into the locking cabinets.

"I put your suitcase in the bigger room. I'll take the smaller one or sleep up here. The view from the boat at night is pretty spectacular."

"Oh, okay," she said. She went downstairs and into the master bedroom and decided to unpack. She felt the boat start to move and chided herself for not helping Graham pull buoys. He was doing everything for her, and she had nothing to offer in return.

She came out of the room and found him behind the steering wheel, playing with the navigation equipment. "You know, Brooklyn never told me how nice this boat was. It reminds me of the boat my parents had when I was growing up."

"Maybe that's why."

"Yeah, I guess." Rennie sat down across from where Graham sat and looked out the window. "How long until we're at the other marina?"

"Not long. I thought we'd fuel up there, grab a few snacks or something for lunch, and head to Friday Harbor. It's a great island. It should take us about four to five hours, depending on the wind."

"No one will find us."

They made eye contact. "He won't find you, Ren."

She nodded. Her purse was beside her, and she felt her phone vibrating. She dug for it and glanced at the notifications. Over one hundred missed calls from Theo and work. One thing she couldn't stand, and the other got on her nerves lately. She stood and walked to the edge of the boat, cocked her arm back, and heaved her phone into the water. She expected to feel some sort of relief, but she felt only anger.

"Don't need it?" Graham asked after she sat back down.

"The only person I care to speak with is standing next to me," she said while staring out the window. It was cold, and she tucked her legs under Graham's sweatshirt. He briefly left the helm and pulled the sliding windows shut all around them and turned on the heat. "I guess boats are really meant to only go out in the summer."

"We'll be fine. I checked the forecast, and there isn't a storm in sight. I'll keep watch." Once Graham was out of the no-wake zone, he pulled the throttle and picked up speed. Rennie longed to feel the wind in her hair, so she went outside, closing herself off from Graham. She stood at the bow, with her hands gripping the railing, and screamed until her throat hurt, hoping Graham couldn't hear her.

TWENTY

It took about an hour to reach the marina. Rennie helped when they came to the dock, pushing the buoys out to protect the boat, and while Graham fueled it up, she went inside and started to shop. He found her down one of the four aisles, with a basket resting on her arm. Graham went to take it from her and hold it, because as soon as you put one item in, those metal bars dug into your skin, making them unbearable to carry.

"Why's it empty?" he asked.

"Everything is jacked up in price," she whispered as her eyes darted toward the front. Graham chuckled lightly at her obvious concern that the clerk would overhear her.

"Once you leave the mainland, prices skyrocket. I'm glad you didn't see what I just spent on gas, because your eyes would've bugged out."

"I'll pay for everything this weekend," she said.

"You will not. We can be a team. Go Dutch. Is *going Dutch* still used these days?"

Rennie laughed. "I don't even remember using that term. Wait, doesn't that mean . . ." Her eyes went wide, and she slapped Graham on the shoulder. "That's gross."

"What?" he asked, as if he had no idea what she referred to. "Do you remember—"

"No, I'm not playing the do-you-remember game. You boys were gross in high school."

Graham laughed. He took the empty basket from Rennie and grabbed her hand with his free one. He stopped at the stand near the door and set the basket down and walked toward the deli counter,

"Okay, this is more my speed, but what will we do for food later?"

"We'll get some sandwiches, grab a few things to tide us over on the ride out, and we'll shop when we get on the island."

Rennie leaned into Graham. She placed her lips on his shoulder and kissed him. "I don't know what I'd do without you, Graham Cracker."

Graham put his arm around Rennie and pulled her close. He pressed his lips to her forehead and held her there for a moment. "You'll never have to know, Ren. I'll always be here for you." He spoke the truth. They may have been out of touch for a good chunk of time, but now that they'd found their way back to each other, being in Rennie's life made sense to him.

They placed their orders, and while they waited, they picked out a bag of chips and grabbed a couple of waters and a few pops, and Graham tossed in a box of cookies for good measure.

Back on the boat, Graham went to the cockpit and started the engine. As he backed away from the dock, Rennie lifted the buoys and set them on the deck.

"Can they stay out?"

"Yeah, might as well, because we're not anchoring; we're docking."

Rennie worked in the galley, putting their sandwiches and chips onto plates, and brought everything over to where Graham was. She sat next to him in a seat that was meant for one person and maybe a small toddler. Graham didn't care, because he enjoyed her company and they had always been like this, back before they grew up and became adults with real-life problems.

"Sorry, I know this isn't ideal."

"It's perfect," he said to her. He set his plate down on the compass display, his bottle of water in the drink holder, and picked up a quarter of his sandwich.

"I thought it would be easier to eat if the halves were smaller."

She was right. It was easier. "Thank you."

They ate in silence for the most part. Rennie would point out another boat or tell him she saw a whale, but the built-in sonar wasn't showing anything on the screen. He wouldn't tell her that, of course. If she thought there was a sea animal out there, and there might have been, he was going to let her believe it.

When they had finished, she got up and took his plate to the galley. He would glance over his shoulder every so often and wonder how things could have been different for them if life had gone their way. He saw her in ways no one else ever would, and despite the fact she was with him, cruising their way out into the middle of nowhere, he wasn't about to let himself think things were completely over between her and Theo. They fought; that was what Graham kept telling himself. By tomorrow, Graham expected his friend to ask him to take her back to Cape Harbor so she could not only buy a new cell phone but find Theo. And he would because she asked.

Rennie came back to where Graham was perched and placed a can of pop in the cup holder, then went back to where she had been sitting, practically on top of him . . . not that he was complaining. She rested her feet on the edge of the console and pulled the tab on her can of pop. She took a sip and then another, all while Graham studied her. She was acting as if last night hadn't happened, as if she hadn't texted him to drive to Canada to pick her up.

"You can ask me, ya know."

"Ask you what?"

"About yesterday."

"I figured if you wanted to tell me, you would. You know I don't like to pry."

She nodded and took another sip from the can. "I need something stronger."

"We can go out tonight," he suggested. "There's a nice bar in town. They have decent food."

"I want to get drunk enough to forget everything."

"Everything?" he asked. Graham kept his hand on the steering wheel, even though he could've sat back and enjoyed the ride out to Friday Harbor. There wasn't another boat in sight, and likely the only ones they'd come across were the ferries.

"The last year, especially yesterday."

"Okay, I'll bite." He sighed. Aside from the fact she had a boyfriend, he would never want to erase the past year, especially the past six months, or even the last few months. Brooklyn's return was in that block of time, which meant it was Rennie's return as well. As of late, he and Rennie were finally close again and growing closer each day. "What happened yesterday?"

Rennie cleared her throat. "The car ride started off awkward, and I think most of that was on me. Since Thanksgiving, things with Theo have been off. I've been off. I've been angry with him about his job, and then out of the blue, he suggests we move to Spokane because his company is there, and it would be easier for him. Never mind the fact that my family is on this side of the mountains."

"Do you want to move there?" Her leaving the area was the last thing he wanted. When he found out she had been living in Seattle the whole time, he wanted to kick his ass for not staying in contact with her all these years. Deep down, he had a feeling Rennie would've pushed him away, though, because of Brooklyn and the secret she kept. Although, to be fair, Brooklyn had no idea Carly Woods hid Brystol (who everyone assumed was Austin's daughter) from his friends.

"No, not at all. I've been there once and didn't like it, and I couldn't imagine not seeing Brooklyn and Brystol whenever I wanted. Now that they're back in Cape Harbor, I'm where I want to be. These past six months have been some of the best I've had in a long time."

"I know what you mean," he muttered. He didn't bother to look at her, even though he could feel her gaze upon him. He adjusted the wheel slightly, making sure the boat stayed the course toward the island.

"Anyway, as I said, I've been off, and my relationship suffered, and I told myself I needed to be better, if not for me, then for Theo. He works hard. We both do. And we'd been looking forward to the trip to Whistler for months. Except when we get there, the reservation for the hotel is under my name, and I didn't make it. I found it odd and believed Theo when he said it must've changed when I made all my spa appointments."

"Believable, I guess." Graham hadn't the foggiest idea about spa appointments or hotel reservations.

"Not really, but I'm there on vacation, and I've sworn to myself I'm not going to let the small stuff bother me. After we checked in, one of us—I don't even remember who—said something about the disconnect between us. We were supposed to go to the room, to *reconnect*, but instead, he wanted to go to the bar, where he proceeded to drink four glasses of wine." Rennie looked at Graham. "Four glasses, Graham. Four! He was fucking drunk within an hour of us arriving. I was so pissed and finally had enough. I signed the charge slip and took his sorry ass to our room."

"And he passed out?"

Rennie adjusted in her seat. "Nope. As I was opening the door to our honeymoon suite, a couple—who, by the way, had given me a dirty look when we stepped out of the elevator—called his name. He introduced me as hotel staff." She looked at Graham and waited.

"Okay . . . ," he said as he met her gaze. She glared. He waited. He didn't know what to say, because he saw Theo's face being pummeled by his hand. He wanted to strangle the son of a bitch, revive him, and do it all over again. "I'm sorry, Ren."

208

"We've been together for over a year, Graham. A fucking year, and that bastard is *married*. Fucking married! Do you want to know the worst part?"

"I think it's obvious."

"It's not." She held his gaze. "I don't even care."

"Does that mean you're going back to him?" Graham was confused. If she hadn't cared he was married, why was he taking her to the middle of nowhere?

"What? No, never. I thought I would be heartbroken . . . *devastated*. I thought I was in love with him, but I think I was in love with the idea of being in love. I don't even miss him."

"You're angry," Graham pointed out. "The hurt will come. The stages of grief, remember?"

She shook her head and remained calm. "I don't think so, Graham. I could've texted Brooklyn to come and get me, but I texted you because deep down, I know I'd rather spend time with you over anyone else. Do you want to know what I was thinking about on the way back from Canada?"

Graham sighed. "How many ways can I ignore Graham?"

Rennie laughed. "I was thinking about the drive up and how I didn't want to be there, and how this past month, the only time I've been truly happy was when I was in Cape Harbor. He wanted to take that away from me, and I almost let him. And I was thinking about his poor wife, Angela; her friend must've called her and told her. What must she think of me? I can't even imagine, nor do I really want to. I don't want her to think I set out to ruin her marriage. Theo did that. From the day I met him, he's been lying to both of us."

"You should probably talk to him, Ren."

"Why the hell should I?"

"Closure?" Graham suggested. "If I've learned anything over the past few months, it's that talking brings closure."

Rennie scoffed. "The only thing I want from him is an answer to why he did this—nothing else. I'm going to be fine, Graham. I really am. I'm relieved, really. He wasn't the guy for me. He was the type of guy everyone expected me to be with, and that's not what I want out of life."

"What do you want?" Not that he'd be able to give her anything on her list, but knowing what she looked for was important to him.

"I want someone who is going to put me first, who cares about me, my thoughts and ideas. I want someone who makes me laugh, even when I'm tired or upset, who can be there with some funny joke or story to cheer me up. The guy for me will accept my independence and encourage my personal growth. He won't order for me or tell me what I'm eating isn't good for me or remind me about the gym membership I pay for but never use. He'll love my family and friends and want a beach house so I can be close to Brooklyn."

He listened as she listed off what she was looking for in a partner. He could give her everything. "What about financial independence?"

"Well, that's a given, right? You gotta be able to support yourself, pay your way. I don't care about lavish vacations, because honestly, I'd rather travel alone. And, I don't want kids."

There it was—the kicker. Graham had enough money to live; that was it. He had cashed out his investments after he left California, bought his houseboat, and put the rest in the bar. He wasn't raking in the cash being a part-time bar owner, even though he was the only one to run the place, and he didn't have the funds to expand or invest in anything that would make him more money. "Sounds like you need a man who is already retired."

Rennie quieted for a moment. "Yeah, you're probably right. At least if he had kids, they should be grown up, and he wouldn't want any more."

Her words hurt only because he'd given himself a sliver of hope she would say, "I want what we never had" or something similar. He was foolish to think they'd ever cross the line from friends to lovers again. They were past that stage in their lives, and honestly, Graham was ready to settle down. He wanted kids and the laid-back life Cape Harbor provided.

Graham leaned back and put his arm around Rennie to give her a one-armed hug. She snuggled into him, gripping his shirt with her fist. "I don't know what I ever did to deserve a friend like you, Graham Cracker."

"I feel the same way, Ren. You're my best girl. Always have been."

And she would always be.

TWENTY-ONE

Graham held true to his word. After they docked, he took a shower while Rennie got ready for dinner. Most of the clothes she had packed were for lounging around the lodge, but they would suffice for now. Thankfully, the fleece-lined pants she had bought online would still come in handy, because it was a bit chilly on the island. Rennie waited for Graham in the upper salon, and when he came up the stairs, he was dressed in a white button-down and a pair of medium-wash jeans. It wasn't what he was wearing that caught her attention. It was the way he smelled. Earlier, when she had showered at his house, she used his soap, hoping to smell like him, but the scent she craved was his cologne. He was old fashioned and wore Old Spice, just like her grandfather had. It comforted her, especially when she wore his sweatshirt.

He led her off the boat and through the marina. They walked side by side up a small hill until they reached the main street. She had never been to Friday Harbor or any of the other San Juan Islands and was already starting to fall in love with the quaint little town. When they rounded a corner, Graham reached for her hand, and she gave it willingly. They walked a block or two until he stopped and held open a wooden door for her.

"Hi, welcome to the Lavender. How many?"

"Two," Rennie said to the hostess, who grabbed two menus and asked them to follow her. The restaurant was dimly lit, and she could hear people cheering from the bar. Rennie almost asked Graham if he wanted to sit in there and watch whatever game was on but also thought Graham might want a break from the bar scene. The hostess showed them to their seats and told them their waiter would be by shortly. The tablecloth was purple with a sprig of lavender in a small jar sitting in the middle of it.

"What is with all the lavender?" she asked him.

"Odd as it may sound, lavender grows here. The soil is perfect for it. There are fields everywhere once you leave this area."

"How did I not know this? I've lived in this state my entire life."

"How much of it have you explored?"

She thought for a minute. "Honestly, not much. I think I need to get out more. Maybe that'll be my New Year's resolution: travel Washington more."

"Sounds like a good one." Graham opened his menu, and Rennie did the same. She scanned the items available, each one making her mouth water, until she came to the seafood. Internally, she gave herself a fist bump. There would be no more complaining about Theo's sushi-eating habits or arguing about where they'd go to dinner. She found herself smiling and chanced a look at Graham, only to see him staring at his phone.

"What is it?" she asked. She saw his thumb move on his phone.

"Brooklyn is worried because you're not answering your phone. She says Theo has been by the house looking for you."

"Oh" was all she could manage to say at first. "I don't want him coming here, and I don't want to see him."

"I know." Graham typed out a message and showed her his phone. She's with me. She's safe and will call you later. Send Theo packing.

"That's a lot. Maybe just say she hates Theo and to shoot him?"

Graham shook his head and took his phone back. "If you don't care about him, why do you care whether he finds you or not?"

Rennie appraised Graham for a moment. He was right. If she didn't care, why keep her location a secret? Truth was, she needed time before she faced Theo, which she hoped would be the first of never. Graham didn't wait for a response.

"Theo has no idea where you are, and Bowie and especially Brooklyn won't tell him. You have nothing to worry about."

"But when we get back . . ."

"When we get back, we'll deal with it. I'm sure he'll be sitting on your steps when you get back to your apartment."

"So, what you're saying is, I should move?"

"I'm not saying anything." He went back to the menu, effectively ending their conversation. Since she'd unloaded everything earlier, he'd been a bit standoffish, and she didn't like it. He wasn't acting like himself.

"What's good?"

"Well, I imagine everything is. This place has a five-star rating, but I've only ever had their steak. It's slow cooked, aged, and all those other fancy buzzwords restaurants like to throw around to make you think you're getting the absolute best cut of meat possible. Plus, it's good. Like really, really good. So, when I come out here, it's always what I order."

"How often do you come out here?"

"A couple times a year. I normally walk on the ferry."

"When was the last time?"

He took his eyes off the menu for a brief second, looked at her and then back at the listing. If he only ever ordered the steak, why was he looking? "This past summer. I came out here for a few days."

She knew precisely when too. Theo was staying with her at the Driftwood Inn, and Graham was conveniently absent that weekend. Rennie looked for him, wanted to touch base, but he was gone, and his bartender wouldn't tell her where he was. Bowie didn't know either.

She wanted to know why he'd escaped to this island when she and Theo came to town, assuming it was because of them. What did this place do for him, or was there some memory here she wasn't aware of? The latter she wanted to doubt, but there was a long period of time when they hadn't spoken. What had happened in those fifteen years?

The waiter came to the table, set two glasses of water down, and introduced himself as Mike. He told them the specials, all of which made Rennie's mouth water. Afterward, he took their drink orders—vodka and tonic for her, and a local IPA for Graham.

"What's her name?" Rennie asked as soon as Mike left.

"Who?" Graham picked up the glass in front of him and took a sip.

"The woman who introduced you to this place. There has to be a story behind it."

Graham fiddled with the glass, and his eyes wandered everywhere but to Rennie. His lips went into a thin line, and it looked as if he was biting the inside of his cheek.

"She must've been some woman."

He smiled or smirked; she couldn't be sure. Graham sat up straight and leaned slightly toward Rennie. "It's tough to date in Cape Harbor. I either grew up with them, they're about ten years younger than me, or they know so much about Grady that they think I'm the same way."

"So, you came here to look for women?"

"No," he said. "I came here because I got sick of people telling me how sorry they were about Austin and Grady. Sure, I may have met a few women, but none of them ever became more than a one-night or weekend thing."

"Graham, are you seriously telling me you haven't had a real relationship since you moved back?"

"That's what I'm telling you."

Rennie sat there, stunned, and before she could ask him to elaborate, the waiter returned with their drinks and asked if they were ready to order. Rennie motioned for Graham to order first. As he said he would, he ordered the steak, which came with mashed potatoes, a vegetable medley, and a house salad. Rennie ordered the same and handed her menu to the waiter.

"What happened to being able to order for yourself?" Graham asked. He had called her out on her earlier rant on how she wanted someone to accept her independence.

"Your order sounded good."

"Liar," he said as he picked up his pint of beer. "You never read the menu because you were too busy grilling me about my lackluster love life."

"Which I don't get, Graham. I remember the first time I saw you. B brought me to some party. It was my first time in Cape Harbor, and Bowie suggested I sit down and play spin the bottle with him. I think he had a little crush or thought we'd hook up or something. You and Grady were there but not sitting next to each other. Brooklyn had told me all about the Chamberlain twins beforehand, so I knew who you were. The game leader called out seven minutes in heaven, spun the bottle, and it landed on you. I watched the old Pepsi bottle spin and spin on the board, and when it landed on me . . ." She sat back and smiled. "Girls were pissed, but I didn't care, because I was heading into the closet with this really hot guy." Graham blushed as Rennie recounted the way they met.

"I remember that night clearly."

"You were my first kiss. Hell, you were my first everything, and there was a time when my mother thought we were going to get married."

"Really?"

"Yeah . . ." Rennie paused when the waiter came to the table with their salads. She and Graham both took their napkins and placed them on their laps and picked up their forks. He dug in immediately, but she waited. She wanted to finish telling him about her mom. "When we went off to college, she told me to be careful, that she always heard the women were a bit wild down there because so much sun made them do crazy things. I remember laughing her off and thinking she had no idea about her daughter. I couldn't wait to party. But as she was helping me pack, she put her hand on mine and said, 'Graham is a good guy and is going to be a great man.' At first, I had no idea what she was talking about until I told her about Theo. Her first question was, 'Whatever happened to Graham? I always liked him.' So, what *did* happen?"

Graham put his fork down, finished chewing, and used his napkin to wipe his lips. "Nothing happened. I fell in love with someone, Austin died, and then she left me because I felt I had a duty to come home and help Grady and my dad. It was like some perverse life cycle I couldn't control."

They were only halfway through their salads when dinner arrived. Graham seemed lost in thought each time Rennie would glance at him. They made small talk, mostly about the area they were in and how long they were going to stay.

"My vacation is over on the third," she told him. She needed to talk to distract herself from her thoughts.

"I don't know if I can be gone that long, but I'll check with Krista."

"Ask her if it's okay if you're gone until the first. I do feel bad keeping you away from work. We can go back tomorrow, if you want. I know you have a life, and I've completely interrupted it. I'm sorry, Graham."

"I'll call her tomorrow and see how she feels working through the holiday."

"You need more staff."

Graham chuckled. "We need more people in Cape Harbor. There are times when I look at the books and ask myself how the bar has stayed open as long as it has, and then I remember the regulars. They come in every day or every other day because they're loyal. Things are great in the summer, but winter hits us hard."

"If Krista is okay with you being gone, I can come work at the bar for a few days before I have to head back to Seattle."

"You want to work in the bar?"

Rennie shrugged and smiled brightly. "Why not? I had a lot of fun when I did it earlier." She stuck her lower lip out in a pout.

Graham shook his head slowly and started to laugh. "You're crazy, but if you want to work, you can. I just don't want to hear you complain about your feet hurting or the lousy tips you're getting."

She clapped her hands in delight. "Perfect. Now I feel like I'm not hogging all your time."

"Why'd you throw your phone in the water?" Graham asked, breaking the silence between them.

Rennie set her fork down and pushed her plate away. "Because the only person I wanted to speak with was with me. Everyone else, including Brooklyn, would coddle me, treat me like I'm fragile. I didn't want to answer a million texts asking how I'm doing or see Theo's name pop up on the screen. I know I could've blocked him, but he'd just call from a different number, and I didn't want to deal with it. I'm also on vacation and shouldn't have to deal with work."

"You only wanted to be with me?"

"When that shit went down, you were the only person I wanted to come to my rescue."

"Why?" he asked.

"Graham, it's like you make breathing easy for me. When I'm around you, I can be myself. I'm not Renee, but Rennie, and it doesn't matter what's going on in my life—you're not going to make me feel like I'm less of a person or force an opinion. You listen to what I have to say. You respect my feelings. You care about me in a way no one else ever has. You're my best friend, and there isn't any place I'd rather be right now other than here with you, enjoying a delicious dinner and exploring a place I've never been."

She wasn't sure, but she thought she saw Graham grimace. When the waiter walked by, he asked for the check.

"No dessert?"

"We still need to go to the grocery store," he reminded her. "We can get some ice cream or whatever it is you want there."

"Booze," she said. "Lots and lots of booze."

"No booze," Graham told her. "We're docked, and the boat will sway more. I don't want you getting seasick."

"Graham Cracker, you're such a buzzkill."

He laughed. "You whine enough as is, Ren. I'm not going to hold your hair back because you decided to drink yourself into a stupor. Believe me; you'll thank me later."

When the check came, Graham threw down a wad of cash and got up from the table. He reached for Rennie's hand, and their fingers intertwined. "Come on—let's go get gallons of ice cream and tell stories all night long."

Rennie slapped his chest, and he recoiled. "Only if I can paint your toes and do your hair."

He shook his head. "Never gonna happen. I will sit outside with you, though, and watch the stars."

She liked that idea, mostly because that was how they spent their first night together when they were teens, under the stars.

TWENTY-TWO

Graham rolled onto his side, wrapped himself up in his weighted blanket, and readjusted his pillow to cover his ear. Whatever animal had decided to take refuge on the dock after nightfall moaned incredibly loud. Coupled with the constant sway of the boat from the choppy water, Graham was restless. There wasn't much he could do about the boat, but in the morning, he would talk to the marina manager and see if the animal could find a new place to serenade. Although, that was unlikely as well.

He sighed heavily and rolled onto his back and spread his arms out wide. All he wanted was a couple hours of sleep, but no matter how hard he tried, it wasn't going to happen. There was too much going on for his mind to shut off, and when it finally started to, images of Rennie popped up, keeping him wide awake.

"Rennie," he said her name aloud and sat up straight in his bed. The lights from the docks crept through his curtains, giving his room a natural night-light. His heart raced as the sound of the animal grew closer. Only, it wasn't some sea creature taking refuge on the dock or on the boat; it was Rennie. Graham listened for a moment before getting out of bed. He dressed quickly in sweats and a long-sleeved T-shirt and sweatshirt and pulled his weighted blanket off his bed. When he stepped out into the small hallway, he noticed her door was open. He didn't need to peer in to verify she wasn't in her room. Her cries were enough to tell him where she was.

On the deck, Rennie sat at the bow, with her back facing the helm. As Graham approached, the sounds that had kept him awake came from her. His steps faltered as he heard his friend wail. He walked faster along the starboard side of the yacht, and when he reached her, Graham draped his blanket over the front of her. He sat down and pulled her between his legs.

"I've got you, Ren," he whispered into her ear. He should've been concerned for the few other boats docked, but no one seemed to be awake. Maybe they, too, thought an animal had beached itself. He warned her about the grief earlier but couldn't predict it would hit her in the middle of the night. It all made sense, though. She was alone with her thoughts, and there wasn't anyone in her room, once they went to bed, to keep her mind from drifting.

She clutched at his arms, her nails digging into the fabric of his sweatshirt. Rennie sobbed. Her body shook. With each new wave of emotion, Graham held her tighter. He hated what she was going through, and he himself wanted to hunt Theo down and pummel him for what he had done to Rennie. He couldn't fathom what was going on in Theo's mind when he decided to cheat on his wife or lie to Rennie. Graham would never be that type of man.

"I hate him," she mumbled. Her words were garbled.

"I know you do, and you have every right to. I'm not judging you." He would never judge her. She hadn't judged him or his family when everything went down with Grady.

"Why did he do this to me?"

"I don't know," he said to her. "I was just asking myself the same thing."

Rennie turned slightly in his arms. "Would you ever do something like this?"

Graham studied her red-rimmed eyes and smeared makeup. He didn't care what she looked like—she would always be one of the most beautiful women he had ever known. She had strands of hair stuck to her face. Graham tucked them behind her ear and brought his hand down slowly from her ear to her neck.

"No, I would never do that to you." He paused and wondered if she noticed how he singled her out. When she didn't turn away, he added, "If I were lucky enough to find a woman who wanted to be with me, marry me, I'd do everything I could to make her the happiest woman alive, and if I wasn't happy, I'd tell her. No one deserves to be cheated on."

Graham felt this deep in his heart. Back in college, when he met Monica, he was torn in half by this growing love for her and his undying love for Rennie. He had to draw the line, decide on his future. As much as he wanted one with Rennie, he didn't see it happening any time in the near future. Monica was there and present. He chose her, and while his heart ached for Rennie, he didn't regret his decision. He and Rennie were as close as ever but miles apart when it came to life. He made a vow to Monica as her boyfriend and kept it. If things had been different, he likely would've asked Monica to marry him. He would've asked her if she'd moved with him as well, but they weren't meant to be.

Rennie snuggled into Graham's chest. He didn't care that his sweatshirt would likely be covered with tearstains and makeup. All Graham cared about was Rennie. If this was what she needed, he would give it to her.

"You're a good guy, Graham Cracker."

Being a good guy was a great quality to have, but where did it get him? Apparently, on a boat in the middle of winter, holding a brokenhearted woman. He should be bothered. Incensed, really, that she expected him to drop everything for her. He was, in a sense, but it was how they worked—coming to each other's aid—no questions asked.

Graham inhaled deeply, taking in the sea salt air. He looked out over the harbor, in the darkness, and wondered what was out there. They were close to where Austin's boat capsized, and that got his mind wondering. Austin's body had never been recovered. Was he out there? Did he have amnesia? Or had he been buried at sea? These were questions that also plagued Grady and yet were never answered.

Rennie shivered and brought Graham's attention back to the forefront. He pulled her deeper into his hold to try and warm her. "We can go inside if you want," he suggested.

"I don't want to be alone."

He nodded and stood. Once he had his sea legs, he helped Rennie up. "Come on." Graham held her hand as they walked back into the galley. He locked up while she waited for him with his blanket wrapped around her shoulders. Graham motioned for her to go down the stairs, and he followed her to her bedroom. They both crawled under the covers, clothes and all, and he held her until they both fell asleep.

Graham stretched and opened his eyes to sunlight streaming through the room. He felt for Rennie, only to find her spot vacant and cold. He listened intently for her and could hear her shuffling around in the galley. She wasn't crying—at least that was what he deduced—so he decided to close his eyes for another few minutes. He was on the cusp of falling back into a deep slumber when the smell of bacon made his stomach growl.

He sat up and moved until his feet were on the ground. He glanced at his attire, and his heart sank at the sight of the black smudges on his shirt. His friend was going through something terrible, and he didn't know how to help her. Holding her while she cried didn't seem like enough. Brooklyn would know, but Rennie didn't want her. She wanted him. And Graham would give her anything she wanted.

What he wanted was a second chance with Rennie, but the timing wasn't right. That was the only thing they ever got wrong when it came to their lives together—their timing sucked. He would wait.

What wasn't waiting was his stomach, and as soon as the second wave of bacon permeated the air, he felt the hunger pangs kick in. Graham stopped by his room, used the bathroom, and changed quickly before making his way up the stairs. He found Rennie in the galley kitchen. She hadn't heard him come up the stairs, so he watched her bob her head to whatever beat played in her head, because the radio wasn't on, nor the television. She danced, shaking her hips as she worked in the small space, making breakfast.

He cleared his throat and said, "Good morning."

Rennie startled and looked at him over her shoulder. She smiled. "Morning. How'd you sleep?" she asked, but before he could even respond, she started talking. "I slept like a log once you brought me back to bed. I can't believe how soothing it is to sleep on a boat. It's like I was rocked to sleep. No wonder you live on the water."

"It's not really the same," he said. He had no idea why he replied with such a statement. Was he trying to discourage her from staying longer, or was there a hint of encouragement in his tone?

"What do you mean?"

"Nothing, just that the house doesn't really move like a boat, unless there's a storm, and then I adjust the mooring, and everything is back to normal."

"Oh." Rennie went back to cooking, and Graham felt like an idiot for the way he responded.

"Sorry, Ren."

"For what?" she asked without looking at him. Graham went to her and placed his hand on her hip to gently turn her toward him.

"I just made what looks to be a perfectly good morning really awkward with my mundane answers. You're happy, and I don't want to dampen your mood."

"You're fine. I'm fine, Graham Cracker. I should be the one apologizing for last night. I don't know what came over me."

"Grief," he told her.

She shook her head. "It's like I had to have that meltdown to exorcise the demon or something. Believe me when I tell you I'm relieved."

Graham wanted to believe her—he did—but he had dealt with enough heartbreak between the accident and his breakup with Monica to suspect Rennie might be hiding her true feelings.

"Do you need any help?" he asked to change the subject.

"No, I'm almost done. Go ahead and sit down; I'll make you a plate." He did as she suggested and turned on the small television Bowie had installed in the corner and flipped through the few channels the satellite was able to pick up. He found a news program and left it on even though he wasn't interested. The background noise should keep his mind from wandering to places it shouldn't. He imagined Rennie cooking breakfast at his house, wearing nothing more than his T-shirt, and groaned. These thoughts needed to stay in his reserve bank and not at the forefront of his mind.

His thoughts had to change, because they were only going to get him into trouble. He reached for the folded paper and noticed the date was current. "Did you leave the boat this morning?" he asked without looking at her.

"I did. I went for a walk. This town is the cutest, Graham. I'm totally kicking my ass for not visiting earlier." She came over and set a handful of pamphlets down on the table and returned to the stove. "Look at those. I thought maybe we could check out the town, visit the shops."

"We can go to the lavender fields today if you want."

"How?" She came to the table with his plate and a cup of coffee.

"Thank you, Ren," he said as they made eye contact. For some reason, at that moment, the desire to pull her toward him, to feel her body pressed against his, overwhelmed him. He resigned his mentality to refer to her as a friend, nothing more, because that was all she could handle right now. She needed him as a friend. Graham shook his head slightly, needing to clear his dreams, but the action failed.

Rennie's hips sauntered back and forth seductively as she approached the table. She sat next to him. Not across, but right next to him, with her knee touching his. The zing his body felt from having her so close was almost too much to bear, but he knew if he moved away, she would be hurt, and he couldn't do that to her. He refused to hurt her.

"How will we see the fields?" she asked, reminding him of her earlier question.

"Well, I thought since we're on a minivacation, we should rent a scooter and cruise around the island."

"I love your enthusiasm and your attempt to make this a minivacation, but it's way too cold to ride around on a scooter."

"We can rent a car instead. I just thought . . ." What he thought was she'd snuggle into him, that she'd need him for warmth. "A car is probably better."

"We'll have to come back this summer and do the scooter thing. I think that would be fun."

He nodded. "It's really fun here in the summer. Maybe we can get the Bs to come over too."

"I called Brooklyn this morning from the pay phone," she said, much to his surprise. "I know she was worried. I would be too. I wasn't thinking straight."

"Everyone understands, Ren. And if you need to use my phone, just ask. You can use it whenever you want."

Rennie smiled. "Thank you. Now back to what we are going to do today. What do you think about checking out the shops? I saw a couple on my walk. They all look so cute and charming."

"Eh, not really my thing. I think there's a game on or something." He flinched before she could even slap him. He started to laugh at the mean face she glared at him with. "Okay, fine. Shopping it is." Graham picked up his fork and started to eat.

"And . . ." She paused, which was a clear indication she was up to no good. She grabbed ahold of Graham's arm and tugged slightly. "When I was out earlier, I saw this bar. They're having a New Year's Eve party tonight. We should go."

"Ren?" Her name came out of his mouth like a warning. He wanted to take her out. They had always had a good time when they were together, but a bar meant drinking, which meant their inhibitions would be lowered. *Screw it.* He wanted to take her out.

Rennie batted her eyelashes at Graham and jutted her lip out. He was a sucker for a cute-and-sexy pout. He relented quickly. "You'll be the death of me, woman."

"Ha," she laughed. "If we were in Cape Harbor, you'd beg me to come down to the Whale Spout."

Graham sighed. "You're not wrong."

They finished breakfast. He got up and started cleaning the galley. It was the least he could do, considering Rennie had made breakfast. He topped off her coffee and took the empty pot to the sink. Graham plugged the drain, added a couple drops of dish soap, and filled the sink about halfway. He didn't want to run out of water for the showers, and he wasn't sure exactly how Bowie had everything pumped. He washed quickly and set the dishes out to air-dry.

Graham expected Rennie to be downstairs getting dressed and ready for the day, but she was still at the table, watching him clean up. The way she was staring at him made him wonder if she had been looking at him the entire time he was in the galley.

TWENTY-THREE

Rennie had never really been a fan of white T-shirts—or anything white, for that matter. Anytime she wore the color, it always ended up with a stain, or after a couple of washings, the brightness dulled, and the item looked dingy. There was one time when living in California that Rennie bought a white duvet with a bright-blue flower on it. She loved it and had it one night before she passed out on it, leaving a makeup stain she couldn't get out. The same for her white pantsuit and the turtleneck she bought for a Christmas party to go with a red suit coat. All ruined within minutes of wearing. She'd sworn off white . . . until now.

The galley on the boat was small, only really big enough for one person, and even then, there wasn't a lot of room to move around. Bowie's boat wasn't one of those massive yachts people always dreamed of owning or spending time on when they would see it go by. It was perfect for his small family and a couple of guests, as long as you didn't mind the close quarters. Of course, not many people traveled by boat during the colder months as Rennie and Graham had.

Graham stood at the sink, washing dishes. Rennie had seen Theo do this chore a few times but never had he made her stop and watch him. She never cared to, but there was something about Graham doing this menial chore that made her stop and pay attention. As Graham cleaned the pan used to cook their breakfast, the muscles in his arms flexed, and her mouth watered. Why? It wasn't like she hadn't seen Graham's well-toned arms before. She had. She was very familiar with them. Maybe it was the white shirt that kept her attention. It wasn't tight, but she could see the muscles in his back shifting each time he moved, and she could see the dark shadow of the tribal tattoo he had showing through the thin fabric. She suddenly found herself in the middle of a hot flash. It was too cold outside, so what was the explanation?

Graham.

As if on cue, he glanced over his shoulder and smirked. Her heart leaped, and she quickly looked away. He was her friend, her confidant. Sure, they had been together before, but that was always just a casual hookup. Yet she couldn't resist turning her attention back toward him, expecting to find him focused on the task at hand. He wasn't. He was watching her, studying her. Who did he see when he looked at her? The woman she used to be? The one where all he had to do was tilt his head to the side and smile, and she'd run to him. Back then, they had this undeniable connection. They were drawn to each other. Others saw it as well, and it made dating difficult for them. When Graham started dating Monica, he put some separation between him and Rennie. She hated him for it but forgave him because she understood why he had done it. Rennie should've done it when she returned to Cape Harbor for the first time in fifteen years—kept Graham at a distance—but she couldn't. Or did he see the broken woman shattered by deceit? The one who realized after finding out her boyfriend was a lying, cheating piece of shit that she didn't care. By all accounts, she should be in bed, exhausted from crying. But she wasn't; she had no desire to see Theo or even hear from him ever again. More so, she felt complete and utter relief he was out of her life. While she thought she should have felt broken and distraught, she didn't. Her heart wasn't aching for him, and her body didn't long to be with him. He put her in an unthinkable situation and expected her to be okay with it. She never would be. Rennie Wallace was not and would never be a home-wrecker.

The more she thought about the past couple of days, the more it hit her. She had fallen out of love with Theo the day she walked into the Whale Spout and saw Graham. To her, he represented everything she wanted to be in life—the fun, outgoing, life-of-the-party person who people wanted to be around. With Theo, it was hard work to be the reserved, dull, and boring person he met the day of the conference. There wasn't a doubt in her mind she was over Theo, and as she accepted this, she felt as if a ton of bricks had been lifted off her body. Rennie could finally be herself.

She stood and went over to Graham. He kept his focus on her until she was by his side, staring into his green-colored eyes that reminded her of emeralds. She suddenly felt like she could get lost in his beautiful orbs for hours. He peered at her intently, never breaking eye contact as he turned his body around slowly. She stepped forward, sliding her leg between his. Rennie yearned to have his hands on her, to feel his calloused hands grip and pull at her flesh. She reached for his hand, and he gave it willingly. They often held hands when out. It was natural for them, but now, as they stood face to face, she took her hand and pressed it to his, and it felt different. Her hand was much smaller in comparison, and he could easily wrap his around hers. She angled their hands, clasping their fingers.

"Graham, what are we doing?"

He hesitated before answering. "It looks like we're holding hands."

Always the smart-ass. His reply made her laugh softly. Was he flirting? It had been years since they spent seven minutes in heaven. The night they played spin the bottle, he took her into the closet while his friends cheered and egged him on. He hadn't cared; she knew that much. The small room, cluttered with boxes and coats, had an overhead light, the type you pulled with a string. When they entered, it was dark, and Rennie expected they would stand there in silence or maybe talk. Graham had other ideas. He turned the light on and told her he wanted to see her, to look at her, because she was the most beautiful girl he had ever seen. After they shared their first kiss, they were inseparable. They hadn't needed a bottle to tell them when to make out. They couldn't keep their hands off each other. Graham rounded the bases quickly with Rennie, the summer after their junior year. Once they started having sex, neither could get enough of each other.

"Why didn't we stay together all those years ago?"

Graham breathed deeply. "Were we ever together, Ren?"

His words stung, but he was right. She'd never wanted the label, and when she went to college, she wanted to be free to do whatever she wanted without having to worry about what her boyfriend across town might think.

"We had a lot of fun in those days."

"That we did."

"I think we should do it again." Rennie waggled her eyebrows at Graham, who remained pensive.

"Ren—"

"I know," she said with a shrug. "I just couldn't let this moment pass me by."

He looked confused by her words. That was, until his eyes went wide and then shut instantly as the white blob of suds moved toward him. Rennie dragged her hand down his face, covering his face from his forehead to his chin. Graham exhaled, and clumps of suds flew into the air.

Rennie giggled like a schoolgirl, and it felt damn good to do it. Graham brought the best out in her.

Graham sighed, shook his head, and turned toward the sink. He looked pissed, and she couldn't understand why. When Rennie leaned in to taunt him, his arm snaked around her waist, and he looked deep into her eyes. They shared a moment until his free hand came forward, and he splashed her repeatedly.

She screamed and tried to get away, but he held on to her. She laughed hard, begged him to stop, and even tried to kick him, but he was far too strong for her. "I give. I give," she said, completely out of breath. Graham set her down and waited for retaliation.

Rennie stood next to him, her chest heaving. She was happy with him, happy when he was around. She ran her fingers over his hair, right above his ear, and rose onto her toes. She placed a kiss on his cheek and lingered there for a moment. "Thank you, Graham Cracker."

Rennie turned and walked down the stairs. When she shut the door to her bedroom, she leaned against it and smiled. They were going to have a good day. She was sure of it.

After she showered, did her hair and makeup, and dressed, she found Graham sitting at the small table, watching television.

"Hey," he said when she appeared.

"Know what I'm thankful for?"

"What's that?" he asked.

"The warm clothes I packed."

Graham chuckled. "Couldn't have planned this trip any better." He turned off the television, stood, and reached for her coat, which she had draped over her arm. He helped her into it and then put his on.

The moment they stepped off the boat, Graham reached for her hand, and she snuggled into his side for a quick second before falling in step beside him. "It's beautiful out here."

He glanced down at her and said, "The view is amazing."

Rennie should not have been caught off guard by his charm. By all accounts, she should be used to it, but his words put a little pep into her step. Regardless of whether he said the words to make her feel better about herself or if he truly meant them, she was going to believe the latter.

They walked through the parking lot of the marina, saying hi to others as they passed by. Every few steps, Rennie pointed at something and said, "Oh, look there" or "Look at this."

"Graham, they have whale watching and kayak rentals."

"It's winter, Ren."

"I know—I'm just saying it now so when we come back this sum- mer, we can do it." She made a list of things she wanted to do in the summer with Graham. He would be a willing participant, or she would ask Bowie to borrow his boat, and she'd kidnap Graham. He needed a little pampering, and bringing him back to the islands could be her way of returning the favor he had done for her.

They walked up Spring Street and stopped in a small café to get coffee, only to walk out with hot cocoa because Rennie loved the smell of chocolate. Their next stop was the Trident Bookstore. When Rennie opened the door and bells sounded, she looked at Graham and winked.

"Do you know what we'll find in here?"

He looked at her quizzically. "Books?"

"Not just any books, but books on folklore, especially mermaids."

Sure enough, as soon as they stepped in, **MERMAIDS AND OTHER SEA CREATURES** was the first section they came to. Rennie walked slowly down the aisle, her finger dragging along the spines of the books. Every few steps, she'd stop and hand her cup to Graham so she could leaf through the pages. Most of them had top-edge gilt, which Rennie loved. For her, the added gold made her feel like the book in her hand was a classic.

Each aisle they visited, either she or Graham found something to share with the other. Graham showed Rennie a book about the history of Washington. He flipped to the page that told the story of the Whale Spout and of how it had been built from a pirate ship. Rennie added the book to the ever-growing pile in her arm.

At the checkout, Rennie added a magnet for her refrigerator and a couple of bookmarks. One depicted the San Juan Islands, and the other had the name of the bookstore on it. After she paid, Graham took the bag and slung it over his shoulder.

"I can carry the bag."

"I know you can." He reached for her hand and wove their fingers together. They continued their exploration of the small town, going in and out of stores, buying souvenirs, and arguing happily when Rennie insisted that Graham buy a whale cut from driftwood.

"It would look amazing over the bar, and you know it. You can't deny it."

The salesclerk looked at Graham and Rennie expectantly.

"You're right. We'll take it," Graham told the young kid behind the counter.

Rennie beamed when Graham said *we*. She thought they'd make a good team, that she could make him happy. She already knew he did the same for her.

When they left the store, Rennie carried the wooden whale sign. It was long and bulky but lighter than the books, and she was secretly elated to carry it. Graham had bought something she loved, and that made her smile.

They crossed the road and went down a side street. Graham stopped them in front of Lou's Lavender. "This summer, when we come back, we'll go to the fields. Right now, everything is dead, but I want you to see what they do here on the island with the lavender."

Rennie rubbed her hands together. "Show me."

He opened the door and motioned for her to go in. Inside, soap, lotion, perfumes, and sprigs of lavender surrounded her. Rennie turned toward Graham. "You know purple is my favorite color," she stated as she held a sprig to her nose and inhaled.

He nodded. "I know, Ren."

Graham took the whale sign from her and set it by the door with her books. They browsed together, smelling the lotions and perfumes, adding soap to their handbasket, and flipping through the photos of the fields.

"I wish it wasn't winter."

"It won't be in a few months," he told her.

Wherever Rennie went, Graham followed. And when she would stop, she knew he was right next to her. His hand would rest on her back, or he would bend toward her and examine whatever she showed him.

After an hour, Rennie settled on a bottle of lotion and a half dozen bars of soap. She took a business card from the stack on the counter and thanked the clerk, who happened to be the owner, for creating such amazing products. They collected their other packages and headed back out into the crisp air.

"I have one more place I really want to show you," Graham said to her. She linked her arm in his and told him to lead the way.

He led them down the street and back toward the marina and into a small ice cream shop. "We'll take one of each, please."

Rennie went to tell him she didn't like people ordering for her, when she finally read the menu. They only served two flavors: lavender and lavender with honey.

"Lavender ice cream?" She wasn't really asking Graham or the young woman behind the counter, but both of them laughed and said yes. "I really feel like I'm in an alternate universe here."

Graham paid and took their two dishes over to the small white wrought iron table-and-chair set. "Dig in." He pushed the cup of ice cream toward her.

Her first bite was small, enough to whet her palate. She let the ice cream rest on her tongue before she swallowed. "Okay, it's good, but . . ." She couldn't find the right word.

"Floral tasting, like you're eating flowers?"

She pointed her spoon at him. "Yes, that's it. I do like it, though. Can I try yours?"

Graham pushed his spoon into his cream-colored ice cream and scooped some out. He held his spoon near Rennie's mouth. She kept her eyes on him as she wrapped her lips around the plasticware until the ice cream touched her taste buds. "Mmm."

"You like?" Graham asked.

"So good. Definitely my preference of the two."

Without hesitation, Graham swapped their cups. The act seemed so innocent yet stuck out profoundly for her. She didn't have to ask; he just did it, because that was how good of a man he was.

"We can share," she told him and pushed her cup to the middle of the table. She was all set to start eating, when Graham held his spoon out again. This time, both flavors sat there. "Seriously?" She leaned forward and took the offering. She smiled and covered her mouth. "You know what would be even better?"

"Chocolate," he said.

She pointed her spoon at him and nodded. "Yes. You know me so well."

Graham didn't reply, but he winked. And sometimes a wink meant more than anything.

TWENTY-FOUR

After they stopped for ice cream, Graham and Rennie strolled the streets, going into boutiques, where Graham became the catchall for their bags while Rennie shopped. They laughed at the whimsical names for the coffee shops and delis, such as the Bait Shop, which promised the best fish and chips for miles. Considering the town they were in was only one square mile, Graham and Rennie found the claim humorous. Graham told Rennie everything he knew about Friday Harbor and San Juan Island, which mostly boiled down to "When we come back this summer." He really wanted to take her to see the lavender fields. To him, they rivaled Skagit Valley's tulip festival.

By the time they arrived back on the boat, they were both exhausted. Rennie took her books down to her room and hollered over her shoulder that she was going to take a nap. The idea of a nap sounded like a good idea to Graham. He waited for her door to shut before he decided what to do, but she left it open—his thoughts started to run rampant. He was back to playing the what-if game.

All throughout the day, they'd flirted with each other, and it felt good. For the first time in forever, Graham felt a deeper connection with her. They were a cohesive unit, always aware of where the other person was, thoughtful, and flirtatious, and she made him feel desirable by the way she would lean into him, stroke his arm, and always look at him with parted lips, which was a tell for her. Rennie didn't have to be a casual hookup; they could build a strong relationship. Of course, she had said she wanted financial independence and didn't want children—but if he was being honest with himself, having children was an idea his mother planted and not one he had ever really considered. Otherwise, he could be the right man for Rennie. He loved the idea of her working in the bar with him, and he could easily return the favor if she needed the work.

Work.

For the past few days he had forgotten about the possibility of someone suing him. He had a sudden urge to know more and made his way down the small flight of stairs and into Rennie's room. He knocked once, even though the door was open, and found her lying on her side, flipping through a book.

"Hey," she said as he entered. Graham sat on the bed and mirrored her position.

"Can we talk work for a minute? I know you're on vacation, but I'm curious about a couple of things."

"Of course." Rennie closed the book, and when Graham saw the cover, he smiled. It was the book he had shown her, which featured his bar. The fact that she chose to read his book sent his heart soaring. "What's going on?"

"This case against me. How will I know when they're suing me?"

"My criminal law is rusty, which is why I'm going to ask my colleague Jefferson to help me again. But from what I remember, the other side needs evidence. You can't just go to a lawyer and say, 'I want to sue someone' without having facts and evidence to back up your claim. I've seen the notes, and unless Donna is hiding information, that's all there is so far—just her notes on what the client has told her."

"How do I defend myself?"

"You'll answer the claim in court, but before that happens, Jefferson, myself, and my private detective will know everything. When we face the judge, and they present their case, we'll prove them otherwise."

"Not gonna lie, Ren. I'm scared."

She nodded and ran her fingers through his hair. "I know you are. Part of me thinks I should've waited to tell you, but I wanted you to be prepared."

"I mean, I'm glad you did, but also I can't believe you have a private detective."

She laughed. "Yes. I use him a lot with my divorce cases."

"Why?"

"Because spouses lie. They hide things that they shouldn't."

"You must see a lot of ugly in your world."

Rennie shrugged. "I do."

"Maybe this is why you're so nonchalant about Theo?"

Rennie scooted a bit closer and placed her hand under her head and left her other one in between her and Graham. "I wouldn't say I'm nonchalant about Theo, Graham. What you witnessed—that was me losing it because of what he did. However, when I think about him and why I'm not more upset, it's because I fell out of love with him months ago and didn't realize it. I'm hurt because he lied to me, and I don't like liars. I'm angry because of the situation he put me in. But I'm not sad, because there is someone out there for me."

Is that someone me? They had missed their chance years ago, and while there could be another opportunity now, he wouldn't feel comfortable starting a relationship with her when her breakup was still so fresh.

"You'll find the right guy, Ren. I'm sure of it."

"I know I will, Graham Cracker." Rennie closed her eyes and drifted off to sleep. Graham studied her until his own lids closed, and sleep took over.

When Graham woke, Rennie lay sprawled out on her stomach, with her hair fanned out. He had never spent any time looking at a woman's hair and wondered what color Rennie classified her hair as. Growing up, she was blonde or dirty blonde, as he remembered her saying. Now, she had a variety of colors mixed in with her natural color. He saw some brown, a hint of red, and some shade between brown and blonde, which he was sure had some fancy name for it.

Graham felt around for his phone and found it down by his knee. They had been asleep for a couple of hours. It was clear after last night that Rennie needed it. Had Graham's presence offered her some sort of peace? He liked to think it had.

He slowly rose and snuck out of the bedroom. Later, in the evening, they would head out to the bar and have a good time. Rennie had been right earlier when she said if they were in Cape Harbor, he would've called her and asked her to keep him company at the Whale Spout. That was how well she knew him.

Graham wanted to try and make New Year's Eve special for Rennie. Regardless of their situation, she was still his best girl, and she deserved to have a special night. He left the boat, locking the door as he slid it shut, and jogged up the dock toward the store. He had an idea in mind but was also aware he was very late in the game to try and implement it. When he walked into the small market, there were a few other patrons in there. Thankfully and much to his surprise, he found exactly what he wanted, made his purchase, and headed back to the boat.

The boat showed no signs of life, which was a great relief to Graham. His goal was to pull this surprise off before Rennie woke. He unlocked and opened the door slowly, trying to remain as quiet as possible, which, given where they were located, was a tricky task. Birds squawked overhead, eager and demanding morsels of food.

He worked quickly and quietly in the galley. Graham opened the presliced meats and cheeses, filled the sink with the bag of ice for the bottle of champagne, and pulled crackers from their plastic sleeves.

After preparing a plateful of snacks, he set it on the table. He stepped back and admired his work. The presentation wasn't great, but it was something they could share while they got ready for the evening.

Now, to wake her up.

Graham had so many thoughts of how to do this. He could go down and tickle her feet. She hated it, but it made her laugh, and he loved hearing that sound come out of her. He could yell her name, but that seemed cold and impersonal. He could crawl back into bed with her, gently move her hair away from her face . . . and he would want to kiss her. The yearning to press his lips to hers started in the bookstore and increased tenfold by the time they sat down for ice cream. There had been numerous times throughout the day when he could've tilted her chin toward him and leaned down to kiss her. Any other time, and not days after her breakup, he might have done it.

Maybe it was time he started listening to her.

He pulled his phone out, brought it to life, and pressed the icon for his music app. He opted for some soft jazz and set his phone down on the table. Graham inhaled deeply and took the steps down to the bedrooms. He paused before he came to Rennie's open door and gave himself a pep talk.

She's hinted. Now it's your turn.

He stepped in and found her sitting up. She would never know how much this upset him, how his heart fell from his chest, and how he wanted to weep because he had finally found the courage to find out if he had read her correctly.

Graham smiled and motioned toward the galley. "While you were sleeping, I stepped out and picked up some light snacks. I figured we'd eat at the bar or whatever."

Rennie slid off the bed and came toward Graham. Her messy hair was now in a ponytail, which tempted Graham to tug on it. "I'm excited to go out."

He laughed. "I know you are," he said as he shook his head. "I have a feeling tonight is going to be crazy."

"Duh, crazy fun."

Her enthusiasm made him feel young and carefree. At least for the night, they'd be the Graham and Rennie of old. He followed her up the stairs and went to the champagne bottle. "Bowie doesn't have much for flutes or anything, so plastic cup or tumbler?"

"How about we save the champagne for later? We can toast the new year or something when we come back from the bar."

Graham had no qualms with her suggestion and set the bottle back into the makeshift bucket of ice. He sat down across from Rennie and helped himself to the food. "You know, I only eat this type of food on holidays, and it only seems to be in the winter. I'm sure Brooklyn will have a plate of these types of snacks for their Super Bowl party." His attempt at small talk seemed trivial and awkward.

You've known this woman half your life; stop being weird.

"Yes, but hers will be cut into little footballs," Rennie pointed out. "I don't even know what she uses to make her platters look so . . . festive?"

"Beats me," Graham added. "I'm the guy you call for a keg. Beer, I can do. Maybe a few bottles of alcohol, chicken wings, or something off the menu."

"I haven't had beer and wings in a long time."

"Six months is a long time to you?" he asked. When she made her grand reentrance to Cape Harbor and came into the Whale Spout, the group of them sat around and drank beer and ate everything off the menu, wings included.

"Now that you've said it, no. But it seems like a lifetime ago. Coming back to town, I fell into such an easy routine. Once we all caught up, it was like Brooklyn never left, and I had always been around."

She opened the door, and he was going to use this opportunity to his advantage.

"Why did you stop visiting? You knew I was there, didn't you?" Graham had always wondered why Rennie never came around.

"Mostly out of respect for Brooklyn. She wanted to put everything behind her and didn't want people asking where she was."

"Even with Brystol visiting all the time?"

Rennie shrugged and picked at the piece of cheese she had on her plate. "The whole situation with Carly was weird. Their dynamic was odd. Brooklyn and Carly rarely talked, and if they did, it was about Brystol and when she was coming to visit. But then, Brooklyn would get a check from Carly for thousands to put toward her business or to pay for Brystol's needs."

"Maybe Carly paid Austin's child support or something."

"The interest from Austin's trust fund went to Brooklyn for support."

"And now, the kid owns everything."

"Even part of Chamberwoods," Rennie pointed out. "What do you think Grady is going to do when he gets out of rehab?"

"I don't know," Graham said, shaking his head back and forth slowly. "I can't offer him a job, obviously. He has one skill, and that's fishing, but I fear he'll have some PTSD from the accident that might prevent him from going out on a boat. I want to help him, though. I don't want him to fall back into the pattern he was in."

"Maybe Bowie has some work for him?"

His eyes went to hers. "That's a great idea. I'll ask Bowie when I get back and bring it up to Grady when I see him next week."

"How is therapy, if you don't mind me asking?"

"Great, I think. We've talked about life, the damage his drinking has done, and skirted around the accident. My only complaint is the drive. It's long and tedious, but whatever gets Grady the help he needs. And my dad is coming around. It's a slow and steady process with him."

"He's a proud man," Rennie pointed out.

"That he is." Graham picked up a cracker and added a slice of salami and a piece of cheese to it before sticking it in his mouth. He looked out the windows and saw ships coming into port and motioned toward the water for Rennie to look.

"Maybe this is a happening place for New Year's."

Graham laughed. "I'm sure it is, Ren. I'm going to go shower."

He got up from the table and went to his room. The shower on the boat was about the same, if not a little worse, than the one on his houseboat. However, he loved that the bathroom was in his bedroom, and he wouldn't subject any of the neighboring boats to anything lewd. He washed quickly, something he was very used to. He chose not to shave, leaving what little growth he had on his face to protect against the wind. Graham used his hand to clear away the condensation from the mirror and examined himself. He combed the scruff on his face down and applied his cologne and turned slightly to the right and then left and smiled. He was going to the bar with Rennie. Tonight was going to be like old times. According to Rennie, it was going to be crazy fun. It had been a long time since he had let loose, and even if he didn't show it, he was excited.

When he stepped into his room, he walked around freely without a towel, and some weird part of him wanted to rejoice and dance around at his ability to be naked. He could still recall the mortified look on Shari's face when she saw him in his birthday suit.

Graham dressed in a pair of jeans and a dark-blue button-down, thankful for the wrinkle-free fabric; otherwise, he would have had to wear one of his T-shirts, which weren't in the best shape. He put on some socks and shoes and then stood in front of the mirror. He looked presentable, and it was the best she was going to get.

When he made his way to the helm, Rennie was there waiting. "Wow, you look better than I do," she said, and he smiled at the compliment, even if it wasn't true. Rennie had on a red dress that stopped at her knees, black heels, and a pearl necklace with matching earrings.

She'd pulled her hair to the side and exposed most of her neck. She looked good enough to eat and was far out of his league.

Gorgeous. "I'm going to have to fight all the men that come toward you tonight."

"Is that your way of giving me a compliment?"

Graham chuckled. "Yeah, I guess I'm not particularly good at relaying my feelings. You're unbelievably beautiful, Ren." He held his arm out, signaling for her to walk out in front of him. As she stepped out, a wave rocked the boat a bit too much, and she wobbled. Graham caught her before she toppled over. "I'm not going to let anything happen to you," he whispered. They made eye contact, and each sucked in their breath. Her cheeks flushed, and he was sure his did as well. She peered at him intently. Was she waiting for him to make the first move? His gaze traveled over her face, and he searched her eyes for the okay to kiss her. His fingers traced along her cheek, downward to her chin. Her lips parted, and his head tilted.

"Happy New Year," someone yelled. They pulled apart and saw another couple on the dock, waving. Graham wasn't sure if he wanted to scream at them for interrupting a moment between him and Rennie or go thank them, because as much as he wanted to kiss her, he still had reservations.

"Same to you," Rennie hollered back. "Shall we go?" she asked Graham as she reached for his hand and tugged him along. He snapped out of the daze he found himself in and squeezed her hand to let her know he was right there with her.

The bar wasn't any farther than the restaurant they had eaten at the night before. He held the door for her, and as soon as they walked in, he realized how overdressed they were. Most of the patrons were in jeans and T-shirts, a few even in sweatshirts. They found a high-top near the back by the pool table, and she asked the couple playing if anyone had the next game. When the woman said no, Rennie looked at Graham, who understood what she wanted and put money down to signal they would play them. Graham knew he and Rennie would have no problem hustling the table away from them. It was almost comical.

Graham and Rennie ordered a pitcher of margaritas, a couple glasses of water, and a plate of nachos to share. Graham made sure Rennie didn't have any issues getting up onto the tall chair, and as he expected, she boosted herself up there like a pro. He had no idea how she managed to move in her heels, but she made walking in them look natural.

The waitress brought their pitcher of margaritas along with two filled glasses, which, judging by the smile on Rennie's face, made her happy.

"What do you think? Do we have this table?" Her eyebrows went up and down, making Graham laugh.

His *Rennie* was back.

Graham glanced at the table and nodded slightly. "I think you can actually take both of them yourself."

She chuckled. "Should we let them play for a bit or just send the message early?"

Rennie hustled. It was what made her stand out over everyone else. However, if they showed their cards too soon, the night could be boring. On the other side of the coin, if the bar filled, they could have to wait awhile to play again.

"Your wheels are spinning."

"I'm thinking."

"Me too. I say we lose the first, but barely. Send a message we're a formidable foe." Graham reached across the table and offered a fist bump to his pool partner.

Their plate of fully loaded nachos arrived at the same time the other couple told them their game was over. The man informed Rennie and Graham he would break. The way he spoke rubbed Graham the wrong way. He also didn't care for the way the guy stared at Rennie.

Graham stood and introduced himself to the guy, who said his name was Jon. They shook hands, and Graham ran his hand along the felt of the pool table, feeling for any bumps and gathering any loose pillings.

"You a pro or something?" Jon asked.

"Nah, just like a clean table." Graham was far from a pro, but he could play a mean game of pool. He motioned for Rennie, who downed her margarita and came over to him. "Pick your cue. You should go first."

"Wife know how to play?"

Graham smirked. "She's all right. Sometimes I have to help her."

Rennie started coughing, and Graham knew it was her response to his joke. She was better than Graham, but Jon and his lady friend did not need to know that quite yet.

True to his word, Jon broke and couldn't knock any balls down. Graham and Rennie walked around the table, and he pretended to show her shots as they spoke to each other in hushed tones. Graham nodded a lot; rested his hand on his chin, as if he was thinking; and pointed a few times until Rennie decided where she would strike first. Their goal: knock in one, maybe two "lucky" shots before missing one, and let the other couple think they had the upper hand.

By the end of the game, more people had gathered. A couple teams had put their quarters down, calling for next game. As it was, Graham and Rennie would sit out two games, and then they'd start running the table on people.

Their plan went off without a hitch, and as Graham lined up the cue to hit the eight ball, he purposely tapped the balls together lightly, leaving the black ball on the edge of the pocket.

Jon rubbed his hands together before he reached for his cue. He added chalk to the end, which Graham thought was overkill. He had set the guy up nicely. All he had to do was tap it in. It almost pained Graham to watch, but he stood next to Rennie and focused on the table.

He found himself holding his breath, wishing the eight ball wouldn't drop. But when it did, Jon and the woman he was with, who never introduced herself, jumped up and down, hooting and hollering. Being gracious losers, Rennie and Graham went to their high-top, continued eating their nachos, and ordered another pitcher of margaritas and more food.

"Probably not how you thought you'd spend your New Year's Eve, huh?" Graham asked Rennie.

She reached across the table and linked her fingers with his. "This is exactly where I want to be, Graham."

With her was where he wanted to be as well. The only difference between his and Rennie's sentiments was how he'd felt when Jon referred to Rennie as Graham's wife. He wished he had asked her a long time ago to marry him.

TWENTY-FIVE

Rennie was having fun. If someone had told her she would be spending her New Year's Eve in a bar in some small island town off the coast of Washington, and not in the mountains of Canada, she would have laughed and walked away. None of her colleagues would appreciate a place like this. Theo would turn up his nose and ask her if she were feeling all right. She was magnificent, happy, and at peace. The person she was when Brooklyn, Bowie, and Graham were around was who she wanted to be. Not stuffy, worried about work, stressed over whether an invite to the social gathering of the year was going to arrive, or always wondering if the man she was with would actually show up at her place as planned. She knew the answer—no, he wouldn't, because he was married.

She sat on the stool, sipped her margarita, and watched Graham play darts with a few of the other guys in the bar, and every so often she would walk over to him and place her hand on his back or his waist and stake her claim. And each time she did, Graham would put his arm around her and kiss her forehead. There were nine or so people gathered in their area, and a few of the women were near Rennie. Everyone was chatting; they were friendly, asking her questions about where she and her husband were from and why they chose Friday Harbor to celebrate

New Year's. Answers fell from her tongue easily—some lies, but mostly truths. She never corrected any of them when they referred to Graham as her husband, and when asked what she did for work, she told them she was in private practice and that they owned a bar in Cape Harbor, and Rennie invited them to come and visit the next time they were in town.

When Graham would return to the table for a refresher, Rennie would flirt heavily, and Graham would reciprocate. Their chemistry was automatic, and it made the other women swoon when he winked at Rennie. He checked in often and leaned down to whisper in her ear each time to ask if she was enjoying herself. She was having a blast, and it was the truth. She couldn't think of any other place she'd rather be.

When it was Rennie and Graham's turn at the pool table, she slowly rose from her seat. Graham must've noticed her wobble and was by her side instantly to help her. "Are you okay to play?"

"It's these damn shoes." She slipped them off and set them on her chair. Renee Wallace would've balked at walking around a bar barefoot, and honestly, Rennie should've as well. But there was no way she was going to let Graham down. They'd lost their first game, and there was no way they'd lose their second.

They were facing two guys this time. Friends from college, they had said, which brought back a slew of memories for Rennie and Graham. They often ran the tables in bars to earn money while in California; they'd had hundreds to choose from and would rarely go back to the same bar more than twice. People always caught on quickly to what they were doing and wouldn't play them, so there was no use in returning.

One of the frat guys broke and knocked down two solids and two stripes. The teams each quietly talked strategy. Graham wanted the frat boys to take the solids because he saw better angles on the stripes, and Rennie agreed.

"We're going solids," the kid yelled out. Graham squeezed Rennie's hand in elation. She was going to shoot first, and if all went well, they'd finish with Graham sinking the eight ball. The first guy missed, and Rennie stepped up to the table. Somewhere behind her, someone catcalled. She tossed her hand into the air and flipped off whoever thought being rude was okay.

Rennie bent slightly to check the angles before she set her stick down on her hand. She moved the cue back and forth, slow and steady, until she was confident in her decision-making. The two balls touched, and her striped ball headed straight for the pocket. One down. She moved to the next and then the next, and so on. Each time Graham was by her side, working through moves with her. Their last shot was difficult, as they had suspected, and she did her best to block the other team.

The college guys were straight-up players. They weren't hustlers like Graham and Rennie, and when they took their shot, they slammed the cue ball into the pile to break it up. These men had no strategy whatsoever. It was Graham's turn, and Rennie coached him. They were a team. They were determined to win. He took his shot, sinking their last playable ball, leaving only the eight. He wouldn't fail; unlike their first game, they wanted to win and run the table. With no hesitation in his stroke, he sank the black ball and turned in time to catch Rennie when she jumped into his arms. She went to kiss him, almost as if doing so should be a natural reaction for them, but he dodged her lips, and she was only able to brush his cheek.

Graham stepped away and went to the end of the pool table. He pulled out the rack and started placing the balls in order, and Rennie went to the other end to prepare to break. She sized up their opponents. Another couple, which didn't matter, because Rennie and Graham were going to take care of them easily. They did, along with the couple after them, the college boys again, and so on. For the rest of the night, the friends visiting from Cape Harbor ran the pool table at the bar in Friday Harbor.

They had either lost count of how many pitchers they'd drunk or the empty ones on their table weren't theirs, and at some point during the evening, they stopped ordering food. Rennie and Graham were having fun. They were laughing, flirting, and being very handsy with each other—and probably a little inappropriate. Neither of them seemed to care, and they really didn't care what others around them thought.

After they won their last game, Graham asked if Rennie was ready to go. It was eleven thirty, the bar had become packed, and honestly, she wanted to go back to the boat. They bid farewell to their new friends and made their way to the exit. When they finally stepped outside, Graham scooped her up into his arms and carried her toward the marina.

"I can walk."

"Why walk when I can carry you?" Rennie wrapped her arms around his shoulders and nestled her head in the crook of his neck. She imagined what life would be like with Graham if they were ever to give in and try being more than friends. They could do the long-distance-relationship thing flawlessly. She'd rather be in Cape Harbor most of the time anyway, and she figured she could work Fridays and Mondays from his home and be in the office three days a week unless she had a court case. No one would be surprised if they started dating either. Their relationship would be natural and long overdue.

Graham carried her onto the boat and set her down when he had to unlock the sliding door. "I have something I want to show you. Wait here." He disappeared down the steps, and when he came back, he handed her a pair of socks and told her to put them on. He also had a blanket draped over his arm. Graham grabbed two cups and the bottle of champagne from the now-melted ice in the sink. "Follow me."

She did, and he led them out to the bow of the boat. The same spot where she had finally let all her emotions out. "What are we doing out here?"

"Earlier, I saw all these boats docking, and I thought it was a bit strange until I heard one of the guys at the bar talking. Out there in the darkness is a barge, and at midnight they're letting off fireworks. I thought this would be a better way of ringing in the New Year, instead of counting down with a bunch of people we don't know."

Her smile was slow to appear, but that was because she was finding it hard not to jump into his arms. She loved fireworks, and he had remembered. "This is perfect."

Graham handed her the cups to hold while he worked the cork off the champagne bottle. Rennie stood back, out of what could be the path of a flying cork.

"I probably should've thought this through a bit more. I don't want the cork to go into the water."

Rennie looked around and saw the blanket Graham had brought out. Worst-case scenario, she would wash it when they arrived back at Cape Harbor. She folded it twice and then held it in front of Graham. "I'll catch it." The idea wasn't perfect, but it would work. Besides, she wanted to spend the night with Graham, and if there was one less blanket on the boat, maybe they'd share a bed.

The cork flew into the blanket, but so did some of the champagne. Neither of them seemed to care. Rennie set everything down and picked up their cups. She held them while Graham poured.

He set the bottle down and took his cup from her. "Happy New Year, Rennie."

"Happy New Year, Graham Cracker."

The loud boom of the first firework startled Rennie. She stood in front of Graham and leaned against his chest. They oohed and aahed, right along with the other people watching from their boats. At some point, Graham had finished his champagne and wrapped his arms around her. She enjoyed the height difference between them. The big-fish-to-little-fish comparison she used to make back in the day.

When the finale lit up the night sky, her heart raced. Rennie was exactly where she wanted to be and had no regrets about what she was about to do. She turned in Graham's arms and gazed into his eyes. She rose onto her tippy-toes to kiss Graham, finally succeeding in pressing her lips to his. She felt his fingers tug lightly at her chin, and she opened for him. It had been years since they kissed, yet it felt like only yester-day they had shared an embrace. Their kiss was anything but chaste as he slid his tongue into her mouth, and his arm tightened around her body. Every part of her zinged with excitement and anticipation. Rennie wanted him. She wanted them together, as they had been in the past. He was familiar. He was home to her.

All around them people celebrated. They cheered loudly and yelled well-wishes from boat to boat, and someone had started another round of fireworks. None of that mattered. Rennie focused solely on Graham.

"Do you want to go to bed?" he asked her.

She nodded and thought about adding something snarky to his sentence but held back. Rennie needed Graham to know she was seri-ous. About him and about them. They left the bottle of champagne, their glasses, and the blanket outside and walked together back into the cabin. Neither of them bothered to close the blinds, but Graham did lock the door. Rennie made her way downstairs to her room and waited for Graham.

Nerves like she hadn't experienced in ages came rushing forward. Her heart pounded wildly, her palms sweat, and her knees wobbled. She felt like she was a teenager all over again. Rennie saw Graham's shadow before he appeared in the doorway, illuminated by the outside lights casting a glow into the room. She stood there with her red dress on and socks on her feet. She laughed at herself.

Graham came into the room and shut the door behind him. He faced her and slowly pushed each button of his shirt through its hole. Inch by inch, the shirt fell away, exposing his toned chest and snippets of his tattoo.

Her mouth watered in anticipation of what was to come. As he approached her, his hand pulled at his belt. "Do you want this, Rennie?" he asked. "Because if we do this, I don't want to stop. Not ever."

Rennie stepped forward and placed her hands on his chest. His flesh was on fire, and she could only imagine it was because he felt the same way. She pushed her hands over his shoulders, taking his shirt with her as her hands trailed down his arms. She worked the buttons at his wrist, and finally the shirt fell to the floor.

She stood in front of him, her fingers caressing his face. "I've wanted this since I walked into the Whale Spout over the summer. I should've never let Brooklyn dictate my life in this way, and I'm sorry."

"For what?"

"For giving up on us all those years ago. As soon as I moved back to Seattle, I should've come to see you. We've missed so much time." Rennie was on the cusp of telling him she loved him, but now was not the time. She had a lot to prove to him. She knew he had reservations about her ex.

Graham closed the distance between them and crushed his lips to hers. His hands bunched her dress into his fist. She lifted her arms, and he pulled her dress away from her body. With deft fingers, he removed her bra next.

Rennie stepped back and stood in front of Graham with only her panties and those ridiculous socks on. She brought each foot up and took each sock off and stepped out of her underwear.

"I liked those," he quipped. Graham swallowed hard but made no move to take off his jeans.

Fear and doubt coursed through her. "Do you not want me?"

"I do. I'm pinching myself to make sure this is all real."

"It's very real, Graham."

With much haste, he freed himself from the rest of his clothes and moved lightning fast toward Rennie. She squealed when he picked her up. His lips were upon hers again, but this time there was an urgency, a need. Graham set her down on the bed. He followed and blazed a trail of kisses down her throat and neck and to her chest.

His hands explored the soft lines of her back, her waist, and her hips while his mouth moved over her heated flesh. It had been years since she'd been aroused this way, needy of a man's attention. One simple touch, and she was ready for him. Her body responded to Graham. It was like her body hadn't forgotten what they used to share and rejoiced when their flesh met.

She matched his necessity with her own lusty, unsated needs. Her hands roamed over the planes of his stomach, his back, and to his rear, where she gripped him hard, pushing him to where she desired him the most.

Graham lowered his body over hers and peered into her eyes. He didn't need words to tell her what he thought. She already knew, and she wanted the same from him.

Forever.

She welcomed him into her body, arching off the bed and into his embrace. They made love, different from what they had done in the past, and it meant something to them, a turning point in their lives. There was no turning back now. She could feel it. They were different.

They were a tangled mess when the sun rose, both lying on their sides, looking at each other. Her body happily ached, and her lips were raw from being kissed all night. They barely spoke throughout the night, and when they did, it was words of pleasure, voiced needs, and wants. Rennie's fingers brushed through Graham's hair while his inched along her side, tickling her skin. They had made love a couple of times and only left his bedroom to get sustenance, neither willing to be away from the other for very long.

Now, the sun had risen, and the water was a bit choppier than it had been. The ferry was active, transporting people from the island to the mainland for their last day of freedom before returning to the workforce. She would have to go back to Seattle—Graham, back to the bar. Their days of being hidden had come to an end.

TWENTY-SIX

Graham returned from vacation with more pep in his step and a plastered smile on his face, and he walked along to whatever song he played in his head. He didn't even care that he had a list of things to contend with from Krista and that it would take him days to go over the inventory and get everything restocked, because he was happy.

When they returned from Friday Harbor in the afternoon of New Year's Day, Graham expected everything to go back to the way things were or revert to their long-ago status of friends with benefits. Much to his surprise, when Graham went to kiss Rennie, she kissed him back, and they made love again in his room before both fell under a heavy sleep.

When they woke, Rennie took Graham up on his offer and borrowed his phone. She went out to the patio to call Brooklyn, and when they were done talking, Rennie came in and told Graham that Bowie needed to speak with him.

Graham and Bowie laughed at how ridiculous the women were being. Secretly, Graham loved it. He was the reason for the smile on Rennie's face. After he hung up with Bowie, he called his parents. His mother was getting ready to meet her friends for a game of bridge, and his father was down at the Loyal Order of the Sasquatch with his friends. Graham hesitated for a moment before asking about Grady.

"How's Grady, Mom?"

"Oh, I think he's doing wonderfully well. He calls when he's allowed, and the other night we spoke while I watched one of my game shows. Grady even participated," she told him. Relief washed over Graham.

After they had both made their calls, they snuggled on Graham's small couch, watched television, and made love in the shower. A place Graham thought would never be possible, and he found it to be the most intense moment of his life. They spent the entire day wrapped up in each other. When the sun rose, reminding them of the outside world, he drove her over to Brooklyn's to get her car. It was there they said their goodbyes. She went inside, and he went off to work.

He thumbed through the notes Krista had left him. One employee didn't show up to work, a couple people came in looking for Grady, there was a list of liquors they were out of or low on and kegs to order, and Don and Mark had left a list of foods needed for the kitchen.

Graham held on to his notes and went into the bar. He turned on all the lights, flipped the open sign to on, and unlocked the door. It was early, and the likelihood that anyone would actually come in was slim. He got to work, first by placing the orders he needed. He would do inventory later and place another order if needed. It would be a matter of weeks before business started picking up again to the point where they were slammed at night and had a nice rush during lunch. Once the gloom of winter passed, the tourists would be out in full force.

The door opened as Graham walked back into the bar with a fresh stack of cleaning cloths. The old-timers were coming in, gabbing about who knew what. Graham stepped behind the bar and retrieved three pint glasses. He pulled the tap for Rainer. It was their favorite, and they were the only reason Graham kept it on tap. It used to be brewed in Seattle until the company sold and ended up in the hands of Pabst Brewing. Graham was surprised they kept the beer in manufacturing. He actually appreciated it because it kept the old men in town very happy.

"Morning, guys."

They gruffly said hello and thanked him for their beer. He thought he was in the clear until R. J. Keel spoke up. R. J. was born and bred in Cape Harbor, a fifth-generation fisherman whose son and grandson now ran the Keel Fishing Company. "Heard you took the Holmes's boat for a joyride."

"Wasn't actually joyriding. It's a bit chilly out there."

Ned Keane added his opinion. "Heard he had a lady friend with him."

The three men laughed. "Hopefully, he brought her back," R. J. snickered.

"Lady in the water," Isaac Davis pretended to yell.

"Ha ha, very funny. A friend and I went to San Juan for a couple of days, and yes, I brought her back."

"Ah, we're just giving you shit, Graham." Ned batted his hand through the air. "How's your brother?"

Graham paused. His usual response would be something sarcastic, but since Grady had been in rehab, things had a positive outlook. "He's thriving," he told the men. Word spread fast about Grady going into rehab. Most people mumbled it was about time, which they weren't wrong to say. Graham was thankful his brother was safe, and therapy seemed to work for Grady.

Graham's pile of notes started to dwindle as the day went on. Each time the phone rang, he tried to pick it up by the second ring, hoping each caller would be Rennie with a new cell phone number or notification that she had a new phone. He was hoping for the former, even though it would be a pain for her to change her number—he didn't want Theo to contact her. One could call it jealousy or a streak of possessiveness, but Graham never wanted to hear the name Theo again, especially where Rennie was concerned.

By late afternoon, the crowd started to pick up. People were coming in to watch the games: college football in the front, and the NBA toward the back. Bowie's crew was in, playing their regular dart game, and there were enough food orders to keep Mark busy in the kitchen. The day was going better than Graham had anticipated, especially when Bowie, Brooklyn, and Brystol walked in.

Graham nodded to them, and after they found a seat, Brystol came to Graham. "Want my help?"

He paused and thought about it for a second and nodded. "Grab your apron," he instructed her. Brystol ran off, and Graham went over to her parents' table.

"It's okay if she works for a bit?" he asked them.

"I'm fine with it. She's still on vacation from school," Brooklyn said. "Wanna talk about these past couple of days?" She waggled her eyebrows at Graham, whose cheeks heated up with embarrassment.

"Can't say I do." But he did. He wanted to know what Rennie had said to Brooklyn. He would have loved to pull out a chair and listen to her tell him everything, but he would never betray Rennie's trust in Brooklyn, no matter how desperate he was.

"Probably for the best, man." Bowie chuckled. "Those two were squealing like schoolgirls. I think one of my eardrums blew." He put his finger in his ear and started to wiggle it back and forth. Brooklyn pushed his shoulder and laughed.

"All I'm going to say, Graham, is you've made her happy."

A feeling of satisfaction washed over him. He took their order with a shit-eating grin on his face and excused himself to go help two others who had sat down at the bar. As soon as Brystol came out from the back, he felt a bit relieved. He could handle the drinks easily, especially with her taking care of all the food orders. They had a good little system between them whenever she worked.

Graham finished helping the people at the bar and took Brooklyn's and Bowie's drinks over to them. He sat down again and sighed. He tried to think of a way to bring Rennie up without looking desperate for information but couldn't.

"What did she tell you about Theo?"

"That dude was beside himself when he showed up," Bowie said. "Pounding on my damn door like I owed him something. Pissed me off." He leaned back, and Brooklyn rested her hand on his thigh. "The guy was yelling into my house, calling for Rennie, except he calls her Renee, which I've never understood, and I'm like, 'She isn't here. Haven't seen her since she left with you,' and then he says she left Canada, that he can't find her, and all I can think is this guy did something to Rennie. Then I started to get really pissed."

"And then I come downstairs and ask what's going on, and he tries to come into the house! But Bowie isn't having that and pushes him back outside," Brooklyn told Graham. "I ask him again, and he tells me he and Rennie got into a fight and that she left. He expected to find her back in Cape Harbor. I was confused because if she were in town, why wouldn't she be at our house, right?"

Graham nodded.

"So maybe you want to fill us in, because the only thing she said to me was that you and she had an amazing time together, and things were going to change."

Graham tried not to smile or think about what her words could've meant. "Did either of them tell you what went down?"

Bowie and Brooklyn shook their heads. "Rennie said you knew, that she'd tell me but had to get back to Seattle for work."

"She texted me and asked me to come and pick her up at the resort. I did. She didn't say a word to me until we were in the middle of the ocean, and then she really let it all out."

"Let what out?" Brooklyn leaned forward and stared intently at Graham.

Graham looked around the bar to make sure everything was okay. "Theo's married." He paused and let the words sink in. "And not in the 'I'm separated and getting a divorce' sort of way."

"What the—" Bowie bit back whatever he was going to say because Brystol approached the table. She set down their order of cheese curds and made her way to the next table. Bowie leaned forward and whispered, "Are you fucking kidding me?"

Graham shook his head slowly. "Nope. There was a couple at the hotel who recognized Theo, and when they approached him, he referred to Rennie as hotel staff helping him to his room because he was drunk."

Brooklyn covered her mouth and gasped. "Oh my . . . Rennie didn't seem too upset when she was at the house this morning."

A smile spread across Graham's face. He hoped he was the reason she was no longer upset. Of course, he also knew how Rennie felt. "I think, regardless of his infidelity coming to light, they would've broken up sooner rather than later. She's been unhappy for some time and said a lot of things over the holiday that led me to believe, even if he was single, Theo wasn't the guy for her." Graham was, though. He was, without a doubt, the man for Rennie, and he was going to do whatever he had to in order to prove it to her.

"That son of a bitch. I was nice to him."

"You're nice to everyone, Bowie. You don't have a mean bone in your body," Graham pointed out.

"Still. He ate my food! Slept for free in our hotel! And this is the shit he does to our Rennie." Bowie threw his hands up in the air. Brooklyn tried to comfort him.

"Graham." Brystol's voice rang out from the bar area. She held the phone up in the air. He went to her, and she handed him the receiver. "Aunt Rennie is on the phone for you."

Another smile broke out. She had called.

"Hello," he said into the phone.

"Hey, I wanted to let you know I'm back at my apartment, and I have a new cell number."

"Decided to go with a new one, huh?"

"I think it was the best decision. Do you have a pen handy?" He did and told her to rattle off her number. He would put it in his phone once they hung up.

"Do you want me to give it to Brooklyn? She's here right now."

"Nah, I'll text it to her. Her number and my parents' are the only ones I had memorized. Although, I could probably download my contacts from a backup or something. If I had done that, though, I wouldn't have had an excuse to hear your voice," she said to him. "And Graham, I really wanted to hear your voice."

His heart soared and pounded loudly. "I know you just left, but when can I see you again?"

"I'll be up on Friday."

He knew his next question might not give him the answer he wanted, but he asked anyway. "Do you want to stay on the houseboat? If you already have plans with Brooklyn, I'd understand."

Rennie giggled. "I want to stay with you. I figure I can hang out with Brooklyn while you work. Whatever. I'm not picky."

"Oh, I'm totally picky. I want to spend as much time with you as possible."

"Me too," she said. "We do need to talk, though—and I don't want you to think it's something bad—but we need to make sure this is right for us, because we have a friendship on the line to consider and our friends. I don't want us to move hastily and regret our actions down the road."

Graham looked out over the bar. His eyes went to Bowie and Brooklyn, in love and happy after all these years apart. It was what he wanted, and he wanted it with Rennie. "We'll talk, and we'll make the best decision for us," he told her. "The bar is filling up. I'll text you, and don't feel like you can't text me back because you think I'm busy. I'll always have time for you, Ren." He wanted to end the call by telling her he was falling in love with her but wanted to give them more time to grow. Instead, he said goodbye and pulled his cell phone out of his pocket. He pressed the app for his contacts and went right to his favorites. She was there, the first on his list. He changed her number and sent her a message. Almost instantly, the message bubbles appeared, and when her words showed on his screen, he was grinning from ear to ear. **Thank you for the most amazing couple of days. I can't wait to see you on Friday!**

Graham smiled at the message. *Amazing* didn't even begin to cover how he felt about the minivacation and Rennie. What started out as an escape for her turned into a life-changing experience for him. They were finally going to give this couple thing a shot.

TWENTY-SEVEN

Luck was on Rennie's side when she pulled onto her street. There was a parking spot available not far from her front stoop. She parallel parked effortlessly, a skill she had mastered from living in the city for so many years; turned her car off; and grabbed her suitcase from the back seat. When she approached her front steps, she fully expected to find Theo there or a note, something he would've left behind to tell her he stopped by. Thankfully, there was nothing. She unlocked her door and, as she did, made a mental note to call the locksmith tomorrow to have her locks changed. She didn't want Theo coming into her apartment, with or without her being there.

Rennie turned on the lights as she entered her place. She called out, "I'm home," even though she lived alone. It was something her father told her to always do when she entered her house.

"Crap," she said aloud. In her haste to throw her phone overboard, she'd forgotten about her parents. She rushed down the hall to her room, pulled her laptop from her bag, and booted it up. While she waited, she started to unpack. As soon as the zipper exposed the contents of her bag, she picked up Graham's sweatshirt and held it to her nose. She missed him already and had a feeling her week was going to drag on until she could see him again. She unpacked and sent an email to her parents asking about their trip and telling them what she did over New Year's.

She also told them she broke things off with Theo, but not why, and how she planned to spend more time in Cape Harbor, figuring it was enough of a hint that her mother would get the underlying message, and closed her email with her new number. She thought about calling her parents but was a horrible daughter and couldn't remember where in the world they were at the moment and wasn't sure her mom would respond to an unknown number, regardless of what Rennie typed out.

After her shower, she sent a message to Graham's phone. I'm home and going to bed. You can text though because I'll be reading for a bit.

Graham texted her right back. I'm jealous of your bed and book.

Don't be. Inanimate objects have nothing on you.

Graham didn't respond right away, which she was okay with. He had a bar to run, and she wanted him to focus on his job and not her. Their time would come when she was in Cape Harbor over the weekend.

When she finally turned her light off, she stared at the darkened ceiling. She couldn't fall asleep and wasn't keen on taking a sleep aid, other than drinking a cup of tea. At some point in the middle of the night, she got up and searched for the sweatshirt she had taken from Graham. She had made him put it back on when they were at his house because she wanted it to smell like him again. The scent of Old Spice welcomed her as soon as she laid her head on the shirt. She thought she would feel his presence, but all it did was make her miss him and miss the weekend they'd shared. She closed her eyes and imagined Graham lying next to her. Surely this would help her fall asleep.

Except her thoughts drifted to Theo, which didn't make sense to her. By all accounts, she *should* be heartbroken over Theo. She wasn't. She was relieved and felt as if she had dodged a bullet, and she was angry. Brooklyn told her the anger would turn to loss and hatred, and at any given moment, Rennie could break down and cry because she missed Theo. Rennie refused to believe her. There was no way a strong, independent woman like herself would cry over the loss of someone who lied and cheated. But she had, and Graham had been there to hold her.

Questions lingered in the back of her mind as to why Theo would do something so deplorable to his wife and her. To tell someone you loved them, to buy them gifts, to take them on work trips, only to live a lie with them made no sense to her. What did Theo expect to happen? Was he going to break up with Rennie? His wife? Was he ever going to come clean to either of them or just lead a double life? What would he have done if Rennie had agreed to move to Spokane? To get those answers, she'd have to communicate with him, and she had no desire to do so, but in order to move on and close this chapter in her life, she would need closure.

And then there was Graham. Her Graham Cracker. The only boy turned man who ever treated her as his equal. To know Graham was to love him. But she never told him how she truly felt, and he had chosen another. That was on her and was something she planned to rectify in the coming months. Sure, in college, she didn't want to be in a committed relationship but thought they would end up together. When he told her he started dating someone, she expected it to last a week—a month at best. That was how long girls stayed around, because they all thought Rennie was a threat to their relationship. When Monica didn't leave, Rennie knew her chance with Graham had gone by the wayside, and it was her fault. In high school, college, and now, Graham Chamberlain was a catch.

And she had finally caught him.

As she lay in bed, she thought about what she would say to Theo when she inevitably saw him. His appearance in her office or at her front door wouldn't be a matter of *if*, but *when*. He had gone to the inn and made a spectacle of himself, demanding to see her. Even if she had holed up at the inn, Bowie would've never let Theo in. Bowie protected Rennie at all costs because it was what Brooklyn would want. Same with Graham, which was why she called him in the first place. She knew he would drop everything for her and do whatever he could to keep her safe and happy, and he had.

Rennie dreaded what the morning would bring. Thanks to her utter stupidity of throwing her phone in the bay, she had no idea what she was walking into at work. She left for vacation early and avoided every call and email. She had needed time to think and feared that if her phone was within reach, she'd look to see what Theo had to say or listen to his voice mails. Graham had been right. She should've just blocked his number.

Rennie had a mediation meeting in the morning with Mrs. Soto and her lazy ex-husband, which Rennie suspected was not going to go very well for the ex with Rennie's frame of mind. She also needed to touch base with Walter in regard to the snoop job she gave him. She wanted to work with Jefferson and find a quick resolution to whatever Donna had up her sleeve regarding Graham. The case was more than personal now, and she needed to make sure it was handled as professionally as possible.

She rolled over, taking the sweatshirt with her, and finally felt a calm wash over her. Graham was there, with her. Her eyes shot open, and she sat straight up in bed. They were an hour from each other—on nights he closed early, he could drive down to her. In her mind, this made perfect sense, and they wouldn't have to wait until the weekends to see each other. Rennie flopped back onto her pillow with a cheesy grin on her face and saw visions of her and Graham growing old together. Rennie could easily be happy in Cape Harbor, but what about her job? Opening a private practice made sense, but how many people were looking for a divorce in Cape Harbor or Skagit Valley? Those small towns with low populations wouldn't yield enough of a client base to support a staff and salary. She needed to stop thinking. Her thoughts weren't doing her any favors.

By the time her alarm went off, she was exhausted. The sleepy-time tea didn't do the trick, and her mind never shut off long enough to let her fall asleep. She started her morning routine, never missing a step, and replaced an existing part of her morning by sending Graham a text, which he would see when he woke up. **Having responsibilities sucks. Let's run away together.**

She stood in front of her closet and looked over her clothes. There wasn't a single thing she wanted to wear in there. She wanted to be comfortable in jeans, but Lex Davey would have a fit if she showed up to work looking like it was Saturday. She pulled out a navy-blue suit with white pinstripes. The ensemble was one of her favorites. Rennie hung it on the hook by her closet and went to her dresser, opened a drawer, and found a picture of Theo. She picked it up, studied it, and waited for the tears to come. They didn't. She stared at it with disgust. He was nothing to her.

Next to her dresser sat a wastebasket. Rennie dropped the photo into it and then looked around her room. There were other images of Theo, some with her in them. She didn't bother to take them out of the frames as she collected them. Each one made its way into the garbage, frame and all. There wasn't a satisfying crunch of glass shattering. She wasn't screaming. She was simply cleaning up what didn't belong in her apartment anymore.

From room to room, she collected things belonging to Theo. Some items were personal, some just random things that had accumulated over time, and she set them all on her coffee table. She'd box those and send them to his work. She didn't care if she was outing him or not—at this point, he deserved whatever came his way. By the time she was done, she had worked up a sweat and an appetite, and she still had to go to work. Rennie went back to her dresser and pulled out a new package of nylons and worked her legs into them. She finished dressing and felt lighter and much better about the day. Maybe she just needed to totally eradicate Theo from her life before her day could start.

Rennie drove to her office, parked in her usual spot, and took the elevator to her floor. When she arrived on her floor, she smiled at Ester and asked her to follow her to her office. Once inside, she shut the door.

"How was your Christmas?" she asked her assistant.

"It was good. I tried calling you."

Rennie waved her new phone in the air. "New number."

"What? Why?"

"Theo and I broke up. Long story short, he's a cad. He's married, and I've been playing mistress for over a year without knowing it. I expect him to call or show up—if he does, put him through, but after today, I never want to see or speak to him."

"Wow." Ester stood there, speechless for a moment. "He seemed so genuine."

Rennie laughed. "You're telling me. So, anything I should know?" she asked as she sat down.

"No, it was pretty quiet. Donna spent a day stomping around because you weren't here, but there's a rumor floating around among the admins."

"Ooh, what is it?"

Ester leaned forward, despite being in a private office, and whispered, "We're pretty sure Donna and Lex are having an affair."

The rumor or news, whatever it might be, broke Rennie's heart. Donna was married, and Rennie liked her husband. And after what happened between her and Theo, she had no respect for anyone who cheated on their spouse.

"Shameful," Rennie muttered. She excused Ester and turned on her computer. Her emails came in one by one, dinging with each new notification. She shut the volume off, having grown tired of hearing the noise, and watched as each one loaded. About half were from Theo, and Rennie deleted every single one of them.

Late last night after Rennie spoke to Graham, she relented and downloaded her contacts to her new phone. As much as she wanted to start over, there were numbers she needed in there. She picked up her phone and called Walter to check in.

"Walter here."

"Walter, it's Rennie Wallace. I'm calling from a new phone number. How are you? How was your New Year?"

"Fabulous. My Lois kissed me at midnight, which is all I could ask for. How was yours?"

"Ah, that's very sweet of her. Mine was perfect; thanks for asking. How's the case coming?"

"In my professional opinion, which you do not hire me for, I can tell you this family doesn't have a case against your friend."

Rennie adjusted in her chair so she could take notes. "Tell me what you have."

"I spoke to her friends and asked where they got the booze. At first, they said the bar, but after some prodding, I got one to tell me the truth. The father of the driver supplied the teens with the alcohol, and it is his idea to pin this on the bar. Apparently, he thinks no one will care if a small-town establishment goes under."

"Does he know the Chamberlains?"

"He's their delivery driver for the distribution company they use."

"Oh, you've got to be kidding me, Walter."

"Wish I was. The family is in financial trouble after the accident. Insurance won't pay because they're claiming their daughter is a victim, so until the lawsuit is settled, they're barely scraping by."

"Were you able to find out how they know Donna?"

"One of the other kids in the car—Donna is his grandma's neighbor."

"So random. Let me know what else you find. Thanks, Walter."

They hung up, and Rennie sat there and stared at her notes. She hated this side of the law, the side where anyone could file a lawsuit and threaten someone's livelihood without cause. It bothered her greatly.

The intercom buzzed, and Rennie's heart dropped to the floor, bounced up, and lodged in her throat. "Yes," she answered, shaken. She wasn't ready for the confrontation.

"Ms. Wallace," Ester said as professionally as she could. "Mr. Wright is here to see you."

Rennie took a deep breath, closed her eyes, and counted to ten and then counted again. "Send him in." She hung up and straightened in her chair. She would be strong and in control.

Theo waltzed into her office, dressed in jeans and a T-shirt. An ensemble she had never seen before. She expected her heart to lurch, a desire to feel his arms wrapped around her, but she didn't. She felt nothing.

"Renee—"

She held her hand up. "If you want to talk, you can sit. Do not come any closer."

He did as he was told and sat across from her. Theo stared everywhere but at her. She sighed and tapped her fingers on her desk.

"I don't have all day, Theo."

"No, I know you don't."

"So, say what you have to say."

Theo finally made eye contact with Rennie, and that was when she saw the remnants of a black eye. His eyes were also red rimmed and bloodshot. "Who hit you?"

"Angela's brother."

"Serves you right."

He nodded. "Look, I never meant for this to happen. The day I met you, it was like I had met my soul mate. Within seconds of introducing myself, I was smitten. Lost in every part of you."

"And married," Rennie interjected.

"Married," he sighed.

"Did you think I'd never find out?"

He shook his head. "I don't know. Honestly, I hoped she would've figured it out that first weekend. I didn't come home. I gave her some lousy excuse as to why I had to stay in the hotel when I lived twenty minutes from there. When the weekend was over, I expected her to yell and scream, but she didn't. She said nothing, and it felt so damn exhilarating because I got away with something so horrible. The thing is, I wanted her to find out because I wanted her to leave so you and I could be together, but no matter what I did, she never suspected a thing."

Rennie herself didn't have a lot of experience with relationships, having submerged herself in her work, but she'd like to think she would question her husband on why he hadn't come home from a local convention.

"I had every intention of leaving my wife that first weekend."

"Why didn't you?"

Theo sat back in his chair. "The thrill. It was exciting. Living this double life."

"All while putting me in danger," she said to him. "While we were together, were you having sex with your wife?"

It took Theo a long moment to answer, and when he did, he barely nodded.

"Unbelievable. Did you ever stop to think what this would do to me? How your actions affect me? My life? My body? How do I know I'm the only one you've been with beside her? How do I know she's not cheating on you? Now, I get why you always used a condom, no matter what I told you about birth control. I figured you were just anal, but after a year of dating, you would think you could trust your partner." Rennie scoffed and shook her head. "I'm the idiot. I should've known something was up earlier."

"I'm sorry, Renee. I really am."

"Are you sorry because you got caught? I mean, where would we be right now if your friends hadn't been at the resort?"

He shrugged. "Not having this conversation," he told her.

Rennie adjusted in her chair. She was ready for him to walk out but had more questions. "What happened at Thanksgiving? Did you fly to Japan?"

Theo cleared his throat. "My in-laws were in town. I flew here to see you and took the next flight back to Spokane."

"And Christmas? Did you have any intention of spending it with me?"

He looked down at his hands. "I really had a business trip to San Diego, but . . ." Theo paused and shook his head. "Angela had a lot of family in town."

There it was in black and white. The man she thought she loved was nothing more than a liar and, worse, a cheater. "Did you ever have any intention of telling me, Theo?"

His eyes met hers, and she could see his answer clear as day. "So, what? You wanted me to move to Spokane and be your mistress? Second wife? I really want to know how this would've played out. Would you tell me you were on a business trip like you tell your wife now?"

Theo shook his head. "I don't know, Renee. I just knew I needed you there."

"Because you had no intention of leaving your wife. Am I right?"

"I think I would've left eventually."

"But not with me by your side, Theo."

His hand reached across her desk, searching for hers. "Can I have another chance? Please? I'll leave Angela and move here. I'll quit my job. Whatever it takes, Renee. I can't lose you."

Rennie shook her head slowly and methodically. "Not in this lifetime. I am not a home-wrecker, yet you've made me out to be one. You're a liar, and I will never trust you. You're exactly the type of man I look forward to destroying in court. Sad thing is, Washington is a no-fault state, which means spouses can do whatever they want with no recourse. Sickens me, really."

"We love each other," he tried to remind her.

"No, Theo. You love the idea of me, the escape, or whatever thrill you got from sneaking around. And the truth is, I fell out of love with you a long time ago."

"Wh-what?"

"The disconnect I felt—it's because I wasn't in love with you, but I hung on because there are things I want out of life, and I thought you'd give them to me. Fool me once, Theo, but that's the only chance you get. I'd like you to leave now. I'll send your stuff to the office. There isn't anything else we need to discuss."

Theo stared at Rennie, who looked everywhere but at him. She didn't need one last look to remember him. He would be the vision in her nightmares. When he finally stood to leave, he walked to the door and turned around. "I love you, Renee." Rennie kept her silence until he walked out of her door. Once again, she counted to ten. She closed her eyes and kept them closed until her intercom chimed.

"Ms. Wallace, there's a Mr. Chamberlain on the phone."

Well crap, she knew three of them.

Rennie smiled. "Thanks, Ester."

"Renee Wallace," she answered, trying to be as professional as she could.

"Damn, that's hot," Graham said into the phone. "Although funny to hear you call yourself Renee."

Rennie relaxed in her chair. "What are you doing calling me at work?"

Graham chuckled. "Because I wanted to hear the sexy Renee voice."

And now she giggled. "It's not sexy."

"Everything about you is sexy. Listen, I was thinking I drive down to see you on one of my days off this week? I'm going to drive over and see Grady, too, and I've decided to hire some help."

"Krista will appreciate having someone else on staff, and yes. I was thinking the same thing. Just tell me when, Graham."

"I will. Have a good day, Ren."

She sighed. "Bye, Graham Cracker."

Rennie hung up, and her fingers danced on her lips. Her days were going to drag on, especially if he was going to call her first thing each morning. The sexy, raspy growl Graham had when he first woke in the morning was a sound she wanted to capture and play over and over. His voice did things to her. Things that shouldn't happen at work.

TWENTY-EIGHT

For the first time in as long as Graham could remember, he was excited to visit his brother. It was midweek when Grady's therapist called and asked Graham if he had time to visit. Without hesitation, Graham agreed. He made the necessary arrangement to switch shifts with Krista and left before the sun rose. The drive from Cape Harbor to Port Angeles was all too familiar by now and seemed to go in a flash. Graham made one stop on his way to see Grady, and that was to pick up his brother's favorite doughnut, a maple bar. Graham was excited at the thought of having breakfast with his brother.

He pulled into the parking lot of the rehab facility at the same time visiting hours started. Visitation wasn't a free-for-all; each one had to be scheduled. Graham gave his name at the door and waited for the all-too-familiar clicking sound to alert him that the doors had unlocked. When he entered, the security guard stationed at the reception desk searched Graham's bag. Graham swore he saw the guard lick his lips but couldn't be certain.

Graham was shown to a room that reminded him of the cafeteria at Cape Harbor High, except the tables were round and not rectangular. Graham chose a table near the window. He liked the view and thought Grady would like to look out. He had no idea what sort of living situation his brother was in but felt confident Grady was being taken care of.

The doors opened, and Graham stood. Grady came toward him, tall and proud and looking healthy for the first time in fifteen years. He wore hospital-issued clothing. He was clean shaven and his hair trimmed. More and more, he looked like his twin. The closer Grady got to his brother, the more Graham could see the changes and what a month without alcohol could do for someone. It was Grady who initiated the hug between the two. Graham held on tightly to his brother and fought back the tears. Why had it taken everyone so long to get Grady the help he needed?

The twins sat down, and Graham slid the bag toward Grady. "What's this?" he asked.

"Maple bar. Still your favorite, right?"

Grady nodded and pulled the pastry out of the bag. He took a bite, closed his eyes, and hummed in satisfaction. Grady still had the feeding tube inserted but only had to use it at night.

"How are you feeling?"

"Odd," Grady responded. "I've done so much of this"—Grady mimicked drinking by lifting his hand to his mouth—"that my hands need something to do, and it's weird because I never had any plans before except to wake up and drink, and now, I'm on this schedule. They're teaching me to be an adult."

Graham wanted to laugh and cry at the same time. Grady at twenty-two was this happy-go-lucky, give-the-shirt-off-his-back-to-anyone-who-asked guy who always had a smile on his face and wore a ridiculous knit hat regardless of the weather. All he ever wanted to be was a fisherman. The man before him had missed out on so much life. Graham wanted to help him get some of it back. He reached across the table and held his brother's hand.

"I'm proud of you, Grady."

"Are you?" he asked, making eye contact with Graham.

"I am. I know I haven't shown it lately, but I'm here, and I'm not going to turn my back on you."

"What if I come into the bar and need a drink?"

"Your H2O game is going to be strong. Maybe I'll create some water competition." Grady laughed, and it felt good to hear him do so. "Seriously, your sobriety means everything to me—to Mom and Dad as well. You have a strong team waiting for you when you're out."

"I have like two more months."

Graham nodded. "It's a little under, and then you'll go back to court. Rennie will do her best to keep you out of jail."

A nurse in pink scrubs came up to Graham and Grady. She put her hand on Grady's back and bent toward him. "Grady, would you like to show your brother around outside?"

Grady looked at Graham and said, "I've been working outside, you know, to keep my hands busy. Would you like to see what I made?"

"Of course!" The brothers stood and followed the nurse to the side door. She unlocked it and held it open.

"I'll be behind you, but you'll have privacy."

"Babysitters everywhere," Grady mumbled to Graham.

"Think of the end prize, Grady. She's here to protect you from everything out there that's trying to take you down."

"And who protects me when I leave?" Grady asked.

The question gave Graham pause. What did happen to people who still needed help after their ninety days in rehab? Surely three months wasn't enough time to cure a fifteen-year addiction. "I'm not sure, but we'll figure it out when the time comes."

Grady led Graham to a rock formation. The stacked thin pieces of slate were formed into an archway. "I did this."

"Wait, what?" Graham asked in shock. "How?"

Grady shrugged. "We can take classes. There wasn't really one I wanted to take, so my therapist signed me up for this gardening thing, and the instructor showed me how to put the rocks together."

"This is amazing."

"Thanks." Grady's smile beamed brightly. "If I continue to do well, I can teach people how to tie flies."

"When is the last time you tied one?"

Grady thought for a moment. "Probably a week before Austin died, but I've been practicing."

"They give you hooks?"

"No, they're these plastic things. Works the same."

"That's great, Grady."

Grady led his brother down the stone path until they came to a koi pond. They sat on the bench, both watching the fish swim around and the water cascade over the edge of the statue to create a waterfall.

"I was surprised to see Rennie in my hospital room."

"She wanted to be there. She spent the first weekend you were in a coma at the hospital with Mom and me. As soon as the police showed up, she intervened and told them you had a lawyer. She's the one who set everything up to get you this help and try to keep you out of jail."

"How come you never married her? Or the one I met the time I visited?"

What a loaded question that was. Graham could make up some story and tell his brother how sometimes things didn't always work out, or he could tell him the truth. Graham sighed, kicked his feet out in front of him, and relaxed against the bench. If he was going to do this, he was going to be comfortable.

"Monica, she's the one you met. After Austin's funeral, I went back to Cali and asked her to move to Cape Harbor with me. She said no, and I really couldn't blame her. As far as Rennie goes, up until Brooklyn's return, I hadn't seen or heard from her. Found out she's been living in Seattle for some time but kept her distance out of respect for Brooklyn."

"You should've stayed in California, Graham."

"Hindsight, Grady. It's a beautiful thing."

Grady chuckled. "Hindsight . . . what if I stopped Austin? How different would things be now?"

Graham was a master at the what-if game. "Okay, let's play this game," he told Grady. They had nothing but time to waste, so why not? "Let's say that night never happens. I stay in California, marry Monica. We probably have kids, and I probably work fifty to sixty hours a week."

"Or?" Grady responded.

Graham laughed. "You're sadistic. Or, Monica and I don't work out, and I marry Rennie."

"Option two sounds more like it. I never understood why the two of you weren't together."

Graham didn't know, either, but their future looked promising. "Yeah," Graham sighed. "Now, to you. Where do you think you'd be?"

Grady shrugged. "Right before the accident, I was going to ask Monroe if she wanted to go out on a date."

"She cares about you, Grady."

"I don't want her to. She needs to move on and stop trying to fix me."

Easier said than done, Graham thought. "You can tell her," Graham said. "I don't want to have anything to do with that conversation."

Grady laughed. "She's persistent, and I love her as a friend, but she's the past, and I don't want to keep living in the past."

Grady's words gave Graham pause. Was that what he was doing with Rennie? Living in the past? Trying to rekindle what they had because it was good then? He hadn't thought about it, but it made sense. He knew nothing of her life now other than she lived and worked in Seattle and that her boyfriend of over a year was married. Everything about Rennie and Graham came from the past.

Graham didn't want to think about his relationship with Rennie, at least not right now. "Have you given any thought to what you want to do when you leave here?"

"Assuming I'm not going to jail?" Grady asked his brother, who nodded. "I'll have to talk to Brooklyn, but I think I'd like to get the company up and running again."

"Really?"

"Yeah. I'd need her permission because she's the majority owner. Well, Brystol is, but she's underage, so I have to go through Brooklyn. I wouldn't be able to have a big crew or anything until I had some capital." He shrugged. "Maybe she'll give me a loan to start with."

"You sure you can go out to sea?" Graham was concerned about PTSD. As far as he knew, his brother hadn't been on a boat since the night of the accident.

"I'm working through some things here. I have to try, at least."

Graham agreed, and he liked Grady's idea a lot. "Let me know when you want to talk to Brooklyn. I'll go with you. And if you need a couple guys to go out on the boat, I can help. Fishing really wasn't my thing, but I can do it."

"You sure?"

He was. Graham wanted to support his brother in any way he could, and if that meant putting on a pair of hip waders and getting up when normal people were sound asleep, he would do it. He had done it today to visit Grady.

Graham spent the better part of the morning hanging out with his brother. He left around lunchtime and made the trek back to Cape Harbor with a lot on his mind. His thoughts focused mostly on Rennie. He loved her, there was no doubt about that, but he couldn't reason if his feelings were new or residual from the life they had before things changed for them and their friends. It made sense that he wanted to be with her. She made him laugh, and she had been his best friend, but there was a time when he chose someone else over her, which had to mean something. He just didn't know what. They had spent an amazing weekend together, although, under the circumstances, their feelings could be vastly different because of the situation they found themselves in. It could be Graham and Rennie were destined to be friends with the occasionally added benefit of sex, except Graham wanted more, and he needed to figure out if Rennie would be the one to move forward with in his life plan or not.

When Graham arrived back at the bar, there was a nice crowd. Per usual, Bowie's crew was there playing darts, and some locals had started up a pool game. Krista was busy behind the bar, and Brystol was there, waiting tables. He'd placed an ad in the paper and online, looking for two people to start right away. He owed it to Krista to find help and planned to promote her to assistant manager. She had earned it.

For a brief moment, Graham stood there and looked out over his establishment and smiled. The winter months were hard for any business in a tourist town, but the people of Cape Harbor and its surrounding communities always rallied to support local businesses. Graham was very appreciative of his neighbors.

He took his spot behind the bar but deferred to Krista. In the past months she had been a stellar employee, and the last thing he wanted to do was step on her toes and mess up the system she had in place. He would follow her lead and do as she told him until Krista passed the bar over to him for the night. When Brystol needed an adult's help, he was there by her side to take the drink orders. He bussed tables, did some dishes, and filled in where they needed him. And he felt good about it. Because of Grady and the help he'd received, Graham's outlook on life had changed vastly. He wanted to see things in a positive light, and in an odd way, Grady's stint in rehab was helping Graham as well.

Graham went to take a case of bottles to the back, and Krista stopped him. "There's a guy at the bar, wasted. He came in about thirty minutes ago, asking for you." Krista nodded toward the man at the bar, whose head was down, and his hand held a tumbler of light-colored liquid.

Graham knew who it was instantly. "What's he drinking?"

"Water, with a touch of scotch. I wasn't going to add to his level of intoxication."

"I'll talk to him, but we don't let him leave unless he has a ride." Graham already had what could be a costly lawsuit dangling in front of him because someone had accused him of not watching his patrons— he didn't want another one, and he definitely didn't want one from Rennie's ex.

Graham went over to the bar, picked up a dishrag, and cleaned the counter in front of Theo. "Can I get you something to eat?" he asked the man.

Theo's head rose slowly, his red-rimmed, bloodshot eyes barely open. He looked like he hadn't slept in a week, which Graham understood. When he and Monica broke up, he cried the entire way back to Cape Harbor and then vowed to let it go.

"How about I put an order in for a cheeseburger and some fries? Would you like that?" Graham didn't wait around for a response. He went to his kiosk and placed the order. He then filled a large glass with ice water and added coffee grounds to a filter to brew a pot of coffee. It was late, and no one would drink it except Theo.

"I don't like you," Theo said when Graham slid the glass of water toward him.

"It's okay; I can't stand you, so I guess we're even." Graham walked away. He wasn't going to get into a tit for tat with a drunk guy, let alone Rennie's ex. He had nothing to gain by engaging in conversation with the man. Because the bar was busy, he found things to do. He refilled Krista's orders, collected her tips for her, and filled drink requests.

When Theo's burger and fries were ready, Krista handed them to him and then stood next to Graham. "Who is he?"

"Rennie's ex."

"Damn, he's taking it hard."

"Hey," Theo shouted over the crowd. Graham turned and smiled. "What can I get for ya?"

"You can tell Renee to take me back," Theo said. "She'll listen to you. You're the only one she seems to listen to."

While Graham would love to think the same, it wasn't true. "Rennie"—Graham drew her name out, knowing how much it bothered her that Theo called her Renee—"is a very independent woman. You should know this after spending the last year and however many months you've been together. She makes her own decisions."

"I love her, and she won't see me. I can't call her, because she changed her number."

"Sorry, man. I can't help you." Graham turned to walk away, but Theo grabbed his arm and held him in place.

"Do you know until last summer, I had never been here? I had never heard of Cape Harbor, and then all of a sudden, she's up here every weekend we're not together, and all I hear are stories about these people she grew up with but hadn't seen in years. They're a priority for her. They're butting into our lives. Interrupting our plans."

Graham pulled his arm free. "Again, I can't help you."

"I know you're the one who came and got her in Canada. I saw you. I recognized you right away. She didn't call her friend; she called you."

Graham stood there. He had nothing to say to the man in front of him. No, that wasn't exactly true. He wanted to scold him for cheating on his wife and for hurting Rennie.

"I'm right, aren't I?"

"Eat your burger. I'll call you a cab."

He left Theo there and walked to the back room, where he pulled out his phone and dialed Rennie's number.

"Hey," she said after the second ring.

"Hey, Theo's in the bar. He's drunk. He's upset. Kind of blaming all of us for ruining your relationship."

"He came and saw me the other day at work—"

Graham interrupted her, "Why didn't you tell me?"

Rennie was silent for a moment. "Not really anything to tell. He came and left right before you called me. He apologized. I told him how he made me feel, and I sent him on his way. I don't know why he's there now. He's the past and not really worth our time."

He thought her answer was dismissive and felt she should've called and told him Theo had gone to see her. Days into their relationship, and he was already upset with her. He shouldn't feel this way. "I think he's looking for someone to blame. He knows I picked you up from the resort."

"Oh."

Graham sighed. "Anyway, I wanted to let you know. I'm going to call him a cab and send him on his way. I'll call you later." He hung up, feeling more frustrated than ever. What in the hell was he doing trying to start a relationship with this breakup so fresh?

He went back to the bar and saw that the coffee had finished brewing. He poured Theo a cup and handed it to him. "Sober up." He then went to the bar phone and called the local taxi service.

Theo took a drink. "I need to get her back."

Graham shook his head. "You're married. I think your focus needs to be on your wife."

"She left me too." He sounded dejected, but it was well deserved. "I'm so in love with Renee. I have to get her back. And you have to help me."

Graham rested his hands on the edge of the counter and made eye contact with Theo. "I'm not your friend. I'm Rennie's. If she doesn't want to see you, there isn't anything I can do, nor would I. What you did, what you put her through—it's inexcusable. You put my friend in such a bad situation, and I don't blame her for removing you from her life. Hell, I don't blame your wife either. You need to figure your shit out and leave Rennie alone."

He nodded toward the door when the driver walked in. "Your ride is here. Your tab is on the house, but do me a favor."

"What's that?" Theo asked.

"Don't ever come back here or to Cape Harbor again. You're not welcome."

Theo laughed. "When she takes me back, I'll make sure she never steps foot in this place again."

"Good luck, man." Graham cleared away Theo's food and glasses and turned his back on the guy. He had a business to run and couldn't waste any more of his time on Rennie's ex. He had a hard enough time dealing with his thoughts in regard to her and what they were doing. Unfortunately for Graham, the negativity crept in, and he spent the rest of the night wondering what the hell he was doing, not only with his life but with Rennie.

TWENTY-NINE

Rennie stood in her kitchen looking at take-out menus. She had tossed the places Theo liked to frequent and kept her favorites. She had poured herself a glass of wine but had yet to take a drink. All week, she had been indecisive about everything, especially Graham. They hadn't really fought, but she had been a bit of a bitch to him when he called her about Theo. The call had caught her off guard. She never expected Theo to return to Cape Harbor, let alone go into the Whale Spout. She didn't like that and took her frustration out on Graham instead of Theo. Her doorbell rang, and she looked up, which really didn't do her any good since she didn't have a clear line of sight to the door. She set her wineglass down and went to answer.

"Graham," she said his name softly. He stood there with a bouquet of flowers in his hand. "Come in." She shut the door after him and locked it.

"Before you say anything, I want you to hear me out. I'm sorry for being snippy the other night in regard to Theo. I know you're dealing with him the way you see fit, and I accept that. I shouldn't have snapped. I'm sorry."

Rennie flung her arms around Graham's shoulders and smashed her flowers into his chest. "I'm sorry too, Graham." She looked deep into his eyes and could easily see herself falling very hard and very fast for him. "I'm happy you're here, but why are you here?" She laughed at her question.

"I had to see you. I didn't want to wait until this weekend, because I have to work a ton. I gave Krista the weekend off."

"Good—she deserves it." Rennie took her flowers and held the smashed petals to her nose. "I think I broke them." She held her hand out for Graham to follow her as she gave him a quick tour. She showed him her guest bedroom, the small bathroom, the living room, the kitchen and finally her bedroom.

"This is cozy."

"I like it. Come on—I was about to order some dinner. Are you hungry?" She walked back toward the kitchen with him hot on her heels.

"Sure."

They stood at the counter and looked at the menus together, finally settling on dim sum. Rennie placed the order while Graham wandered around her living room. When she hung up, she went to him and pulled him toward her favorite oversize stuffed chair. He sat first, and she crawled onto his lap.

"I'm happy you're here."

"You are?"

"Absolutely." She caressed the side of his cheek and leaned in to kiss him. Within seconds, passion ignited between them. "I want you," she told him, only to have him pull back.

"Can we talk?"

She could only nod, because her heart was in her throat.

Graham adjusted in the seat, turning slightly so he could look at Rennie. He smiled, but she didn't see his eyes light up like they normally did. "I saw Grady the other day, and he said something to me that got me thinking."

"About?"

"Us. He said it in reference to him and Monroe. Roe has always liked Grady and has cared for him a lot over the years, but he wants her to move on, because she is part of his past. I know his situation is different from ours, but we were all affected by the accident, and I fear that things between us could be residual feelings. The last thing I want for either of us is to jump two feet in and then start to backpedal because we don't really know each other. I know Rennie Wallace from age sixteen to twenty-two, but for the past fifteen years, minus the last six months, I don't know the Rennie sitting on my lap, and I want to know. I want to know her more than anything, but she needs to know me too. I'm not the same guy I was all those years ago."

Rennie looked away and let his words sink in. She hated everything Graham said but respected him greatly for saying it.

Graham brought her chin toward him so they could look each other in the eyes. "I want to fall in love with you, Renee Wallace. But I want to do it because it's right and it's what we both want. I think rushing into a relationship isn't healthy for either of us. You're just coming off a long relationship, and I have Grady . . ." Graham paused. "I want to be the man you deserve, not the one who has to cancel on you or changes plans because his brother needs a little extra help right now."

She cupped Graham's cheeks and noticed he had tears in his eyes. "I don't deserve a man like you—I really don't—but damn I respect the hell out of you right now. Ever since I returned, I've had this lingering feeling something was off. Not with you, but us. It's like we missed a step, and you're right; we need to date. You need to wine and dine me; show me the world, Mr. Chamberlain, because I'm about to do the same for you. I believe in us, Graham."

He pulled her close and held her to his chest, where they stayed until their food arrived. They ate together on her couch and talked a bit more about his session with Grady. When Graham stood to leave, Rennie protested.

"You can't leave."

"I have to. If I stay, I'm taking you to bed, and that defeats the purpose. I want to be your partner in life, Rennie, not your hookup, and if we have sex, we'll never figure out if we can hack a relationship together. To me, that's more important."

Rennie stood and stared into his eyes. "When did you become so wise?"

He pushed her hair behind her ear and smiled. "It was Grady. What he said made sense, and I want us to work."

"Me too." She rose up and placed her lips to his. She kept it chaste, knowing the last thing either of them needed was more temptation. Rennie walked Graham to the door, and they promised to talk later in the week. She stood on her stoop and watched him walk down the street with tears in her eyes. Her heart broke with the thought that they might have missed their chance at happiness together.

When the sun rose on Monday, Rennie did as well. She went about her morning routine. She showered, applied lotion to every part of her body, drank her coffee, dressed, and did her hair. After Graham left, she had turned off her phone, worked from home on Friday, and spent the weekend curled up on her couch with a blanket, his sweatshirt, and a couple pints of ice cream. They weren't broken up but were not exactly together. They were going to date, which meant she'd see Graham when she went to Cape Harbor or on the off chance he drove down to visit her. It wasn't good enough, and she felt like her world had fallen apart in a matter of days. It was the beginning of the year, and she already wanted a redo.

On her way in to her office, she turned on her phone and waited for the onslaught of messages to come through. There weren't as many as she'd thought, and she didn't know if this was a good sign or not.

She read the one from Brooklyn, which said to call her if she needed anything, and there was nothing from Graham.

"Good morning, Ms. Wallace," Ester said when Rennie stepped off the elevator. Ester handed her boss a file folder and followed her into her office. "Good weekend?"

"Not really. What's this?"

"It's a report I came across on Friday. It was left on the copier, and I thought it was something you'd like to see."

Rennie sat down and read the documents in the file. Case notes about the potential suit against Graham. As far as Rennie could tell, it was all circumstantial evidence and hearsay.

"Ester, you're a little devil, and I love it."

"Thank you." Ester bowed. "I have something else. This came to me on Friday." Ester handed her boss a printed email with a medical report attached to it. Rennie read it over twice.

"No way."

"Perfect timing, right?"

"Couldn't be better. Nice job. Can you ask Mr. Perkins to come and see me before our staff meeting?"

Ester nodded and excused herself. Rennie kept poring over the document and wished her divorce clients would hand her smoking guns like this. The knock on her door startled her. She jumped and closed the file before she looked to see who it was.

"Oh, Jeff. Come in." He closed the door behind him and took a seat across from her. "Remember my pro bono case?" He nodded. "My client is in rehab, thanks to your strategy, and he's actually doing really well, according to him and his therapists. But his brother, who owns a bar, is the subject of a witch hunt." Rennie went over everything Walter had told her when they spoke and handed Jefferson the file from Ester.

"Who did he piss off?"

"Odd, right? It's like Graham has an enemy, which I don't get. He's literally one of the most loved members of the community. The same for his brother, despite everything. This is a stand-up family, and this delivery driver is trying to frame them for something they had no part in. Can they do that?"

"That's the thing about civil suits. You hash them out in court or pretrial. It's up to a judge or a jury to find if there's fault."

"Even if the plaintiff is lying?"

Jeff nodded. "Do you remember the OJ Simpson case? He's found not guilty by a jury of his peers, but when it comes to civil court, the families are awarded millions. It's all in how the case is presented."

"That's crazy."

"It is. Do you want my help with this? I'll gladly take it over and keep you in the loop."

Rennie leaned forward and lowered her voice. "Donna is going to fight you on this. She'll tell you that you can't keep the case because of her client."

Jefferson laughed. "Let her. I'm not scared of her. Besides, we have a signed contract from your client—well, now mine—saying we represent him. She can cry wolf, whine to Lex. I don't care. I'll happily take her on in court, but by the looks of this, one conference and the plaintiffs will owe the Chamberlains money for harassment." He rubbed his hands together. "I do love countersuits." He picked up the folder and tapped it on her desk. "Let your clients know I'll call them by the end of the week."

She hoped this would be the day her Soto case finally ended. She was optimistic when she went into the conference room and saw her client Kelly seated at the table. Kelly was a tiny woman with stick-straight, long jet-black hair. When she first came to Rennie, Kelly had given her a book to read and told Rennie that she wrote it. Since then, Rennie had read every novel her client had written.

"Hey, Kelly," Rennie said as she entered. "How was your holiday?"

"Actually, it was nice. Andrew wished me a merry Christmas."

Before Rennie could respond, Andrew and his lawyer, Thomas Krouse, entered. "Good afternoon, gentlemen." Rennie hated that term because these two were nothing close to gentlemen. They sat down across from Rennie and her client, and Ester sat at the end of the table with her pen poised and the tape recorder ready.

"Are you ready to start?" Rennie asked. She opened her binder and waited.

"Our settlement option remains the same," Krouse said.

"Which is fine." Rennie pulled a sheet of paper out of her folder and slid it across the table to Andrew. "Mr. Soto, can you please tell me what this is?"

Before Andrew could read it, his attorney took the document from his hand. His eyes went wide, and he leaned in to confer with his client. Kelly looked at Rennie with confusion written all over her face. Rennie waved her hand a little and hoped Kelly understood that what was happening before them needed to play out.

Thomas Krouse cleared his throat. "My client is willing to negotiate a twenty-five percent stake of Ms. Soto's current and future royalties. Same conditions as before—gross wages, of course."

"Of course, Mr. Krouse. But I would like for you to turn to page three of our already agreed-to stipulations and look at item five. I'll read aloud for your benefit. 'If at any time Mr. Soto, during the five years this stipulation is in effect, is to marry or father a child, he will forfeit his right to royalties.' Your words, Mr. Krouse."

"You got someone pregnant?" Kelly blurted out. She reached forward and took the paper from the lawyer's hand and read the results of an amniocentesis done on Andrew's behalf. "Wow, Andrew. Doesn't she live in the apartment next to you?"

The next stack of papers Rennie pushed across the table was the original divorce settlement assuring that Kelly retained 100 percent of her company and royalties. "Let's go ahead and sign these so my client can move on with her life, and yours can build a crib."

"I still want money," Andrew yelled. "I'm entitled."

Rennie wanted to laugh, but she kept things professional. "I'm sorry, Andrew. You already agreed to the stipulation, and we're not willing to change it. You can sign the papers, or we can go to court."

Thomas leaned over again and whispered in his client's ear. Andrew grabbed the pen hastily and signed where he needed to sign. Once he signed, he abruptly left the room.

"I'll have your copy sent over later today after we file," Ester said as she gathered the documents.

"That was shady, Renee. Even for you," Thomas said as he packed his briefcase.

"I'm not the one who asked for the clause. That's all on your client."

As soon as Thomas left, Kelly tackled Rennie in a fierce hug. "How did you find this out?"

"I didn't. As part of the divorce proceedings, we requested medical records. I had to see if he was ill or needed treatment for anything that you'd normally provide for. Because of this, when he had the test done, everything was sent to us."

"Freaking brilliant. I'm going to use this in a book someday. How am I ever going to thank you?"

Rennie didn't have an answer. "Keep in touch, Kelly. I'm interested in your career."

"I will. Thank you, Ms. Wallace."

"Congratulations. You'll be a free woman soon. Now, go sign that contract."

Rennie bid her client farewell, dropped her files off on her desk, and decided she needed some fresh air. She grabbed her purse, made sure she had her phone, and checked messages on her ride down to the lobby. She was in the midst of texting Graham, telling him about Jefferson taking over his case, when she heard her name. She stopped and looked around and saw a woman approaching her.

"Are you Renee Wallace?"

Rennie froze. She'd seen one too many movies where someone answered yes, and they ended up with a shotgun hole in their chest. She remained quiet, her mouth and brain unable to work properly.

"I'm Angela Wright. Do you have a place where we can talk?"

"I have nothing to say to you." Rennie sidestepped, but the woman grabbed her arm.

"Please."

Rennie could see the desperation in her eyes. They were crystal blue but lacked life. She gave the woman in front of her a good hard look. Her hair was limp, and her clothes looked frumpy. Theo had done this to her, his wife. Reluctantly, she nodded and told Angela to follow her. Rennie led them to a restaurant attached to her building. It was late enough that they missed the lunch rush and were able to get a booth in the back, which gave them some privacy.

"Did you bring my husband here?"

With that question, Rennie reached for the strap on her purse and started to leave, but once again, Angela held on to her arm. "I'm sorry. That was rude. I'm just . . . I'm lost, and everything hurts."

"I don't know what talking to me is going to do for you."

"Can you answer my questions?"

Rennie was hesitant. "I reserve the right not to answer anything, especially if it might incriminate me in a divorce hearing."

"I understand. Maybe you could give me some legal advice?"

She shook her head. "Hire a lawyer. A good one. A shark. Take him for everything he has."

Angela nodded. A server came over and brought them menus. Rennie pushed hers aside. She had lost her appetite. "The people you ran into at the resort—they golf with my parents. Karen called me right away to tell me. Part of me wishes she hadn't, because then maybe Theo would tell me when he got home. I tried calling him, but he didn't answer, and he never returned any of my messages. I spent four days wondering what the two of you were doing. Crazy thoughts, ya know.

Like, how many times did you and my husband make love while you were in Canada? Did you wear lingerie? Shower together? Is he spontaneous, or does he schedule everything? Does he act animalistic and throw you against the wall? Every time I tried to close my eyes, all I could see was the two of you making love, and I had no idea who you even were, and I couldn't understand why he took this woman to where we spent our honeymoon."

Angela's statement made Rennie's stomach twist. Theo was the worst type of man she had ever known. "I wasn't there," she told her. "I left right after the encounter with Karen."

"That's not what Theo told me. He said you stayed."

Rennie huffed. "He's a liar. I spent the weekend in the San Juan Islands with a friend."

"Then where was my husband?"

"Well, I know he went to my friend's house looking for me, but I don't know much after that."

"Are you still seeing him?"

"Hell no. I'm not a home-wrecker."

"But you went away on a trip with a married man."

The fact that Angela was referring only to the trip confused Rennie. She convinced herself Theo was lying to his wife. "Listen, I don't know what Theo has told you, and I don't care, because I want no part of his life. We didn't just go away for New Year's. We've been dating for over a year. We met at a college job fair thing in Spokane and have been together ever since—well, at least until I met Karen. He never once mentioned he was married. If he had, I would've kicked him in the balls and bailed."

Angela sat there for a moment and then started to cry. Rennie was torn on whether to comfort her. She chose not to and kept her hands to herself. Rennie felt terrible for the woman but wanted to avoid their marital issues.

"I remember that weekend. He called and said he wouldn't be home, that he needed to stay there. I was so confused because we live down the street from the convention center, and he could've easily been back first thing in the morning. Did you sleep with him that night?"

She had nothing to gain by being dishonest. Rennie nodded.

"And the next day?"

Rennie nodded again.

Angela looked at her in disbelief. "And the following weekend, right? He had a business trip. You know, I'm just going to assume that every time my husband was out of town, he was with you. He wears a ring. Why wasn't that enough to stop you?" Angela pointed out.

"Like I said, I didn't know. He may wear one when he's home, but the day I met Theo, he did not have a ring on and hasn't since that day." Which made her wonder if she was truly the only woman he had cheated on Angela with. The more she sat there, the more she hated him.

"You know, I'm sitting here and wondering why *you*. What do you have that I don't? What did my husband, my high school sweetheart, see in you that he doesn't see in me? I've given him everything, and I don't understand why he's done this to me."

Slowly, Rennie shook her head back and forth. "I don't know. From my experience at work, sometimes it's nothing. Sometimes, men cheat, or women do. Some say they're bored or their partner isn't satisfying in bed. Others do it because they don't get caught. I can tell you anything you want about our relationship, but as to his state of mind and why he's done this, I don't have an answer for you. If I knew he was married, I would've never entertained the idea. I would've walked away. I deal with divorce on a daily basis. I'm not going to be the catalyst for one. That's not who I am as a person."

"Are you in love with him?"

Rennie adjusted in her seat. "At one time, yes, I was. But we drifted apart a little. We planned the trip for a few months, and we were going to use it to reconnect. Again, I knew nothing about you, so I had no idea you spent your honeymoon there."

"Whose idea was the trip?"

"His. I don't ski. I agreed because it was something he wanted to do." Rennie paused and contemplated what she was about to tell Angela. "You should know, he asked me to move to Spokane, to live with him. And a few days ago, he sat in my friend's bar, demanding my friend help him get me back."

Angela nodded. "So, no business trip?"

"I don't know. I haven't seen or spoken to him since the beginning of last week." Rennie reached for her bag again. "Look, I'm really sorry. I am. If you decide to stay in your marriage, I wish you the best of luck, but if you decide to leave him, you'll need a damn good lawyer. He's a manipulator. I really have to go." Rennie walked away. She left Theo's wife at the restaurant and never looked back.

THIRTY

The saying "The writing is on the wall" never meant much to Graham. He wasn't the type of guy who looked for signs or omens or believed in superstition, which hadn't made a ton of sense since he ran what many considered to be a haunted bar. Graham chalked those stories up to old wives' tales or stories that had been embellished over time. He likened most of them to the game of telephone that he played in kindergarten. By the time the message got to the last kid, it was nothing like the way it had started.

It had been weeks since Rennie had visited Cape Harbor. She was busy; that was the excuse she gave Graham every Thursday or Friday. Her caseload was heavy, and she didn't have time to drive north; she had court, too many meetings, mediation. When Graham suggested he come down, her excuse was that he would be a distraction. He tried not to let the rejection hurt, but it had, and he had gone back to the ridiculous what-if game. What if he had told her no when they were on the boat? What if he had dropped her off at Brooklyn's instead of bringing her to his house? Graham could come up with a dozen or more questions, all with no answer. His hindsight game was strong, and at this point in his life, he should've made a career out of it.

As much as Rennie's absence bothered him, he refused to show it. He went about his day, returned her text messages when she would return his, and made every-other-day trips to see Grady. For everything Rennie was doing to Graham in regard to their relationship, he couldn't be mad at her, because she was there when he needed her most, and because of her swift actions, she had brought Grady back to Graham.

Grady thrived in rehab. Their weekly family therapy sessions weren't always serious. There had been a lot of laughter, jokes, and overdue apologies. Grady was apologetic for what he'd put everyone through, and they, in turn, were sorry they'd waited so long to get him the help he needed.

When Graham arrived at the facility, he carried a box of doughnuts. Bringing one to Grady had become a habit, and he told his brother that the staff hinted they would like one. Graham was happy to oblige and started bringing a dozen. He checked in, waited for the security guard to take his doughnut, and then made his way to the rec room, where visitation started.

It wasn't long until Grady came in; he was looking more and more like Graham every day. If someone who didn't already know they were identical twins met the brothers now, they'd at least know they were related. Grady looked like an older version of Graham. But he was healthy, and that was the only thing that mattered.

"They're seriously going to miss you when I get out of here," Grady said as he sat down. He chose his maple bar and took a bite. Following Grady's last checkup, Dr. Field informed the family that Grady's organs were healing, but he needed to stay clean. One relapse would kill him. Thankfully, they removed Grady's feeding tube, and he could start eating more substantial meals.

"They'll have to con someone else into bringing them treats."

Grady looked at his brother and smiled. "You visit more than anyone out of everyone here."

"Really?"

He nodded. "I appreciate it. I've missed being your brother."

Graham reached across the table and squeezed Grady's hand. "Me too, brother." The boys shared a moment, and when Graham pulled his hand back, he had to look away. He didn't want his brother to see him cry. "So, you have about a month left."

"Yeah," Grady said as he picked at the pastry. "I have a new lawyer. His name is Jeff something or other. He works with Rennie. She said he's more equipped to handle my case. I like him."

"Rennie does too. She said he had helped her with your arraignment."

"Jeff said I wouldn't serve any jail time. He worked out a deal with the state or whatever. One-year probation, license suspended for a year, and two years community service, plus three years of court-mandated treatment."

"Wait, you have to stay here for three years?"

Grady laughed. "No, like AA or whatever. The state will assign me a counselor and all that."

Graham understood now. "Maybe it can be in Skagit Valley or somewhere close."

"Yeah, I'll ask."

"Grady." Graham spoke his brother's name softly. "I'm really proud of you. I thought you would've fought us on this last push to get you into rehab, made things hard, but you're doing really well."

Grady stayed silent and focused on his breakfast. When he finally spoke, he said, "I'm going to need a job."

"Already on it," Graham said instantly. "I've spoken to Bowie. He has a spot on his crew if you want it. Dad has spoken to the guys on the docks. There's a job there as well. And there's an opening at the fish market. So, you have options."

"Fishing would be good."

"It would, but, Grady, I'm concerned about you being on a boat. You haven't been on one since the accident."

"I think I'll be okay."

"Thinking and knowing are two different things. Maybe if we talk about what happened that night—"

Grady's eyes shot up, angry and intense. "I will not talk about it. I live it every day."

Graham held his hands up. The accident was a topic the therapist had trouble scratching the surface of. Each time he asked, Grady shut down. He refused to discuss it or tell anyone what truly happened that night.

"I just worry about you being out there and all." Graham sighed and changed the subject. "So, you have a couple prospects, which is a good start."

"Do you still live on the houseboat?"

"Yeah. There's a recovery house in Skagit Valley that you qualify for, or Mom and Dad's is always an option." There was no way Grady could come live with Graham. The house was too small, and they both needed their own space.

"Guess I have a few weeks to figure it out."

"And I'll help. You have a strong team supporting you. We won't let you fail."

When visiting hours ended, Graham and Grady hugged. "I'll see you in a couple days," Graham told his brother. As well as Grady was doing, Graham feared a setback, especially when Grady returned to Cape Harbor. With his refusal to talk about the night of the accident, Grady still battled a lot of demons, and it was those demons that led him to drink. Something had to be done, but he wasn't sure what, if anything. There wasn't a law saying Grady had to tell his therapist everything, and if he couldn't get Grady to open up, who could?

Graham made it back to Cape Harbor in record time. He'd become a pro at making it to the ferry when it was time to board. Instead of getting out of his car, he used the time it took to get across the bay to take a nap. Exhaustion was Graham's new friend.

Once the ferry docked, he drove home. He had to work later but wanted to take a shower and relax. When he got to his door, he saw a note taped there.

Meet me at the pit

Ren

Graham wasn't sure what to think about the note. Part of him found it cute, but the other half of him wanted to know why she hadn't called and told him she was in town. Graham got back in his car and drove over to the Driftwood Inn, which was the easiest place to access the firepit. Throughout his life, he had spent so many spring and summer nights in this spot. Many of his memories included Rennie.

He parked along the side of the road to not only avoid the valet at the inn but to also cut through the shrubs. He didn't want to run into Brooklyn—and Bowie, if he was home. Graham went down the stairs and trudged through the sand until he came upon the driftwood-log formation. There were a blanket and a pair of shoes, but no Rennie. Graham looked out over the horizon and saw someone standing near the water. He went toward the person, hoping it was her. When he got closer, he could see her multicolored hair, which he loved picking the colors out from, blowing in the wind. She was dressed in shorts and a long-sleeved shirt and stood barefoot in the wet sand.

"You're going to catch a cold out here." It wasn't the first time he'd had to warn her about getting sick.

Rennie turned and smiled. When Graham was close, she wrapped her arms around his waist and held him tightly. He hugged her back.

Neither of them spoke; they just stood there in each other's arms and absorbed the moment.

It was Graham who finally said something. "I'm kind of surprised to see you, honestly."

"I know. I'm sorry for being so absent."

"How come you didn't tell me you were coming up?"

Rennie tilted her head up and smiled. "I wanted to surprise you. The lawsuit against you, totally bogus. You will have a new delivery driver, though, from the distribution company. Your normal driver saw you as an easy target, concocted this whole story to get money because the insurance company wouldn't pay for his daughter's care because she was at fault. She wasn't even in the area at the time of her accident. The whole thing was really convoluted and has really left a bad taste in my mouth with the firm. Donna wanted to waste resources and money to bring the case to trial, but we had enough evidence to shut her down."

He couldn't deny it; he liked her surprise, and he was relieved, but something else bothered him. Her lack of communication. She rose to kiss him, and he allowed it but didn't deepen the kiss. He pulled away and enveloped her with his arms. Graham looked out over the ocean, hoping to gain the strength and encouragement he needed for what he was about to say.

"Ren, we need to talk."

He felt her move, and when he looked down, she stared at him. He bent forward, kissed her nose, and then took her and led her back to the pit. He sat down and expected her to sit next to him, but she sat between his legs, like they were seventeen all over again.

Graham pulled the blanket over her to keep her warm, like he had on the boat. He wished they had a fire, but it would take too long for him to start one, and it would likely attract people from the inn, and he wanted as much privacy as possible.

"I saw Grady today," he started. "He really likes his new lawyer. Said things are very promising?"

Rennie nodded against Graham's chest. "That's good." She inhaled and then exhaled slowly, gathering her thoughts. "I'm in this funk, and I don't know how to get out of it. I know I'm shutting you out—Brooklyn too. I'm trying to find a way to deal with everything."

"Do you remember when I told you I thought you needed time to get over Theo?"

She nodded against his chest.

"I want you to take the time, Rennie. You need it, and I need to focus on Grady. And I think . . ." Graham paused and fought back the tears. His heart ripped in two, and he prepared himself for what he was about to say. "I think we need to remain friends. I had come to you with the idea that we date, and you blew me off. I really feel like I'm giving so much of myself to you, being here, but I can never say no to you. As stupid as this sounds, I know I could take you back to my house, and we'd have sex because that is what we've been used to. Don't get me wrong; the sex is great—but it doesn't tell me the kind of person you are. I want to know who you are now. I don't want to rely on memories. And as much as I love you, we're not on the same path. The list of qualities you want in a partner—they're not me. I'm never going to be financially stable; hell, I'll probably die behind the bar. Sometimes I think I want a wife and a kid or two, and that's not the life you want, and I'm okay with that because you'd be enough in my life.

"What we had when we were younger—it was great. The best time of my life. But if Grady's rehab has taught me anything, it's taught me that I can't live in the past, and that is what I see when we're together." She had heard all this before, but he figured he'd repeat it, maybe help her accept she wasn't ready for a relationship, at least not the kind he wanted to have.

Rennie pulled Graham's arms tightly around her. They sat there for hours, watching the surf until the sun went down. When she finally moved, she got on her knees and placed her hands on Graham's cheeks. "I love you, Graham Cracker. Don't ever forget it." She kissed him, stood, gathered her things, and walked away.

THIRTY-ONE

"I have never, in my life, been to a dry party." Rennie sat in the sand while putting bottles of water, cans of pop, and juice boxes into a cooler.

"It'll be good for you," Brooklyn replied. "You can cleanse like the rest of us."

That was what everyone vowed to do: cleanse. According to Brooklyn, Graham had approached the group of friends and asked if they'd be willing to forgo drinking for a bit, at least in front of Grady, to help in his sobriety. And when Rennie called Brooklyn to tell her she was coming up for the weekend, Brooklyn filled her in on everything that had happened in the last month.

After Rennie left Graham on the beach, she returned to Seattle, spent two days passing her cases off to other lawyers, and put in for some time off, and then she went south to Malibu. Much to her surprise, the shack she had rented back in college was still there, although updated—but still not worth the money to rent it for a month.

Each morning, she woke and took a run on the beach. After she showered, she strolled along the main road, browsing through the shops. She would take whatever book she planned to read that day with her and find a bench to sit on and read or return to her one-room shack and lie in the sun. She kept her phone off and made sure to leave her laptop back in Washington. The only people who knew where she was were her parents and Brooklyn. None of whom would divulge her whereabouts.

Rennie also wrote in a journal. Each day, she'd put her thoughts down, hoping to cure whatever ailed her. She wrote angry letters to Theo, tore them up, and wrote them again. Each one was the same, asking him why he chose her over everyone else? At times, she felt sorry for him, his wife, and herself. He was, at least to her, the worst kind of human.

She also wrote to Graham. She put her feelings down on paper and recounted their love story. Rennie mailed this letter and prayed that when she returned from her trip, they would talk.

> Dear Graham Cracker,
> It's funny, as I write the nickname I gave you, I wonder if you ever truly appreciated it or understood where it came from. You see, before I met you, s'mores were my favorite snack. During the winter, I used to make my mom turn on the gas burner so that I could roast a marshmallow to perfection. I loved the ooey-gooey goodness.
>
> Then, I met you, and you became my treat. Even at sixteen, you're the one I craved. You were the only one I needed. I always waited for you to ask me to be your girlfriend. I know, I know, I told you many times that we were just friends or having fun, but it was because I was afraid that was how you truly felt. Pretty stupid now that I think of it. All this time, we could've been together, raising a family, and living our lives.
>
> Along our journey, I made mistakes. My first one, telling you (even though we were "friends") that

I didn't want a relationship in college. Dating was hard because I compared every single guy to the one I couldn't have and was afraid didn't want me. My second mistake was not telling you how I felt when you started dating Monica. The night you came over to tell me about her, I should've professed my love to you, and I didn't because I thought I had already lost you. My third was ignoring you for all those years. I can't tell you how many times I thought about driving to see you, but I didn't because of B. I think deep down, she would've understood. My fourth, not leaving Theo last summer after I saw you for the first time in years. I knew the minute I laid eyes on you again. You were the one I'd been waiting for my entire life. And to think, I could've had you.

Graham Chamberlain, you are the love of my life, and it's okay if I'm not yours, but I had to let you know. It's the reason I called you to come and get me. You were, and still are, the only man I want to spend my time with.

By the time you receive this letter, I'll be on my way home. But you should know, I'm sitting on our beach, the one in Malibu with the tiny shack we rented for all of us that one time. It's been updated but it's still rickety, the roof leaks, and the same man still owns it. Oh, the price changed. It's astronomical but worth the cost to come back to a place we shared.

I hope that when I return, we can talk.

Love,

Rennie

The day she mailed the letter, it poured. The rain reminded her of home. She was sad her trip had come to an end but was hopeful and excited to see Graham. When she returned to Washington, she went right to Cape Harbor to spend some time with Brooklyn and Brystol, not knowing about Grady's release and welcome-home party.

Rennie looked up when she heard either Bowie or Jason grunting. The guys carried a steel drum barbecue down the stairs and placed it just outside the canopy Bowie erected earlier. It was still too cold to have parties on the beach, but they were determined to make it happen.

"You guys okay over there?" Rennie asked. She got up, wiped the sand off the back of her yoga pants, and went to them. Jason started loading the briquettes while Bowie secured the legs with mounds of sand.

"We're old," Jason told her. Jason Randolph was the only one from their group of friends who'd left Cape Harbor and stayed away. He went to medical school and now worked as an ER doc in Seattle. He didn't visit as often as he wanted but made sure to be here to see Grady.

"You may be old, but I'm not," Rennie quipped. Although, at times, especially after a hot yoga session or a miles-long run, she felt old.

Bowie doused the charcoal with lighter fluid and then tossed a couple of matches in. The flames roared instantly and, after a few seconds, died down. It would be a bit before they'd be ready to cook.

Brooklyn appeared with an armful of blankets from the inn's shed, which wasn't far from where they'd set up. Rennie took half and set them on the driftwood logs. They were there for anyone to use. Bowie came over to Brooklyn and kissed her. "I'm going to get the fire started," Rennie heard him say. It was her cue to run back into the house and grab her bag of provisions—everything she'd need to make s'mores.

When she and Simone reemerged, the group of people had grown, and everyone had clumped together. "I think Grady is in the mix," Rennie said to Simi.

"I think you're right. They're liable to freak him out."

Rennie watched the group from the outskirts, letting the friends and family congratulate Grady. It wasn't until she felt a tap on her shoulder that she turned around. "Hey, Grady."

He didn't say anything to her. He wrapped his strong arms around her and lifted her off the ground. "I don't think I'll ever be able to thank you." Grady set her down gently and stepped away.

"All I did was help out a friend."

"The fact that you even consider me a friend means everything to me. If it weren't for you, I'd be in jail right now."

Rennie briefly touched Grady on his arm. "I'm so happy you're healthy and clean."

The next to hug Rennie was Johanna, who held on to Rennie as if her life depended on it. "If you ever need anything, please let me know."

I need your son to love me back, Rennie thought to herself.

"Dinner, tomorrow night at our house. I won't take no for an answer."

"I'll be there, Mrs. Chamberlain."

Johanna waved her hand. "None of this *Mrs.* crap. Call me Jo or Johanna. As far as I'm concerned, you're family."

Next, George stepped forward. He was much more subdued than his son and wife had been. He shook Rennie's hand and thanked her before he went to rummage through the coolers. The rumor was George stopped drinking the day Grady went into rehab because he wanted to support his son and finally realized he hadn't done a very good job of it.

Graham stood off to the side, watching Rennie interact with his family. When they made eye contact, she smiled and then diverted her eyes to the sand. She felt him approach but didn't look up.

He placed his hand on her hip and stepped close to her. "Can we go for a walk?" Rennie nodded and finally lifted her gaze toward Graham. His green eyes sparkled, and his crooked smile was back. Graham led her away from their friends and toward a large rock formation, which formed different alcoves and inlets of water.

Graham found a place with privacy and motioned for her to sit on a rock while he stood next to her. He leaned against the rock with his hip and reached out to touch some strands of hair that had fallen from Rennie's ponytail.

"I got your letter in the mail. I have to say, getting fun mail when it's not my birthday or a holiday is quite the treat."

Rennie smiled and let out a tiny laugh. "I can't remember the last time I wrote a letter. Everything is text or email these days."

"How's the shack?"

She laughed harder this time. "Still the same shithole it was when we were in college, but very nostalgic. I'm glad I went. I needed the time away to clear my head."

"Is it clear?" he asked, and she nodded. "That's good . . . good." Graham hesitated before continuing. "I want you to know I read your words a few times, actually. I wish like hell we could go back to the night we spent in the back of my truck under the stars. I had no idea what the hell I was doing. I just knew that every time I was around you, I had this ache, and you were the cure. I never wanted our first time to be in the back of the truck, but it was, and I've never forgotten that night. I should've told you then that I was in love with you. I knew from the moment I met you I wanted you to be my wife. I was embarrassed, though, because guys don't talk like that, so I kept my mouth shut.

"When you said you planned to study law in California, I looked for schools near you. I thought we'd live down there, and us becoming a couple would be a natural progression. I could see it all playing out in my head. We'd become roommates, and before long, you'd be in my bed every night. We'd fight, make love, and finally grow up enough to tell each other how we felt."

"What changed, Graham?"

He looked away and fiddled with the rock Rennie sat on. "The week before I met Monica, you and I were at this party. We were dancing, making out like we usually did. You took me into the bathroom, which wasn't out of the ordinary for us. What was, though, was what you said. It caught me off guard and really made me take a step back. Do you remember that night?"

Rennie shook her head.

"You said, 'Make it quick.' That's when I realized we were nothing more than fuck buddies."

"Oh, God." Rennie covered her mouth. "I'm so stupid."

"We were young, in college, and having fun."

Rennie shook her head and looked off into the distance. Her smart mouth had finally done her in, and now she knew why Graham chose someone else over her. Who would want to bring a crass college chick home to their parents, no matter how many times she had met them before?

Graham's thumb gently brought Rennie's face toward him. "I don't want to live in the past, Rennie. It's not healthy. But I want you in my future. I want to date you. I want to take you places, spend every minute we can together. I want to wake up in your arms on Sunday morning and read the paper together. I want to call my mom and tell her I'm bringing my girlfriend over for family dinner. I want to show up at your house in the middle of a rainstorm just so we can dance together outside."

"I want those things too, Graham."

"Can you live with me being a bartender? Knowing this is my life. It's the life I chose out of duty to my family. Is this going to be okay with you? I'm not rich, Ren, and I never will be, but I can love you until my last breath if you'd let me."

Rennie sprang from her seated position and launched herself into Graham's arms. She kissed him deeply and wrapped her legs around his waist. His hands went to her hair, back, and finally under her shirt, where she shivered from his touch.

"I love you," she said as she pulled her mouth away from his. "I love you so damn much it hurts."

"I love you, my Rennie."

THIRTY-TWO

It was the middle of the summer when Graham asked to borrow Bowie's boat for a long weekend. He loaded it full of food, made sure to grab bedding, and told Rennie to pack light. They were going sailing to celebrate the end of Rennie's employment at Rhoads PC and the start of her new private practice. Main Street in Skagit Valley had a new resident, Wallace Law Firm, with two employees, Rennie and Ester. Rennie had fretted about asking Ester to join her new endeavor. She was a single mom and depended heavily on her income. One night, when Graham and Rennie were over at Brooklyn's, it was Bowie who suggested a compromise. Rennie would do all his legal work, and in exchange, Ester could live in one of the small cottages he and Brooklyn recently renovated, rent-free as long as she paid utilities. The deal was too good to pass up, and Ester agreed to move.

Before Rennie submitted her resignation, she started taking a couple night classes. She wanted to expand her knowledge of the law and work as a general practitioner, which would allow her to help anyone who walked through the door. Her colleague Jefferson had also resigned, and she promised to send any criminal cases his way. Working at Rhoads PC had become overwhelming, more so after the frivolous accusations toward Graham were found untruthful. Ester had uncovered the real reason Donna's attitude toward Rennie had changed—Rennie's promotion. Donna had felt Rennie wasn't ready or deserving, and when she was promoted, Donna wanted to send a strong message to her former mentee. When Rennie found this out, she had no choice but to quit.

While Rennie focused on her career, Graham poured his attention into his house. If he and Rennie were going to live together, changes had to happen. He worked with Bowie and Brooklyn to create a bigger space and then took the necessary permits out to start construction on his houseboat. They would add four inches of width and up to thirty inches to the length, giving them a lot more room. The plan, as it stood, would be to add two additional bedrooms, one of which would double as an office. It was an absolute must that the bathroom be expanded, as well as their living space. They wanted to live together, but neither was willing to pass up the views and ambiance the houseboat provided. With the additions, they'd be able to live comfortably.

As soon as Graham had everything secured on the boat, he jogged back over to his house. His neighbor Shari was outside; they waved at each other before Graham ducked inside his home. He was still too embarrassed to speak to her after the incident last year. When he told Rennie about it, she laughed and went over to introduce herself to Shari. The two were now friends, which made Graham feel even more awkward.

"Hey," he said as he stepped inside. He went right to Rennie and pulled her into an embrace. He hadn't seen her in a few days, as she'd had loose ends to tie up in Seattle, but she was back in Cape Harbor and didn't have to leave.

"I made sandwiches."

"Perfect," he said as he kissed her again. "You ready to go?"

Rennie nodded, bagged up their lunch, and grabbed her things. Graham waited for her to exit first before pulling the door shut and making sure it was locked. While they were gone, construction would continue.

"The work crew will be by while we're gone," Graham could hear Rennie tell Shari. He smiled as he passed by but kept his head down.

"You know, you're going to need to talk to her someday."

"Nope, I don't think so."

"Stop being such a baby."

They walked hand in hand up the ramp and through the parking lot until they came to the gate for the docks. Graham typed in the six-digit code and waited for the lock to disengage. He opened the door, and Rennie went through and led them down to Bowie's boat, where she stowed her things.

"I'll untie and pull the buoys," she said as Graham started up the craft. When it came to boating, she was still a novice but learning. Graham had shown her a few tricks on how to coil the rope and fold the tarp, but he mostly did it for her. He appreciated her help, though, and always thanked her.

They set sail toward Friday Harbor. Graham was making good on a suggestion—not a promise, as he liked to remind Rennie—that she see the lavender fields in bloom. They would dock for the night once they reached the pier, visit in the morning, and then head south toward Puget Sound and then turn north to head home. Four days at sea, with nothing but each other.

Much like their last trip, Rennie worked in the galley, plating their lunch, and sat next to Graham in the extrawide single-person chair. Unlike their previous trip, Rennie was happy and in love . . . with Graham.

"Thanks for lunch, babe." He turned and kissed her on the cheek.

With the navigation set, Graham relaxed a bit, and the boat cruised along the course. The last time they came out this way, there wasn't another boat in sight; now they were everywhere.

"Think Grady's out here?" Rennie asked as she looked out the window.

"Nah, I think he said they were headed toward Alaska."

Rennie shook her head. "I can't believe how far he's come in these past few months. You must be so proud of him."

"We all are." Graham placed his arm around Rennie and pulled her closer. He had to give her a lot of credit where his brother was concerned. If it hadn't been for her, there wasn't a doubt in Graham's mind Grady would be in jail. As it was now, Grady had a stable job on a fishing boat. After he had a talk with Brooklyn about starting Chamberwoods back up, she suggested he work for a bit to make sure he still had his sea legs. If in a year he was sober and thriving, she, on behalf of Brystol, would invest in the company and hand over majority ownership to him. Much to Graham's surprise, Grady agreed. When Graham heard what Brooklyn said, he thought for sure Grady would go off the deep end, but he hadn't.

Rennie cleared their plates away and cleaned the galley before she stripped out of her clothes and went to lie in the sun. He was jealous of everything: that he had to drive the boat, of her swimsuit because it touched her, of the other boaters who saw her. He wanted to be with her, always.

When they reached the pier in Friday Harbor, it was time for dinner. Rennie cooked while Graham paid their slip fee for the night. They had talked about going back to the bar, but neither had really drunk since Grady got out of rehab, and it really wasn't their scene. Although they liked the idea of hustling the pool players, they also feared someone would remember them from New Year's. They ate an easy dinner of chicken and sautéed vegetables and sat on the deck and spoke to people as they came down the pier.

"I feel like we're old."

Graham laughed. "We're not even forty yet."

"Look at us, Graham. I'm dressed in white shorts and deck shoes, with my striped pullover sweater. I belong in the catalog for what retired women should wear when boating."

"You're ridiculous; come with me," he said as he got up. He walked up the stairs into the galley and then down the small flight to where the bedrooms were. He went into the master bedroom and waited for Rennie to join him.

"What are we doing?"

He closed the door and then went around to make sure the windows were closed as well. "Strip."

"What?"

"Get naked," he told her as he dropped his shorts. Rennie gawked at him and slowly undressed. She stood before him, naked. "Now, lie on the bed. I'm going to show you how sexy and not old you are."

She did as she was told. Graham lay next to her, resting on his elbow. Slowly, he touched every part of her body, saying he loved the spot behind her knee because it was so ticklish and how the curve of her hip fit his hand perfectly. Each time he'd get to a random part of her body, he would comment and massage or kiss the area. By the time Graham came to her neck, she was panting. She wanted him, but each time she reached for him, he batted her hand away.

"Graham," she drew his name out through ragged breaths.

"Ren," he replied. When they'd finally figured their lives out, he'd promised never to call her *love* or *darling*. Both nicknames triggered fits of anger in her, and he never wanted her to be upset with him.

"Can you?" Her chest heaved up and down as his finger trailed over the goose bumps on her skin. "I need . . ."

"What do you need?"

"You. I need you."

"Okay." Graham dropped his hand onto her waist and pulled her toward him, hitching her leg over his thigh. He cupped her face between his hands, and she gripped his wrist, as if to hang on. He flexed his hips and watched her intently. Her eyes fluttered, and as soon as her mouth opened, he kissed her.

When the sun came up the next morning, Graham was thankful they only had one thing on their list to do. The rest of their vacation would be on the boat, just the two of them. He rose early, showered, and made his way to the rental agency, where he was able to get the scooter he wanted. When he pulled into the marina, Rennie was waiting for him in the parking lot.

"Oh my. Is this safe?" she asked as she slipped her helmet on.

"We aren't going far," he told her.

Rennie climbed on the back and wrapped her arms around Graham's waist. He drove them out to the field he had shown her back in January, and when he pulled into an open parking spot, she jumped off the scooter and walked toward the fence.

"Graham, this is beautiful," she said after she took her helmet off. "These fields are so vibrant."

Graham secured the scooter and took Rennie's helmet from her and set both helmets on the seat. He reached for her hand and started them off on the trail that would take them deeper into the lavender.

"I can't believe it's taken my whole life to see this place."

With those words, Graham turned and got down on one knee.

"What are you doing?" she asked him.

In his hand, he held a black-velvet box, and he said to her, "I can't believe it's taken me this long to ask you to be my wife. Rennie Wallace, will you marry me?"

Rennie covered her mouth with both hands and nodded. "Oh my God, yes. So many yeses," she told him as she tackled him to the ground. They lay there laughing at her exuberance for a moment until Graham rolled them onto their sides. It was an awkward position, but he was able to slip the halo solitaire onto her finger.

"I'm sorry it's taken me so long to do this." He kissed her hand once the ring was in place.

"Are you kidding me? We're so much stronger now than we would've been. We needed to grow up, be stupid, and find our way back to each other. I love you, Graham Cracker."

After their hike through the fields, they returned the scooter and made their way back to the boat. Graham caught Rennie holding her hand out, angling her ring so the sun would hit it, and each time it sparkled, she would giggle.

When they boarded the boat, it was business as usual. Graham started the engine while Rennie untied them from the dock. Once they were out in the open sea, Rennie curled up on the couch and opened her book. Every so often, Graham would glance over and find her looking at him.

Their road to happiness had not been easy, but if Graham had his say, their future would be.

EPILOGUE

The bonfire crackled, and small embers flew to the sand, leaving black soot marks scattered around the area. People sat on the driftwood logs, some stood, and others wrapped themselves in blankets to keep the mid-September night chill away. Others sat in the sand, and a few people had chairs. The group had started small but grew in numbers as the night went on. Every time someone new joined, there were squeals and statements such as "I haven't seen you in years."

Rennie stood near the fire, trying to keep warm. Every time she tried to sit down or find Graham, an old classmate came up to her. They hugged, talked about what they'd been doing for the last five years or so—however long it had been since their last high school reunion—and pestered her with questions about her upcoming wedding. A few of her old classmates gushed about how handsome Graham was; a couple had asked if he had a brother, and Rennie had pointed toward Grady, but when these women asked if she would introduce them, she blew them off. Rennie was protective of her soon-to-be brother-in-law, and the last thing she wanted and felt he needed was a relationship. They were complicated and messy, and Grady was working his tail off to keep his life on track. To date, he hadn't slipped up, even though he talked about it, especially when the anniversary of Austin's death rolled around. At her and Brooklyn's insistence, Bowie, Jason, George, and Graham took

Grady camping for a weekend. Just the guys. No cell phones. No wives, girlfriends, or Johanna making sure her boys were well fed. It was good for the guys to get away and even better for Grady to be surrounded by his friends.

Strong arms wrapped around her from behind, and she was comforted instantly by the smell of Old Spice. She closed her eyes and placed her hands on his arms, holding him as best she could. Rennie had all but forgotten about the woman she had been talking to until she heard her clear her throat.

"Oh, sorry," she said as she opened her eyes. Rennie wasn't embarrassed. She was in love. After years of not having the man of her dreams, now that she finally had him, she couldn't get enough of him. "Jen, this is my fiancé, Graham."

"Nice to meet you." Graham stuck his hand out to shake Rennie's friend's.

"Wait, I know you," she said after Graham let go. "You're the bartender at the place not far from here, right? My friends and I stop in all the time when we're sailing."

"We actually own the bar," Rennie corrected, even though she didn't need to. When the conflict between Donna and Rennie became public knowledge at Rhoads PC, Lex Davey had given Rennie an excellent severance package, which she'd used to buy out Graham's parents' stake in the Whale Spout. Graham tapped Rennie on her waist, a sign from him that she needed to tone her jealousy down a little bit. She couldn't help it. Once she moved to Cape Harbor, she saw firsthand how many women flirted with Graham. She was thankful he was oblivious to it all, but it still got on her nerves.

"We appreciate you and your friends stopping by. When you're in next time, say hi." Graham kissed Rennie on the cheek. "I love you, firecracker." He laughed and stepped away.

Rennie continued to talk to Jen for a few more minutes before she excused herself to find Brooklyn. "Hey," she said as she sat down on one of the logs. "I can't believe you invited everyone from high school to your wedding."

Brooklyn huffed. "I didn't mean to."

"Tell me again how this happened?"

Brooklyn covered her face with her hands and groaned. "Stupid social media. I created an event for the weekend. I figured it would be easier if all the information was in one place. Except I didn't make it private, and I sent invites to *all*, along with the ones I sent our friends. I had no idea what I had done until people started RSVP'ing."

Rennie bumped shoulders with her best friend. "You know what this means, right?"

"That only Brystol can do my social media from here on out?"

She laughed. "Well, yes, I would agree with this, but also you'll get a ton of presents tomorrow at your reception. So many freaking presents."

"You're ridiculous."

"And yet, I'm your best friend, and you love me no matter what. Seriously, that's why I tell Graham we need to have a huge wedding and invite every single person we know."

"Have you set a date?"

"We've talked about next year, but we also talked about going to Vegas during the winter to elope."

Brooklyn gripped Rennie's forearm. "You can't do that. Not without Bowie and me."

As if on cue, Luke the black Lab barreled through the crowd and found Brooklyn. He sat at her feet while she petted him. "Seriously, Ren. I have to be at your wedding."

"And you're saying you and Bowie can't fly to Vegas?"

"Oh, phew. I thought you wanted to do it by yourself."

Rennie shook her head. "Oh, hell no. You have to be there. So does Grady." Rennie nodded toward the area where Grady stood. He wasn't engaging in conversation unless someone came up to him, which

Rennie understood. Most people walked on eggshells around him, except for her.

"Are you ready for tomorrow?"

Brooklyn looked into Rennie's eyes and nodded. "I am. I'm so ready. I love Bowie with my whole heart. I love the life we have together and how he's this amazing dad to Brystol. Everything is so perfect, I just—"

"Stop," Rennie interrupted. "Stop thinking the other shoe is going to fall. Both are planted firmly on the ground. It's taken both of us a long time to get our princes. I say *get* because we found them when we were teens but were too wild and rambunctious to see that we had a good thing . . . well, you weren't, but whatever. What I'm saying is, Bowie is the right man for you, and you need to put whatever lingering thoughts about Austin away and keep them there."

"You're right."

"I know I am. I'm going to talk to Grady and then try and convince Graham to take me to bed. I'm tired."

"Liar," Brooklyn said with a laugh.

"I know, but it sounded good." Rennie hugged Brooklyn and told her she'd see her in the morning. Even though Rennie and Graham could walk back to their houseboat, they were staying at the inn, along with everyone else. Rennie wasn't exactly keen on the idea, but it was what Brooklyn wanted, and as maid of honor, Rennie would do anything for her friend.

Rennie avoided everyone on her way over to Grady. He stood on the outskirts, holding a water bottle. As soon as he saw her, he held it out for her.

Only she refused to take it. "I trust you." She looked forward to the day when Grady wouldn't feel like he had to prove he wasn't drinking anymore.

"Thanks."

"Is someone giving you shit?"

He nodded toward the crowd. There were so many people she had no idea who in their right mind would say something to Grady about his sobriety. Rennie had firsthand knowledge of the efforts he put in. Grady met with his probation officer, passed every surprise test, never missed a therapy appointment, and went to AA twice, if not three times, a week.

"I'm going to need a name, Grady."

"It's Mila, but I think she's drunk."

Everyone in their close-knit group of friends refused to drink around Grady. They were all trying to do their part to help him out, and Grady stayed away from the Whale Spout, and the staff there knew not to serve him alcohol if he did come in. There were times when he'd come in to see Graham. He'd sit at the bar and drink pop or water, never once asking for a drink. On those days or nights, Graham would come home and tell Rennie how proud he was of his brother.

"Eh, gotta look at who is saying crap and ignore. You know you're doing awesome. I'm proud of you. Jefferson tells me all the time when he gets reports from your PO how well you're doing."

Grady raised his water bottle and took a sip. "I know I've thanked you before, but I'm really appreciative of everything you've done for me. I know you've helped Brooklyn out with the contract and stuff she wants me to sign, so thank you."

"You're welcome, Grady. Next summer will be an exciting time. Do you know what you're going to name your boat yet?"

"No, not yet. Everyone tells me I have to name it after Austin—"

Rennie cut him off. "No, you name it after whatever you want to. Austin's gone. He has been for a long time. It's time everyone bury him and move on. You could call your boat the *Jo* or *Johanna*. I bet your mom would love that."

Grady laughed. "I think I might try for something comical. I don't know. Once I get through winter, I'll start thinking."

"Hey, are you trying to steal my woman?" Graham hollered as he strode toward Rennie and Grady.

"I think she pays more attention to me than you anyway," Grady teased his brother.

Graham leaned down and kissed Rennie. When she stood between the two of them, she felt like a shrimp among giants. The Chamberlain twins were tall men with piercing green eyes, and both were currently wearing their hair a bit shaggier than she was used to. From afar, very few people could tell them apart. But up close, Graham carried himself with confidence, while Grady slouched most of the time. The years of alcohol and drug use had done a number on Grady's skin, but he was slowly healing and looking more and more like Graham every day. He was a work in progress.

"I'm glad you're here. I'm ready to go inside. Are you?" Rennie asked Graham. She would never take him away from his friends or brother and was more than willing to head in by herself.

"Yeah, I'm good. Grady?"

Grady looked over Graham's shoulder and nodded. Rennie tried to see who he looked at, but no one stood out. The three of them walked up the wooden stairs to the inn. Once inside, Rennie insisted they take the stairs to the third floor because she still didn't trust the elevator. More so with the twins inside.

When they reached the third floor, Grady stopped halfway down the hall and wished them good night. "I'm so happy I'm not anywhere near your room. The last thing I want to do is listen to you guys all night long."

Rennie slapped Grady on his shoulder and rolled her eyes at him.

Graham, on the other hand, asked, "Are you jealous?"

Grady sighed. "Yeah, I am, actually. I'd like to fall in love someday."

"You will, Grady. It just takes time." Rennie hugged him and told him they'd see him tomorrow.

In their room, as soon as the door closed, Graham picked Rennie up and set her on the bed. He hovered over her and gazed into her eyes. "I love you, Ren."

"I love you too, Graham Cracker. Now, show me how much."

He did exactly as she demanded.

Rennie held her hand out for her niece, Brystol. Together, they twirled in front of Brooklyn and her mother, Bonnie, along with Bowie's mother, Linda, and Simone. Everyone clapped for the little dance party going on in front of them.

"Those dresses are gorgeous," Linda said to Brooklyn. Rennie wore a floor-length, modern, short-sleeved A-line gown with thick straps and a slit that she insisted Graham would appreciate and be very thankful for. Brystol wore a simple A-line, knee-length dress that flared when she spun in circles.

"All Brystol," Brooklyn said, making sure to give her daughter credit for everything. When it came time to plan the wedding, the women in Brooklyn's life sat around a table for a weekend, scouring bridal magazines for inspiration. It wasn't until Brystol opened up one of Brooklyn's paint swatch books that they finally found what they were looking for. An obscure but trending color of blue. Referred to as *dusty blue*, it was a light navy, which was one of Brooklyn's favorite colors. From there, they decided the men would wear navy-blue suits, and all the decorations and flowers would be blush colored.

"Okay, ladies. Let's get the bride into her dress."

Everyone clapped and took their positions. Rennie stood on a chair and held Brooklyn's long locks up while the two moms helped her step into her blush-colored boho sweetheart A-line dress. The day the wedding crew went shopping, Brooklyn had her mind set on something simple. No fuss, no lace. She wanted a plain dress. That was until she saw the strapless boho dress on the mannequin with all the embroidery and appliqués, everything she didn't want, and asked to try it on. As soon as she stepped out of the dressing room, she had tears in her eyes, proclaiming that was the dress.

"I got the zipper," Simone said. With the zipper up, Rennie let Brooklyn's hair go. She had chosen to leave her hair down in soft waves and held the front back with a diamond headband. Brystol wore one to match.

"Oh, Mommy," Brystol exclaimed. "You're so beautiful. Can I hug you?" Brooklyn nodded and pulled her daughter into her arms.

"Don't either of you start crying," Bonnie warned.

"We won't, Grandma."

Linda stood off to the side, dabbing her tears. "My son is one lucky man."

"We're the lucky ones," Brooklyn told her.

"Okay, let's get this bride down to the beach to marry her groom." Simone took charge. Someone had to, or the women would've stayed in the room and gushed over dresses all day.

One of the valets waited for the bridal party at the end of the staircase. When he saw them coming, he ran off to the back to signal for the music to start. The group walked toward the back and met Brooklyn's father, David.

"You look . . . Bonnie, help me out."

Bonnie put her hand on David's arm and said, "She's gorgeous, honey."

"Yes. Yes, she is."

Bonnie patted her husband's arm and then followed Linda and Simi out back. As much as Rennie wanted to rush, to get a glimpse of Graham in his navy-blue suit, she waited until the moms were out of sight.

"Come on, Little B, let's go do our thing." Rennie took Brystol's hand and started for the steps. They had practiced going up and down the stairs a few times because Brooklyn and Bowie decided to make their wedding fit their life. At the bottom of the steps, Bowie waited for his daughter, right along with Luke dressed in his own tux. Once she was down, he walked her down the aisle.

Rennie came down the stairs and paused. She took in the scene in front of her. The white chairs, tulle occasionally blowing with the breeze, and the lanterns with their fake candles glowing. Blush-colored roses marked the aisle, and at the end of it, standing next to the groom, was her man.

Soon, we will have our day, she thought as she took each step toward the altar. When she was close enough, Graham winked at her, and she blew him a kiss. Sometimes, he made her feel like a teenager all over again.

The music changed, and everyone stood. It took a moment before Brooklyn came into view, but when she did, Rennie watched Bowie. He dabbed at his eyes and rocked back and forth on his heels. Her eyes went back and forth between him and her best friend and her niece. Everyone was crying.

When the music stopped, the minister stepped forward and spoke. "Who gives this woman to this man?"

Brystol came out from behind Rennie and said, "Luke and I do."

Everyone laughed, but it made sense, especially to Bowie and Brooklyn.

Brooklyn stood next to Bowie, holding her blush-colored peony bouquet, which she'd had specially made for her wedding. Rennie wanted to catch it at the end of the night, even though she was already engaged—she was in love with the flowers and wanted them for the houseboat. She had visions of fighting all the other single women at the reception for it, which was ridiculous because she could order her own. But that wasn't the point, at least not to her.

When Brooklyn handed Rennie her bouquet, it dawned on her she might want to pay attention to the ceremony instead of imagining a battle royal later on.

"When I look at you, it's hard to remember what my life was like a year ago. I was lost, barely surviving, and then you were here, and it was like everything was right in my world. Once I saw you, I knew I wasn't going to let you go again. You are the absolute best of me, Brooklyn, and you have given me the best gift I could ever ask for in our daughter. I love you both so much."

Rennie dabbed her eyes. She couldn't even think about what Graham would say to her when they had their turn. The minister directed Brooklyn to give her vows.

"Bowie, you've seen me at my best and loved me at my worst. When I pushed, you pulled. When I asked you to forget about me, you told me memories never went away. You reminded me what love was and showed me how to live. You've guided me through heartache and were there when I was adamant I didn't need anyone. You're the best dad, both human and dog; the most amazing partner; and the love of my life. I'm so happy you want to continue to make memories with me. I love you."

"I love you too, Dad," Brystol yelled out, causing everyone to laugh.

After Brooklyn and Bowie exchanged rings and promised to love each other no matter what, the minister pronounced them husband and wife. "Bowie, you may kiss your bride." Bowie took Brooklyn in his arms and kissed her. It took ten seconds until everyone started clapping. Rennie handed Brooklyn her bouquet; she and Bowie turned and held their hands up in the air. All their family and friends stood and clapped as they made their way down the aisle. Once they reached the end, Graham and Rennie stepped forward and linked arms.

"What do you think? Still want to go to Vegas?" he asked her.

"Nah, I want a wedding. I want my parents there. Your parents. Grady. Brooklyn and Bowie. I want our friends there to celebrate."

They came to the end of the aisle, and Graham stopped. He placed his hands on Rennie's cheeks and kissed her. Judging by the hooting and hollering going on behind them, everyone approved. When they parted, he looked into her eyes.

"A wedding we will have. I don't care where or when, just as long as I become your husband." They stood there until Luke barked, reminding them it was time to party.

ACKNOWLEDGMENTS

Thank you to everyone in the Beaumont Daily for the everyday encouragement, laughs, and support. The Whale Spout crew—your conspiracy theories about Austin are the best! I can never thank you enough for your support, encouragement, and love for Cape Harbor. You ladies are the OG crew and will always have first dibs at the bar.

To Lauren Plude, I absolutely adore you. Thank you so much for the opportunity to work with you. Many thanks to the amazing team at Montlake, and Holly Ingram, whose red pen makes everything prettier.

To my agent, Marisa, for encouraging all my harebrained ideas.

And finally, to Madison and Kassidy. I love how brilliant, creative, and giving you are. You girls are my reason for everything. I can't wait to follow the path you blaze in the future.

ABOUT THE AUTHOR

Heidi McLaughlin is the *New York Times*, *Wall Street Journal*, and *USA Today* bestselling author of the Beaumont Series, the Boys of Summer, and the Archers. Heidi turned her passion for reading into a full-fledged literary career in 2012 and now has more than twenty novels to her name. The acclaimed *Forever My Girl*, McLaughlin's first novel, was adapted into a motion picture by LD Entertainment and Roadside Attractions starring Alex Roe and Jessica Rothe. It opened in theaters on January 19, 2018.

Originally from the Pacific Northwest, McLaughlin now lives in picturesque Vermont with her husband, two daughters, and their three dogs.

Designed by David Cole Wheeler

Copyright © 2009
Peter Pauper Press, Inc.
202 Mamaroneck Avenue
White Plains, NY 10601
All rights reserved
ISBN 978-1-59359-848-8
Printed in China
14

Visit us at www.peterpauper.com

PETER PAUPER PRESS, INC.
WHITE PLAINS, NY